BILLIE'S KISS

BILLIE'S KISS

ELIZABETH KNOX

BALLANTINE BOOKS • NEW YORK

A Ballantine Book
Published by The Ballantine Publishing Group

Copyright © 2002 by Elizabeth Knox

All rights reserved under International and
Pan-American Copyright Conventions. Published in
the United States by The Ballantine Publishing Group, a division
of Random House, Inc., New York, and simultaneously in
Canada by Random House of Canada Limited, Toronto.

Ballantine is a registered trademark and the
Ballantine colophon is a trademark of Random House, Inc.

www.ballantinebooks.com

LIBRARY OF CONGRESS CATALOGING-IN-PUBLICATION DATA
is available upon request from the publisher.

ISBN 0-345-45052-3

Text design by Holly Johnson

Manufactured in the United States of America

First Edition: March 2002

10   9   8   7   6   5   4   3   2   1

ACKNOWLEDGMENTS

I would like to thank Jill and Viv de Fresnes for their hospitality. Jill and Viv encouraged me to visit the Western Isles, and it was at their kitchen table in Loch Morarside, I first heard about Lord Leverhulme. Lord Leverhulme's relationship with the Island of Lewis and Harris formed the basis of the fictional relationship between Lord Hallowhulme and the Island of Kissack and Skilling. All Hallowhulme's other attributes are my invention.

In memory of my father, Ray Knox.
1926–2001

1   ⚚   THE *GUSTAV EDDA*

THE CROSSING WAS ROUGH, AND EDITH UNWELL. BILLIE couldn't read, so she sang to her sister. Edith kept her eyes closed and her face turned into the pillow. Billie saw sweat beaded beneath the reddish down on her sister's cheek, the down that had grown gradually darker, from cheekbone to jawline, as Edith came nearer her time. It seemed to Billie that her sister was turning into another kind of creature, with furred skin and an extra layer of soft fat on her arms, her midriff firmly tight, not laced and nipped, as it had been, but convex. Even Edith's hair had changed, now so luxuriant that her unpinned plaits were as thick as Billie's forearms. But these changes weren't Edith's whole alteration, and as Billie sang to her sister she kept her right hand against Edith's belly, between belly and supporting pillow, to feel the other thing, the motion, strong and irregular, and as invisible as the ocean.

The flame was fairly steady in the binnacle lamp on the ceiling of the cabin, for the lamp itself rocked on its gimbals, moved in counterpoint to the heaving ship. All the room's shadows tilted this way and that, as, no doubt, any person on deck at that time would have done.

Beneath Billie's hand and her sister's skin the baby seethed. Billie paused between verses to whisper to herself: "Let the cat

1

out of the bag." It was an expression she'd always liked. Of course they weren't fully ready for the baby—*they:* Edith, Henry, Billie—and cats out of bags meant trouble. But, as a child, whenever her father had turned to her, his index finger barring his mouth before he whispered, "Don't let the cat out of the bag," Billie would imagine the cat—the abducted feline—on the sill of an open window, fur upstanding, haloed in darkness, framed against a garden, and looking back with eyes like embers.

Edith squeezed Billie's arm and gasped. "Why did we have to go on *today?*"

Edith had been content to travel by train, but balked at the idea of a sea voyage. So her husband, Henry Maslen, planned a journey that used the Inner Isles as stepping-stones, and ferries that crossed at all the narrowest places. In Henry's plan they were to cross from Dorve, in the Inner Isles, on a steamer small enough to navigate the crooked way among the reefs that lay between Dorve and Southport, on the southeast coast of an island called Kissack and Skilling. Dorve to Southport was a short, fair-weather journey. From Southport it was only a day's travel north to their ultimate destination, Stolnsay, Kissack and Skilling's only sizable town. But when Edith and Henry Maslen, and Edith's sister Billie, arrived in Dorve, it was to a harbor whipped up by wind and a reef not to be chanced. Not for several days, they were told. It was suggested that, if Mr. Maslen liked, he could take his family overland to the port of Luag, where they would coincide with the arrival of the *Gustav Edda*. The *Gustav Edda* was a big, Swedish-owned steamer that passed through the islands every month on a circuit that began and ended in Stockholm. Henry Maslen had hesitated before rushing off to catch the bigger ship. He hesitated and his sister-in-law watched him hide his worry and his calculations, watched his lips move against the heel of the hand with which he screened his mouth. Then Henry dropped his hand. He looked at his sister-in-law. "Billie, you and Edith *could* keep our room here and follow me when the weather's calmer. But . . ."

But they were short of funds, and he wanted to have his wife settled before the baby came. Its arrival was imminent. Henry's new employment had come at exactly the right time, but the journey hadn't. Mr. Johan Gutthorm, who, in his own words, handled Lord Hallowhulme's "indoor business affairs," advised Henry to come before summer. Since Mr. Maslen meant to bring his wife and her sister it was, Gutthorm wrote, "better by far to make the most of the best of our weather." Henry had read Johan Gutthorm's letter to Billie and Edith as they sat in the tiny parlor of their cottage in Crickhowell. Edith said, "We should all go at once. We're very crowded here."

They were—spring damp breaking in on them, making black stars of mildew on the paintwork around the windows—crowded out by Edith's belly, Henry's books, and Billie's upright piano, and by a tortuous cyclonic current of feeling that could neither be borne nor gone with. That afternoon in Crickhowell, Henry had agreed with his wife. He repeated his salary offer, pounds and shillings, but warned that there was no guarantee that they wouldn't find themselves again crowded at Kiss Castle in Stolnsay. Henry looked at her then—Billie—but his eyes said: *"Edith."* He could say her sister's name without moving his lips. Henry appeared sad. The flaring ends of his fair muttonchop whiskers—minus moustache—were shaved to terminate exactly parallel to the lines beside his mouth: two defined lines that always made his face seem sober, his mouth bracketed, braced, and disciplined. What had he been looking for in looking at her, Billie wondered, encouragement or warning?

The ship pitched and tossed, and Billie sang to her sister: hymns, love ballads, a comic song from the music hall. The ship yawed and the swinging light chased the shadows into a corner of Edith's bunk, where they concentrated into such thickness Billie expected to see them coalesce, leaving something solid sitting there.

Edith rolled over, showed a whole perspiring face, and asked, "Why do you say that? 'Cat out of the bag'?"

"I was thinking of the baby." Billie stroked her sister's abdomen.

"Honestly, Billie. Why would a baby bring to mind a cat in a bag? People put cats in bags only to drown them." Edith's lower lip trembled, then she said she was sorry, she hadn't meant to be sharp. Could Billie go up on deck and see how near they were to that headland the captain had explained would afford some shelter from the north? The ship surely couldn't still be out on the open water. "And send Henry down," Edith said. "And take the bucket out and empty it. Please, dear."

Billie got up. She said that she'd heard that the saying was nautical, or naval anyway, the "cat" was a lash. Then she had to swing the zinc pail back at her sister's urgent signal. Edith's mouth filled, and she leaned over and spat out another gob of ropey bile. The wet rag with which Billie had been wiping her sister's face was already in the bucket, so Billie turned up her dress hem and found the scalloped cotton edge of her petticoat. She wiped Edith's mouth. "I don't like to leave you."

Edith said, weakly, that Billie could give her some hope. "See where we are," she said again. "But leave Henry up in the fresh air if he's ill."

Billie wrapped her shawl around her head and carried the pail from the cabin. She crept along the passage, her free hand braced against the wall. By the hatch an oblong light skated about, probing the darkness, sliced by the rungs of the ladder, whose own shadow surged so wildly that it seemed dangerous to climb. Billie went up, one rung at a time. She didn't dare put the pail down above her.

The sea was higher than it had been, and its waves were streaky, but the wind was now only stiff. Last night's gale had passed. Billie steadied herself, took hold of a shroud. The hemp thrummed in her palm as the wind drew its long, smooth bow across the few ropes and cables on the steamer. It made a mournful sound, and seemed to be missing something. The wind shoved the stack smoke down, so that several hot smuts hit Billie's cheeks—like snow in Hell. Billie thought of another phrase and imagined the coalesced shadow from the corner of Edith's bunk, a black cat, step out of its jute bag and onto the black ice of a Hell frozen over. Billie shook her head.

Henry was at the rail, his back to a group of well-dressed gentlemen—two youths and two men. One of the men was just putting his pipe back in his pocket with the air of one who has tried and failed at something—igniting it, probably. The boys were in the uniform of a military academy, their greatcoats gray and piped with black, the facings of their collars crimson. They wore their scarves high, halving their faces, and their caps pulled low. The second man wore a long astrakhan coat, its blurrily black sable collar turned up around his ears. He held the collar in place with one black-gloved hand. His head was bare, and his thick, phosphorescently pale hair blew forward.

Billie passed the huddled group, nodded to them, cordial. She didn't catch any eyes. She felt a little self-conscious seeing them so uncomfortable, for this party had formerly occupied the cabin in which Edith was now lying.

It was the first of June, and in summer the journey from Luag to Stolnsay took around ten hours and was undertaken from midnight till morning. The *Gustav Edda* had come on from bigger mainland ports, and there were no cabins empty for its outermost journey. When Henry and his hugely pregnant wife had presented themselves unexpectedly at the quay at Luag the captain of the steamer had Henry write several letters petitioning "the gentlemen" who had the ship's four cabins. Three were friends, with a cabin each, and the captain imagined they might be content to bunk together.

Yet it was the letter carried to a hotel adjacent the harbor that was the only one answered. "Dear Sir," Henry read. "My party is happy to oblige yours. I wish you, and your wife, as comfortable a crossing as can be hoped for in a northerly gale in the bight. Yours etc. MH." "Mr. Hesketh," the captain said. "A cousin of Lord Hallowhulme. Hesketh was an officer in King Oskar's household cavalry. Now he sees things done for Lord Hallowhulme. There's no love lost between Hesketh and the islanders. Lord Hallowhulme is full of plans, and they say he's a good-natured fellow, that his heart's in the right place, but his cousin is the one who keeps the plans in motion whenever they stick."

Now, although they were on deck together, Henry had his back to the obliging Mr. Hesketh and party. Henry was stooped over the rail, but when Billie stopped beside him she saw he wasn't unwell, but was hiding, shy.

HENRY. EDITH HAD MET HIM IN HER FIRST SITUATION, with the Lees family at Falmouth. Henry was a tutor. Edith wrote to her sister that a Mr. Maslen had come to prepare the boys for better things. "To meet their maker, in the shape of Eton, he says. With the twins now at Latin and German with Mr. Maslen, I have just the three girls in my charge. But I don't have more *time* on my hands. Mrs. Lees and I spend our afternoons printing bookplates and pasting them in every volume in the library. We began on the bottom shelves till Mrs. Lees saw the value in dusting as we go. Billie, the dust has drawn the youth from my hands—you should see them, worse than they are even after Aunt's spring cleaning." (This Edith put in to tease Aunt, who always had to read Billie her mail.)

Henry Maslen, it turned out, was a cataloguer, a man who knew his books—or other people's—and where to put them. When Mrs. Lees abandoned her bookplates to nag the kitchen about preserves—the apricots and peaches being ripe and overabundant—Henry and Edith worked together. "Mr. Maslen arrives in the early evening and as well as keeping me company keeps me quite entertained explaining what he's about. I've taken to teasing him a little, and call him Mr. System. He takes it very well—rather like a nervous horse in its best blinkers—and explains in good faith as though *if only* he can make me see the sense of his cataloguing decisions, and the authority of other cataloguers behind him, I'll stop mocking him. Of course I only mock because, although it's quite right to be serious with the work, it really isn't much good being serious to me after my long hours with those dull girls. I *miss* you, Billie. The longer I live and teach the more baffled I am by what father would unkindly call your obtuseness (as though it were *willed*, some resistance you put up to the world, not the bewildering trouble it is). The Lees girls are pleasant, but in no way quick or perceptive or witty (as you are). But they do read. They read, but they read like they eat soup, not like *you* listen to *me* reading."

When Edith and Henry came to an understanding it was, of course, Billie who first heard of it. In fact, it was only Billie whom Edith told when she was home for Christmas. She couldn't tell their great-aunt, with whom the Paxton girls had lived after their father died. Aunt Blazey would have thought an "understanding" improper between a governess and a tutor employed in the same house. She would have considered it somehow dishonorable in relation to the family employing them. Edith suspected that her employers might share this feeling—so had persuaded Henry to hide even their friendship. She told him to deceive people about his regard for her, to conceal his feelings. On her visit home Edith confided to her sister that she was a little disturbed by how good Henry was at dissembling. "The girls suspect feelings on *my* side. If he surprises me I blush or trip over my words, or fumble my cup and saucer, and the Lees girls peer into my face as if they're watching for the moment of reaction in a chemistry experiment. But *Henry*—he never turns a hair. It's dreadful! The girls are all interested, and sympathetic, and sorry for me."

"They'd always be mistaking me for being in love," Billie said, "if those are the signs they look for. I'm forever blushing, fumbling cups, and tripping over words."

"You do it the other way around, dear. You blush because you fumble."

In the new year Henry found a situation teaching in a school. He gave his employer notice, and his sweetheart a gilded silver ring to wear. Then he put his trunk on the carrier's cart and went with it to Crickhowell, in Wales. Edith told her employer that she planned to marry in June, and that she hoped that would give the Lees ample time to replace her. But Mrs. Lees seemed to feel that she had been deceived and told Edith that her employment was terminated and she must leave immediately. Without a reference. "Carrying on a romance right under my roof!" said Mrs. Lees. And Edith, defending herself: "But we waited to become engaged. We waited till Henry had gone. Is it wrong to fall in love?"

Edith was sent home without a reference and followed by a letter to her aunt about her deceitfulness and impertinence. It was the second such letter Aunt Blazey had received—Billie's even shorter foray into paid employment had ended in her dismissal after only four months. Aunt Blazey was ill, and worried for both girls. She had so little to leave them. Their rooms would go—with her late husband's chandlery, above whose premises they all lived—to her husband's nephew, also a chandler by trade. That left only a little money, forty pounds apiece, and Edith would have to keep Wilhelmina's till the girl came of age. Forty pounds, and a silver tea service, the china, the linen, a few little pieces of jewelry. It was the best Aunt could do. She *had* hoped the Paxton girls had inherited some of her own good sense, or that at least Edith had. Aunt Blazey did declare her intention to give Henry Maslen a good looking-over before she died. The moment he was able to take the time to travel from Crickhowell he must present himself for inspection.

Aunt Blazey died that spring, before the end of Henry's first term. She never did look him over. Henry stayed in Crickhowell and found lodgings, a cottage with a small back bedroom off the kitchen for Billie. He wrote describing the place and his plans for it. He and Edith published their banns. Edith made arrangements with the vicar who had buried Aunt.

That summer Henry came south for his wedding, and to take possession of both sisters. He found Edith alone, on a hot day, settling saucers among the sheets and pillowcases in a trunk in the rooms above the chandlery. She made him tea and had him promise he'd stay put—wasn't he tired?—while she fetched Billie, who, since she was gone so long, must have climbed around to the cove beyond the arm of the harbor. Edith kissed him, put on her hat, and went out.

Billie always imagined it this way, imagined the scene, the steaming kettle, Henry settled before the pewter pot and one of the two cups still unpacked, with the cracked jug they weren't going to take before him also, filled with milk and under its beaded cover—her handiwork, both the crack and the beading. Edith kissed Henry, put on her hat, and closed the door, and Billie imagined that Henry got up to follow Edith's progress along the road from the parlor's bow window. Billie's elaborations on these events were her picture storybook, the story being how Henry and she first met. Billie liked to imagine it from his point of view.

This is what happened to her. Aunt Blazey was six weeks in the ground. Bilious, crotchety Aunt Blazey, whom her nieces had always rather enjoyed, for whom they felt liking rather than tenderness or dependence. Now that the weather had become close and hot, Billie was really regretting having dyed her second-best dress black. The dress had come out a rusty uneven black, yet it still sucked up the sun's warmth and conveyed it into the redundant crush of corset—Billie wasn't fleshy, she had nothing to hold in or to hold in place. Billie wore her dress, a corset, petticoat, chemise, drawers, stockings, and boots, and was sweltering under all of it. The day Henry came she had walked around the harbor by the donkey track, and had left the track to climb the zigzag path the whelk gatherers used to get down the crumbling cliff face. She left her boots at the top, and her clothes at the bottom, and went into the surf in her chemise and drawers.

Billie could swim. Her father had taught her how when she was five, in the south of France, where he took his daughters on his flight from his debts. They had lived in one room of a hotel in Beaulieu-sur-Mer, where Billie's father taught her to swim on a bet. The men he bet against, fishermen and fishmongers, let Mr. Paxton borrow a boat, and they all followed him out a little from shore, where the water turned from aqua over gold sand to deep blue over red seaweed anchored on darker rocks. Edith sat on the shore, her shawl held up to shade her fair skin, and the shade turning her dark red curls black. Mr. Paxton took off his youngest's shoes, stockings, frock, and lowered her over the side into buoyant, salt-saturated water. She held on to the stern board while he rowed, her flimsy underclothes transparent over her thin, freckled body, her hair drawn out straight in the sea and darkening from strawberry to a kind of translucent pink. Mr. Paxton rowed, Billie laughed and kicked the sea and let go to dangle one hand, then let go altogether while the boat bobbed near her and she tilted her head back and dog-paddled, the wavelets breaking against her sealed lips. Billie's father shouted, "Oh dear! I've lost a barnacle!" Billie smiled at him, and wriggled in the water, while the two boats of onlookers applauded and called out in French, words of praise and admiration. For a whole summer Billie made a profession of swimming, or possibly of acting. Paxton would take his daughters by train to Nice, or Villefranche, or San Remo and, while strolling the stone jetty or promenades overhanging water, and on some signal from him, Billie would slip and fall and the water would close over her head. Mr. Paxton would cry out her name, shed his coat, kick off his shoes, and plunge in after her. Billie would let him clasp her, and he would wade out, sobbing with anxiety. She'd let herself be passed from person to person, would feel strangers touch her face and loosen her soaked clothes. She'd revive and there'd be thankful tears. All Edith could ever manage was to hang back, pale with shame that passed quite well for shock. Billie submitted to blankets, more tears, watered brandy, warm chocolate—and at some point in the proceedings Edith would recover her father's jacket and shoes and Mr. Paxton would discover his pocketbook gone. *Taken* by some heartless opportunist in the confusion. The Paxtons never came away from one of Billie's swims with anything less than dinner and several days' living expenses. And, to Billie, swimming came to mean many things. It was a secret between her father and herself; she was thrilled by his pale, alert face, his sly, sidelong look, and the wink that was a signal for her self-abandon. She liked to fall, fast through the air and slowly and noisily through the water, liked to come up through deep-voiced and hissing bubbles and surface into the sound of screaming: *"Au secours! La petite! Vite!"* She'd shriek and slap the water, then roll facedown in time to see her father's long, trouser-covered legs and stocking feet come toward her. Then he'd pick her up, drenched and dazzled. She'd flop and be cradled and stroked and breathed on, then could pretend to cry and be nursed for hours. It was wonderful.

And Henry first saw her swimming.

Billie was in the water twenty feet from shore, the steep shingle beach, and beyond the cold shadow of the cliff. She heard her name called and turned in the water to see Edith, on the clifftop, where the path began. Edith's dress, over the mandatory two petticoats, stirred jerkily, like a dense bush in a gust of wind. And Billie saw Henry behind her sister—or she saw a man she guessed was Henry. He had come up on Edith, was for a moment undiscovered by her, his footfalls inaudible in the wash of waves on shingle. Billie knew he could see her, because he half turned away. She saw his head averted and body swing side-on to her. And then she saw his face turn back. Billie kicked out for the shore and came out of the waves with her arms wrapped around herself. She ran into the shadow, out of sight of the summit, and found her clothes. She climbed the path holding up skirts heavy with seawater, transferred from her wet drawers and camisole. Her bodice was still only half-fastened, her feet bare, and her hair in long salty ropes. She scrambled up the cliff face. She wasn't presentable, but was eager to meet Henry. Edith's dear Henry. He was blushing, and shy, and eager, too. "You're much too old to be doing that now," Edith scolded her. "You might be seen. Or followed." Edith pushed her sister's hair back and finished buttoning her bodice. "She's such a creature," Edith said to Henry, a challenge and a complaint.

Henry smiled and took their hands, one each in his, so that they stood there in the wind and noise of the surf, at the edge of something, a cliff, their new lives, in a moment of intimate solidarity, which told Billie that Henry had heard all about her already—her virtues and her failings—and that he meant to be her friend. And she was able to tell him why she'd been swimming, despite the risks and wrong involved. "It was the last time," she explained. "I wanted to say good-bye."

IT HAD BEEN FULLY TWO YEARS SINCE BILLIE HAD BEEN IN over her head. She was now twenty. But she couldn't read, and had trouble telling time till Henry bought her the silver ring she wore on the little finger of her right hand so that she could tell by standing face-to-face with a clock whether its minute hand was descending to the half hour or ascending to the hour. She couldn't read, and she was still clumsy doing some things—for instance, she could run and jump but not dance, she could bake bread and bind books, knit and embroider, but couldn't be trusted with the pony and trap. Between them, encouraging each other, Edith and Henry had taught Billie to read music. She could already reproduce a tune by ear. Now, given time, she was able to puzzle out a song from a thruppence sheet. And, once she'd picked the tune out on her piano, she had it in her head for good. Her playing improved and, with Edith and Henry's help, she even learned how to transcribe a few simple tunes of her own. Billie had grown and made progress, she was cherished and necessary, but often it seemed to her that nothing had yet appeared to compensate her for no longer being borne up on the steep peak of an unbroken wave or rolled about in the chilly fizz of a smashed one.

BILLIE SET THE BUCKET DOWN AT HER FEET AND LEANED on the rail beside Henry. He had one hand on top of his hat. Its knuckles were white, but only with cold. "That is Alesund Head," he said to her. "Do you see those rocks?"

The headland was beside them, too close, an immense wall of brown turf, with a lighter living tan where the heather was coming into bloom. All of it seemed broken, scoured and stony, and empty.

"Those rocks are Kissack gneiss. Kissack gneiss is the oldest stone in the world," Henry informed Billie. "Some two thousand, eight hundred million years in age."

It looked as though nothing much had happened to the rock in the intervening time. Except the intervening time.

"Once we're clear of the headland we'll be able to see Stolnsay," Henry said. His face was wind-reddened, his lips dry. He pointed to the headland's end, around which a small steamer had appeared, its smoke a kinky plume as it lurched from side to side. "I think that's the pilot's boat. The one we were to catch Thursday morning, except it couldn't come through the reef." Henry directed his sister-in-law's gaze back to the shortish stretch of silver water between Kissack and the Inner Isle, whose mountains from here looked less like a geography than piled thunderheads. The reef was visible as a receding series of tucks and pulls in the sea, as though the water was a piece of weaving with uneven tension in warp or weft. "The pilot's boat appears to be in the Wash now. The Wash is a famously unpredictable current that flows around Alesund Head." Henry supposed the pilot had come out because the sea was still bad. Or perhaps he always met the steamer at the harbor's mouth. Billie said she hoped the *Gustav Edda* wouldn't be told to stand off. "Edith isn't well. She sent me to fetch you—if you're not in need of air yourself."

Henry put his hand on her back. "I'll go," he said, then, "Remember the pail, Billie."

Sometimes she did have to be reminded. She could remember faces and conversations from years before, faithfully, freshly, as though she'd only just turned away from a person, a scene— for instance, her father in a little room in a hotel, its ceiling covered in scaling plaster, and its wrought-iron balcony spotted with rust. But Billie often had trouble remembering just what she meant to do next—the order of daily tasks, what she'd come to market to buy, or whether nutmeg went in *before* sugar in frumenty pudding.

Henry left her. She watched him, saw how small and neat he looked as he passed through the huddle of men between the galley and wheelhouse. Their coats were dark and thick and heavy— quality, Billie knew, but Henry looked quick and unencumbered moving between them, one hand still on the crown of his hat, the other raised to touch his hat brim. The men nodded, parted, let him by. They were all taller than Henry. She and Edith were slight, but both were nearly the same height as he was. He'd always laugh about his size, and congratulate himself and them on it whenever they had to pass each other on the steep narrow stairs of the cottage in Crickhowell.

Billie found herself watched. That much she was able to see past several tentacles of her long, collapsed curls as they got out from under the shawl and whipped before her face. She saw a pale countenance turned her way, a kind of shapely luster above the rich black of sable collar and the supple ridged pelt of astrakhan.

Billie turned back to empty the bucket and, because she wasn't thinking, she threw the pint or so of cloudy bile out into the wind. The wind caught the mess, stopped it in the air then flung it back toward Billie, who ducked. Nothing nasty hit her. She stood straight and cleared the few pinkish tendrils of her hair away from her eyes and found herself looking again at the beautiful sable collar and astrakhan coat splattered with ropes of grainy bile.

Billie dropped the pail. It made a clang and rolled away from her feet. She stood with her mouth open, trying to hear. Her ears were ringing.

He had spread his hands, his arms, too disgusted to touch, and was looking down at the front of his coat. Billie watched the wind part his pale hair, like water pouring into water. He looked up at her as she went to him. She lurched against him, unsettled by her numb clumsiness and the motion of the ship. Billie pulled her shawl from her head to mop at his coat. The ends of her hair rushed in front of her and got into the mess but she kept on mopping, folding, finding a clean spot on the shawl to soak up more filth. She could see how the fluid left smears, like the snail trails on the brick steps of the cottage at Crick-howell. She couldn't speak, knew she'd only stammer if she tried.

He stopped her, brought his arms up slowly between them, so that her hands were moved aside. But he wasn't trying to master her hands; he put his own gloved ones together and used his clean sleeves to push her hair up and back, so that his arms were crossed behind her neck, and her hair was out of her face. He moved slowly, apparently concerned not to frighten or offend her, and with the effect of someone lifting something heavy, or capturing something lively—her hair.

"I'm so sorry!" Billie said. She was more miserable than embarrassed. She was tired of her own stupidity, tired of being conscious enough to suffer shame for it but unable to correct herself. Then she dropped the shawl and ducked out of his arms. She scrambled away from him, got up, and struck her head on one of the short craning turrets that ventilated the engine room. Her eyes filled and she glanced back at a blurred block of darkness that was all those coats. Those men. She fled to the far side of the steamer and pressed her back against the wheel-house wall.

From this retreat, as she collected herself, Billie watched the pilot come alongside, both ships backing their engines. A boat was put down from the pilot's vessel, and a line thrown from the deck of the *Gustav Edda*. The *Gustav Edda*'s captain waited for the pilot, and another man, to climb the rope and wood ladder that two seamen had rolled over the side.

Eight bells were struck.

The fair-haired man in the astrakhan appeared, followed by his servant. Billie flattened herself against a closed door. But he wasn't interested in her. He wanted to know what the problem was. He was, apparently, one of those people who wouldn't acknowledge any problem unforeseen by him as an actuality. "What *seems* to be the problem?" he said. It was another expression whose usage Billie had always found intriguing—the possibilities of concession provided by "seems to be," as opposed to the inconvenience of "is."

The pilot asked the captain for the cargo manifest. He glanced at the tarpaulin-shrouded shape firmly roped to the stern deck. The captain explained that it was Lord Hallowhulme's new automobile. He'd find its seats and doors in the hold—where they had been put in order to preserve their leather from the elements. The pilot said he was more interested in how the coal was stowed. He told the captain that the Wash was particularly wicked today. The captain said all the cargo was fast, but let the pilot and his man go down to look for themselves.

The person Billie had drenched in Edith's bile lost interest in all this and went back into the sheltered place between the wheelhouse and galley. The pilot eventually reappeared. He was followed by his man who was, Billie saw, oddly engaged—the man was tucking in the tail of his shirt, as if he'd had some cause to unbutton and unbelt his trousers while below. Billie was intrigued. The pilot seemed satisfied. Then he saw Billie and she believed he asked the captain who she was.

"Miss Wilhelmina Paxton," Billie heard the captain say, "who is traveling with her sister and her sister's husband, Mr. Henry Maslen."

The pilot said he had thought that Mr. Maslen and his womenfolk would wait another few nights at Dorve. He had been supposed to ferry them over. Their haste was unnecessary. He said it loud enough for Billie to hear, seemed regretful, as if he was aquitting himself of some blame. Perhaps he'd mistaken the pallor of Billie's mortified embarrassment for illness.

The pilot and his man went back down the ladder to their boat, and rowed back to the small steamer which, after a minute, was under way again, on a shallow curving course, to the headland and the Wash. The *Gustav Edda* followed.

Billie remained on deck, on the windward side, away from the other passengers. Without her shawl she was very cold. As the *Gustav Edda* came into the Wash and began to toss in a strange watch-winding motion, Billie gripped the thick guide ropes against the wall behind her. The steamer came around as if kicked into place by the current, then made its laborious way around the headland. The sea gradually became calmer.

Fifteen minutes later Billie had her first sight of Stolnsay.

The land around the town wasn't in any way distinguished from the rest of the "countryside"—if you could even use that word. It was virtually treeless, except for a quarter-mile stretch along one arm of the harbor. Those trees were a witchy wood of lichen-blanched beech, birch, and hazel, framing a gray limestone castle. The castle was newish, a folly of ornamental battlements and towers, inlaid stonework shields, sphinxes, dragons, griffins, and lions. The castle had two wings which lay somehow awkwardly, like a taxidermist's guess at the anatomy and posture of a creature he'd never seen living. Except for the wooded point there were only a few trees by the town's three visible churches. The remainder of the landscape was stone, shaped stone, houses organized out of hills where the green-and-bronze turf looked rubbed away from rock, as if each hill was solid stone under a meatless, fatless pelt of turf.

It wasn't an ugly town, but it looked dour and unfriendly, grown up around the long notch of a fishing port. The tide was right in and the fishing vessels moored along the wall of the inner harbor had their decks less than ten feet from the quayside. Beyond the quay there were several streets of two-story houses. On the slope above these were whitewashed cottages, all separate, with nothing between them, not even fences of stone. Stolnsay was the biggest town on the island, but looking at it Billie could see no public buildings other than churches and a post office. She knew at once what this would mean—that there would be no retreat from indoors outdoors, no gardens, shaped trees, hedgerows, garden seats, no porches even, nor enclosed lanes. No retreat outdoors from in—and indoors there'd be Edith and Henry.

Billie had, in the two years of her sister's marriage, so far been able to take a hat and shawl and walk away from their private moments, their private happiness. Or there were indoor retreats, the kitchen clock's bold, definite tick, a kettle talking on the coal range, or her songbird piping away in the tiny bedroom off the kitchen, whose walls, around her zinc child's bedstead, were papered for extra insulation with the varnished pages of the mercantile gazette. Billie thought of her retreats, and what she was in retreat from. Edith, on the settee, turning up her petticoats to pick at loose threads, a new run in the soft cotton. Edith's expression: smug, tolerant, exclusive. And there was the soft, luxurious look Edith wore sometimes when Billie brought her up a cup of tea in the morning. Billie had often wondered whether it was embarrassment she felt, or envy. She *wasn't* excluded. Henry and Edith would each take one of her arms when they went out walking together. She sat between them in church; and Henry would always make sure to set their one good lamp so its light fell, divided but equal, on Edith's mending or Billie's music—while he'd lounge on the floor himself reading, his back against Edith's chair and a foot braced on the square pilaster leg of Billie's upright piano. When Billie would pass Henry on the stairs, on her way up with tea for Edith—who was of late sick to her stomach, or sleepy and waxing full—Henry would stoop quickly, his eyes warm, to kiss Billie's cheek, or once, her ear, his lips catching a few wispy hairs at her temple and setting her whole scalp aprickle.

Beside the wheelhouse, on the deck of the *Gustav Edda*, Billie Paxton scraped her loose hair back to look at her new hometown. Her hair pushed heavily against her cocked arms and flickered around them. She caught the two uniformed youths staring at her. They appeared to consult, to egg each other on, then they came over. The boys removed their caps, but the strong wind was only able to set up a telegraphic quiver in their cropped hair. One spoke, the other merely gazed. The one who spoke had slightly protuberant pale blue eyes, but was otherwise good-looking. He was perhaps fifteen years of age. He introduced himself—Rixon Hallow, and this was his friend Elov Jansen. He said he hoped Mrs. Maslen was comfortable in her cabin. Billie nodded, speechless. She felt the wind poke a cold finger through a split seam under her arm. The boy blushed. He was waiting for something. Billie realized that, as it was this party who'd given up their cabin to the Maslens when they arrived unexpected at Luag, they might expect her to acknowledge it. These boys had been obliged to walk the deck for the ten hours of the voyage. Surprised into it—and despite herself—Billie dropped into a jerky, curtailed curtsy; she bobbed, as she'd used to do to her employers when she was briefly in service. She resented this, that she'd been reminded to show gratitude, found ungrateful, or hesitant—again.

"Mr. Hesketh says he'll send your shawl on to you once it has been laundered," said Rixon Hallow. He was still blushing.

"Thank you." Billie excused herself, said she must go help her sister get dressed.

The engines had slowed. The ship was making not for the deep, sheltered water within the harbor proper, but for a berth at the sea side of the longest pier. Billie saw that the pier had been constructed as a causeway to a much older castle, a small fortress really, on what must once have been an island of rock. Nearer to, the fortress showed dilapidated, its lower walls thick with salt scum, its unglazed windows protected by bars in the form of rusty iron arrowheads.

Billie walked between the boys before they had replaced their caps. She ducked her head and darted around the wheelhouse, watched only her step, her hand on the rope rail along the wheelhouse wall. The sea was quiet enough now for her to hear the ash smuts from the ship's smokestack drop hissing into the waves. She glanced toward the sound and saw the water, clear and almost grass green over stretches of sand between rocks maybe thirty feet down. The sea turned gray again over the rocks, but green was the true color of its dense transparency. The ship was backing its propellers and Billie saw wind-pushed wavelets crisscrossed by smaller wrinkles, water disturbed by the engine, the crosshatching a border between natural wind-driven, and unnatural submarine turbulence. Perhaps because of its color, or its texture—this novel sign of engine's muscle moving water's weight—the sea suddenly seemed strange to Billie, as it hadn't since she was a small child.

Henry met her at the hatch. He said he'd been sent to fetch her. Edith had told him Billie had the buttonhook. Then he said, "Look at our new home."

"I looked."

He touched her cheek. "You must be tired, dear. And cold.

Have you been up here without your shawl?" His hand was warm. Billie tilted her face momentarily into his cupped palm. Then she went by him and let herself down the ladder into the gloomy passage.

Edith was upright on her bunk, with her face clean, and an unpinned hat perched on her damp hair. Her feet were in her shoes but unfastened. The cabin stank of vomit, sweat, and distress. Billie crouched at her sister's feet and got the buttonhook from the bag at her belt and began to prize the kid-covered buttons through their stretched holes. Edith's feet were swollen, fat and tender to the touch. "Please God don't let me have to spend the rest of my time lying down," Edith said. "I'm afraid they'll have to carry me off the ship. What an embarrassment."

"It's Lord Hallowhulme's cousin whose cabin we've taken," Billie said. "There will be a carriage for them, surely."

"But *we* were expected at Southport, Billie," Edith said. "On Thursday."

"I mean, we can take their carriage as well as their cabin."

Edith smiled. She drew her foot away from her sister's hands. "Leave it a little undone at the ankle, or I'll be crippled. My feet are all pins and needles." Edith showed no sign of moving. She said she'd wait till the ship was at a complete stop.

Billie went to find Henry. She was concerned that they would have to carry Edith between them. Henry met her under the hatchway, and they paused in the now-motionless square of light by the foot of the ladder. Henry said that the sailors, who had carried his writing case, microscope, and leaf press onto the ship, could be trusted to carry his burdened wife. He took Billie's hands and told her to stop fretting. "It's unlike you."

The *Gustav Edda* quivered as its anchor chain played out.

"You must compose yourself a little," Henry said. "I think I saw Hallowhulme himself on the pier. Waiting for us. Wearing a frown."

"He's waiting for his cousin and the boys in uniform," Billie said. And then she burst into tears. "The water looks so cold," she sobbed. "And where are the trees?"

Henry tried to make her raise her face. He pressed her shoulders softly back against the timber wall, then touched her chin. "Love?" he said. "My poor girl." He cleared a tear away to kiss her gently under one eye.

Billie turned her head so that their lips brushed. Henry started back, a fraction of an inch, broke contact. They exhaled together, and their breath mingled and encased their faces, warm and moist like summer in the south. Henry stared at her, his face pale and shining, then moved nearer again. He touched his mouth to hers, parted his lips, and something passed from his mouth to hers.

The mooring lines were made fast. Billie heard—registered hearing—an order about the gangplank. She pulled away from her brother-in-law, shoved him aside, and swarmed up the ladder. She stepped once on her own hem, fell into the opened hatch cover, and heard stitches part. Henry caught her ankle. At his touch Billie felt a crippling spasm somewhere inside her. She jerked her foot free and stumbled onto the deck, her legs clumsy, the space between them filled as if something there had swollen to twice its normal size.

The cold wind burned her face.

Billie plunged through the four gentlemen. One of the cadets staggered, his cap fell and rolled on its brim. A hand caught at her arm—Hesketh, incensed and implacable. She threw her whole weight back to break his grip, and fell on her hip, sucked air and a whiff of the tar between the timbers on the deck, then sprang up again and ran.

She made for the gangplank, which two seamen at the rail were still guiding into place. The plank's far end was yet clear of the stones, a foot both ways, a foot beyond, a foot above. Billie wanted to get off the ship. She wanted to get off the shore, too, Henry's "home," a town without trees or fences. She wanted to jump as if the ship and shore were both stepping-stones with some firmer place beyond them, some viable future. Billie vaulted up between the men, then past them. Her feet came down neatly in the center of the gangplank—and the men dropped it. For a second it hung on its hinges as the *Gustav Edda* edged by stately inches toward the pier, then Billie leapt again, the gangplank depressed and tilted, a hinge broke, and the plank's end jammed against the lip of the stone pier. The whole thing splintered. But it was behind Billie already, the plank, the shouting men—the stone was only inches under her feet. She gathered herself to land and to run some more.

Then, instead of arriving, touching down, or being snatched back, Billie felt a hard blow. Some force shoved at her whole body. Her hair flew in front of her face, her legs jerked wide, and she flipped over, flew forward, eyes wide-open. She saw the pier, its slabs of green-gray stone abruptly beneath her head. She glimpsed splinters of white painted wood, pieces of the gangplank, passing under her inverted crown, pushed across the stone faster than she'd ever seen thrown daisies sucked under the weir at Crickhowell. Then she saw rope webbing and jute-covered bales beneath her, and she put out her arms and fell into them.

BILLIE LIFTED HER FACE FROM THE PALLET OF MUSTY hemp. Her left ear was ringing, but into her right ear rushed the sound of the sea. The sea was filling her head, and was screaming like steel on stone. Billie looked back, and saw the funnel of the ship, its black barrel trained right at her. It spat out a cloud of smoke and burning embers. She felt two dozen light touches, then lancing pain. She scrambled up—she'd lost a shoe—shook her hair and clothes, shook off the coals before they caught. She couldn't walk straight, but crawled and clambered out of the smoke.

The next thing Billie saw was a woman in a red cap, her mouth stretched wide. The woman was standing, shouting, but—Billie thought—not putting out much sound. The woman was looking at the bulk of an overturned carriage, two horses down and struggling in tangled harness. They were squealing with pain and fright. The noise was appalling. But it was worse seaward. Billie watched as the *Gustav Edda's* stack impacted on the pier and collapsed. It unrolled like a collar that had popped its stud, then it was dragged out of sight. A cloud of steam came up, ragged and dissolving fast in the wind, a kind of quick smoke. Through the steam Billie glimpsed an impossibility—the ship drifting backward from the wharf propelled by the water boiling in its stack. She saw a mooring line snap at the pier and recoil to flick a figure off the perpendicular starboard deck. The port deck was underwater, the ship rolling over at its berth, water boiling around it and flooded with jets of fire. There were people in the sea. And there were people hoisting themselves over the starboard rail and onto the gleaming side of the ship. Billie watched as two seamen clambered, slithering, toward the bow and then slid into the sea and struck away from the rolling hull as fast as they were able to swim. Fishermen were running to their boats, but these were on the harbor side of the pier. The pier was solid stone and couldn't be passed under.

There was a group of men on the ship's flank. They struggled to keep their hold on the steel, but the ship was still rolling. The man in the astrakhan coat, Mr. Hesketh, turned against the slope and pushed the two boys up it before him. Their feet made catches in the smooth slick of water running on the hull. He paused, straddled the keel, and put a hand back to his servant. Shouts rose above the howling of steel and a horrid roar of water filling the ship—a roar that rose in tone as water displaced air. The *Gustav Edda* shuddered. It shook Hesketh's servant off into the water and then began to roll, serenely at first, then with a sudden rush, down upon him. Hesketh, still dry in his beautiful coat, leaned into the roll, after his man, for only a moment, looked into the churning sea as his man was ploughed under it, then flung himself the other way, tumbling down the far slope of the hull even as it was reversing its aspect. Billie didn't see where he landed. She couldn't see Henry at all. She just watched as the ship spun right way up for a moment, its deck swamped and white water rushing out of its galley and wheelhouse. It seesawed briefly, then plunged into a roll again and pushed its way down into the sea, with an awful muffled roar, giving up air at every aperture, air whitening the water, and steam whitening the air.

The small boats that had rounded the long pier made quickly for the spot, and the quickest had to stand off out of the suction and explosions of flotsam. They circled, and men with gaffs pulled people from the water, some bodies lively, and some limp. There was a crowd on the wharf. No one seemed to know who was in charge, but things began to happen, things that looked like order and action, succor and good. Billie stood and stared. Something pulled at her neck and hair—blood, drying already. Her unshod foot was very cold. She limped to the pier's edge and looked down at the boiling sea. There was less air to escape now, and the water was slowly coming clear. The black side of the ship was perhaps only ten feet under. It was still alive, exhaling.

Billie waited for something else to come up.

Then someone clasped her and drew her back, a woman whose hands smelled of fresh herring, and who wrapped Billie in her own harsh woven wool shawl, and gargled at her soothingly in an unknown language. Other women came to help and they made to lift Billie between them. Billie tried to free herself. She said her sister's name. Then that name was the only thing in her universe—her whole life collapsed into her cry—it was all she could recognize. *"Capital E," Edith had said, "is always easy to recognize. It looks like the head of a garden rake." And she wrote, on Billie's slate: "Edith."*

"Edith!" Billie screamed. "Edith! *Edith!*"

2 ⚜ STOLNSAY

MURDO HESKETH WASN'T CAPABLE. THEY SKINNED HIM
before lifting him. They left his sodden coat like a skin in the
bottom of the boat and carried him into the shelter of some
wool bales, out of the wind. There weren't enough blankets, although even from the shelter, and with only one ear, Murdo
thought he could hear a sound very like stones pouring down a
wooden sluice—people in pattens hurrying down the stone
streets of Stolnsay to the harbor to help. A herring-boat man at
Murdo's side used his knife to slit a wool bale open, then pulled
greasy fleeces out to tuck around Murdo and Rixon, his cousin's
son. The man worked tenderly and, despite the cold, Murdo felt
himself catch fire, a half-drowned man in a nest of fleece like a
coal in dry moss. Kindness often enraged him. But this was an
impartial kindness, it was purely circumstantial.

Murdo couldn't move his jaw or hold the cup they offered
him. Young Rixon Hallow was better off, shivering hugely, slop-
ping his tea, but able to speak. He said that his friend Elov had
come ashore in the herring boat with him and was alive. He said
it several times, but, "Where is he?"

A woman with bare forearms glistening with fish scales was
trying to get tea into Murdo's mouth. Murdo realized that he
was reading Rixon's lips and that the rattling of pattens on

cobbles had blended into a high-pitched squeal in his one good ear. He pushed the mug aside and demanded that the woman help him up. She and Rixon reared back. Murdo realized he was shouting. The woman compressed her lips, but did as he asked. Rixon, mistaking Murdo's intentions, stood, too. The boy probably imagined Murdo meant to find Elov Jansen.

The girl with the beautiful hair had leapt from ship to shore only a second before the explosion. She'd blundered past them, white with fear, picked up her skirts, and jumped. Murdo tried to catch her—because, in careening past, she'd winded him, shoved her sharp, insolent elbow into his ribs. He had staggered, snatched at her, then watched her do something wild as if desperate to escape great danger. Then there was a thud, and the deck twitched and rose. It was an explosion in the hold of the ship, on the side against the pier. Murdo had felt hot air push his face and saw it lift the sailors who had been fumbling after the unhinged, overburdened gangplank. It blew them over backward with bloodied faces. Rixon's hat flew off, then the deck began to tilt down toward the large hewn stones of the pier.

Murdo, half-deaf, his strength broken by shuddering, grabbed the arm of a passing man. He asked—shouted—"Where is the girl? The one who jumped?"

The man shook his head.

Rixon peeled off—he'd seen Elov. His young face quivered, smiled, then collapsed. Still susceptible to reprieve, the boy burst into tears and cast himself at his friend. The bloody-nosed cadets squeezed each other till water started out of the thick cloth of their uniforms. Murdo trudged on. He yelled his question, till finally, to his great relief, he came on Rory Skilling, who was on his knees by a half-drowned sailor. Rory Skilling worked for Lord Hallowhulme but was under Murdo's management. Rory sprang up smartly to hear what his manager wanted. He listened, his neck braced with his hand, and made a few timid dampening signs until Murdo dropped his voice. "I can't hear myself," Murdo said, deafly. His ears popped and whistled.

"Can you hear me?" Rory asked, sounding like someone whose head is buried in honey.

Murdo nodded. He said, "Find her. Keep her."

"I have to *know* her, Mr. Hesketh," Rory said. Murdo caught it the second time. He told Rory, "She's young. She has red hair. Or pink—more pink. You will know her by her hair."

Rory Skilling left Murdo, who hunkered down on a salt barrel and dropped his face into his hands.

He saw again his servant's alarmed face, saw the moment in which Ian Betler realized that his efforts to climb were outweighed by the downward progress of the ship. Murdo saw the feeble flurry of Ian's arms, like a kitten tumbling off the edge of a chair, its claws failing to find an anchorage, muscle nothing against momentum. Murdo saw alarm turn to horror, and then saw the familiar figure churned under the hull, caught between the rollers of ship and sea. Ian's hands went last, patting and paddling helplessly at the slick steel plates. For an instant Murdo had leaned out into this latest loss, hovered above it. Then he threw himself back over the keel and fell, scrambled, finally thrust himself free. He saved himself.

Somewhere nearby, and inaudible to him now, the boys, Rixon and Elov, were probably still sobbing and swapping stories, shocked, appalled, grateful—and all Murdo could feel was a kind of disappointment, as though he'd missed an opportunity, or failed a test. It made him queasy. It made him want to shed his cold, deaf, bruised self as he'd shed the coat. But he was curious, too—if this savage suspicion could be called curiosity. His consolation would be to discover *why* that girl jumped. Her. His culprit.

Murdo was suddenly fallen upon and pummeled by his big, clumsy cousin, whom he hadn't heard coming. "Murdo! My dear fellow, are you all right?" James Hallow, Lord Hallowhulme, was shouting. He was excited. He pawed Murdo, all the time issuing orders, making suggestions, giving advice to the people crowded around him. They were mostly men from the castle, all looking eager, as eager as hounds looking at the man with the horn, the master of the hunt. Hallowhulme *managed* Murdo to his feet, supported him, his big arm clasped across his cousin's back. As he propelled his cousin along the pier, Hallowhulme continued to check and palpate and stroke Murdo's neck and face and chest and stomach, saying, over and over, "Not hurt? Not hurt at all?"

"No. I'm not hurt at all," Murdo said, too loud, and saw James wince. "I want to question that girl."

James's meaty, pleading face formed one of its most characteristic expressions—he looked at Murdo as if his cousin were an apparition, an unexplained phenomenon, and somehow as productive of indignation as of surprise. *"Girl?"*

Murdo explained. He mentioned her name.

James Hallow's cheeks and forehead suffused with blood—he flushed as though humiliated. "Good God!" he said. "My cataloguer! He wasn't supposed to be on the *Gustav Edda*."

"The girl is to blame," Murdo said; then, with some effort, "I suspect."

"Are you quite sure?" Lord Hallowhulme was frowning mightily. He looked like a tot straining on a chamber pot—part pained, part delighted. "Surely not. Surely it was the boiler. Some fault with the boiler."

"No." Murdo was stubborn. His rage was stubborn. He shrugged off the supporting arm. "Why did she jump if she wasn't to blame?" He felt stifled, felt the good air drain away from his thinking. Air, or red blood. He was sick of being shown concern. He couldn't feel any pain, only violent impatience. Around him and Hallowhulme lay figures in clothes dark with seawater and wrapped in blankets. Some were sitting, some supine. A stretcher went by with a sailor on it, up on one elbow and cradling his other arm. There were shapes motionless under dirty sailcloth. Others were lying with men at work on them, lifting their arms up and over, up and over, as though the rescuers were teaching the dead to row themselves across that final river. Murdo saw that boats continued to patrol the stretch of water above the wreck, which was still simmering in escaping air. The scene began to shrink, then faded to a red-shot darkness. Murdo hoped no one would catch him and, as he fainted, he thought he heard or felt his cousin abruptly stop fussing and take a step back. Murdo went down in a heap on the stones.

HE CAME TO IN HIS OWN BED. JAMES'S WIFE, CLARA, WAS by him, sitting in a straight-backed chair several feet away. Beyond Clara her maid Jenny stooped over a table and tray, conjuring steam in a bowl. Jenny was a lady's maid but had, on this extraordinary occasion, deigned to descend to dispensing beef-tea.

The curtain was open and Murdo could see an odd red radiance out on the pier.

Clara got up and came to the side of his bed, but she didn't kneel, or even incline a little his way. "Can you hear me?" she said.

Murdo could, but shook his head. He could postpone everything until daylight, until he was strong enough to get up. If no one told him what had been done in his absence—his stupor—who had taken charge, for instance, then he'd be able to pursue his own investigations. In the morning.

However, Clara seemed not to believe him, and kept on talking. She said that it had grown dark too soon. There were seven still unaccounted for, three from the "black gang"—stokers—and four passengers. James had sent to the mainland for divers. Some of the island men had been down in the dark with a line and air hose, without any luck. Clara paused, said again, "Can you hear me?" Then she called Jenny over, with the beef-tea. It was Jenny who got Murdo upright. Clara rearranged his pillows. But then Jenny disobligingly handed her mistress the bowl and Clara had to sit and assist Murdo at getting it to his lips. Clara told him his coat had followed him to the Castle. It was hung up in the drying room, and already looked like a weeks-old seal carcass. "And we had to cut your gloves off. They shrank."

His valise and two of his best suits and shirts and shoes were all in the submerged hold of the *Gustav Edda,* and his watch was on the table by the bed, case open, cogs stilled.

Clara said, about his clothes, that she imagined it all represented quite an investment of time and money. She asked Jenny to bring her brush case (his was gone). "One less thing for you to manage tomorrow by yourself."

Jenny, who was at the door already, started and stared and blinked at Clara's latest remarks—her mistress rubbing salt in her cousin's wounds. Then Jenny let herself out, the door only opening wide enough to let her skirts past, and nearly closing on their hem.

Murdo pushed the bowl away from him.

"Enough?" Clara said. Then, "Can you hear me, Murdo?"

"Yes," Murdo said.

"Rixon told me that it was his impression that his father found and fussed over you before even looking for him." Clara waited, then asked, "Since when have you been such a favorite?"

IN THE MORNING NO ONE CAME TO OPEN MURDO'S CUR-tains, came carrying a hot kettle to take the chill off the water in the washbasin. Or, rather, Ian didn't come.

For some minutes Murdo lay in the ruddy gloom—there was sun coming through a crack in his red brocade curtains. He couldn't hear whether the house was up; his ears still buzzed and fluttered. But he supposed that it *was* up, and he felt forgotten. He had been only Ian Betler's business. Now he was no one's business.

Murdo kicked off his covers and thrashed out of bed like a child in the throes of a tantrum. He found himself on the rug in the middle of the bedroom floor, his muscles pulled and cramping. Even his bones seemed bruised. His fingertips were still bloodless, yellow-white, and when he put them in the basin to splash his face he found that the overnight water felt warm. He dressed himself, shook scenting sprigs of thyme out of a good cotton shirt, wrestled his shoes off the shoe tree, and sat on the edge of his bed to put them on. It took him five minutes to brush the knots out of his hair, and he found only a quarter inch of macassar in the bottle on his bureau. The better stuff French—was in the harbor. Murdo darkened and slicked his hair—which resisted, as usual.

Breakfast was in the dining room by Clara's small conservatory. Past the begonias in their hanging baskets was a view of the black, wet tree trunks of Lady Hallowhulme Park. The sun had gone now, and the air was full of rain that the islanders, more droll than optimistic, persisted in calling "mist."

On his cousin's appearance James Hallow got up from his place, wiped his beard thoroughly with his napkin, and came around the table. "We hadn't expected to see you up so soon," he said. He took Murdo by the elbow and showed him to his chair, drew it out, and pushed it in against the back of Murdo's knees so that he sat rather abruptly. The butler, posted by the sideboard and the chafing dishes, made a few awkward and aborted movements, trying to make James feel his presence, and his *own* place. Lord Hallowhulme paused beside the butler and, without meeting his eye, patted the man several times, squarely, his big fingers drumming on starched shirt front. *Stay put.* James took up a plate and began to displace covers and spoon out scrambled eggs, sausage, blood pudding, and kedgeree. He heaped the plate high, then laid it before Murdo quietly, without a flourish. At least he allowed Murdo to deal with his own napkin.

During this performance everyone at the table was silent, but once James was back in his own chair he resumed speaking. He was telling his son's friend, Elov Jansen, about his kippering houses down at Southport. How far forward the construction was. "I'll show you the plans after breakfast, shall I? There's a new pier, jetty, and half a dozen houses for my managers. While you're here we must get up a party to Southport. Overland, so you can appreciate some of the fine Paleolithic sites between here and there."

Elov nodded, bewildered. His food had long since ceased to steam; he hadn't been able to tell when he might be called on to make an alert response.

James Hallow turned to Murdo and told him that the divers

he'd sent for were not expected till the following day. There were times when it really was no virtue to be so out-of-the-way.

Elov Jansen gratefully turned his attention to his plate. Murdo watched the boy. Elov was, like Rixon, bruised beneath the eyes, waxy and unsteady. He seemed relieved that he had lost his host's attention and felt reassured by the quiet sobriety of Lord Hallowhulme's latest remark.

Hallowhulme took a forkful of sausage into his mouth and chewed with mighty appetite, as though giving a demonstration of chewing. The fork's tines thrust into a mound of rice and clashed on the plate. All James's big noises and deliberate movements seemed to be saying "Come on, buck up," to all of them. He swallowed, and started talking again. It was a shame, he said, that all those fellows on the pier hadn't thought to use their hats. "Use their heads, and use their hats." He waited a decent interval, and with increasing delight, to be sure that no one knew what he meant—knew what *he* knew. "A hat makes a capital life preserver," he said, and then put down his fork to poke a finger in the air. "Provided it's the stiff sort, silk or beaver or thick felt—a straw boater just wouldn't be up to the job. No—a stiff hat and a pocket handkerchief are all a person needs to make a life preserver. In a pinch." James pushed his plate and cutlery aside to mime, and the invisible objects of his lesson immediately assumed real dimensions, real substance. He was pink with enthusiasm. "First you spread your handkerchief on the ground, then put the hat on it, brim down. Then you tie the handkerchief, careful to keep the knots upward and in the center of the crown." He looked up, in turn, at his son Rixon, Rixon's friend Elov, and at his daughter, Minnie, who was listening with a calm politeness that was obviously a cue to the bewildered Elov Jansen. "Then"—James half rose from his chair, making his demonstration—"seizing the knot in one hand and keeping the opening of the hat upward, you can fearlessly plunge into deep water despite being unable to swim." He sat down again, dusted his palms together, to dissipate the particles of the imaginary hat and handkerchief. "There's not enough emphasis in education on learning all the little tricks and devices that make us able to render assistance to our imperiled fellow creatures," James said. "There are boys and girls all over this island getting their catechism off by heart—in one of two flavors—but frankly, I think that the churches, having them for an hour on Sunday morning, should teach a few practical matters not related to mending nets, sowing barley, or cutting peat."

Elov opened his mouth to say something. "But—" Then he jumped.

Rixon had prodded him under the cover of the table. Rixon knew not to say a word, knew that it made no difference if you disagreed, agreed, asked a question, tried to turn the subject— there was endless potential energy in his father's talk, and one word, one touch, would only set it rolling on again.

Lord Hallowhulme called for a fresh pot of tea. His daughter, Minnie, had patted her mouth and risen a few inches from her seat, so that the butler hustled up behind to draw back her chair. She said, "My lessons, Father."

"Yes, Minnie. Are you fully fortified?"

"Yes, Father." She shook the napkin off her sticky hand and came around the table to kiss him. Minnie was short and slight and had to balance a hand on one of her father's big shoulders in order to lean in to his face. Then she circled behind Murdo, who was sure he could feel her gaze breeze the back of his head. She touched her lips to her mother's cheek, checked the door before it was fully ajar, checked the footman's white-gloved hand to discourage him from opening it farther. The footman audibly caught his breath, possibly because of the touch, possibly he was shocked to have forgotten one of the household's habits, or preferences.

James Hallow had remembered that the new telephones, and telephone line, and batteries, had been in the hold of the *Gustav Edda*. He had been *so* looking forward to its installation, the Isle's first telephone line, between Kiss Castle and its gatehouse first, then between the castle and the post office, possibly the Rectory—Mr. Mulberry being willing—and there would certainly be a telephone line to the factory. "Another factory," said the smirking James to Elov, who blinked and blushed. "At Scouse Beach, near here. A factory to extract alginate from seaweed. It's the food of the future, you know."

Elov nodded, as if he did know.

James's wife Clara said that she must go and write to her friend Jane Tegner, who, considering the accident, might decide against bringing the twins to visit Minnie. She hoped they weren't on their way already.

Rixon muttered that at least he and Elov would be excused from Minnie and the twins' ambitious theatricals.

"I'll ask what Jane thinks," Clara said, but she didn't get up.

Murdo did and, as always, the butler anticipated his movement. Murdo looked over his shoulder at the man. He said thank you. He saw sympathy. "I'm going to speak to Rory Skilling," he said to James.

Clara stood. "And I'm going to visit the people in Mr. Mulberry's 'infirmary.' "

"I'm going there, too," Murdo said. "Eventually."

"Good morning, then, to both of you. Good work," James said. He beamed at his wife as she came gliding up the room to kiss him, and held her as she did so, his hand on the artificial fluted curve of her waist.

Jenny was waiting in the hallway with her mistress's coat, hat, and gloves. She helped Clara into the coat and they both turned to the big dark glass above the hall table to settle the hat. Clara rolled down the hat's veil over her dull-skinned, handsome, worn face. Murdo saw that she was watching him in the mirror. He told her that Rory Skilling had a suspect in custody at the gate-house. "The suspect jumped from the ship directly before the explosion. Before the gangplank was down."

Clara wormed one hand into a glove, settled the leather over her wedding ring.

"I think James underestimates the islanders' antagonism toward himself and his ideas," Murdo said.

"Antagonism?"

"Hostility."

"James wasn't on the *Gustav Edda*," said Clara. She put her other glove on and took the bag from Jenny. They left the house.

Murdo went back to the dining room, opened the door and asked James if he had the *Gustav Edda*'s cargo manifest—and if not who would have it?

"I thought of that yesterday evening," James said. "Anticipated your interest."

Murdo waited in the doorway. He brushed the door lightly with his shoulder so that it opened farther.

"There wasn't anything explosive on the ship—except the coal, of course," James said, his brows knitted. He began to fidget with irritation. "For God's sake, cousin, either come in or go out!"

"Where is it? The manifest," Murdo said.

James Hallow leapt up. The blasted paper was in his office,

he said. He hustled his cousin out of the doorway, closed the door firmly, gave the door handle a couple of fast turns to make sure it was firmly latched, and, taking Murdo under the elbow, led him to his office.

The room was dusted and polished, and the window glass sparkled with the lead from the ink in the newspaper used by the maid for its final polish. But there were papers everywhere, notes and plans, books stacked on chairs, and two unfinished canvases precariously sharing James's easel. The cargo manifest and other papers pertaining to the ship had not yet worked their way under the sediment of documents. "I do have a copy to spare," James said, and gave the manifest to Murdo, who thanked him. James drew his cousin to him by his elbow, so that their hips bumped, but he didn't look at Murdo. He said quietly that of course Murdo must satisfy himself about the accident, but he should bear in mind how little James could spare him, Southport and Scouse Beach being at a crucial stage in their development.

"I'll be everywhere, James," Murdo promised, then, amusing himself, "You won't see me."

"Of course, of course," James said. He released Murdo's arm, gave him a shying and sideways look and a slap on the back.

Murdo went to speak to Rory.

A LONG, PARTLY GRAVELED ROAD RAN IN A LOOP through the edge of Lady Hallowhulme Wood and then down between the seawall and a sloping lawn before the castle. The road continued around the edge of the shallow, notched corner of the harbor—where the sea lay only at high tide—and terminated at a stagnant waterway straddled by a bridge on which perched Kiss Castle's gatehouse.

Murdo walked from the graveled drive and along the road whose surface was rutted, leaves in a deep layer in each rut and the grass tall on either side. The road seemed to say, soberly, that it wasn't recreational, was only for expeditions either into or out of the grounds of the castle. As Murdo went he watched water draining back into the mush of leaves where Clara's trap had passed and the road was recovering its composure. Below the seawall the tide was out and the rocks of the seabed were draped with a tissue of tender green sea cabbage and brown Neptune's necklace. The notch was in the shade, rank and slippery, its air grainy with midges.

Murdo knocked and was admitted to the gatehouse. Three men were lounging in its kitchen—Rory's fat female friend was busy at the range. All had glasses of porter by them.

The men were overseers employed on Lord Hallowhulme's Stolnsay projects under Murdo's management. They were islanders, but only two were locals. Rory—like his surname—was from over the mountain range that had divided the island throughout its history.

Stolnsay was the largest settlement on Kissack, Southport the largest on Skilling. This "on" was deceptive—since Kissack and Skilling were one island. One—but because of the dividing mountains, Kissack had been invaded, settled, and ruled by Norsemen for several hundred years of its history, whereas Skilling was, for a long time, under the protection of an Irish chief. Both Kissack and Skilling later became the territories of two mainland clans, but while Kissack, looking to the northeast, embraced a combination of Scandinavian Lutheranism and the Knox Church, Skilling, facing southwest, remained an outpost of the Church of Rome. Rory Skilling was a Catholic, and was thus even more Murdo's man—not because Murdo was a

Catholic; he was not—but because, as a Catholic, Rory was scarcely tolerated in Stolnsay.

At the gatehouse Murdo sent someone up to see if his prisoner was awake. Then he drew Rory aside. "Can you do something for me?"

The man turned his mouth down; he was surprised, not disapproving, perhaps pleased to be asked for help instead of given an order. He was favoring Murdo with his most attentive, serious look.

"Would you go into town and buy me some shaving tackle? Mine went down with the ship."

Rory began to shuffle.

Murdo gave him some money.

Rory palmed it but continued to shuffle. He sighed, said, "You do know that I live *here*, Mr. Hesketh. Here in the gatehouse."

"Yes?"

"My Fiona"—he indicated the fat woman at the range—"brings us bread, and eggs, and fish, and ale, sir. The landlords don't like us at the bars. And the grocer has long since stopped serving me. I'm sorry, Mr. Hesketh." Rory unclenched his hand and gave back Murdo's crumpled money.

Murdo hadn't been aware, till then, that his men were so ostracized. He was astonished, and uncomfortable. He must send them down some whiskey later.

The other man reappeared and said, "She's awake."

Murdo went upstairs to see her.

3 ⚜ AMONG THE DEAD

BILLIE WOKE WHEN THE KEY TURNED AND OPENED HER
eyes to see a man peer around the door.

"Miss?" he said. Then he came into the room and fished in
his patched jacket. He placed a comb beside her on the bed. He
apologized, he had no mirror. He went out again.

There was dusty white grease in the teeth of the comb. Billie
looked at it—waited as though for animation—before turning
her eyes to the other recent appearance in the room: a mug of
tea, its heat long gone and a dark skin on its surface. This skin
shook and wrinkled as the floorboards quivered. Another man
came into the room. Billie looked only at his shoes. They were
black, with a high polish on the black leather-covered buttons of
their gaiters.

Had she not slept? he asked, then came close enough for her
to see his hands, too, to see the one with the wedding ring lift the
blankets that were still folded on the foot of the bed—lift them
as though he was looking for something stowed between them.
Then he planted himself in front of her and reached down to
touch the filthy comb.

Billie raised her head just high enough to see his waistcoat,
watch chain, fob—all black, the chain made of beads, basalt and
jet, the fob a heavy jet heart embossed with the glittering facets

of an eight-pointed star. Billie checked her own hands, the silver ring on the little finger of one. His wedding ring was on his *right* hand, she saw, and he was in mourning. She looked up into his face.

His face blinded her. It was, simply, the wrong one. She turned her head.

"You will need shoes," he said. He went back to the door and called down the stairs: "Rory, send Fiona up here, will you?" Then, a moment later, and in a lower tone, to a nearer person: "Could you go up to the castle and tell Mrs. Deet that there is a girl from the ship with no shoes who needs to walk somewhere. Tell Deet the girl is approximately the same size as Miss Minnie."

He came back to stand over the bed. He asked Billie why she had jumped.

She made an effort, but only to say that she couldn't talk to him—didn't care to.

He asked her how she did it.

Jumped? Took flight? Flew? She was in the cabin with Edith still, and was singing. She jumped and she hit her head. Oil fell from the lamp in little rags of fire. There were holes in the wool of her skirt, coin-sized, with brittle scorched edges. She was in the cabin with Edith still. The shadows swung and pooled against one wall. Black water. The light had gone out. She was in the cabin with Edith still—

He asked how she *knew*? Why she jumped when she did?

Billie tried; she opened her mouth and got it wrong. "The sip shank," she said. Then she said, "Stupid," to herself. She was gagged by stupidity. She ventured a look and saw his curled upper lip.

"You disgusting creature," he said, softly.

Billie was being misunderstood and it mattered to her. That

surprised her. She began to shake. She found she wasn't in the cabin with Edith and the song was just something wheedling away in her sore ear. She touched her ear and felt, all down her neck, a lock of hair plastered with blood, set as hard as the grain in a branch of sea-dried tortured willow.

Billie moved back against the wall, drew her feet up under her skirt, and wrapped her arms around her knees.

THE GIRL MOCKED MURDO'S QUESTIONS, THEN CALLED him stupid, and then squirmed back across the bed and folded herself up away from him, fastidiously hiding her bare toes. The room filled with the faint smell of old vomit, stirred up from her skirt when she moved. There were holes in her dress, as though made by a dropped cigarette.

Gooseflesh formed on the skin of Wilhelmina Paxton's flat breastbone. In the dim light her hair was darker, a red without its own radiance, matted at the back, separated in thick chunks, and so long its curls still managed to form hooks against the bed-clothes on either side of her hips.

"Speak up," Murdo said. "Why did you jump, Miss Paxton?" Then he went on to say that, while the island operated under the laws of the land, there was no representative of that law on the island—unless one were to count his cousin, James, who was a magistrate.

"Henry was coming to take up employment as cataloguer of Lord Hallowhulme's library," the girl said. Then, "I was happy to hear his name had two Hs. I couldn't turn it around. I didn't have to practice." Then she finally answered Murdo's question. "It's no business of yours why I jumped." She hugged herself tighter, put her forehead on her knees, and muttered that she couldn't bear to wear anyone else's shoes.

Murdo said he imagined she might need shoes to follow a coffin.

Miss Paxton grunted. She said, "Uh!" in the true timbre of her voice, which wasn't deep but dense and furry somehow— Murdo had heard that when she'd apologized after her clottish mistake with pail, vomit, and prevailing wind. Miss Paxton grunted, and came off the bed with the same speedy competence with which she'd jumped from deck to gangplank. She crashed into Murdo and pushed him right across the room and against the wall. The room shuddered, and a panel cracked. Miss Paxton was small but solid, like a young dog, all power and muscle; the only feminine things about her were her hair and her fine upholstery of body fat. Murdo caught her. He didn't fall. He held her fists away from his face. She called him a pig—a mist of warm spit hit his chin. Then she went limp, lolled, and he turned her so that she fell against him, her head on his shoulder.

Murdo righted himself and walked her to the door, touched the back of her bare ankle, her tender Achilles' tendon, with the toe of his boot. She moved. He walked her down the stairs. Every man in the kitchen was on his feet, red-faced with stove heat and booze, but blotched, the faces turned to him like cards in a high straight hand.

"Mr. Hesketh," said Rory.

"Be quiet!" Murdo said, savage. He sat Miss Paxton on the stairs, her arms held crushed against her body. Then he released her. His hands hurt from the exertion of his grip.

"Is the young lady—?" Rory tried. Murdo glared at him, then at the top of Wilhelmina Paxton's drooping head. He said

to her that he simply could not believe that the explosion was
only coincidental with her jump.

"But, sir—" Rory persisted. "Why would a young lady go
to those lengths to—" Then, with difficulty, "Who on that ship
had enemies so desperate?"

Murdo shrugged this off. He'd possibly never have imagined
that the ship was sabotaged if the girl hadn't jumped. He told
Rory that he didn't have to explain his thinking. But then he
did. Perhaps it was the *cargo* the saboteur had wanted to send to
the bottom, the tools and materials for Lord Hallowhulme's fac-
tories. Perhaps the explosion occurred too soon. The fuse was
poorly timed. She set it, then saw her mistake, and ran.

Murdo saw that Rory Skilling looked dubious. He also saw
pity. He leaned forward, held his weight for a moment on his
trembling arms, then sat on the step above the silent, drooping girl. He looked at her hands—her grubby, grazed palms, stiff
with scabs, and curled like cooked shrimps. Then he closed
his eyes and regarded what he cherished—a plausible picture—
Wilhelmina Paxton setting a flame to a fuse, the dynamite
packed between the plates of the hull and something unyielding,
perhaps the crated parts for the Scouse Beach generator, or
James's telephones, their batteries, and bales of cable. He saw
Miss Paxton check her watch to time the fuse. And, persuaded
by his picture, he opened his eyes to look for the timepiece,
around her neck or pinned to her breast. He touched her and she
brushed at his hands, absently, as if brushing at a fly or scratchy
foliage. Murdo opened the bag she wore on her belt—found a
mesh miser's purse, a pewter pillbox, a comb, a manicure set, a
hinged buttonhook and shoehorn, the steel horn engraved on its
inside curve: Janet Blazey. She hadn't a watch, of course, and so
Murdo let it go—her purse, and his picture.

"It was the boiler," Rory said, consolingly.

"Edith," whispered Miss Paxton.

For several minutes nothing was said or done. Murdo remained beside the girl, his head hanging, too, his men looming in the passageway and teetering a little like skittles grazed by a bowling ball.

Fiona came back with two pairs of shoes. Worn dancing shoes, one pair red, the other white. "These can be spared, says Mrs. Deet." Fiona was out of breath, with anger as well as hurry. She said to Rory, beginning quietly and ending up broadcasting: "Deet was in a fluster. I suppose because these shoes were poor Miss Ingrid's. Still, a respectable woman would have asked *why* the girl was in the gatehouse, and noticed that, with me gone, the girl must be in the gatehouse alone"—Fiona gave Murdo a mollifying but totally unmeant smile—"with one gentleman, and three ruffians." She was making it quite clear she'd modified her first thought—*four* ruffians. She knelt to fasten the shoes on Miss Paxton's feet, first removing Miss Paxton's one remaining shoe. "And where are you taking her, Mr. Hesketh?"

"Mr. Mulberry's church."

"She should have been there from the first," said Fiona.

"But Fi, she was never in the water," said Rory Skilling.

Murdo could feel his rage going, taken by reason and the force of circumstance. He had felt that he'd come ashore on the girl, that his imagination followed her jump—but behind him was the water, and Ian, under the water. Only his spite had vitality; it pulled him up and on again. Miss Paxton's scabbed palm was against his own; he hauled her to her feet as Fiona finished fastening the shoes. Miss Paxton stumbled around the kneeling woman. Murdo hauled her out the door.

They walked from under the arch of the gatehouse and onto

the road. Murdo's men followed them, a few paces back, except Rory Skilling, who stayed just behind Murdo's shoulder, and whispered to him, "God help you, Mr. Hesketh."

Murdo ignored him. He didn't have to drag the girl. She went on nimbly enough, kept pace with him. Her arm was at its fullest stretch, but her shoulder never pulled forward. The worn leather soles of poor Miss Ingrid's slippers slapped and scuffed.

MR. MULBERRY'S CHURCH HAD BECOME A MAKESHIFT IN-firmary. Some pews had been moved together to make beds and others had been pushed back to the walls to make way for cots. There was a detached draining board balanced on the font, car-rying a kettle, a basin, a pot of soup, and a basket of bread. There were around ten town women in attendance on twelve near-drowned people—Mrs. Mulberry in charge of all.

Billie stood where she'd been let go, in the doorway, and listened to the doctor, to the minister, Mr. Mulberry, and to Murdo Hesketh. Hesketh was now all politeness, patience, and propriety. The doctor told how he had the four worst cases back at his house—those who showed signs of bronchopneumonia af-ter their immersion. Three had been "pumped" on the pier yesterday. Emptied of water, and had air pumped in by a bellows inserted in one nostril. There were many "dry" drownings—the shock of sudden and unexpected immersion in the icy water had simply stopped hearts. All the dead were next door, in the sac-risty. Seven bodies were as yet unrecovered.

"Your cousin wouldn't let me look you over," the doctor said to Hesketh, grave. "Or the young gentlemen. He was in a hurry to have you off the scene and safe at Kiss Castle, and he couldn't be made to see sense." The doctor pointed the porcelain cone of his stethoscope at Hesketh's buttoned waistcoat. "Do you mind?" Hesketh gazed disdainfully over the top of the doctor's head, but submitted to his touch, stood rigid as the doctor unfastened six waistcoat and three shirt buttons and put the stethoscope in against his heart. The doctor then inserted a hand, fingers shaped like a parrot's beak, to sound against Hesketh's ribs. Billie saw Hesketh hold his breath, as he was told, then let it out so that it stirred the wispy, unoiled hair by the doctor's left ear.

"You're fine," the doctor said, himself reassured. Then he moved out of the knot of men, came to Billie, frowned at her, concerned, and pushed down her bodice a little to place the skin-warmed porcelain cone against the top of her chest.

"She wasn't in the water," one of Hesketh's men said, informative and acid at once. Billie recognized the man as the one with the same name as the other half of the island—Skilling.

"I've brought Miss Paxton to help identify some people. Wherever they are." Hesketh spread his hands rather like the evenhanded, sloe-eyed Christs in the Last Judgments frescoed on walls of the churches Billie had seen as a child. Churches in San Remo or Portofino, or the chapel near La Brigue— Christs with hands spread to say, *Behold! The damned and the saved.* Hesketh was apparently too refined to say, "Among the living or the dead."

Billie, who knew well enough where in a church a sacristry generally was, took herself there. The men hadn't expected this independent movement and, by the time they caught up, Billie was already in the doorway, and faced with two rows of wrapped forms, on the flagstone floor, around a massive, immovable table in the center of the room. The only light came from the church behind Billie and two tall and narrow windows of alternating, diamond-shaped, violet-and-amber panes. The minister's wife appeared beside Billie, a lamp in her hand. She took Billie's arm and led her in among the silent shapes. Mr. Mulberry, Mr. Hesketh, and Rory Skilling followed them.

The corpses wore their names printed on brown paper and pinned to their shrouds. Billie looked at the paper on the shape nearest her, then glanced helplessly at Mrs. Mulberry. "What is it, dear?" said the minister's wife. "Do you know this man? He's Gunther Hathrenson, ABS—which means able seaman."

"I can't read," Billie whispered.

"Who are you looking for?"

"Edith—and Henry."

Mrs. Mulberry nodded and led Billie farther in. "I've forgotten myself," she said. Her voice trembled. "Forgotten all the names. I helped write the labels last night and I've forgotten."

The room was full, but breathless. The women's skirts hissed against the sheeted figures at their feet.

"She might mean the young fellow in Irish tweed," Mr. Mulberry said, in a hoarse whisper from the doorway.

The women had come about at the stained-glass window, arm in arm, as though they were taking a turn around the parlor on a sodden day. And there was Hesketh, barring their passage, halfway up the room, his arms out on either side of him, not very high, but nevertheless forming a barrier. His pale skin and hair and eyes gave back the lamp's light, grew lamplike as the women came closer to him. "Thank you, Mrs. Mulberry," he said, and took the lamp from the minister's wife and placed it beside him on the table.

Billie looked down at the body he was guarding, but Hesketh put a hand below her chin, fingers fanned—he didn't touch her, but screened her gaze. She moved her head, but his hand followed, stayed between her and her view. Mrs. Mulberry blushed and began to breathe fast.

"Go on, madam," Hesketh said.

The minister's wife drew back a pace, but didn't leave Billie.

Hesketh placed a cold hand on Billie's wrist and squatted, pulling her down into a crouch. He used his free hand to move the sheet veiling the head of the corpse. Billie stared—for a moment she couldn't see the total, only the dry surfaces of bared teeth, dull, like the tea-stained inside of an old porcelain cup. She thought of remedies, like baking soda.

"See the gooseflesh?" Hesketh said. "It's as though his skin is still trying to raise some life and warm him."

The face was dusky and mottled. The man's jacket was drawn down and his shirt had burst at the shoulder seams to reveal red patches of hemorrhage. Hesketh followed her gaze: Billie felt it—his bright eyes on her face. He said, "It looks as if he was the victim of assault, doesn't it? But it was only his struggle that injured him. He was looking for something to hold on to. You see, water yields, but wins." He went on to say that, while the skin was rough, it wasn't swollen and wrinkled. "He was only a few hours in the water. And it was cold." Hesketh stooped, as if to look in under the man's partly open eyelids and, doing so, leaned a little weight on the overinflated chest. The white foam that crusted the man's lips and nostrils burst fresh from each, exuded thickly, a white tinged with pink. Hesketh drew back sharply. Both he and Billie stayed kneeling, stunned and penitential. Above their heads Mrs. Mulberry said, "But— this is Ian Betler."

Billie got up.

"I think we should go have a look at the young man in the Irish tweed," the minister's wife said, and beckoned, very gentle. Billie followed her. As they walked, Mrs. Mulberry read out the rest of the labels.

Henry, however, was among the living, though scarcely conscious. Billie was taken to the doctor's house, where they found Henry wrapped in bare wool blankets, before a fire, and smelling powerfully of both liniment and brandy. Billie sank to her knees beside his couch, but found herself unable to touch him. There was something between them, it seemed—or nothing between them, an impassable barrier made of an absence.

Mrs. Mulberry carried a wrapped warm brick from the fireplace, lifted Henry's blankets, and put the brick at his feet. A few minutes after that the doctor appeared and uncovered Henry's chest, which was marked by a number of red, fluid-filled blisters. The doctor explained that he had injected peppermint water. "To help him revive." Billie watched the doctor warm his hands and sit on the edge of the couch. He spilled some spirits into his warmed hands and began to rub Henry's sides, so vigorously that the flesh made a whooping, flapping sound. Henry gasped and moaned.

"He did revive after an hour or two," the doctor said, above the sound his hands made chafing Henry's skin. "But now fever has set in." He finished his massage and closed the blankets around Henry's slight form. "Now he must be kept quiet and warm. When he wakes perhaps he might drink a little broth." He was addressing Mrs. Mulberry now. He shook his head. "It's too close and crowded here."

"Can he be moved, Doctor?" inquired a woman.

Billie looked up at the tall figure. The woman removed her

veiled hat, looked about, and balanced it on the horned top of a big case clock.

"We'll see, Lady Hallowhulme. I don't have room to run a hospital. It makes more sense for *me* to move between my patients. I anticipate five to ten serious chest cases following on from the accident. The rest—I don't know. Any man who has not come back to himself by now I can't hold out much hope for. I've a woman over here already starting to swell up—her kidneys having had a mortal shock."

"Doctor—this poor man is Henry Maslen, whom my husband has employed to catalogue the castle library. And this young lady is—I think—Mr. Maslen's sister."

"His wife's sister," Billie said. "Miss Paxton."

The woman gave Billie her bony, gloved hand. She was Clara Hallow. "We must find out what you need, Miss Paxton, and what can be done for Mr. Maslen."

Billie said she'd stay with Henry. She had been looking for her sister, Edith, but hadn't found her.

Lady Hallowhulme's thin, shapely face, trying to hide sadness, looked as if she had just encountered a bad smell. She glanced at the doctor, then at Mrs. Mulberry. "Hannah?"

"Mrs. Maslen hasn't been found, I'm afraid."

Billie was thinking about a boat ride she'd had, in San Remo, with some Italian boys. Edith had scolded and begged and tried to drag her back on the beach, but Billie took off her shoes and socks, climbed into the boat and went out with them. She was eight. The boys had wanted to touch her hair, and check the speckles on her legs. Billie sat on the seat in the bow and let them lift and drop her curls, look into her eyes, or at her ears, *"Piccolo!"* She let them unbutton a cuff to caress her wrist, and lift her skirt to touch her ankles. But when they wanted to do more than touch, to *move her about*, she capsized their boat and came up underneath it to press hands and feet on its sides, her head up in the trapped air. She listened to them call and search. She watched them clumsily try to dive down—their buoyancy a kind of leadenness—their legs' ineffectual soft scissoring, shoes shedding bubbles, and suits ballooning. She breathed compressed air, listened to the little waves slap the wood. After a minute one of the boys finally thought to look underneath the boat, and seized her around her waist, tearing her out of her anchorage. Between them they got her ashore. She let them struggle—stayed limp, as she'd been schooled to. They put her down on the shingle and dripped on her, sobbed, and prayed. It was a chilly day in May and the shore was empty. Only Edith came—kicked the boys and cursed at them. They ran off. Edith understood that her sister was acting. She wouldn't speak to Billie, but went off to sit on the terrace near the casino and wait for their father to come out.

There had been light in the upturned boat, aqua light from beneath, light in the shape of a church window, the shape of a boat.

Thinking of this, Billie said to Lady Clara and to Mrs. Mulberry, "Even if there was any air, it would be wholly dark in there. In the ship."

Lady Clara put a hand on Billie's arm.

Billie considered the dark, the cold water—how cold?—Edith's impediment of belly. "Edith's dead, isn't she?" Billie said to Lady Hallowhulme.

"Almost certainly, I'm afraid, my dear," the woman replied.

Billie looked about for Murdo Hesketh and his men, and

realized she'd come over to the doctor's house with only the minister's wife.

"These aren't my shoes," Billie said to Lady Hallowhulme, who frowned at what seemed an odd, additional remark, and at the possibly familiar footwear. "You look ill. You must rest." Lady Hallowhulme looked to Mrs. Mulberry for help. "Hannah?"

"I think it may be difficult to persuade Miss Paxton to leave Mr. Maslen. What we must establish is how soon Mr. Maslen can be moved to the castle."

"Yes."

"It's a case of wait and see," the doctor told the women.

"Would you like to wash your face and hands, dear?" Mrs. Mulberry asked. She got Billie up and showed her to a basin in the corner of the crowded room. Billie washed. They gave her something to eat.

Fed, Billie went back and settled by Henry. Her hand lay next to his, but she didn't touch him. She watched his face, at last at leisure to do so. There was no pleasure in her watching, nor patience, she merely waited, waited to be the one who had to answer what Henry's face, even asleep, was asking—"*Edith?*"—because he was Henry, so where was Edith?

MURDO STOOD ON THE PIER, ABOVE THE WRECK, AND watched the local men diving with their rope and makeshift airhose. He recognized the *Gustav Edda*'s captain in the bow of the boat that floated above the place where air occasionally came up in small batches of bubbles.

He saw that a salvaged mailbag lay beside the captain in the bottom of the boat. The fisherman holding the end of the hose said to Murdo, "It's not so good with no pump." He made a pumping sign, not entirely certain he had the right word.

"Is it danger?" Murdo asked, in his apt but ungrammatical Gaelic.

The man nodded.

"But divers are coming from the mainland." Murdo went back to English. He supposed that the locals would continue to dive themselves till the divers came. Perhaps they couldn't be satisfied there was no one trapped and alive until they saw all the bodies.

A young man surfaced, first appeared as a watery mirage, man-shaped, against the ship's black side, then turned his wide face up to the light, and broke through. He was pink-skinned, chubby, wheezing with cold. He was hauled into the boat, and immediately wrapped. The rowers set out for the pier and the young man was helped into a topless tent where women with steaming kettles were filling a small zinc bath. The man stripped, his friends closing the tent with a blanket, which, once he'd dipped, and washed himself in the warm water, they folded around him. Since he had emerged he'd been shaking his head. The rope he'd carried into the wreck was still taut between the pier and the depths. When the man got his breath he said he'd managed to open the engine room door. He had a body on the rope but couldn't shift it back through the hatch. He'd not had enough breath.

"Can you see the boiler? Does the rent let in light enough?" the captain asked.

The man nodded. Coal and coal dust had settled on the bottom of the engine room, he said. "On one wall, really, like treacle in water. I could see everything. The boiler is whole. There are three bodies in the engine room. And I saw a woman wedged behind the ladder—" He shook his head again, perhaps trying to dislodge water in his ear, it was so abrupt a movement. He blinked and blinked, and glared at his friends, and then began to sob. He said that he'd seen a baby hanging within her skirts.

Murdo walked away, walked back around the harbor and along the promontory to Kiss Castle.

AT DINNER JAMES HALLOW ASKED WHETHER HIS COUSIN had remembered to write to Mr. Betler's kinfolk. Murdo lied. He hadn't been able to finish the letter. He'd felt he needed to know more about the cause of the accident. "The locals who have been diving into the wreck found the boiler intact." Murdo thought that might deflect his cousin's interest. It seemed to, but not in the way he expected. He'd imagined that his cousin would begin to speculate, would launch a flotilla, a *fleet* of theories about the sinking. But James said, "Indeed." And then attended to his food.

Murdo was forced to understand that he'd run out to look at his suspect and had forgotten his duty. He excused himself from the dinner table before dessert was served and went to his room to write his letter, only one, to Geordie Betler, Ian's older brother.

On his bed Murdo found a parcel, wrapped in brown paper. Brushes and combs, macassar, soap and shaving tackle, a pig's bristle brush, a razor and strop. He sat on his bed and handled the gifts, then carefully laid away the razor. His razor had been an object that, for the last several years, would sometimes shine at him a steely invitation. Murdo considered his hopelessness. Considered the silence of his room, a silence not only of privacy, but of neglect. He saw Ian beating up shaving foam in a cup,

Ian's care, his hand testing the bathwater, his form crouched at a hearth laying a fire in a humble room, his figure wrapped in blankets on the far side of the fire and near the picketed horses. Murdo saw Ian sleeping, sleeping and *there*, his apt attention, his ready ear.

Murdo covered his face with his hands.

4 ⚜ THE ELDER BETLER

IT WAS MEELA TANNOY, HIS EMPLOYER'S WIFE, WHO
stopped Geordie Betler. When he reached for the door handle
she leaned forward and placed her hand on his arm. She gently
pressed him back beside Tannoy and put up the heavy leather
blind that covered the carriage window. It was around ten in the
morning, and the sun was out, but mist still pushed against
the blind arches of Carrick's Folly and poured over its rim.

Meela Tannoy told the men that she would take the
footman—to beat off thieves, or curiosity seekers—and walk up
to the high street. Her eyelids were heavy and her look droll. She
said that since she was in Oban she might as well take a look at its
little shops. She opened the door, and the footman was there,
folding down the steps before her stout boots. Quayside idlers
stirred and stared. Mrs. Tannoy fished two folds of her silk sari
out of the collar of her long Paris coat and drew them up over
her head. She paused to look back in, not at Geordie, but at her
husband—a quick look that carried several clear instructions, and
her confidence in him. Then she left, the footman following
her figure in its weird mix of nipped-waisted wool and amber
gossamer.

Andrew Tannoy raised the other blind and a long halt of
sunlight ran through the carriage. The dust looked lively.

Geordie and his employer regarded the ship. It was still taking on cargo and signing new crew, three of whom had paused, canvas sacks on their squared shoulders, facing the cargo that was still waiting its turn, a collection of empty boxes which had to go on top, couldn't take too much weight, or sit too close to other goods and contaminate them. Contaminate with bad luck, for the cargo the new crew stood and eyed waited stacked in four hearses—coffins for Stolnsay, whose own coffin-maker hadn't enough seasoned timber to house the *Gustav Edda*'s eighteen dead crewmen and passengers.

"The wind is sharp," said Andrew Tannoy. "Parky." He didn't say, *"You need not go yet, Geordie. We'll wait here till you embark."*

Geordie felt comfortable with this restraint, for Geordie Betler was a butler, and a model of propriety. Well—it was axiomatic, all butlers were proper, but Geordie had been seven years with Tannoy and the rules of Tannoy's house were relaxed and informal. Informal, not unnatural; relaxed, but not lax. Andrew Tannoy put no stock in the niceties that had often worked to exclude him even as he made his fortune. He didn't oppose, but ignored them. Tannoy was an educated man. The son of a poor parish minister, he had starved his way through a degree in mathematics and a pinch-penny post in a Glasgow firm of engineers. Then he went to India and built bridges on a Himalayan railway. Tannoy had retired at thirty-eight, his health imperiled by a fever. He came home to Scotland with a yellow complexion and an Indian wife. "I was on the bones of my bottom," he'd once told Geordie. "But we rented rooms and I used my little bit of money to build my first steam shovel, then I put in for the patent."

Andrew Tannoy now had a factory in Glasgow, and a big house in Ayrshire, a tender liver, and his white-haired, soft-spoken Meela. He had friendly tenants and a few good friends—enough for a busy shooting season. He had a well-paid, comfortably housed butler whom he was loath to lose. And he knew enough to be worried.

Geordie could see that his employer was trying to think how he could coax his butler to talk. Andrew Tannoy was concerned—and in need of reassurance. Geordie was fond of his employer, but he was also curious about him. Tannoy was an original, and Geordie wanted to see what he'd do, how he'd manage both his anxiety and the impropriety of fussing over a servant.

Andrew Tannoy rubbed his forehead. Then he blurted, "He's no idler."

This was a novel approach. Geordie turned in his seat, and looked attentive.

"Well, of course, I am. Played out. Or, I play as men do when they've made a fortune and want a quiet life."

Andrew Tannoy was talking about Lord Hallowhulme. He was making his foray into Geordie's near future—but on *his* side, as a segregated stallion, who must watch his mares and keep pace with them along his side of the fence. Geordie and Andrew Tannoy were servant and master, but for Mr. Tannoy the barrier was more of a ha-ha than a fence—a recessed, stone-lined ditch that stops sheep and cattle from wandering into the garden and eating up tulips and grape hyacinths, hellebores and honesty, a barrier invisible from the parlor, a barrier that presents no impediment to the view.

Tannoy went on. "Of course, some of what Hallowhulme does *is* a kind of play. But it takes a great deal of wealth. He's no Mellon or Carnegie, but—" Andrew Tannoy blushed. He fiddled with the fringed pull on the leather blind. It swung back and forth before the view, a hypnotist's fob watch. Geordie focused on it and was again able to lose sight of the stacked coffins.

"Meela and I were invited to Port Clarity once," Andrew Tannoy volunteered. "You know, Port Clarity, Lord Hallowhulme's model town? The town he built near his soap factory in Hull. It has workers' cottages, all plumbed, two up, two down; it has a library, museum, observatory, swimming baths; it has parks, schools; a hospital, and an employees' health plan. A marvelously progressive project." Mr. Tannoy mused. "He's an enlightened man."

"So you've met him?" Geordie said.

"Yes."

The undertakers were waggling the end of the first coffin to ease it out of the hearse. Andrew Tannoy watched them, then said that they could do with some recessed rollers along the bottom of that vehicle. "But they'll think of it themselves," he added in a strange, cold voice. Then he said, "Forgive me. I've wandered rather from the point. Betler, I am sorry that I never met your brother. You kept up a regular correspondence, I believe?"

"Yes, weekly. Ian liked to get letters. Liked to write them, too. I've been hard put to it sometimes to keep him entertained. I have enough to do, but my life is quiet. Ian had rather more color and incident in his. But he never forgot me, he always reported to me. When he was a boy and I was a big lad he'd come out to meet me when I was on my way home from school. Sometimes I'd find him three or four miles from home. This was when he was only seven. I learned not to dawdle. I'd go on as fast as I could so that he wouldn't come too far."

They were silent a while. The mist was turning dilute in the blue sky, only a smear against higher, sunlit clouds, clouds with some architecture, as imposing as the public buildings of empire.

"He got a peerage on top of his knighthood," said Tannoy. "Four years ago. And he added the 'Hulme' to his name. He was a grocer, then an inventor, now he's a philanthropist—a great man, really." Mr. Tannoy glanced at Geordie. "I do admire him. And he's bought that island in order to give it back to the crofters. And to start a few industries, to make work for all."

"But?" said Geordie, amused, despite his trembling hands, heavy eyes, sour stomach. Despite the view he had.

"But nothing, Betler." Tannoy blushed again—that is, his complexion went an orange shade. "I *approve*."

"My brother disliked him," said Geordie. "Ian was very attached to Mr. Hesketh."

They watched a procession of three empty coffins carried, lightly, up the angled gangplank to the steamer's deck. "Will they stow them there in the weather and in plain sight?" Geordie said, exasperated.

In the breeze the blind's tassel tapped and tapped on the top of the carriage window.

"So—did your brother feel he had to choose between them?" Andrew Tannoy asked.

"Hallowhulme and Hesketh? No. Lord Hallowhulme paid Mr. Hesketh's debts. Or *bought* them. They're cousins. So is Lady Hallowhulme a cousin. All cousins. Clara and Murdo Hesketh twice over, since both their fathers and their mothers were siblings. The two Hesketh brothers, Lars and Duncan, married two Vega sisters—white-haired Swedish lasses, the daughters of a baron. Lars and Duncan's sister Mary, the eldest Hesketh, married a grocer from Durham, Edward Hallow. They are all very near kin. But—you see—Mr. Hesketh liked his independence."

"Fellows who value their independence are usually more careful with money," said Andrew Tannoy. "They don't gamble and think God will make an exception of them."

Geordie looked hard at his employer. Why, he asked, did Mr. Tannoy think it was gambling?

"I'm fishing, Betler. Angling. I had heard Murdo Hesketh was ruined."

The coffins had gone below, after all. The undertakers came back down the gangplank, showed for a minute like black cormorants against the sparkling water.

"It was more misfortune than mismanagement." Geordie confided that much. He said, "I must be off, Mr. Tannoy."

Andrew Tannoy nodded. They both got out, and Mr. Tannoy put up his arms to take Geordie's bag from the coachman. "If we can be of any help at all," he said, speaking for his wife, as well as himself. He handed Geordie his bag.

The ship's whistle sounded. Two boys running past stopped dead, covered their ears, and joined the whistle, screamed along with it.

"That's enough now!" roared Tannoy. The boys looked at his frown, startled, speculative, then went on running. Tannoy's scowl deepened. He looked at his butler and said, "You mustn't be offended if I attempt to press a few pounds on you, a little extra for the unexpected. You don't want to put a hole in your savings."

Ian's grave. A hole in his savings.

Geordie took the purse; he took it to be kind. Both men shuffled, looked awkward. And then Meela Tannoy appeared, breathless from running, the two layers of amber silk blown back from her white hair. The footman was puffing and blowing in her wake. She took Geordie's hands and said, "Please take care.

Be as long as you need, but please let us know how you are." She squeezed his hands.

Geordie boarded the ship for the fifteen-hour trip from Oban to Stolnsay.

MISFORTUNE, NOT MISMANAGEMENT. A BAD INVESTMENT, a court case, an illness, two funerals. One thing on top of another. A big rock balanced on a cliff top.

The ship was in the Minch, its open water, the voyage half-gone, the sun going. It was a white evening, white and gold, white and rose, the sky an expanse of godly flesh, its white solid and warm. Geordie hooked his arm over the rail and looked down into the water in time to see a seal surface, its sleek head turned to look at the looming side of the ship whose engines were a discomfort that flushed it out from the waves and its pursuit of fish. It was a fur seal, not a sea lion, small, and soon lost again to Geordie's eyes. How delightful it was, Geordie thought, just to look down and chance to see something alive in the water.

Ian had been, by profession, an officer's orderly. The first man he worked for, a major in the Black Watch, had, on his retirement, recommended Ian to a friend of the family. Ian had wanted to travel. Murdo Hesketh, whose mother was Swedish, was a captain in the household cavalry of King Oskar. Ian did have some trouble learning a new language, but there was quite a group of "Scottish Norsemen" in the household, and he took an instant liking to Captain Hesketh, a charming, clever but reckless young man. They had their adventures—the excesses and hard play of bored men in barracks, the fierce games, the pranks, intrigues, romantic diversions. They went about the countryside on royal warrants and traveled with the young princes to Russia and Denmark, Holland and Norway.

Ian was, with people, as a keen reader is with books—he lived on his observations, he took everything in, he enjoyed the life around him as the audience of fiction will the play of character. Gossip wasn't quite the right word for what Ian did, because he seemed to need to share his observations only with his elder brother.

Ian and his employer had five good years, then Murdo Hesketh gave up the army and began to look around for some unstrenuous and gentlemanly occupation. He had money, a modest inheritance, and the pay he'd saved. He stayed in Stockholm—where he had some hopes of a young lady. Besides, his sister was there, his younger sister, Ingrid, and her husband, Karl, who was a friend of his.

This is what Geordie knew. What Ian had told.

It was this Karl Borg who persuaded Murdo to invest money. It wasn't Borg's own financial venture, but that of a friend, a man in whom Karl had complete confidence. The business had, Ian wrote to Geordie, looked sound on paper. He had even thought to put a little capital in for himself, but he had so little, and looking at the figures—no huge profits were promised—it didn't seem worth the paperwork, or the worry. Ian *did* worry, he didn't quite know why, but wrote later to his brother that, on meeting "the man," he had found himself unable to *read* him. "He was like a certain kind of clergyman. A man with a very clear conscience. His brow was utterly unmarked by lines—odd in a man of forty. It was as if he had never bunched his brow muscles, had never been moved to frown, had never lifted his eyebrows in surprise at the world. When I say I couldn't read him, Geordie, I was looking for *lines*, as one looks for the story under the headlines in a newspaper."

Murdo and Karl lost their money. Had it lost for them. Ingrid was with child, so Karl resolved to protect her from knowledge, to hide his distress. Murdo let Ian go, and moved to small rooms, while Karl kept up a silly pretense of solvency for a few more weeks. Ian wrote, "Borg seemed more afraid of being shamed in his wife's eyes than of sin or bodily danger." Then, on the morning men came to remove the Borgs' furniture to pay their creditors, Karl walked out. He walked past the carriers, the bailiffs, Ingrid and her gray silk gown, stippled lines showing all along its seams where she'd had it let out. Karl went to the place his friend had gone when he fled arrest—Karl knew where to find him. They met, there was an argument, and Karl drew a gun from his coat pocket and shot his friend. Shot and killed.

Ian read about the murder while sitting in the tearooms of a station in Copenhagen, waiting for a train to Brussels—and, eventually, a boat to Dover. Ian did what a friend should, folded his paper, paid for his tea, cashed in his ticket, and went to find his former master.

Murdo Hesketh was living in two dim rooms up three flights of stairs in a street within the invisible noisome capsule of a new tannery, where a block of fine old residences had become one of neglected boarding establishments. Ian walked up to the house through the unmown grass of an overrun lawn, sat on the steps to bash the paste of mashed browned birch leaves from the soles of his shoes, then knocked. He was shown up, hat in hand, by the landlady. Murdo was waiting on the landing. He said, "Oh—Ian. I thought it was the post." His voice was dull.

Murdo's sister had shrunk around the determined swelling of the child. She asked Ian to sit, but didn't say anything further.

Murdo talked. He'd been writing letters to anyone who might help. He glanced at his sister. "We've had advice," he said.

"About the whole matter of the money—any number of people could come forward to shed light on all that. And, of course, we have testimonies as to Karl's character." He jumped up, fetched a stack of letters, and winnowed them—let them flutter down into Ian's lap.

Murdo looked again at his sister, who only gazed at the uneven mended edge of the hearth rug, the floor there glossy with wear and ingrained soot.

"My cousin Clara's godfather, Peter Tegner, the judge, is coming from Malmö to attend the trial," Murdo added. "We expect him shortly."

Ian's paper had said that the trial was set for the beginning of the following month. Ian looked at Murdo's sister in her corner, against a stack of shelves, almost empty, but still bowed down by the memory of books. The corner looked blurred and distorted— Ingrid, too, like an oil painting prematurely faded, one that has lost the red pigment which lends life to painted flesh.

Ian suggested that Mr. Hesketh might like to consider taking his sister somewhere quieter, more salubrious, with fewer flights of steps. Murdo stared. He said they must remain in town for the trial. Murdo said he had thought Ian *gone* already, then, "When do you travel?"

Ian said he had a few things to do before he left. He asked could he call again? Then he saw himself out.

Over the next few weeks Ian would go to that street and watch the boardinghouse door till Murdo departed, then he'd visit Ingrid, let her make him tea, and share the bread or bacon or cheese or apples he'd brought. He played the part of a good guest, someone who wouldn't arrive empty-handed. He didn't insult Mr. Hesketh and his sister, never came carrying ingredients—

eggs, or a joint of meat, or vegetables—nothing that needed preparation. He'd eat some of what he bought, would come with his appetite as well as his donation, and play at conviviality. Then the trial commenced, and Murdo and his sister were at the court-house every day.

Once during the trial Ian saw Murdo meet with the young lady of whom he'd had some hopes. She was waiting outside the courtroom, her brother in escort. She stepped up to Murdo and unveiled her face, her brother tipped his hat, then turned his gaze. She and Murdo spoke briefly—he once raising his voice so Ian overheard, ". . . in that case, I'd like my letters back." She be-gan to weep, replaced the veil and stood for a time, handkerchief inserted between veil and face, dabbing, dabbing. Her shoulders shook. Then she let her brother lead her away.

Karl Borg was found guilty and condemned. "The guillo-tine," Ian wrote to Geordie, "They have it here, although one tends only to associate that contraption with the French." It was only after the sentencing, when pity made him indelicate, that Ian asked his former employer *how he could help*. "I almost begged him to be able to. And he only looked at me with that look he has, like blue light leaking out from under ice." (Ian had once slipped through two cracked and tilting plates of pack ice and gone under in Kalmar Sound. Murdo saved him. As Ian told it he came back to consciousness, bundled up in a stranger's travel rug, still on the shore, being scorched in places by several hot bricks in leather-lined velvet bags. The rug and bricks had been donated by a matron and her five pink-nosed daughters, who stood lined up like fence palings along the road, beside their sleigh. Murdo was draped in a horse blanket. He had his shirt off and his skin was so rosy he looked boiled. "He was steaming, as if he'd just stepped out of a sauna," wrote Ian.) He was look-ing, Geordie supposed, with eyes that didn't seem able to show concern or warmth—only alertness.

Perhaps a week after his offer of help, Ian had what he referred to as "a moment of inattention." He'd had certain things fixed in his sights: the day the sentence would be carried out, and after that, the week around which Ingrid Borg's child was due. Her time. Her husband's time. One afternoon Ian arrived at the boardinghouse with a packet of pears and cheese. The land-lady bustled out of her room when he was halfway up the first flight and said that the young lady had been taken to hospital. She had begun to bleed.

Ian reached the ward only an hour after the end, when In-grid Borg's face was covered, but before she was moved and the bloody sheets were stripped from the bed. Murdo was in the cur-tained cubicle, on a chair by her bed, his elbows on his knees and hands in his hair. His cuffs were blood-soaked, his hands stained and still tacky—so that, when he raised his face to stare at Ian his hair caught in the blood and came free in a fidgety, stag-gered fashion, some locks standing out from his head in clotted points.

Murdo said to Ian, hoarse and hesitant, "It won't sink in. She was unwell yesterday and I fetched a doctor instantly. She gave me her ring to pawn. I sent the doctor up to her, and ran around the corner to pawn her ring. I paid him—but he didn't see far enough ahead to save her."

Murdo lifted the covers to show Ian Ingrid's left hand, bloody and white, with a whiter circle of tender, shiny skin where the ring had been. Then, to Ian's horror and pity, his former master raised the covers further to share what was burning in him, burn-ing like a new sun into the orbit of which everything former now had fallen. Murdo pried open a toweling parcel that lay in his sister's bloodied lap, and there was the baby, all mousy down and soft fat—dewy, pliable, motionless.

Ian wrote: "I couldn't do much more than shake my head. I wasn't uncomfortable, in that tent of sheets he'd made inside the tent of bed screen, it was peaceful in a way. And I was relieved to think that he would now let me offer some assistance, that I wouldn't have any more trouble for a time with his pride."

Ian took over, tended to his master—redeemed Ingrid's wedding ring and Murdo's watch. He paid the landlady's bills, the week's rent Mr. Hesketh owed, and for the replacement of a bloodied mattress. Ian rented another room, along the hall from his, and went with Murdo about his business. They buried Ingrid. They visited Karl and dissembled.

Ian was with Murdo on Karl Borg's last day. They were not permitted a visit on his final night—which he spent with two jailers and a minister in a small snug room right beside the courtyard and its contraption, under which the bare ground showed a light snowfall of quicklime. On that last day Karl seemed to have become hard of hearing. He shook constantly, and said his ears were ringing. Murdo stood at the bars and loudly recited Ingrid's latest message—all fabrication.

Later Ian went out for "more news" of Karl's wife. In fact, for an hour he walked up and down in the dusk before the prison gates. He was there when a guard emerged through the postern door, yawning, and tacked up the articles of execution. The man asked Ian for a match. They stood together for a time and sucked on their pipes, then the guard went back inside. The paper fluttered, Karl Borg's name blinking in and out of existence.

When enough time had passed—an interval sufficiently

plausible for Ian to have learned something momentous—he knocked and was readmitted. As soon as he entered the room beside the condemned cell, where Karl rocked back and forth against the solid bars, Ian whispered in Murdo's ear. The jailer got up from the table and announced that it was time for all visitors to be gone. He puffed up and slapped the taut cloth of his uniform jacket. "Yes," he said, "you gentlemen must leave now."

Karl lunged at the bars and clasped Murdo's wrists. He was quaking as if convulsed. He sobbed—Murdo must *do something*. "Don't leave me!" he begged. "It's inhuman!" He hauled his brother-in-law against the bars and smeared Murdo's hand with tears and phlegm and kisses. Then, when Murdo tried to withdraw his hand, Karl abruptly bit him at the base of one thumb. Murdo snatched back his bleeding hand. Ian came to his rescue, caught hold of and controlled Karl's clutching hands, and drew him near enough so that Murdo could whisper the news Ian had stepped out to "learn." "Ingrid has delivered," Murdo said. "She's tired, but well. You have a son, Karl. You're a father." Then the jailer came forward, swollen with significance, and bustled Murdo and Ian out of the room.

Ian wrote to Geordie, "The dead child was a girl. It was as if Mr. Hesketh couldn't bear to tell anything but an ideal lie."

Murdo asked for Karl's remains and had the three buried together: his sister, her husband, and their daughter. He hadn't money for a headstone—but it was too soon anyway, the ground had to settle. Ian told Geordie how it was he who wrote to Lady Hallowhulme, who had been Clara Hesketh, the older cousin with whose family Murdo had spent every childhood summer. The answer came, with its prospects: an offer of work, a banknote to cover certain necessities of travel, and a pledge by Lord Hallowhulme to buy his cousin's debts. "And he did write *buy*,"

Ian told his brother, "not *clear*, or *cover*. When I read the letter out to Mr. Hesketh I read *clear*—to be kind. And why wasn't he reading it himself you ask? Because he wouldn't let me make a light in the corner where he sat."

(The room was a mess of dropped clothes and dirty crockery. The fireplace was cold, full of silky, shrunken coals. Ian recited Lord Hallowhulme's letter, then put the pages down from his face and peered at the figure in the corner. Murdo's hair was dirt-darkened, his cheeks frosted by blond stubble. On the cabinet beside Murdo there glittered the black reptilian coil of Karl Borg's jet-encrusted mourning watch and fob—and something else, another gleam, of oiled steel. Ian crossed the room, picked up Murdo's revolver, and pocketed it.)

AT 11 P.M., TWELVE HOURS INTO GEORDIE'S JOURNEY, IT was as dark as it got in early summer at that latitude, 55° north. Geordie was still at the rail, eyes wide, looking at a long island, hills against a sky not quite dark. Some radiance below the horizon made the sky seem semitransparent, several layers of black silk with a light behind them. The landmass was the southeastern coast of Skilling—a Chang to Kissack's Eng. Though the ship was now in the lee of the land and sheltered, Geordie knew that only these two entities joined at a hip of high mountains, this island of hills, bog, and bared rock, stood between him and a great stretch of inhospitable sea: the North Atlantic, across which every other Betler had gone, the Betlers of Nova Scotia and Newfoundland, from whence no letters now came. Geordie Betler stared and shivered, and thought that he was the last Betler left to go west—frozen at the rail of a ship going westward.

Geordie inverted the bowl of his pipe and knocked it against the rail, to dislodge the clot of cold ash. Then he went in out of the air.

The steamer's salon was full of solid warmth, a smell of the coal in its stove, and of tea, scalded milk, damp wool. There were only four other passengers—a mother, two daughters, and a maid, who was asleep, her back braced against a large wicker hamper. Someone had covered her legs with a travel rug. The sisters were twins, young ladies in their minority, but exactly where in that minority Geordie was unable to map, since they were stout, round-faced, swathed in shawls, and perched on by fur muffs as sturdy as tomcats. These two watched him, blearily, as he took the top off the hatbox into which Meela Tannoy had insisted Cook put three brown-sugar pinwheels, two pork pies, four boiled eggs with a saltcellar, a now fused stack of chocolate fudge, a hard cheese, several ripe pears, a knife, fork, spoon, and napkin, and, finally, a bottle of damson sherry. The box was packed like a puzzle, but Geordie had been at it, and had eaten a hearty lunch already, only because of his inability to repack it so that all fitted and the lid could close. His lunch had been at three, nearly eight hours earlier, and he was hungry again. The twins watched him eat. Their mother, a fragile, papery woman with very fine black eyes, caught them staring and spoke to them. She didn't tell them off; she only made conversation, retrieved their attention. Her voice was low, scarcely audible to Geordie, except that he stopped chewing and found himself listening. She was speaking another language, but Geordie was sure her sentence ended, ". . . poor Ingrid."

Poor Ingrid?

The twins nodded at their mother, a gesture doubled, a more intense assent, and intensely solemn. Then both pursed their mouths and squirmed in their seats.

For a moment Geordie did nothing, then he had to prize the pastry off the roof of his mouth with the tip of his tongue. He swallowed. He brushed the crumbs from his coat and crossed the salon, made his bow. Could he offer the ladies anything? He was so generously provided for.

The lady accepted a small glass of the damson sherry. She was sorry she couldn't open their hamper—she gestured with one tight-skinned, arthritic hand at the sleeping servant. "But we do have a tin of very succulent muscatels," she said.

Geordie established that she was the widow of Paul Tegner, a justice of Malmö in Sweden. She established that he was the butler of Tannoy, who owned a machine works in Glasgow. They soon learned that they were going to the same place—Kiss Castle. Jane Tegner tendered her deepest sympathies. She and the twins had thought to postpone their visit on account of the accident, but Minnie Hallow was a dear friend of her girls, and very lonely for the two years since her poor sister had drowned . . .

And Geordie realized that, of course, they'd been talking about the *other* Ingrid in Murdo Hesketh's story—not Hesketh's sister, but Ingrid Hallow.

5   ⚜   KISS CASTLE

BILLIE, IN A STRANGE PLACE AND A HAZE OF MISERY, STILL recognized that, in leaving her and Henry alone as much as possible in those first two days of hushed peace in his sickroom, the Hallowhulme household was being kind. There was always a servant on hand, at times in the room, otherwise posted on the landing at the end of the hall, where there was a large linen press holding all the household's sheets, quilts, bath towels, and sundry other cloudy whitenesses. The maid would keep herself busy by keeping order in the press—she folded, made inventory, and watched for Billie to put her head around the door. She was a quiet woman, near in age to Billie, an islander, soft and hesitant in her speech. She kept her distance, clearly shy of Billie's grief, of what had happened to her.

Lady Hallowhulme came in the morning and evening, made her own kind inquiries, and carried others' polite ones. "My husband has reminded me to assure you that he still regards Mr. Maslen as engaged. He says that this engagement must by no means be considered an *obligation* and, if Mr. Maslen would prefer to return to the mainland, he shall, all expenses covered. However, if Mr. Maslen decides that the cataloguing task could prove an occupation that helps him through this sad and difficult period, then my husband will be more than pleased to hear he will stay on." Clara smiled at Billie. "That's the meat of my husband's message. If, when Mr. Maslen returns to himself, this assurance of an *imaginable* future offers him some comfort, please do convey it to him." Lady Clara frowned faintly, her eyelids down and brows raised. "But I'm sure James will come and put it all to Mr. Maslen himself when Mr. Maslen is able to attend."

Billie said yes, she thought Henry would be glad of something to do. She fiddled with the matted fringe of the shawl that hid the gaping neck of her borrowed dress—her own surviving one was being cleaned. The one she wore was too big for her, but a good dress—the height of fashion three years earlier, a young lady's garment, with a bustle that rustled and, as Billie walked, made passes at the air behind her as if it had its own appetites and interests.

Clara, Lady Hallowhulme, was decent, but stiff, her manner awkward, immobile, as if it gave her pain to sit near another person, to speak and meet their eyes. Billie was feeling something similar. When the young islanders came and changed the water, removed dirty crockery, and mended the fire—all tasks Billie usually performed—she'd watch them work, look defiantly at their activity, which showed up her inactivity, her uselessness. If they turned their eyes toward her, she'd look away.

She slept in a slippery nest of two big silk-covered quilts on a daybed across the room from Henry. Sometimes she just lay and watched the rain spill from one lattice to the next, collecting against each horizontal of lead like tears on the rim of an eye. On the stone sill the tears were again only rain, the stone pitted and ominously lace-trimmed with yellow lichen. It seemed to Billie that she was in a new world, a world made of Henry's harsh breathing, and the sickroom stink of sweat, stuffiness, and various medicines that managed fever or congestion. The room was all unfamiliar luster and deep color, carved wood, and ornately patterned carpet and upholstery. Billie's daybed was covered in a fabric decorated with nut bushes in full leaf, with simultaneous blossom, fruit, and fat squirrels. There were no plain things in Billie's view, except the black lead between the windowpanes and an outdoors that—when Billie lay down and looked up—was all soft gray sky. There was no ceiling to the clouds, only a skin of still mist, through which the rain seemed to strain like whey through a cheesecloth, leaving its pale solids still in the sky.

The doctor was in and out. He seemed satisfied by Henry's progress. He said to Billie, to Clara, that he judged it better not to tell Henry of his loss till he'd come back to himself sufficiently to ask.

"He is asking," Billie said. "He's calling for her."

"No, my dear, we must wait till he asks rationally. Right now he has no idea where he is, or what has happened."

Billie held Henry's hand and listened to him, waited for some sign that he'd begun to orient himself in time and place. She knew that *she* had been three nights at Kiss Castle and one in the gatehouse. But she had forgotten what to expect. So that when, on the afternoon of her fifth day, the latch clicked and the door opened and Lady Clara put her head and hand around only to signal Billie to follow her, Billie was reluctant, unready to go out into a world through which she could walk and walk and not ever expect to fall into step with her sister.

"Come out, Miss Paxton," Lady Hallowhulme commanded.

Billie followed her. The landing was empty, but Billie could hear soft, hurried steps going down the carpeted stairs below. Determined to find a movement to go with the sound, Billie's eyes darted away from Lady Hallowhulme's to follow the flight of a pair of blackbirds which started up from the sill of the hall window, and dropped out of sight. Billie felt they were flying from her, these birds—and the hurrying footfalls. A door closed. The landing was still and silent. Billie looked down to find a hand closed around her wrist, a cold manacle of flesh.

Lady Hallowhulme told Billie that they had found Edith's body. It had been retrieved by the divers from the mainland. Clara Hallow walked Billie to a seat across the hall, a red velvet love seat with two bays that, when they sat down, kept their bodies apart but pressed their knees together. Clara placed a bundle in Billie's lap. It was a man's handkerchief in which was wrapped Edith's brooch of silver filigree and a cat's-eye like an iris fogged by cataract; Edith's miser's purse, a mesh that was clinched closed by rings, its ends weighted with red amber beads; and a third thing, a button, plain plaited pigskin over brass—a button from Henry's jacket.

"Your sister was wearing the brooch and purse," Clara Hallow said. "The button was in her hand."

Billie asked Clara if she could see her sister.

"We think you shouldn't," said Clara.

"I think I should," said Billie. Then, very plain, but desperate, "I must stop wanting to look for her. Don't you see? I keep wanting to walk out and find her."

Billie was taken out of the castle, told to "at least cover your hair." She thought of the church, but Jenny and Lady Hallowhulme had only meant that her hair was a fright.

THEY MADE THEIR WAY TO THE CHURCH AGAIN, THROUGH a crowd of people, bright sunshine, the stones still wet, a street full of reflected light. Billie shaded her eyes and followed Clara

Hallow into the church, into gloom, and points of light—candle flames, and those flames reflected in the eyes staring at her. The church smelled of beeswax, bad meat, and the perfume of some branches of wilting wild azalea that lay on the pews near the door. Clara paused, took something from one of the women lining the aisle, and passed it back to Billie—a small gauze sachet of the sort used to scent stored clothes, this one full of thyme and lavender. Clara put the sachet in Billie's hand, then applied Billie's hand to her nose.

There was a line of coffins on the floor below the altar, all sealed. Two empty coffins inclined upright, like tired sentries on either side of the sacristy door. Billie followed Lady Clara down the steps between them, through the short passage, which was full of people, it seemed. Billie didn't so much see Murdo Hesketh as sense him, right beside her, a change against her skin, the temperature of moonlight. Billie looked and saw him press back against the wall and turn his head hard sideways to avoid meeting her eyes.

A man removed the lid of Edith's coffin—and there she was, so changed that it wasn't strange to see her there. (Billie and Edith's father, after his final illness, had merely looked tired and uncomfortable, his broad shoulders pushed together in the incommodious crate that was all his daughters could afford. His shoulders were raised; he'd seemed to shrug, hapless, careless, as nonchalant as ever, wedged in his last bed.) Edith's *hair* was Edith—even frosted with salt, a red so dark that it was black in the deep curves of its curls. Her face was dark, too. The first diver had disturbed her so that she'd spent two days with her back pressed against the bulkhead but facedown in the water. Edith's hands were livid, but her face was fat and a cyanotic blue. Billie stooped nearer—she thought she saw something else, that her sister held something like tiny scraps of paper in her hands . . .

Clara held Billie back, gripped her hard under the arms, and braced one foot forward so that she trembled with effort. Billie was hauled around sideways, but not before she saw what Clara had seen, and had recognized sooner, that the "scraps" were Edith's fingernails, coming away from the tips of her fingers. But Billie wouldn't unbend and hadn't finished, for instead of Edith's bump there was a bundle. A neatly wrapped, damp bundle lying in the hollow of Edith's lap.

"You shouldn't," someone said, very firm. Arms circled her waist, then pulled her back a few steps, still doubled over.

"It's the baby, dear," said Lady Hallowhulme. She sounded breathless.

"It's too sad a sight," said the man who held her. She straightened against him and turned to glare. He was just her height— Henry's height—little and wiry, neat and gray.

"What kind of baby?" Billie asked, then, explaining herself, "Henry will want to know."

The man looked around, inquiring. Billie heard Mrs. Mulberry, the minister's wife, say that the baby was a boy. Then she heard someone laugh, a short, stifled, unhappy laugh. She was sure that it was Murdo Hesketh, though she had never heard him laugh before.

"Come away now," said the man. He released her, but kept his arm up, a barrier between Billie and the coffin.

Mrs. Mulberry asked Billie would she like a lock of hair? Billie said yes, and watched the minister's wife bend, lift a long red rat's tail of hair, and cut it with a pair of embroidery scissors. She laid it across her knee, fetched thread from a pocket in her apron, and bound the hair at its severed end. Billie received it, remembered to say thank you, as Edith would have reminded her, and let herself be led away.

Billie pressed her cheek to the window, smeared the pane with oil from her forehead and nose, her ears and hair. She rubbed her head back and forth across the glass, felt the lead dig in against cheek and browbone. She waited for Henry to wake.

There had always been someone to do the difficult things for her, to speak for her. There was always an advocate: Aunt, or Edith, or Henry. Now the hard task was hers alone.

Henry still ran a fever. That morning she'd had to mime gathering a skein of rope, a cable he said, in which he was tangled. "It's holding my legs. It hurts," he whispered. Billie stood over him, her arms out, baling a cumbersome invisible rope. He thanked her, his eyelids drooping and, before he sank and lost his shape again, disappearing into his hot ground-mist of fever, he turned his head to look at the other side of the bed, where there was an empty chair, and said, "Where is Edith?" But then he was under, and Billie didn't have to answer him.

The question was harder than ever to answer. Perhaps tomorrow, after the funeral, Billie would only have to point at a patch of ground: "There she is." For, until she was found, Edith had receded only in time—unseen for five days, dead, yes, but a dead Edith. Billie *had* had to look, she'd had to see, but the altered Edith had stolen Edith's possibilities. The substituted changeling horror in the church wasn't Edith. Billie felt that her sister could only be Edith again in Edith's grave.

Through the window, waxy with oil, Billie saw the colors become more solid; the waving stems of marshmallow, fuchsia, and vetch flowering in an angle of the walled garden were eclipsed by a more animal motion. Billie found an unclouded pane and looked out.

There were five young people in the garden, two round-faced bosomy young women, a slight dark-haired girl, and the two cadets from the *Gustav Edda*, now in civilian attire. One of the stout girls had a notebook and pen. She and the one who looked like her sister walked about, looking at this and that cluster of flowers and making notes. The boys had gone farther, swinging their rackets, onto a lawn, where one cast up the fletched cone of a shuttlecock and they began to bat it back and forth. The other girl set up an easel, positioned a blank canvas on it, and balanced a paint box across the top of an urn full of drooping anemones. Then she waited. After a moment a servant came out of the house with a pitcher of water. The girl took it, set it by her feet, laid her extra brushes on the grass, and began to dip a brush, and mix paints.

The plump sisters—so alike that Billie decided they must be twins—tired first, and one slipped the notebook into the pocket of the painter's apron. The other craned over the painter's shoulder and made gestures of appreciation. Then they barged the boys aside, wrestled for the rackets, won not by use of force, but by touch. The boys seemed disconcerted to be jostled by hips and breasts and backed off, blushing. The twins began to whack the shuttlecock about, less nimbly than the boys. It was retrieved from a tree, then from a green pond. The lace trim on the three-quarter sleeve of one girl's white dress dripped, mucky. The boys idled, then, as it became overcast and still, began to shrug and twitch, bothered by insects. The twins, when they paused to catch their breath, shrieked, began to slap their own necks, then ran indoors.

After an hour, when Billie looked out again, only the painter remained, absorbed, her canvas flowering with forms and colors something like those before her—but without the fat glow of sap and green ichor. The blues, yellows, and reds of flowers with scent and substance were, in her picture, Billie saw, transformed into paper lanterns, transparent, a light behind them perhaps, but paper still.

Billie watched as the girl stepped to one side, her arm over the easel, to look at the flowers. Then she caught up her brushes, washed them together, and flicked the cloudy water across the grass. She regarded her picture once more, sidelong, then inclined at the waist, leaned gradually and delicately till her hip connected with the easel and it collapsed. The picture lay faceup on the grass and the girl swayed over it, looking at the flowers. The real flowers. Then she swooped on a stand of flag irises and embraced them, gathered their thick stalks together so that their yellow and purple crowded up around her neck like the flaring frill of a lizard. At that moment it began to rain. Billie watched as the girl released the irises, snatched the easel up by its ankles, and the painting by its edge, and ran indoors.

THE FOLLOWING MORNING, FIRST THING, LADY HALLOW-hulme arrived in the sickroom with the maid, Jenny. Jenny bore a garment in her arms. A dress had been made up for Billie on the pattern of her own. It was of fine black wool, fitted, shaped by row after row of tiny vertical tucks. It buttoned at the back, and the buttons were real jet—warm and weightless. Lady Clara stayed a minute to explain her gift. She explained it as respectable and well suited to the weather, without mentioning the occasion of its appearance. Then she left her maid to coax Billie out of her borrowed clothes, and to wash Billie's hands, arms, and throat with warm water and soap.

Billie's hair was dirty, dark at its crown, but Jenny simply sat her down at the mirror and brushed it, then plaited and pinned the plaits up into a winding crown on Billie's head. Then the maid helped Billie lift the new dress over her head. They settled it, and Jenny hooked all the buttons closed.

"Your waist isn't so small," Jenny said, "but you don't really need a corset."

Billie couldn't tell if this was criticism or praise. She felt the woman touch the muscle over her shoulder blade before fastening the last fifteen buttons. The touch wasn't a caress, but a push, a firm push, as though she were being tested for ripeness.

A movement in the garden caught Billie's eye. It was a gardener and the painter girl. The girl was directing the gardener to cut the stand of irises she'd attempted to paint. She discovered her paint box, flicked its lid closed, and carried it indoors, held out from her black clothes and oozing red and yellow and blue across her fingers and onto the flagstones.

There was a knock on the sickroom door. It was the first time Billie had noticed someone knocking for admission. Maybe they hadn't before and the knock was for Jenny, not her or Henry—who at the moment could no more be knocked for than the dead. Billie watched Jenny in the big oval glass in front of which she'd been stood. Jenny gave Billie's reflection a last, long, assessing look, and wet her finger to smooth the hair about Billie's ears. Then she went to the door.

It was Clara again, this time accompanied by a dark, well-built man, who stopped in the doorway and frowned at the window. Jenny bustled past Billie and opened two sections in its broad bow. Cool air came in, and the smell of rain.

Clara introduced her husband. He came in and, taking his wife by the arm, repositioned her in the room. "In attending sick persons," he said, "it is best to stand where the air passes from door to window, never, Clara, between the invalid and the fire, for the fire will draw any infectious vapor toward it." He sniffed, looked at Jenny, and inquired, "Acetate of lead?"

"Yes, Lord Hallowhulme," said Jenny.

Hallowhulme finally looked at Billie. He colored up, a blush as sudden as a change in the light. She was reminded of someone— then, rather confused, realized that it was Murdo Hesketh. In the church Hesketh's turned face had worn the same shade of rosy blush on a clenched jaw muscle like the convex side of a dent in otherwise smooth metal.

"Are you ready, my dear?" James Hallow said. "You're to come with us."

Lady Hallowhulme shook open the shawl she carried and wrapped it around Billie. Then she pinned a square of beaded black net on Billie's hair. Billie could feel a bead tapping her brow as she walked. Lord Hallowhulme linked her arm with his and closed her hand in both his very warm ones.

THERE WAS A SCARCITY OF HEARSES, OR EVEN RIGHT-SIZED carts to serve. The island was rich only in two-wheeled traps— the ends of which any adult's coffin would overhang. Apparently, Murdo said to Geordie Betler, no one had had the sense to borrow one of the big drays from the construction site at Scouse Beach.

The coffins were carried from the church to the new grave-yard above the town. Murdo walked with Geordie Betler behind Ian's coffin, which was borne by the four big men from Kiss Castle's gatehouse. Before and behind Ian in the procession were two of the drowned stokers. One was a mainlander and had his wife in attendance, the other, a Swede, had to make do with Mrs. Mulberry and a knot of Stolnsay parishioners.

When Murdo and Geordie reached the stepping-stones over the small burn just before the new graveyard, Geordie remarked that this wasn't very *satisfactory*. The stones were wet, and Geordie had placed his foot a little too far forward on one so that the water backed up in several glassy ridges around the toe of his shoe. He got to the far side and shook his feet, as if his shoes weren't protected by rubber galoshes. Murdo looked at this sidelong. Ian's elder brother was something of an old woman, fastidious and spinsterish, and coaxingly *fishy* in some of his conversation.

Nothing could be done about the slope of the new cemetery. What little flatland there was behind the town was cow pasture. Higher up, where the slopes leveled off, began the vast peat bogs that made up most of Kissack. The graveyard was on a strip of heath—and a twenty-degree incline. Murdo reached its wall, looked at the heath rising before him, and saw that the fresh graves, in their two rows, appeared as neat in shape as the slots in a baking pan.

They went on up. Rory Skilling and the others set Ian down beside his grave. All the mourners drew back, leaving the ground between the rows empty. Only Mr. Mulberry ventured there, passing slowly up between the graves in his white surplice. The rain had stopped, all umbrellas were closed and stowed under arms. Nobody stood near the excavations themselves, which looked unstable, for there was water at the bottom of each and water oozing out of their earthy walls. Mr. Mulberry's surplice snapped and fluttered above the more dulcet rustle of wool skirts and shawls and coat-tails. Murdo for once couldn't hear that sound he hated—the island's one ceaseless noise—of heath hissing, like someone cooling a burned tongue by straining air through their teeth.

Mr. Mulberry read to the gathering—the order of service. Then a piper beside the minister resuscitated his bag and wound them all up into a hymn. Murdo looked down at the raindrops elongated on the lid of Ian's coffin, seeping into the grain of the undressed wood. He remembered Ian starting a fire with wood shavings, a resinous smoke, coffee, Ian's clever iron pot with its clawed feet that could sit in the embers of an open fire . . .

Murdo didn't know the words of the hymn.

Wilhelmina Paxton stood across from him. James and Clara Hallow were behind her, with their son Rixon, his friend Elov, and the newly arrived Tegners behind them. Of all the colors on that slope, mostly mossy plaid, the Kiss Castle family was the only concentration of deep black. Ostentatiously solemn and purposeful, their black was like time stopped—time stopped with a will, and with wealth. These people could afford to sit still, fold their hands, lay down real life to mourn. They had taken Miss Paxton in, and dressed her as one of them. Murdo stared at her. The hem of her skirt was sopping wet—she had neglected to lift it as she crossed the burn, or she'd missed the stones and blundered through the water—he could imagine that. Her young face was shut. Stubborn. Murdo supposed she was trying not to cry. Murdo then saw that his cousin James's eyes were fastened on the back of Miss Paxton's neck and, as he sang, they darted from side to side, as if he were reading words there.

Minnie Hallow, separate from her family but accompanied by a Kiss Castle groom and two gardeners, came up the slope between the rows of graves, stopping now and then to place a handful of pink mallow, or irises, on the bare coffins. Minnie must have stripped Kiss Castle's garden. Minnie liked plays and pageantry and, aware of this, Murdo watched her with suspicion. He watched for signs of pious self-consciousness. He tried to see Minnie's father in Minnie. But, placing her flowers, Minnie seemed completely unself-conscious. She had no point to make. There was no challenge, no reproach, no pride in her action. It was simply right, graceful, and good.

Murdo held his breath and sank back into a fizzing orange mist. He felt Geordie Betler seize his arm and steady him, then he was walking past the sexton's spades and wheelbarrow on the downhill slope, guided by Betler, behind his family in their dazzling black, and looking at Miss Paxton's white neck below her crown of plaits, her glowing corona.

At the stream James Hallow, who didn't usually think to do those things, turned around, waited for Miss Paxton, and lifted her over the water. Despite himself, Murdo caught them up, and was in time to take Minnie's arm as she teetered on the slippery stepping-stones. "Did you *ever?*" she said, her face shining up at him as if he was someone quite different, someone to share a joke with. Then she gripped his arm and pointed out Rory Skilling's young son. "I found Alan again, Murdo. He's got the same coat on he wore all last year, though its sleeves are halfway to his elbows. I've employed him, as you suggested, at a penny a day."

It *had* been Rory's son behind one of those armloads of cut flowers.

"I'm sure he'll be glad of your patronage," Murdo said and, having seen her safely across, he went on after the elder Betler.

They were in Ian's room. Ian's salvaged bag was in the middle of the floor, damp with drained seawater, its leather sunk into the shape of its contents. Geordie Betler was sleeping in Ian's room. "I did have to insist," Geordie said to Murdo. "Lord Hallowhulme pointed out that it was—in fact—only your dressing room. He said he thought I might not be pleased by the proximity. He reminded me that I was a guest, and that there were a number of guest rooms empty despite the seasonal, and *unseasonal*, influx."

Mr. Betler managed to be both delicate and confiding—but Murdo wasn't about to be involved.

"What do you think?" Betler asked. Murdo could feel eyes, feel himself peered up at. Geordie Betler went on, "I think Lord Hallowhulme is concerned I'll simply fall into the habit of seeing to you." Betler's voice was blithe and polite. From the corner of his eye Murdo saw the spread hands, a gesture of helpless concession. "I reassured him, of course. It would be no trouble to me, I said, in the short term. And that you'd be in need of—ah—if not a friend, at least an ally—"

Despite himself Murdo met Geordie Betler's eyes. And he didn't see deference or fussiness, but shrewdness, compassion, and patience. It pulled him up short; he felt himself bridle, like a horse checked at the very moment it takes fright.

"I've made a start," Geordie Betler went on—on another subject already. "Ian had so very little." He got down on his knees, gingerly, to open the sodden bag. Murdo, who had spent too much time in the past days walking about a room paved with corpses, flinched at the sight of the clear mucus that seemed to cover all of Ian's clothes. But its source was only a burst container of foot powder.

For a while Geordie Betler delved among folded shirts and other necessities of travel. He found a few ink-mottled papers, carefully peeled them apart to lay them out to dry. He made to get up and Murdo went to help him. "Thank you," Geordie said, and gave Murdo's hand a couple of firm, friendly pats.

"I'll leave you to your sorting," Murdo said. But Geordie retained his hand, tightened his grip, said, "Wait." He released Murdo, then opened a drawer, and took out a worn chamois, gray with oil. Geordie carried the bundle to Murdo, unwrapped the chamois, and put a revolver into Murdo's hands. "This is yours, I believe?"

Murdo couldn't remember when he'd last seen the gun. But he did remember the moments, the hours, when he'd been aware of its absence and, in pain, his mind would act out what, lacking the gun, he wasn't able to do. He might be sitting on the edge of his bed in his room in Kiss Castle, immersed in a tank of night. His hands would have no object to act on, but in his mind he'd break open the gun's chamber to load it, slowly. He could *feel* the machine-tooled concentric circles in the brass at the bullets' blunt ends like fingerprints against his fingertips. He'd smell the gun oil, sweet in the open works, the six empty slots, would hear the small click as each hole was plugged, and feel each little increment of weight as the gun filled. Only a *rake*, a show-off, would spin the chamber of a pistol they knew to be in good working order—so, in his trance, Murdo never set the chamber spinning. He would come back to himself, his hands empty, the gun gone. His imagination had to go back and do it over—press bullets into bullet-sized blanknesses again and again.

"Yes, I believe it is mine," Murdo said.

AFTER THE FUNERAL BILLIE RETURNED TO THE SICKROOM. But Lord and Lady Hallowhulme pursued her up the stairs and, after a moment when she was sure they were only speaking to each other and that she must pick up her pace and hurry out of earshot, she realized that they hadn't finished with her. They pursued her into the sickroom. Lord Hallowhulme hesitated a moment on the threshold, but only to set the door back deliberately against the wall.

"Miss Paxton," Lady Hallowhulme began. Then she paused, frowning, as her husband crossed the room and pushed one window wide.

The doctor was with Henry, Henry's wrist limp in his hand, checking Henry's pulse against the circuit of his watch's second hand. Because he was figuring he ignored their entry, their precipitation.

"Miss Paxton—we have another room ready for you. This really isn't at all satisfactory—" Clara began, and gestured at the mashed cocoon of white silk quilts that was Billie's nest on the daybed. Lord Hallowhulme, by the window, put his hands down into the cushiony billows and stood absorbed.

"James," said Clara, sharply.

The doctor replaced Henry's hand under the covers. "Miss Paxton," he said, "it's my opinion that you haven't the stamina to be a sick nurse. You've suffered a terrible shock. You're entitled to care for yourself, and to rest."

"You must trust us a little more, Wilhelmina," said Clara.

"Billie," Billie corrected her.

James Hallow withdrew his hand from the bedding and looked up at her. "Billie," he said. "The doctor and my wife are quite right. Mr. Maslen will be better off in the care of a round-the-clock, trained nurse. I have acquired that nurse. I propose you come downstairs and meet that nurse. You are *reduced*, dear girl. And you are my guest, not a refugee."

Minnie Hallow barged, panting, into the sickroom. The door *was* open after all. She skidded to a stop, her heavy black skirts catching up with her and carrying on, swinging forward under their own momentum then settling with a rush that was like her breathing. Minnie glared at her father. She'd been deceived by the open door perhaps and hadn't thought to find him there. "I just wanted to say—" she began.

"Minnie! Moderate your voice!" her mother chided.

"Minnie, are you aware that it isn't advisable to enter the room of a sick person in a violent perspiration? The moment your body cools it will absorb the sickness." James Hallow delivered this little rebuke in a mild, toneless voice.

"Oh, I'm going directly." Minnie was impatient.

"What did you come about?" her mother asked.

"Never mind," said Minnie. She glanced at her father, then frowned at her mother.

"Minnie," said Lord Hallowhulme, "could you please show Miss Paxton to her room?"

Clara touched Billie's arm and said she'd send Jenny along to see if there was anything else Billie required.

Billie stooped over the bed and kissed Henry's forehead. She whispered to him that they were taking her away from him. There was sun in the room and his skin glistened, dewy and yielding.

When she stood back up Billie felt time start. It was as though she jumped from something in motion onto something firm, from a ship onto the pier. Time was starting again for her—or, at least, a period of time in which certain things would happen, like the twelve days and nights of Christmas, a time *apart*, but with events in sequence. After the sequestered time-lessness of the sickroom, the thought of *events* made Billie dizzy—motion sick.

She heard Minnie say to her parents, "I *do* know which room you mean." Reproachful. The girl came up to Billie and took her arm. "Come along, Miss Paxton."

The passage was intersected by one of those strange short flights of steps, four down then up again, where two passages met and one cut through the other like a dried streambed. They turned a corner, and there was a view of the water from the window at the end of the hall. Minnie walked with her head in-clined, so that all Billie could see was the back of her thin neck and the knuckly ridge of her cervical vertebrae. Minnie was slight, slope-shouldered, and had her father's frizzy mid-brown hair—Minnie's was pinned into a beaded snood. Billie heard her say, "After all—they already have you in her shoes."

Billie's new room was redolent with fresh beeswax polish. Stacked coal glowed in the shallow grate. The fireguard wasn't yet replaced, and the water in a glass ewer was still moving, see-sawing faintly. Whoever had made the room ready had only just left it. The bed was made, the wardrobe open and empty, the mantelpiece without ornament but dressed in a red velvet drape, with scalloped edges embroidered with swans made of mother-of-pearl, and lilies and bulrushes of silk. Only one thing in the room seemed stale, and that was a shawl, once very fine, now a withered skin of yellow silk draped across the glass of a full-length mirror on the far side of the room.

Minnie strode over and pulled the shawl from the glass. A plume of dust hung in the air between fabric and mirror. Minnie went out past Billie, pausing to smile, a knowing, clever smile. She was fingering the embroidery along the shawl's hem—once red roses in bud, and daisies with yellow hearts, now scabs of faded silk in the shape of flowers. "I do hope you'll be comfortable," Minnie Hallow said.

6 ⚜ BILLIE IS EXAMINED AGAIN

Billie, in tears, sitting on a chair in the passage outside the sickroom, was only consoled by the familiar sight of the toes of her own boots peeping out from under the hem of her own gray wool dress. The doctor and Lady Hallowhulme had just left her, Lady Hallowhulme to see the doctor out herself, to hand him his hat and have a private word. He'd made a point of reassuring the patient's sister-in-law that the patient was making progress. Perhaps Clara meant to ask what Billie hadn't—was Henry making the *expected* progress? He hadn't come back to himself, not far enough to fully understand his loss. The night before, when Billie arrived in his room, she found him awake, his face relaxed under a condensation of sweat. She took his hand and he asked her, "Is Edith dead?" Then, to account for his question, "She hasn't been here." Billie nodded—he echoed her nod, and turned his face away, his cheeks drying, tearless. But in the morning the fever was back and he was asking again for Edith.

How many more times would Billie have to break the bad news?

She dried her eyes. She found she was looking down at someone else's shoes, their toes pointed toward her own. It was Minnie Hallow, standing over her with an expression of pitched determination. "I think you need to go out and get some air,"

the girl said. "You need to avoid all those endless directions about where to stand—between the invalid and window, or
window and fire, or the invalid and the fire—you must be
worn-out."

Finding herself with a representative of the family, Billie said
what she had forgotten to say to Lady Hallowhulme. "My room
is very comfortable, thank you."

"Oh, hell!" said Minnie, then, coaxing, "Anne Tegner and I
are going out. My boy will drive. I suppose I should call him 'my
odd man'—Alan Skilling. Anyway—you should come with us.
You can simply sit on a hillside for an hour or two and think of
nothing."

Billie got up.

"You'll need a wrap," said Minnie, trailing after Billie,
who was going to her room to shut herself in, away from invitations and kindness and this girl's clear, well-bred voice. But they
reached the room together, and Billie couldn't bring herself to
close the door in Minnie's face. She collected a shawl—one of
her own, washed and dried but faded a little where salt water had
collected in its folds.

In the driveway a low trap was harnessed to a short-legged,
broad-backed, hairy pony. The driver was a spindly boy whose
skin, hair, and eyes were all the shade of brown sugar, and whose
nose was like a round bead sewn in under his skin. His shirt was
too big and frayed at collar and cuffs; both shirt and skinny torso
were forced together into a jacket made for a child several sizes
smaller. He had the reins wrapped around his fist and raised tight,
as if he thought his little horse was skittish. But the pony and
cart remained motionless, even when the boy wriggled around
to appraise Billie.

Anne Tegner—one of the twins Billie had observed earlier—

was already seated. She wore a handsome fur hat and jacket and carried a large jar on her lap. Minnie rearranged her easel, sketchpad, a different paint box—this one pristine—and made room for Billie. "Room for one more," she said, in a managing tone, and to no one in particular.

"It'll be you tumbling off the back if your *one more* has Kirsty overbalanced and dangling between the shafts with her feet off the road," the boy warned, darkly.

"Nonsense, Alan," said Minnie. "I'll set my back against yours and you and I will be the center of gravity, the pivot point, if you follow me."

"You pay me, Miss Minnie, so I follow you."

The boy tapped the pony with the tip of his long whip. The pony's skin twitched, but it didn't stir. "Get on, would you," he said. Kirsty set off at an ambling walk. Minnie made introductions. "Miss Paxton, Miss Tegner." Minnie had perched herself above them on the buckboard, her back against the boy's. She was in some danger of displacing him with her weight and height.

"Could you shift your arse a little?" the boy said, amicably.

Minnie made an adjustment, and the pony plunged forward a jump to keep her feet.

"I can't answer for us on the hill," said Alan.

Billie offered to get off and walk behind, and earned a look from the boy which told her that, if she did, she would be robbing him of a pious cause.

Kirsty picked up her pace. The morning was fresh. In the seven days Billie had been on Kissack this was only the second of sun. Everything glistened, the stones on the roadside, the trunks of the trees furred with refreshed moss. The trees were in late spring leaf and, with the moss, were fully green in foliage, branch, bole, as though some painter had been at work with a sadly limited palette. The harbor was nearly empty, all the fishermen still out, and from the road along the point the long stone pier seemed crowned with frozen gray smoke—the skeins of drying nets. These seemed to have a catch of shadows—old men standing behind and plying awls to mend them.

The cart passed through the open arch of the gatehouse, which dripped on them.

"Is your father at the Scouse Beach site today?" Minnie asked her driver.

"I think so."

"Are you sleeping here now?"

"The gatehouse, Miss Minnie?"

"Yes."

"I am."

Minnie was impatient. "Is it *comfortable*, Alan? Are you glad to be able to keep your father company?"

"Glad, Miss Minnie. And grateful." His tone was teasing.

"I didn't ask you to be grateful," Minnie Hallow said.

"Aren't I allowed to do something without you asking?"

"You know that isn't what I mean. You're impugning my motives, Alan. I mean to help, not to inspire gratitude." She was affronted.

"Don't go on, Miss Minnie. Kirsty has enough trouble with the noise of the town." The boy was very reasonable.

"This," said Minnie Hallow, rigid with scorn, "is *not* a town."

The boy glanced back at them, dropped his jaw, and said that those *big* towns must be a staggering spectacle indeed.

"Be quiet, Alan Skilling," said Anne Tegner.

Alan was quiet.

Not far beyond Stolnsay, where the few pastures came to an

end, there was a final stone wall along the brow of the hill, a new one, not yet settled, and as they came up the road beneath it Billie could see the sky shining through its piled stones as if they were only knotted lace. She looked back at the town and saw, in the still air, exhalations of hearth smoke going up like slack strings, which seemed to anchor the few motionless clouds. She could discern the wreck, under green water, a salvage derrick on the wharf above it. The *Gustav Edda* didn't look like a ship. It looked like its own shadow, the shadow Billie had seen on the sandy seafloor as the ship had maneuvered slowly into its berth, shortly before she went below and met Henry at the ladder, and Henry had pressed her back against the wall.

The dogcart passed over the rise and pulled in where the road branched, turned one way into the hills and out across a vast stretch of rolling bronze bogland, and the other way down a narrow valley, crossing and recrossing a wayward watercourse that had scattered stones around itself like a trail of crumbs. This road was eventually smudged out in bracken-covered sand hills. Through these Billie saw a beach with golden sand.

Minnie climbed down from the cart. She removed her easel, canvas, paint box, and set them on the roadside. She said to Anne Tegner that by the time they got down to the beach the tide would be well in, and they should be able to find some pipefish in the shallows along the shore. Alan would help.

Billie got down, too, and without a word walked away onto the heath. Around her feet was thyme and budding heather—in blooms only by stones whose radiating heat had brought some flowers on early. Billie saw thrift and clover and mountain speed-well and tough tawny grasses. The heath was a springy patch-work dotted with smooth stones, none the same composition or color. It was all so pleasing and varied, it was as if it had been planted, planned. It was lovely, so lovely that Billie wasn't watching her step and stumbled again and again. She waded and staggered, and then dropped down among it, and the heath buoyed up her body and hissed in the breeze, a hiss made of the ringing of dry bells.

Nearby, but invisible, Minnie Hallow said, "It's beautiful, but none of it is tender. I like tender plants."

Billie stroked a stiff sprig of some herb, resinous and aromatic. Then she sat up. The cart was some way away down the road to the beach, Anne Tegner holding her hat and hunched around her jar. Minnie said, "I have to get my fill of tender flowers before we come."

She had set up her easel and was at work already, testing the tip of her brush on the sleeve of her white smock. "We follow the spring north," she explained. "We see it first in London, then Port Clarity, then Edinburgh, then here." Minnie said that Billie would have liked Scouse Beach. It was warmer than the hill. And none of the bays nearer the castle was any good. They were all stony and cold and coated with sulfurous weed.

Billie lay down again, sank into the low room of heath.

Further silence. The angle of the light was such that the sky wasn't the deep drawing blue it would be on a cold day. There seemed to be a fine and flawed white screen between Billie and the blue. She pretended she was alone. She listened to the sifted air. She nearly slept, but her body jerked, as if the ground had given way and dropped her—twice—and at each fall she snatched something, first a plaited pigskin-covered button, then the untucked tail of the shirt of the man who came onto the *Gustav Edda* with the Stolnsay pilot. Billie heard her sister's voice, right at her ear, hoarse with cold and calling. "Billie!" said Edith.

"Miss Paxton," said Minnie, scarcely distinct, as though she'd waited for some sign Billie was asleep and only then addressed her. "Miss Paxton, we have something in common."

Billie sat up again and had to tear her hair out of the heath—her head was taking root.

The dogcart had gone out of sight. She had no notion how long she'd slept. Minnie was seated on the ground now, her paint box shut and propped on her knees, in use as a desk. It was covered in paper, a thick sheaf of pages, the breeze thumbing their top corners.

Billie said that maybe she would follow the others. Minnie stopped writing and chewed her pencil. When Billie got up and moved a little her way, unintentionally, for she was groggy and unsteady on her feet, Minnie hunched over the papers. Billie saw this and looked sharp. *A love letter*, she thought.

Seeing Billie looking at her pages, Minnie told her that she was making several fair copies of a play by the well-known playwright George Bernard Shaw, for her theatricals at the castle. But even the illiterate Billie, who had never heard of George Bernard Shaw, could see no printed text from which Minnie might be *copying*. The excuse seemed curious, too hasty to be true.

"Miss Paxton," Minnie said, frowning at her, "perhaps you should go and see how they are."

The road was uneven, the burn that it repeatedly looped to avoid still crossed it a number of times, dropping its crumbs of stone. Billie went easily but was pleased when the road petered out into several sandy tracks through the bracken. She took the broadest of these, where the wheels of vehicles heavier than the dogcart had plowed a way through between two dunes. But its churned sand was heavy going, and Billie left it for a narrower one, sprinkled with dry sheep droppings. This track came out on the crest of the dune, where bracken gave way to cropped grass, above the long gentle curve of Scouse Beach. Far out, the sea's dimpled blue passed imperceptibly into the cobalt blue of the mountains of one of the Inner Isles. Closer to shore the water was placid, and completely clear.

Directly below Billie stood the dogcart, the small pony drowsing in harness. Kirsty was snoring into her feed bag, and had blown chaff up into her eyelashes.

At the near end of the beach Anne Tegner was up to her ankles in the water, her thick flounced skirts bunched around her thighs. She was attempting to direct Alan Skilling, who was in over his knees and treading the sand as though stamping out a vintage.

Billie scrambled down the dune with more impetus and less stealth than she'd planned, so was obliged to go join them.

Alan had discovered that a certain kind of sand, collected below miniature headlands of rock, had somehow, when submerged, remained infused with air. If he stamped, he sent up a fizz of bubbles. When Billie arrived he was busy speculating to Anne about how the sand had trapped the air. The water was very cold and his knees were bright red, the rolled ends of his trousers wet through.

"Look!" he said to Billie, and tramped in a circle, the water boiling about him.

"All the pipefish will be up at the factory by the time you're through," said Anne. She waved an arm at the far end of the beach and the construction of new, raw stone—buildings and a breakwater. Lord Hallowhulme's alginate factory.

Billie sat down to take off her shoes and stockings. The bands of sunlight in the water were warm and rhythmical, a balm like a repeated caress, too subtle to be tactile, perhaps only a sound like a cat purring. Billie hitched up her skirt and waded in, away from Alan and his agitation.

Anne said, "Isn't it cold? My anklebones are aching." She got out. Alan invited Billie to try the bubbles. She surged his way, wetting her hem and petticoat at once, and found her feet breaking a crust of sand that wheezed and then released air. The fizz brushed her skin. Tiny bubbles caught in the small transparent hairs of her legs, coated and fattened them like a silvery mold. Billie felt a laugh behind her teeth, in her sinuses, a chortle, a snort—she shut her teeth on it and stomped about, her lower half loose, but face set. Then she stopped, ambled away, trailing her skirt. Anne Tegner pursued her, waving a small net. Anne gave it to Billie, explaining that pipefish were a sort of streamlined seahorse, without flounces or armor or a coiled tail. "They're dark, brown or black, with delicate horse heads."

Billie went on up the beach, wading, passed a beached blob of water, wholly transparent, a jellyfish, wobbling like a stone in someone's thirsty delirium dream. She saw a stripped fish skeleton, still cohering, bobbing about in the ripples of the crowning tide. Then she saw her first pipefish. It was drifting rather than swimming, the two rippling fans of its gills the only apparent voluntary motion. She tried to scoop it up, but it flicked away from her, pouring over the rim of the net.

Billie saw Alan's raggy shadow before she heard him. He came up beside her and they began together to herd the pipefish, with water, into Anne's big jar. Billie saw that her hands were red after only a moment immersed.

She asked Alan Skilling if people ever swam here.

No, they only paddled. But Mr. Hesketh had been seen to swim last summer. And young Mr. Rixon's friend, Elov Jansen, tried only yesterday. But *they* were Norsemen. It warmed up a little by July, and in the hot weather—*if* there was any hot weather—folk did go in the sea for a dip. No one *swam*. The island's fishermen made a point of never learning. It was considered bad luck, futile, for after all, if they fell in off their boats, or if a boat capsized, the water was so cold that they wouldn't stand a chance. "Better to go quickly, than to tread water and freeze," said Alan Skilling. Then after a moment he said, "I do know that your sister drowned. I don't mean to cause hurt, only I was so keen to tell you about us that it slipped my mind."

Billie looked up at his young, tense face and said not to worry. He was clutching the jar where the pipefish flowed about then, confused by how its whole sea had become an all-round surface, impenetrable except to light, it stiffened and became a streak of black wax dropped into cold water.

"Would you like me to teach you to swim?" Billie said—and then she straightened and shaded her eyes with her hands.

There were men at work on the site of the factory, several unloading lumber from a dray, others busy with trowel, mortar, and brick.

"If there's ever no one about," she amended.

"Everyone keeps the Sabbath," Alan told her. "Even the castle must because of its servants. Stolnsay's congregation is stricter than their minister—they always have been." Then, in an outbreak of astonishment, "Can *you* swim?" He followed this with an apology, or an explanation. "I'm a Catholic, you see. We are of Skilling—my father and me."

Billie looked at the water; at this temperature she'd likely be breathless after ten strokes. The bands of sunlight flowed, bright gold over green gold, the water an icy paradise, compressed, a dense medium, but it seemed more habitable than the air, the steep treeless hills behind her.

"I mean," said the boy, uncertain as to whether he'd made himself understood, "Stolnsay is strict about the Sabbath, but *I'm* not expected at church, and maybe you're not either. And I'd like you to teach me to swim."

Billie stood peering at him, the net dripping on the dry upper part of her skirt. She didn't say yes or consent to arrangements. She didn't know if the boy was being kind, by giving her something to do, and she should resist his kindness, or if he was only hungry for advantage, the advantage any skill would earn him. She did ask if Anne Tegner would be content with only one pipefish.

"One will do, though I think she means to paint it as two. Paint a picture of it. But anyway it'll be me down in the cove at all hours of the day and night fetching fresh seawater so that her fish won't stifle."

Billie gave him the net to carry—and some advice: he should charge Miss Tegner for running around after her fish, surely Miss Minnie's money didn't cover that? Then she set off back up the beach to collect her boots.

Anne Tegner plonked down beside Billie to put her own on, and Alan arrived on her other side, so that she was flanked, as Henry and Edith had always seemed to flank her. Billie had taken it as kindly shepherding, but now she wondered, did this boy and girl think she was in danger of breaking out, running mad?

THEY COLLECTED MINNIE, WHO, BILLIE SAW, HAD CON-cealed her papers and was packed, ready and waiting for them. But once they were all aboard and the cart was hurrying the poor little pony down a dip—Alan's knuckles white on the brake handle and the brake squealing—Anne asked Minnie, "How is the play?"

"If you and Ailsa could make another two copies," Minnie said, "we'll be closer." Then to Billie, "We always put on a play. I mean, we have most summers we've been here. My brother makes a fuss as a point of honor, to save face with his friends, but really he likes it, too." Minnie paused, then went on, her tone airy. "This year we'll put on a very little-known work by George Bernard Shaw, titled *Fortune and the Four Winds*. It's about a man's first meeting with his grown-up children."

"Has he been in India?" Alan asked, facetious, and only to get attention. He was told to be quiet. Minnie asked Billie whether she'd like to help, maybe make a fair copy—six or seven were needed.

Billie paused, then explained that she couldn't write. She didn't blush—and it was the first time ever. Edith could no longer be shamed by their failure. It was only Billie's shame now, and as only hers it seemed a smaller thing, a lesser form of orphanhood than being without Edith.

But Minnie was blushing. She apologized, said that since Miss Paxton's sister was a *teacher* . . .

"Yes. I know. Edith and Henry tried. But I can't see the words right."

Alan was plainly intrigued. "How *do* you see them?" When Billie didn't answer he began to guess. Was it poor eyesight? Did she mistake her letters—like, at dusk, he might mistake a rafting flock of guillemots for a bed of bull kelp?

"You know, Miss Paxton, I would have taken a simple 'no' for an answer," Minnie said, sulky.

"I'm being honest, not rude," Billie told her.

Minnie reddened more. Even Alan was quelled. They went along in silence.

Two horsemen appeared behind them. The rider on the taller animal was Murdo Hesketh, his bearing both natural and martial. He looked like a hussar. The other man was well bundled, wore a bowler of not quite the right sort to be a riding hat, and rode with his elbows stuck out.

"Well," said Anne, "Hesketh hasn't any reservations about Scouse Beach." She looked at Minnie, then burst out, "You *should* have come down. It was lovely. Sheltered and mild."

Minnie turned to Billie and explained. Her own older sister Ingrid had drowned on Scouse Beach two years before. "*That's* what we have in common."

"He has business there," Alan Skilling put in, clearly defending Murdo Hesketh.

"Father had already planned to build his alginate factory on the beach before Ingrid drowned—and Father is unswerving in his plans," Minnie said.

Billie asked if Mr. Hesketh only minded Lord Hallowhulme's business, or did he have an interest. "He is kin, isn't he?"

"He's Father's cousin. And Mother's. On Mother's side I think he's my first cousin once removed twice." Minnie pulled a face and laughed at what she'd said. Billie found she was laughing, too. She choked out, "Was he *very* persistent?"

When Minnie had done laughing she explained that her grandmother and his mother were sisters, her grandfather and his father brothers. Which made him, by her calculations, a first cousin once removed twice. He'd been part of the Hallowhulme household since that summer. The summer Ingrid drowned.

Anne told Billie that the accident was directly after the Tegners

last visit. "We all put on *Twelfth Night* that year. Ingrid was Olivia."
Anne paused, then asked if Miss Paxton knew Shakespeare.

"*He who has but a tiny little wit . . .*" Billie sang, as Henry had
taught her.

The horsemen were gaining on them. Minnie said to Billie,
"The other man is Geordie Betler, Ian Betler's brother. Mr.
Betler has rather made himself at home. He dines with the family
sometimes, and sometimes in the kitchens. He's quite comfortable in either place—which Father has noticed and admired. My
father is very egalitarian, he doesn't believe in 'breeding' as in
background, though he does believe in blood, as in *inheritance*, what
one's parents bequeath one in terms of health, soundness, ability.
But I'm sure he'll tell you himself."

They all watched Murdo Hesketh's smooth rise and fall in
his stirrups. Minnie fixed her eyes on him, frowning. "I believe
he had something to do with Ingrid's death," she told Billie.

And Billie: "What? He *killed* her?" Believing him capable of
anything.

THE DOGCART WAS BURDENED AND SLOW, AND THE
mounted men soon came even with it. Geordie reined in. He
walked his horse in order to ask Miss Paxton how she was, and
Miss Anne and Miss Minnie if they'd enjoyed their outing. Perhaps he'd even ask to view the progress of Minnie's landscape.
She might say something astonishing. She had when he'd last
spoken to her.

The day before the funeral Geordie had pushed himself up
the wet road to the brow of the hill above Stolnsay Harbor, in a
still spell between two scudding fronts of cloud. He had found

the dogcart, Alan Skilling roosting in its lee, his head wrapped in his jacket, and Minnie sketching at her easel. Geordie stopped to catch his breath and admire the view. Minnie said, "Good day, Mr. Betler," then put her diminishing glass up to her eyes and looked down at the town—removed the glass, added a few lines to her picture. Geordie asked if he could look at the instrument, and she passed it to him explaining—as he peered down its double-barrel at the clouds coming in, a great flotilla at the height of the hill—that artists used diminishing glasses to "compose" a landscape. Did Mr. Betler see the measuring marks to one side of his field of vision? That was the device's science—but mostly what the glass did was make the landscape more manageable, make it more like its own portrait.

Geordie gave the instrument back to Minnie, and she made her astonishing remark. Her father could be said to view things through a diminishing glass. "His landscapes always look like his designs for them. Otherwise, he simply doesn't see them. Things are as they should be, and managed, or they are in need of management." The girl looked at Geordie from under her brows, her chin down, as if she was accustomed to peering over the top of reading glasses. "You do know that Father owns this island, Mr. Betler? Both entities—Kissack with Skilling. He's *given* the crofters their houses and land on the condition that they'll consent to benefit from his industries and other planned improving institutions—on the condition that they'll *play* with him. He's purchased a whole population as playmates."

Today, as he approached the dogcart, Geordie was expectant. He drew rein and tipped his hat. But all the cart's occupants were looking at Mr. Hesketh, passing on their other side, straight-backed on his big bay horse. All—but Billie Paxton. She glowered at the road between the pony's ears.

Murdo Hesketh checked his pace so that his mare paused in her flowing trot and capered a few steps to one side of her straight course, her glowing neck bowed. "Good day," Murdo said, merely polite, "Alan, Minnie, Miss Anne, Miss Paxton."

Miss Paxton hunched up. It wasn't a flinch, but a blunt thickening of her whole body. "Pig," she said under her breath, without looking at him.

His horse surged forward, made a number of pretty parade-ground jumps, responding to her rider's clenched muscles, then set off again at an even trot.

Geordie was at a loss, so put his hat back on and followed.

MISS PAXTON OBEYED LORD HALLOWHULME'S SUMMONS and appeared at dinner. Clara Hallow asked after Mr. Maslen and Miss Paxton said that she and the hired nurse thought that he was less feverish this evening.

Billie Paxton sat opposite Geordie and he saw that, although she felt awkward, and was there without any expectation of plea-sure, he wouldn't have to give her secret signals about which utensil to use for which course. Geordie looked across the six-foot breadth of white linen, silverware, crystal, tureens topped by tumbling nasturtiums in bright glazed ceramic, and white soup bowls full of creamy mulligatawny. He saw that, despite her dull lowering look, and her foulmouthed frank opinion of Mr. Hesketh, Billie Paxton was an unpolished but reasonably well brought-up young woman. He also saw that, between the road into Stolnsay, and the dinner hour, she'd had a bath and washed her hair. He'd seen her hair plaited, a pale red corona. It was now loose against her back and, when she moved, as alive and radiant as coral. Geordie considered—was Billie Paxton pretty, or a plain youthful girl with beautiful hair? Her jaw was set, and even her strong throat looked stubborn, blunt, above broad shoulders and a flat compact chest and waist. *Yes—a plain girl with stupendous hair,* Geordie thought till, seeing herself appraised, Miss Paxton's nostrils twitched and her light brown eyes caught a candle flare, hot rather than hard, and Geordie saw that she was an odd beauty, like the maned, staring women in the pictures Meela Tannoy admired and would buy. Pictures by Rossetti or Burne-Jones. Billie Paxton was odd, striking, but not enervated or drowsy, ill or bewitched, like a Burne-Jones or Rossetti model. Geordie saw also that Billie Paxton was *afraid* of Lord Hallowhulme's table—its beauty, bounty, its company—but that she was in vigorous rebellion against her fear. He watched her thrust her strong, tapering fingers into her bread roll and tear it open. He caught her eye and then passed her a plate heaped with dewy whelk shells of shaved butter.

Lord Hallowhulme was talking, solving his and other people's problems. The phone cables and batteries had been salvaged but were already set to corrode hopelessly. He'd had his secretary, Johan Gutthorm, order more. Hallowhulme nodded at the desiccated man seated on his left. At this acknowledgment Johan Gutthorm lifted his chin and pursed his lips. Hallowhulme said that the replacements would ship in next to no time—his plans were only a few weeks behind schedule, no harm done. The alginate factory was coming along—thanks to Mr. Hesketh. Here Hallowhulme addressed himself to Geordie, his eyes sliding over Billie Paxton, who had just remembered to tilt her soup plate away from her, as she should. "As you must by now have divined, Mr. Betler, I'm something of a visionary. A man like me needs someone practical near him. A man like me, with dreams and schemes and funds in abundance needs a canny executor, someone to deal with all the details, who will do what needs to be done. And here is my cousin, Murdo, the excellent Mr. Hesketh, whom I treasure."

Geordie responded to this with a polite nod. It was disturbing. Lord Hallowhulme was diligently salvaging the means of his plans—his cables and batteries—while there were people at his table whose losses were irreplaceable.

Hallowhulme went on to say he was concerned about progress on the herring cannery in Southport, at the other end of the island. He'd have to go there very soon.

"Father, please do take account of the date of the performance of our play," Minnie said. She smiled at the man who removed her soup plate.

Her father asked was the performance at the end of July, as usual?

Rixon moaned.

"Wait till you read it," his sister told him. "I'm making copies."

"Have you thought of using Mr. Gutthorm's typewriter?" Hallowhulme asked. "Of course I can't volunteer his *time*. We're far too busy."

"May I use it?"

"Ask Johan, Minnie."

Johan Gutthorm bowed slightly and said Miss Minnie was welcome to use his machine.

"I've done two fair copies already. Rixon, you and Elov can have yours this evening." Minnie turned to the salver of greens and took the tongs. She served herself. "It's a modern play, by Mr. George Bernard Shaw. You'll like it. It's called *Fortune and the Four Winds*."

Clara wanted to know if it would be performed on the lawn,

or in the ballroom. If outdoors, the gardeners would have to clear all the nettles out of the ha-ha.

"Indoors," said Minnie. Then to her brother, "I wish you would read it tonight. You *can* choose whether or not you'd like to do it."

He seemed astonished by this offer.

The serving dish came to Geordie, and he plied the tongs, smiled at Robert, the footman who was serving. Robert had eaten already. Geordie had a standing invitation in the kitchen and Robert had wanted to know why Geordie would choose to eat in *there*—the dining room. He said, "We have almost the same."

"Saving the wine," said Geordie, and saw that the footman might like to add that he wouldn't want to join the family, even for the wine, but that theirs was too short an acquaintance for Robert to offer opinions of this sort.

Lord Hallowhulme was tendering more advice. Had his daughter thought to enlist Miss Paxton? He only glanced at Billie, with a stiff baring of his teeth, more grimace than grin. "Copying would be a quiet occupation for the sickroom."

Billie Paxton was silent. Geordie supposed she was puzzling over how to decline, and still seem polite.

Ailsa Tegner said, "Miss Paxton can't read." The twins were watching Billie intently. Apparently they had formed some notion of helping her.

Several people spoke. Some only to ask her, "Is that true?" Clara Hallow disbelieving—hadn't Billie and Edith received the same early education?

Billie put down her knife and fork—her hands were trembling, Geordie saw. She folded them in her lap, then gave a very brief account of her trouble, its history. Her father, sister, great-aunt, and Mr. Maslen had all tried to teach her. "At a very poor return for their efforts," Billie said. "Once people see that I'm not *very* stupid, they begin to imagine I'm stubborn. But really it's a mystery."

Lord Hallowhulme was quite motionless, then he abruptly jabbed at the air with a raised index finger. He'd thought of something. He motioned Johan Gutthorm toward him and had a word in his ear. Everyone watched. Gutthorm removed his napkin and went out with his instructions—inaudible to most of the table. Hallowhulme fell to eating again. He kept silent, and chewed thoroughly, all with an air of suspenseful significance.

Elov Jansen began to look bilious.

Acquitted, Billie resumed eating.

AFTER THE DESSERT WAS CLEARED THE LADIES RETIRED. Geordie moved closer to the head of the table. Rixon asked his father if he and Elov could please have a small glass of port. They were allowed, and the boys watched Robert pour, their eyebrows up and urging him. Robert was scrupulous, but tantalizing; he took his time and gave the decanter a flourishing twist to spin the last hanging drop back into its neck. He smiled at the boys.

Gutthorm came back with what Lord Hallowhulme had wanted—a number of the *British Medical Journal* for the year 1896.

Murdo declined the port. He pushed back his chair and slid down in its seat, extended his legs and crossed them at the ankles. He lit a cigarette and tilted his head right back against the headrest. He asked Gutthorm if the accident report had been typed yet. His understanding was that it had to be ready for the investigator sent by the *Gustav Edda*'s insurers.

"Yes, Mr. Hesketh, it's done. You can have a copy tonight. But I don't think you'll find anything new, as it is largely based on *your* notes."

"I do need to see it in total, Johan. To have the full story."

Geordie watched Murdo. He knew one salient fact about the wreck—its boiler was intact. He and Murdo had discussed it, or, rather, they had discussed how Murdo had acted on mistaken evidence—Miss Paxton's still unexplained flight. Geordie knew that Murdo Hesketh had never altered his opinion—that the explosion was an act of sabotage. Murdo was only waiting for certain submerged facts to surface, like air bubbles on a long journey from a great depth. Murdo's relaxation, the still silvery brown lashes of his closed eyes, all gave the somewhat menacing impression of patient appetite. He was waiting for something to come up. He was a white bear poised over a seal hole in pack ice.

"Here it is!" Hallowhulme made his announcement to the whole table. "Doctor Pringle Morgan: 'Congenital Word Blindness.' " He was quiet, reading. He read solidly, for ten minutes, during which time Rixon, by licking his lips and dancing his eyebrows at Robert, inveigled another small glass for himself and Elov. Geordie noticed that both the boy and the footman knew that Lord Hallowhulme wouldn't see.

Johan Gutthorm waited behind his master's chair. He didn't read over his master's shoulder—something Geordie would never have been able to resist in the circumstances—after all, it couldn't be an indiscretion to read the *Medical Journal*, which was in the public domain, even if its reader's thoughts at that moment were not.

Hallowhulme put the journal down, and his hand fell on a letter that the secretary had placed by his port glass. "What is this?"

Gutthorm said it had arrived in the morning mail. He hadn't passed it on at once because he wasn't sure where the guest was lodged.

"Capital!" said Hallowhulme, eyeing the address—then, "Awkward." He glanced sidelong at Murdo. He cleared his throat and told Robert that they would join the ladies now, and were all ready for the coffee and cake. Rixon and Elov, startled, knocked back their glasses.

As everyone got up, Murdo said he had some business.

"Nonsense, Cousin, leave it for now. Come in and have coffee." Hallowhulme collected Murdo as he passed, wrapped an arm around his cousin's shoulders, and led him into the parlor.

Geordie followed, intrigued.

In the parlor Lord Hallowhulme stopped abruptly; he looked angry and at a loss. "*Where* is Miss Paxton?"

"She went up to sit with Mr. Maslen," said Clara.

"Send for her, Clara. I have something for her."

"Surely it can be carried up to her, James?"

"Certainly not!" Lord Hallowhulme wouldn't sit. He posted himself by the mantelpiece and fidgeted. Clara kept him waiting, she let the maid who carried the coffee settle the tray before sending her out again with a summons for Miss Paxton.

When Billie came in Lord Hallowhulme took his seat. And, as soon as the fireplace was unoccupied, Murdo carried his coffee over to it and faced the fire, not the room.

"Sit down, dear," Clara said to Billie. "Do have some cake."

Miss Paxton was watchful; her chin tilted down, she looked at them from under her eyebrows. She appeared to have guessed that she hadn't just been fetched for her share of the cake.

Then Lord Hallowhulme shuffled forward on his seat and asked her to attend a minute. He held up a knife. It was not a cake knife, Geordie saw, but one of the triangular knives from the dining table. It had a dull smear on it where Lord Hallowhulme had licked it clean before putting it in his pocket. "What is this?" he asked.

"A knife, sir," Billie said, in a cautious voice, but as if she was used to being asked odd questions.

"What kind of knife?"

"A fish knife."

"And this?" He pointed to a groove incised the length of the blade.

Billie hesitated.

"Yes?" James Hallow said.

"I believe it's a gutter of sorts."

"Ah. And what would you call it on a ship?"

Billie seemed puzzled. "A knife, sir."

"No. A gutter—"

"Oh. I think maybe the scuppers." She smiled faintly. Perhaps she was thinking of the drunken sailor.

James Hallow stooped, peered at her hard, then straightened and asked her if she could point to something in the room which could be described as a vertical.

Billie Paxton took a few steps and touched the window frame beside the silk bellpull.

"What about upright?" James Hallow said.

She dropped her gaze, then turned her eyes up briefly and glanced through her lashes at Murdo Hesketh. She looked for long enough so that it seemed, when she looked away again, that he'd been patently rejected. She pointed at a standard lamp.

Minnie was laughing.

Lord Hallowhulme said, "It is difficult with people, of course, when you have to take moral qualities into account," explicating her joke—as if it was *his* joke, as if he could see that what she'd done was funny, but not that she'd *meant* to be. Hallowhulme gathered himself again, held his breath, and concentrated on the young woman in front of him. He directed her to the large, dingy, pastoral landscape above the mantelpiece. Murdo moved out of her way. James Hallow followed her and actually tapped his finger against the small gold mound of a painted haystack. "What is this?" he said.

Billie Paxton looked, her eyes darted from the haystack to the many other objects around it. Her jaw set. "I can't think," she said, after a time. "I know what is, but I can't think of the word."

"It's a haystack, dear," Lord Hallowhulme said, kindly. Then, "Can you find the harrow in this picture?"

She found it straightaway.

James Hallow cleared his throat. "I shall have to write to Dr. Morgan Pringle," he said.

Billie was defensive. She said, "I can't always think of the name of the thing if I'm shown its picture."

"And you're quite a bright girl," he said.

"Yes, I am!" Billie fired up, passionate, with the first sign of tears anyone had seen. For a moment Geordie had a sense of her enormous frustration.

Lord Hallowhulme told Miss Paxton that she was a scientific puzzle, which was to say that science had recognized her problem but knew neither its cause nor its cure. "However," he said, in a remote, regretful tone, "it *is* considered congenital." He gave her arm a conciliatory squeeze. Then he told her that a letter had come for her, from Cornwall. Had he her permission to open it?

Billie nodded.

Lord Hallowhulme used the fish knife to slit the envelope,

shook the letter open, and some other papers dropped into his lap. He read, and his neck colored up. "Cousin," he said, and held the letter out to Murdo. "Could you read Miss Paxton's letter to her?"

Clara said, "James." She put her cake fork and her as yet untouched wedge of cake back on the table and held out her own hand for the letter. James Hallow seemed neither to hear nor see her. Clara slowly lowered her hand—she cooled, grew dull, a dying coal under a forming skin of ash.

Murdo took the page from his cousin.

Clara told Rixon and Elov that they needn't stay—since they'd finished their cake. Elov leapt up, brushing crumbs from his front. Rixon joined him. Clara told Minnie and the Tegner twins that, if they also wished to go—

"I'd like another piece of cake. Thank you," Minnie said, loudly. It was a sort of bugle call, Geordie thought, not a charge, perhaps a call to muster. The Tegners hesitated, looking at Minnie, then, checked by a gesture from their mother, they left the room. Minnie cut herself another fat slice, conveyed it to her plate, sat back down, sighed in contentment, and tucked in.

Was the letter improper? Geordie wondered. Billie Paxton looked more alarmed than embarrassed. Geordie saw her steel herself, as though she expected an attack.

"I'm afraid that at least one newspaper was inaccurate in its reportage of the accident," James Hallow said. "Miss Paxton, you have friends who believe that both your sister and brother-in-law are drowned."

"Who?" Billie asked. "Henry has friends. Edith and I only a very few."

"Read Miss Paxton her letter, Cousin." Lord Hallowhulme

took out his handkerchief and dabbed at his eyes. His cousin and wife watched this, skeptical.

"The letter is from a Reverend Vause," said Murdo. "It is dated this Monday."

"And the fellow has overpaid the post," muttered James Hallow. "In his concern, no doubt."

"The Reverend Vause writes: 'My Dear Miss Paxton. I cannot say with what shock and sadness my sisters and I read the report of the unfortunate accident which has claimed the life of my former classmate Mr. Maslen and your sister. Please accept our sympathy and our regrets for your loss. To be deprived of a family in so sudden and summary a way! But, Miss Paxton, you have friends, and your friends—Mrs. Wood and Miss Vause— join with me in asking you to accept an offer of protection, comfort, and assistance. We entreat you to come to Mulrush, where you can rest and recover yourself with people who wish only to assist you. We're deeply concerned for your well-being, and do hope you will write directly and draw on the enclosed order . . .' " Murdo broke off.

"There's a bank draft—the sum would cover a sea voyage and second-class rail, I presume," Hallowhulme said. He held the order up to his secretary's eyes. Gutthorm nodded. "And there is a further page, with times and connections copied from railway timetables. So you see, Miss Paxton, the Reverend Vause has done all he can to do your thinking for you, if not your reading. Is there any more, Cousin?"

" 'In expectation of your reply' . . . 'sincere condolences' . . . and so forth. Which newspaper was it, James, mistaken in its facts?"

"That's only an assumption of mine, Cousin. I can't otherwise imagine how such a misunderstanding could arise."

Murdo handed Billie her letter. "I'm sure Clara can write to this Vause and tell him that you're still in possession of a protector."

"Yes. I'm sure he'll be happy to hear Mr. Maslen was spared," Clara said. "And how he does."

"Who *is* he?" Lord Hallowhulme said, waving the money order. "This Vause of Mulrush?"

"I was in service. Mulrush is his sister's house. A Mrs. Wood. That's the real connection—but it's true that Henry was at school with him."

"Mrs. Wood and her brother were kind to you?"

"No, Lord Hallowhulme, they were unkind."

James Hallow took this in his stride. "Do they mean to make amends then? Or do they want another opportunity to be unkind?"

"I'm sure the Reverend Vause's offer is meant kindly," Billie said. Then she asked Lady Hallowhulme if she would help her reply. "In the best way."

Geordie, watching all this, was making more of it. Billie was frank. *"They were unkind."* And she was a good girl ready to make the right reply. She confided in Lord Hallowhulme, and then conceded, asked Clara's help. But there was something unmalleable under it all—and he imagined her backed against a door with her teeth bared. The image shocked him, it seemed to belong to no feelings he had about her. It was as if the image was an infection, something he caught from someone else's bad air. It was something Murdo might have seen—but Geordie believed Murdo was now in sympathy with Billie Paxton, as far as he was able; at least he didn't cast her as a culprit anymore. Geordie looked around. Gutthorm was watching the girl, with the look of a lean dog on a short lead. Clara was refreshing the girl's cup. Murdo was consulting the coals in the fireplace. Minnie was picking cake crumbs off her front and putting them in her mouth. While Lord Hallowhulme—well—Hallowhulme, like a lockkeeper turning his lock key, was opening up, letting in a cloudy flood of talk that thickened gradually, gained speed and volume. He suggested to Clara what she should write. Said that the contact made should be maintained; Mr. Maslen and Miss Paxton should cultivate these alert and generous friends. It was as if she had never confided their "unkindness." It was as if Hallowhulme hadn't demonstrated something, grief or mortification, on reading the letter, hadn't been unable to read it out himself or entrust its—his actions suggested—*improper* communication to his wife. Was Lord Hallowhulme such a sentimental man? Geordie wondered. Or was it that he just must manage everything? Hallowhulme talked, and they all bobbed up, unharmed, to a higher level of the waterway. Hallowhulme opened the second lock. He changed the subject—said something about a visit to his salmon hatcheries—moving them all on.

7 ⚘ THEFT AS A SERVANT

AT SIXTEEN, IMPATIENT WITH HER DEPENDENCE ON
Edith and Aunt Blazey, Billie had demanded to be allowed to do
what she could. She couldn't teach, but she could go into service. Aunt Blazey advertised, and Billie found a place, only eight
miles inland, among the staff of twelve belonging to the household of a widow, Mrs. Wood. Mrs. Wood lived with her two
daughters, and an unmarried sister, Miss Vause. Billie left Aunt a
week after Edith had gone to take up her own post. Though she
missed her family—and the sea in the cove beneath the cliff—
Billie wasn't unhappy. She'd had more than her share of strange
beds—top and tail with Edith on some rustling horsehair pallet
in a room on the back streets of French or Italian towns in the
Ligurian Bight. She wasn't afraid of change, and had never yet
been lonely so was unafraid of loneliness. Her work wasn't hard;
she'd been engaged as a sewing girl but did other upstairs work.
She ran to answer the bells in the top row, she carried trays, made
beds, corked stains on woodwork, packed away furs in their
cedar boxes, and wool dresses with packets of camphor, snuff,
and Persian insect mix. She cleaned mirrors with blue powder,
and polished them with the deceased Mr. Wood's tattered silk
handkerchiefs. Billie liked to be earning as Edith was, and learn-

ing some of the skills of managing a household. She couldn't hope ever to manage to marry the figures in the cash book and daybook, as the Woods' housekeeper did in her big black ledger, but she did learn how to dress leather shoes with castor oil and wash hairbrushes with hartshorn. As she came into practical knowledge Billie felt herself increase. She was satisfied, and felt herself satisfactory.

But something went wrong. Afterward, when she talked it all over with Edith, she tried to uncover her first error, what it was she did or failed to do that caused Mrs. Wood, or Miss Vause, to lose confidence in her. It seemed to Billie that her trouble started the moment any of them first looked at her for longer than the duration of a request or instruction. It was Olive Vause who first noticed her—one morning when Billie was busy replacing a chipped crystal button on the back of Miss Olive's rose silk dress.

It was a sumptuous dress, heavy, overornamented with machine-made frills, ruffles, and superfluous tucks. A dress so sculpted that it could almost stand up by itself. It was all one fabric—its saving grace, perhaps even its glory—a heavy silk, which spoke whenever it moved, sighed and whispered. Olive Vause had come back into her bedroom from the dressing room with more mending for Billie, who sat in the best light by the bay window. Billie broke the thread with her teeth, put the needle in her pincushion, and stood to carry the rose dress back to its hanger. Quite unconsciously, she pushed the frock's waist against her own, and put out one leg to look down the cascading frills. Miss Vause asked Billie if she liked the dress. "Yes," Billie said. Miss Vause said she wasn't sure that she did—it didn't do much for her. "I doubt you'll see me in it," Miss Vause said. "People *don't* see me in it." And then Miss Vause said to herself that she should give the dress to Billie. "Yes, I think I will," she said. "If I haven't put it on before the end of summer, it will be yours."

But the very next day Miss Vause scolded Billie, quite rightly, for using the wrong brush on a velvet jacket and taking the nap off a patch on one sleeve. The hard bristles were for *topcoats only*. Although Olive Vause corrected Billie sharply, she didn't go on. But Billie would tell Edith later that it might have been from then—the wrong brush—or from her momentary careless admiration of her own foot emerging from under the frothy hem of the rose dress. Or—or perhaps the trouble dated from the previous Sunday when the Reverend Vause spoke to her.

They had met already. He'd been there when she'd first arrived. She remembered him saying that he hoped she'd be comfortable with Mrs. Wood, and then he had given her a little book, an illuminated Scripture textbook, with a quote and a tiny colored panel for every day of the year.

Billie got out the book and showed Edith, who found her way to the date of Billie's dismissal, the 11th of August, and Hebrews, chapter thirteen, verse five—the picture of a sad individual hiding in the shelter of a high hedge: "I will never leave thee, nor forsake thee." "Humph!" went Edith. Then she found the date Billie's employment began, the 24th of May, and St. Luke, chapter 12, verse 15. The picture was of a pile of money bags, as orange as pumpkins. The text: "Beware of covetousness." Edith shook her head, closed the book and said, "So—the Sunday he spoke to you . . . ?" to prompt her sister.

The whole Wood household had gone to church. It was the Reverend Vause's parish. He was the younger brother, younger than Miss Olive. His sisters were rather proud of him—Trinity College, Cambridge; three years in East Africa. The girl he'd meant to marry had tuberculosis of the bone. They were still waiting—Billie thought—when Billie first met him. "He had her picture on his piano."

"And *when* did you have cause to see his piano?" Edith inquired.

Billie was once sent to the rectory with a message—that was sometime *after* she made the fan of rook feathers in the churchyard—and he'd offered to let her play his piano. She'd never had cause to linger in the Wood parlor—though there was a Sunday afternoon when it rained so hard and they'd all stayed away from church. The widow Wood had read to the assembled household—a few chapters of Paul to the Greeks—and Billie had played hymns. The Wood girls knew nothing so pedestrian as hymns, and couldn't play without a score. "That was the only time I was allowed to touch the Woods' piano," Billie said.

"The rook feathers?" Edith reminded her sister.

It was just as well Edith was interested in each incident, not in the order in which they came. For, once she'd begun to consider a cause of her trouble, Billie was beset by memories of irregular incidents. But with no sense of progress—like the progress of a disease from infection to crisis.

It was in the churchyard that Billie first spoke to the Reverend Vause. "Properly—not just to say 'Thank you, sir, for the little book.' " She passed him greeting his parishioners in the church doorway after the service. She bobbed, tapped his palm with her gloved fingers, and drifted away from the knots of talkers. She was to go back in the trap with the other maids. But they weren't yet ready to go, so Billie walked among the graves and found a feather from a pheasant cock then, under the tall elms, a scattering of rook feathers. Billie sat down on a headstone to make a fan with the feathers and a piece of straw. She took off her hat and slid the straw-wrapped shafts of the feathers in behind her hat-band. The Reverend Vause appeared before her. He asked her what she was doing.

"And?" Edith, expectant.

"I said I was only fiddling."

"And I don't suppose you thought to get up off the head-stone?" Edith asked.

"No."

The Reverend Vause made conversation. Billie couldn't re-member its content, but he was pleasant to her. "Then his sisters came to carry him off in the carriage, and I ran after the trap."

"Oh, I can see that," Edith said. "You, with your hat off, running after the trap."

Billie wondered whether her occasional unconsciousness was a fault, or merely an irregularity? Edith always said that if Billie had been able to remember their mother, she would have learned to check herself. *Edith* always checked herself—in the mirror on the wall at the foot of the chandlery stairs, at the street door. She'd check her hair, her hat, that she hadn't transferred printer's ink from the newspaper to her chin by propping it with her fin-gers as she read. Edith said: "I can remember mother telling me, '*Look* at yourself!' when I'd made a mess on my pinafore, or had mud on my shoes or twigs in my hair." Edith said that Billie had to learn to rein herself in, to hear a voice saying "Look at your-self!" when she was about to run after a trap, waving her hat and scattering feathers.

Billie continued to do her work, diligent, alert, and her at-tention wandered only occasionally. But she was being watched. After the rook's feathers, or her misstep with the rose dress, or the wrong brush, Billie felt eyes on her. Her odd lapses didn't escape notice. There was a day when, cleaning the mirror, she turned it a little at each pass of the cloth till, noticing the light in the room magnified, she saw she'd turned the glass to face another, on the far wall, so that she could see herself, crouching, arms upraised, infinitely repeated, like a motif on wallpaper, a figure that someone had got *right* and was worth repeating. Studying herself, she inclined her face against the glass, and her cheek made a cloudy imprint, smooth but slightly furred.

Olive Vause, watching from the doorway: "You'll have to do that over."

Billie imagined Olive complaining to Mrs. Wood: "So many lapses. Just think of all those she'll have made unobserved."

The housekeeper had Billie into her office to warn her that she wasn't giving satisfaction. And Billie was moved to remark that on the contrary, her lapses seemed to give Miss Vause and Mrs. Wood enormous satisfaction.

"That was wrong of you, Billie," Edith said.

"I know. But then everything settled, Edith. I was *circumspect*—as you're always telling me to be. I liked talking with the other servants at the kitchen table, although I did feel that I wasn't yet wholly one of them. And there was a lovely day when we all put our feet up and played cribbage—the afternoon of the Sunday when the roads were mired and Mrs. Wood read the service and I was asked to play hymns. But they all knew each others' stories—the family ailments and weddings and births. They had letters from brothers in Australia. I'd talk about you, but that seemed to put their backs up. They couldn't see how come I was cleaning combs and you were a teacher. They couldn't accept that I was—well—simple. They thought I must be lying."

Edith had visited Billie once when her employers took a detour to see the famous church at Hayle, within a mile of Mulrush. They dropped Edith off at the Woods' gate. Edith went to the front door, fully conscious of where she stood in the world. She rang the bell, and asked the butler, and waited in the hall. She had no notion of the quake she caused, arriving as she did, a single tremor like that in a bowl of jelly given a sharp knock. Everything moved, but nothing altered. Billie was in Miss Vause's dressing room, standing on a low stool, wearing the rose dress, while its hem was being put up to the right height—an inch below her anklebones. She was happy—as happy to have this assurance that the dress was hers as she was to feel that this meant she was forgiven, that at last people understood her and were making allowances for her oddness. She had heard—but hadn't taken in—the remark of her fellow maid, the girl pinning the hem. The girl said what a good thing it was that Billie was the same height as the elder Miss Wood. Then Billie was called. The housekeeper put her head around the door, and said, "Wilhelmina, your sister, *Miss Paxton*, is here." Billie didn't hear the mockery—that she was Wilhelmina, while Edith was Miss Paxton. She didn't hear the implication, that one of them was dishonest, either Billie wasn't entitled to her inclusion in that little tribe of maids and footmen—didn't belong with Bronwen, Gladys, Owen—or Edith wasn't entitled to her elevation to "Miss Paxton." Billie didn't hear. She jumped off the stool, picked up the stiff, talkative skirts of the dress, and dashed out of the room. Edith was in the lower hall, smiling, her arms held out. Edith had always been beautiful, but that day Edith's beauty made Billie falter in her flight—she stumbled and caught the banister. Edith was breathtaking—possibly always had been, but Billie had never seen before, had never been surprised by the sight of her sister, hadn't penetrated the haze of her own love. Billie threw herself at Edith and they sat down together on a long padded bench with their backs to the stairs. They talked, arms around each other's waist, Billie curved into her taller sister. Then the reverend came down the stairs behind them. He'd been up to see Mrs. Wood, who was in bed with a cold. At the sound of his footfalls Edith looked back over her shoulder. She gave a faint gasp, and Billie felt her own hair moved—Edith put a hand behind her and gathered Billie's hair together on her back. Billie became aware that she was in the rose dress, and that its buttons were unfastened, and it was open all the way to the small of her uncorseted back. But she *was* wearing a camisole, and Edith was being overanxious. Edith did think about propriety—in a rather fitful, startled way, for her upbringing hadn't equipped her with what other young women of her class tended to have naturally: the art of knowing exactly what was permissible in most ordinary situations.

Reverend Vause went right by them. Billie said, "It's all right," to Edith. But then the reverend reappeared with a lamp. It was gloomy in the hall. "I thought you might like a light," he said, and put the lamp down on the table beside them. The rose dress came alive. And Edith's hair—before as dark as the old oak of the stairs—gave out its full bloody luster. Edith got up to give him her hand, thanked him, introduced herself, and asked if her sister could be let off for an hour to walk her back to the church at Hayle, where she would rejoin her employers.

The reverend said yes, certainly.

And Edith, droll: "Quickly, dear, run upstairs again and change out of that magnificent dress. And remember to tie your hair."

When Billie came back down Edith and the reverend were on the front steps. Edith was saying, ". . . he was a very affectionate parent, and we were never really unhappy. In hindsight I can't hold him entirely responsible for our difficulties. It's hard to say. You know—*post hoc ergo propter hoc.*"

"Do you know Latin, Miss Paxton?"

"It was my patrimony, Mr. Vause, a patchy classical education."

"And red hair," said Billie.

The reverend smiled at her.

From somewhere overhead came the carrying sound of Mrs. Wood's tight cough, and several startled sparrows flew from the face of the house.

Edith began to stroll toward the gates and the reverend followed. She told him that she'd had the opportunity lately of polishing her Latin. Or rather her Latin had been buffed up some in the course of the general polishing going on in the Lees household, where Mr. Maslen was preparing the boys for Eton. And it turned out the Reverend Vause had gone to school with Henry Maslen. "And it wasn't Eton," the reverend said. Edith told the reverend about Henry's cataloging, his love of systems, and the reverend said he could recall Maslen's enthusiasm for memory palaces—the medieval memory system, where facts are made to live in an imaginary "palace" according to their rank.

At the gates they went different ways, and the reverend said that Edith must say hello to Henry from him, then, to be correct—Billie supposed—to the general ceremony of parting, he shook her hand, looked at her boots, and said that it was good to see her suitably attired for a long walk.

"Oh—the dress," said Billie.

"Billie just sometimes forgets herself," Edith said, explaining. They walked off their separate ways, Billie already chattering to Edith about the sheet music she'd bought with just a little of this quarter's pay, and how she was being *given* that gorgeous dress.

In Billie's experience all situations improved once Edith had *explained* her. After Edith's visit, Billie relaxed. She was cheerful and forthright at the below-stairs table, and fearless going about the house, about her work. She was trusted, it seemed, and given the better tasks. For instance, she carried a letter to the rectory. She waited while the Reverend Vause wrote his reply, and drifted some as she waited, toward the piano, the piano itself—not the picture in pride of place. The reverend looked around, got up, and came across the room to pick up the photograph of a girl with a thin face in a nimbus of fine blond hair. They had been engaged, he said, she had tuberculosis of the bone. She'd wanted to break off the engagement, had thought she was being generous, but he thought it was possible to have a too finely developed sense of duty. Billie, who had only intended to stroke the keys, recognized this confidence as complimentary somehow, and confided in her turn. Her father had died of his lungs. The same disease. But his sense of duty was questionable. "He usually kept enough back to feed us. He was a gambler. Sometimes he won, then we lived like royalty." She smiled at her memories of new clothes, fine meals, fireworks. Then she did stroke the keys, and said she liked his piano. She told him she'd bought some new songs— couldn't wait for her Sunday off, when she'd be able to try them out on her own piano. It took her *such* a long time to puzzle out a tune from a song sheet. She sighed. The reverend wanted to know why, and Billie told him that she found those sorts of things very difficult. "My father used to say I was a stone. Impervious. In every way but one."

"What on earth did he mean by that?"

"No, my mistake. I mean, sir, a *stone* in every way but one. I never sink."

It was then that the reverend asked if Billie would like to come sometimes and try her songs on his piano.

"If Mrs. Wood can spare me," she said.

He finished his letter, she ran back to the house with it, and, that evening, she asked the housekeeper how she might best approach Mrs. Wood about the Reverend Vause's kind offer.

Billie said later to Edith that she thought the important thing was to remember to use the word "kind" of the reverend's offer—to show gratitude.

The following day Billie accidentally knocked a box of loose face powder off Miss Olive's dressing table and onto the floor. Miss Olive was angry at first, then she laughed, because her terrier, who had been lying on a dark blue rug by the dressing table, and who had leapt up and run, emitting pinkish clouds at each leap, had left a dog-shaped silhouette on the rug. Billie cleaned up. But that afternoon she was called to the housekeeper's room and informed that Mrs. Wood was "letting her go"—would pay the balance of her wages, but was letting her go. Billie asked why. Because, the housekeeper said, her work wasn't satisfactory. The woman counted out coins and made Billie sign the ledger. Baffled, shamed, and angry, Billie picked up the cash and went upstairs to the attic room she shared with another girl. The rose dress was hanging from a hook on the rafters. Billie had been finishing its hem, to her height. Billie hauled her bag out from under her zinc bedstead and hurriedly packed her possessions. Then she bundled the dress and pushed it in on top.

She carried her bag downstairs and had to find the housekeeper again—in the kitchen—to ask her for information about the trains. She listened, committed times to memory, then stared for a long moment, her eyes peering, at the blank, seamed face of the clock. "Is that the right time?" Billie asked, and the butler pulled out his watch, and said, "I have a minute more. It's a quarter after two."

Billie left the house. She was at the gateway when the butler and a footman came up the graveled drive at a rasping run and stopped her. The butler wrenched her bag out of her hand, and both men turned her and marched her back to the house. She was taken to a drawing room and asked to wait. The footman, Owen, waited with her. "I'll miss my train," she said to him.

"That's nothing to do with me," he replied.

Mrs. Wood arrived, with Miss Vause and the housekeeper. The ladies seated themselves, Mrs. Wood on the sofa and Miss Olive erect in a Queen Anne chair. They talked about time. It would take ten minutes for the message to reach him. He'd drive over. He'd be here any moment.

Mrs. Wood produced her handkerchief and wiped her eyes and nose. She said that times like these brought her loss sharply back to her.

The Reverend Vause arrived, pale and winded, and the court was in session.

Billie's bag was opened and the rose dress burst out, in a gleaming foam, like a silk scarf from a magician's top hat, striking, especially when one has expected three broken eggs and a mess of shells and slime.

Olive Vause stood up on a slow intake of breath.

"You said I could have it," Billie told her. Then she looked at Mrs. Wood and said, "Miss Vause gave me the dress." Yet her first thought wasn't to defend herself. She wanted to say to Olive Vause, "You went up to the attic the moment I was gone." How else had Olive known the dress wasn't still hanging from the rafters?

"Olive?" said the reverend.

"It *is* true that I said to Wilhelmina, sometime in May, that if she were good, the dress might be altered for her. I should, of course, suppress these whims of mine, but—Wilhelmina, you have known since Friday that you were making the alterations for Miss Deborah."

Billie shook her head. She told the Reverend Vause that Miss Olive told her that she must make the alterations *in her own time.* "Why would she ask me to do it in my own time if she didn't mean it to be mine?"

"I said it was worth the reward. You knew I meant to put a little extra in your pay."

The Reverend Vause asked his sister Olive whether it was possible there was a misunderstanding?

"Oh—I suppose it's possible," Olive said. "It's so hard to know, William. With good diction one expects acuity, but—"

"And why on earth was Wilhelmina dismissed without—" the reverend began.

"Without asking *you,* William?" Mrs. Wood said. "Dear—while I value your advice, particularly in an awkward situation of this sort, I'm quite capable of seeing to the day-to-day management of my own house. Including letting go a servant who—after all—was only in her trial period."

"This 'awkward situation' might have been avoided if you'd come to me with your complaints about Wilhelmina *before* dismissing her."

"And have you try to talk me out of it? I have no intention of changing my mind, or my course of action. Why should I let you make me uncomfortable for it? Really, William, you force me to remind you that you aren't on your own ground."

"At least let her work out her pay period. She's due home for a holiday in two weeks. If you send her back when she is not expected, she'll be humiliated."

"She *was* paid till Saturday," the housekeeper put in. "I told her I expected her to work till Saturday. And she went straight upstairs, hid Miss Olive's Paris dress in her bag, and walked out of the house."

"You told me to go. I asked you about the trains." Billie interrupted at last.

"Where on earth did you hope to *wear* the dress, Wilhelmina?" Miss Olive asked, almost compassionate.

And Billie went wild. She grabbed the bag, turned it upside down and shook it so that the rose dress spilled, with an explosive rush, onto the carpet. Of course everything else came out, too, her good shoes, her hairbrush, socks, drawers, camisoles, the stays she left off whenever she could—they unrolled with a flap and whipped at Miss Olive's feet with the ends of their laces. Everyone but Olive drew back. Olive Vause leaned forward a little, anticipatory as, after a pile of unironed handkerchiefs, the little illuminated Scripture book, and the bag's own felted lining, Olive's silver-backed brush and mirror fell on top of the pile, the mirror landing faceup and angled so that Billie could see the Reverend Vause in its glass. She thought she saw a smile—but his face was inverted, and after a moment she read his expression correctly, as distress.

Mrs. Wood was aggrieved. She was reproachful. This was far worse. This was theft, outright. Was it, she mused, a matter for the police?

"Just let me go!" Billie yelled. Billie wanted to be where she'd be believed. Edith would believe her. Billie saw she'd been outmaneuvered, she saw a confidence trick, the words with double meanings, statements that seemed candid one-to-one, but ambiguous when there were witnesses. She saw she'd been practiced upon, taken in. She had helped her father do these things to other people—but her father's "marks" were usually gulled into their own good nature, their better nature, and his game was always for material profit. Billie understood that she'd been fooled—but not *why*.

"A matter for the police?" Olive took up Mrs. Wood's remark, turned to her brother.

"I'm going!" Billie threw herself at her belongings and began piling them together and shoveling them back into the bag. She pushed the dress aside and it unrolled with a lazy, conclusive hiss like the only big wave on a calm day. The mirror spun on its back across the rug, the hairbrushes, Olive's and Billie's own, made off in the opposite direction, skittering on their bristles across the parquet. Billie got up, but stepped on the hem of her own dress and pitched down facefirst—as she'd done countless times.

Mrs. Wood then, disgusted and peremptory: "Please pick her up, Owen."

The footman helped Billie to her feet. She was crying.

"Waterworks," said Olive Vause.

Billie didn't often cry, but when she did her tears were copious; also copious was the thin salt water her nose made. Tears stung the carpet burn on her chin. Owen steadied her.

"Give her the bag," said Mrs. Wood. "I'm afraid, Wilhelmina, that in my letter to your aunt I really am obliged to mention the theft."

"Let me speak to her." The Reverend Vause didn't mean Billie's aunt. "In order to learn to—to resist cupidity, she has to repent her—her defiance."

"I'm sure," Olive said. "Well, of course, it's your duty to set her on the right path."

"You could accompany her to the station, William." Without waiting for her brother's answer Mrs. Wood gave some instructions to the footman for the groom—the Reverend Vause had ridden over, but would like to see Wilhelmina to the station. He'd take the trap.

"No," said Billie. Bag in hand, she walked out of the room.

THE REVEREND VAUSE CAUGHT UP WITH HER A QUARTER of a mile from his sister's gate. He was alone in the trap. Billie kept on along the road, her bag banging on her shins. He turned the horse to bar her way. Billie stood still and stared through the horse at the road ahead. She waited for him to get down and relieve her of her luggage. He put his hand under her elbow and asked her to climb up. She obeyed him.

As they went, the Reverend Vause said she must see how important it was for her to maintain a good character. He saw her difficulty. How hard it was not to covet what she couldn't have— to be surrounded by beauty and expected only to keep it in trim.

Billie said, "I took the dress because they turned me off."

"That's better," he said. "No more of that nonsense about a promise."

"I was led into it," Billie said. "She was kind, then unkind. I was anxious to please her."

"Olive?"

Billie didn't answer.

The reverend went on. He said "accept our lot," he said "know our place."

Billie raised a brow at his "our." She said, "There is so little I can do. Aunt and Edith support me." She put out her hand to pull an apricot off a tree whose branches overhung a wall by the road. Then she laughed at the look the reverend gave her. "It isn't theft, it's foraging." She thought for a moment of "knowing her own place" and laughed again at what came to her—what usually came quickest—the memory of motion. "Edith would say I haven't learned how to be careful. That caution hasn't been cultivated in me. She believes our father made bad choices, and was the helpless victim of his habits. Well, of his gambling. But I think—I think I now *know*—that he found life dull when he wasn't in danger." She told the reverend that she had laughed just then because she'd remembered how she and Edith and their father had caught a boat in a bad swell. The boat put into Corniglia, but couldn't land. The man on the shore threw the line right back at the deckhands. But Billie's father had seen a man who owed him money, and he was determined to get himself off. He bullied the sailors, and they took the boat back in, but not far enough to endanger it. Mr. Paxton pushed his daughters up onto the bow. The bow was going up and down, straight up six feet and down four in relation to the pier. Mr. Paxton took Edith by her waist and tossed her off on the downward roll. Edith dropped only three feet, but with some propulsion. She twisted her ankle. Billie remembered detecting the limp as Edith moved out of the way. The stone was surging past, up and down. Billie's father picked her up and jumped, at the beginning of the upward pass so that they were tossed up almost level with the pier and right onto it. *How dark the water was,* Billie remembered. She saw it still, the shadow of the boat's sharp prow like the chopper at the end of the "oranges and lemons" poem. "Father was owed far more than five farthings," she added, nonsensically. "You see," she explained to the reverend, "Edith thinks of our father as a desperate man, driven here and there by bad habits and bad planning. And, in a way, she's right. There was some of that. But he just did dangerous things without thought and without fear. Like breathing," she said. But her description seemed inadequate alone, so she added, "Like breathing or swimming or sucking the stone clean." She threw her apricot pit back over the wall and into the orchard. "Do you want one?" she asked the Reverend Vause, and stretched out to catch at the next cluster they came upon.

"Leave them, Wilhelmina."

Billie sat straight again. "I'm *Miss Paxton* now, thank you."

"I worry about you, Miss Paxton. What will you do? Where will you go?"

"I have Aunt, and Edith," Billie said. And she said that, one day, when she had enough money, she would take a boat and train to that coast. The coast shared by France and Italy. She'd arrive after dark and sit on the beach turning over smooth stones to find the ones underneath with the heat still in them. She rubbed her fingertips against the balls of her thumbs, smiled, and added, "Like freshly boiled eggs." Then she asked the reverend what time he had—the next train was at ten after four.

IN THE SICKROOM AT KISS CASTLE BILLIE PUT THE REVER-end's letter down by Henry's hand. Henry picked it up, and while he read his head lifted from the pillow. He said, "This fellow thinks I'm dead!"

"I think he hopes you are," Billie said.

Henry's head dropped again.

Billie told him about the incorrect newspaper report.

"Well, at least it flushed out your 'friends.' " Henry was wry—was himself for a moment. "But we can't have you falling into the pawses of the Vauses," he said, which made her smile. Then they both became conscious of his "we," and Billie saw him clench his teeth to block the first syllable of her sister's name.

◆   ◆   ◆

Henry knew what he'd lost, but was still too weak for his grief. He lay propped on pillows and opened his mouth for the spoon. He was obedient—accepted the doctor's orders as a duty. "You'll be up before too long," the doctor told him. But Henry felt no embarrassment, no obligation to Lord Hallowhulme, no pressing need to get up and take care of his surviving family. He had listened, dull, and with only a few tears, to Billie's account of the accident. He didn't remember it. He didn't remember the voyage—only recalled the embarkation at Luag and Mr. Hesketh's handsome offer. He did recall the sailors helping hand Edith down the ladder to their cabin. Remembered holding the instep of her boot in his hand, helping her foot to find the rungs. But nothing further.

No mutual reckoning, Billie thought. He'd been spared in more ways than one. She had fallen in love and fought it. But they had kissed, and Edith drowned. *Silly* Billie—as if their kiss was a match to a fuse. They kissed and the ship sank and Edith drowned, and Billie was the only one who knew to be culpable. Henry, bereaved but not bereft—not enough life in him for that—was, it seemed to Billie, no longer her sister's custodian. Edith was hers again. What would Edith have said about the kiss?

No. No, Billie.

And what about the kiss followed by her death? When Billie asked herself this, it was as if she'd asked Edith, and her sister was there, inside her, enclosed and suspended, and angry with the dark water. Billie felt that Edith had forgotten the kiss, too. What was a kiss to the dark water?

8 ⚜ SCOUSE BEACH

A FRIDAY WITH WICKED WEATHER—THE WIND FROM THE
south, not cold, but a steady force that made a melee in the
crowns of the trees of Lady Hallowhulme Park, a close-fought
battle with casualties. The trees were knocked about and dropped
their deadwood.

Billie had gone out for a walk. She went through the garden,
her shawl tight around her ears, pushed the narrow gate open,
and ran along the footpath. The wind broke a little on the crest
of the long, wooded promontory—the Nose—and Billie was
only a little blown about herself, the breeze making constant impatient tugging rearrangements to her skirt. She couldn't gauge
how strong the wind was forty feet above her head in the gnarled
and malnourished branches. Billie was headed for a clearing she
could see through the dark trunks. The sun came out and
the wood became a tumult of light, of leaf shadows. The grass in
the clearing appeared quite still in comparison, smoothed down
by the wind, moving in long ripples. The trunks of the trees on
the far side of the clearing were pale. Dark close to, but pale farther off, as if there were two forests of different composition,
beech and birch, not just two sections of the same forest, and sun
stopped against a breakwater of tree trunks in a grass surf.

Above Billie came several large cracks, and a rustle. The air filled with chaff, fragments of bark and lichen, then a large tree limb landed with a crash on the road before her. She came to an abrupt stop, and because she'd stopped, her two pursuers caught her up.

"Miss Paxton!" said Rixon Hallow. "We were calling you."

Minnie panted behind him, staggered, held her chest with one hand and flapped the other at the fallen branch.

"The park isn't safe in a strong southerly." Rixon's explanation was somewhat redundant. They turned Billie around, each took a hand, and they rushed her back the way she'd come. All the time Rixon craned up at the trees, and flinched as a hard gust knocked them together. They went the quick way, straight down the slope, crunching through layers of old moss-covered windfalls, and came back to the small gate at the corner of the walled garden. Their feet were wet, as were the hems of Minnie's and Billie's skirts.

Rixon told Billie why the park's trees were fragile. The man who'd had the land before his father, and who had built Kiss Castle, had brought shiploads of topsoil over from the mainland in order to cultivate a forest. So, fifty years before, the trees had had a good start, but the goodness was gone from the topsoil now, and they were slowly starving, dying back.

Rixon and Minnie took Billie through one set of French doors in the long wall of the ballroom. Fires were lit in all six of the room's hearths, casting melting pools of orange across the highly polished floor. The room was empty of everything but several chairs and a piano. There were five piles of paper inside the circle of chairs, Elov Jansen and the Tegner twins sat on the floor before three of them. It was a rehearsal for Minnie's play. Or—Minnie explained—a "read through."

The Hallows went back to their places. Rixon actually seemed eager. He took off his damp boots and slid them under a chair. Billie went to the fire, shook twigs and flakes of lichen off onto the hearth. She stood close to the flames, and a steamy wool smell came up into her face.

Minnie was reading the part of the patriarch's most ardent admirer, his "man of affairs." Minnie—in the part of the man— was explaining to the patriarch's houseguests that they weren't, in fact, strangers, and Mr. Goodwin's invitation wasn't just a rich man's whim. They were his heirs. Mr. Goodwin—a visionary man—believed only in *monetary* patrimony. It was one of his tenets that parents were the people least equipped to raise their own children. All sorts of bad habits, like timidity, or false humility, or fear—always excused as "upbringing"—were what prevented individuals from reaching their fullest potential. "The admirer should say it as if he's quoting Scripture," Minnie said. "He quotes Goodwin: 'Money is a precious patrimony, but family culture is private doom.' And: 'Character is an artifact.'"

"You know, Minnie," said Rixon, "the young people who meet in the train and like each other, aren't they brother and sister?"

"Yes. But that only highlights the most obvious flaw in the patriarch's experiment."

"I don't want to be *scandalous*," Anne said.

Minnie slapped her script on her leg. "I want the audience to anticipate trouble all the way through. Imagine—human life organized around an idea!"

"I think the patriarch is a bit of a charmer," said Anne Tegner. "And I think that his first appearance should come before that of his 'man of affairs.' I mean—should he seem bad? Or should only his ideas seem bad?"

"I don't think I can do him," Elov said. "Why did you give me the part?"

"Well *I* can't," Minnie said. "It isn't 'a trouser role.' I can't walk around with one of my curls stuck to my top lip. It just wouldn't work."

"It's a pity Alan Skilling is still so small," Anne said.

"Alan has the character for it," Ailsa finished her sister's thought.

"Alan has far too much character without our cultivating it further," said Minnie.

"No. Look," Rixon said. "To turn it all right way out—let me ask you: Is Francis Galton *wrong*?"

Billie was so busy listening to the young Hallows and their friends argue that she didn't see Geordie Betler till he was beside her. She touched her hair and explained that she'd been out in the wind. Mr. Betler said he'd been looking for her. And while doing so he'd had the pleasure of meeting Mr. Maslen. "He sent me down to the library to fetch him the latest number of a periodical. I left him looking at its index as though at a menu in a fine restaurant."

Rixon was saying, "They're not called Mendel's *laws* of heredity for nothing, you know. Intelligence and idiocy and criminality certainly do seemed to be passed down."

"Look, Rix," said Anne, "if Minnie meant to disprove an idea, she wouldn't do it by showing its opposite in a bad light, would she? You don't need to defend Dr. Galton."

Geordie Betler spoke up then. They all turned, and froze. He said he'd always thought Mendel was discussing peas.

They stared at him. Then Minnie asked had Mr. Betler heard of Francis Galton and his Artificial Selection?

"I can't say that I have," said Mr. Betler.

"Society's sympathy for the weak thwarts proper evolution. Since the weak are allowed to reproduce, natural selection no longer applies to humankind," Rixon said, as though repeating his catechism. Then he blushed and added, "That's the gist of it, sir. And I think there's something to it." He glared at Minnie.

"I don't care if it's the Eleventh Commandment!" she said. "It's not what I'm on about." She explained to Mr. Betler. "In our play the patriarch believes something quite different. He believes that the only inheritance is what is *taught*. He believes it so strongly that he thinks children should be taken from bad parents."

Elov Jansen said, "He sent his own children away as an experiment. Which becomes rather complicated once they've grown."

Geordie Betler thanked Minnie and Elov for their explanation. "I see," he said. "And the point of Mr. Shaw's play is that *any* overarching idea, even if pursued rationally, is productive of evil?"

"Yes!" said Minnie.

"This Shaw is a moralist," said Geordie Betler. "I *like* this Mr. Shaw." He smiled at the rehearsal in general, then touched Billie's sleeve. "Mr. Hesketh has sent me to fetch you. He wants a quick word with you."

Billie just glared at Mr. Hesketh's messenger. Then she looked at the fire and felt the heat drying her lips. She put her tongue out to wet them.

He said, "I'll be present, Miss Paxton. I want to hear what you have to say—about the Stolnsay pilot. I wasn't there. And Mr. Hesketh tells me he wasn't paying attention."

He had begun to steer her out of the ballroom. She went, her wet dress clinging to her wet boots.

At the door Geordie Betler glanced back, his face warm. "They're such intelligent children. So earnest. And both uncannily like their father."

"Everyone here is intelligent," Billie said.

He dipped his head to look into her face. She could almost feel the fire's heat still radiating from him—although they were now out in the dark hall, in an unsteady light, raindrops casting crawling shadows on the walls. "Except you? Is that it?" he said.

"Except me." Then she grinned. "And Mr. Hesketh."

GEORDIE COULDN'T REMEMBER EVER HAVING SEEN TWO people treat each other with such careful neutrality. The moment he let Billie into the library ahead of him she announced to him—and to Murdo Hesketh, who was waiting there—that she wouldn't sit. Murdo nodded, then told Geordie that he needn't stay. Geordie reminded Murdo that two heads were better than one. He heard himself, breezy, whereas they were very correct and guarded.

Billie Paxton turned herself so that she faced both men and folded her hands against her skirt.

"Miss Paxton," Murdo began, "I believe you saw the Stolnsay pilot come aboard the *Gustav Edda*."

"Yes."

"He came aboard . . .?"

"Yes."

Geordie wondered if Billie was being stubbornly monosyllabic, or if she was only refusing to be led. But Murdo showed no sign of impatience. He scarcely showed interest—wasn't concealing eagerness, didn't glance aside or slow himself down with any other business, he didn't take out his cigarette case and tamp the end of a ready-made against its silver lid. He only waited.

After a moment Billie said, "You were there."

"I do recall asking the pilot why he'd come aboard," Murdo said.

"You said, 'What *seems* to be the problem?' "

"Yes. You have my tone exactly, Miss Paxton. You're a good mimic—but how good is your memory? I said, 'What seems to be the problem?' and the pilot then asked the captain for the cargo manifest." Murdo paused, then asked, "Why do you think he did that?"

"He wanted to make sure everything was stowed securely. I believe that's the reason he gave."

Murdo nodded, then his gaze became a little less neutral. His eyes—even in the soft yellow lamplight—grew blue. "How long were they below? Do you recall?"

"The pilot and his man—we haven't mentioned his man yet, have we?"

"The man with the pilot isn't in the pilot's employ. He's a Stolnsay herring man. One Duncan Macleod. His boat was in the harbor that day—owing to the weather."

"You recognized him?"

"No. I made inquiries."

"You asked the pilot?"

For a moment Billie and Murdo stood quiet, looking into one another's faces.

"Mr. Hesketh is exercising discretion in his investigation," Geordie said, with the distinct feeling of casting a cat among birds. And then his mind strayed to those intelligent Hallow siblings, and Minnie's problems casting the part of the patriarch in her play. And it was as though he had run his hand along a dusty lintel above a door and found the expected key. It was all too trustingly easy—as if no one had died, and no one was responsible for deaths. *Tomorrow,* he thought, *I'll find some way of having Minnie hit on* my *idea* herself.

"If Mr. Hesketh is exercising discretion, then he can't be secure in his suspicions," Billie said.

"Perhaps I'm learning from my mistakes," said Murdo. "But let us continue—how long do you think the men were in the hold?"

Billie put her head down to think, and Geordie watched her twining her fingers. She said she wasn't sure—she wasn't much interested at the time. She had watched them go down through the aft hatch, and saw them when they reappeared. But she wasn't sure how long they took.

Murdo shrugged, and looked at Geordie, then he laughed—and Geordie understood that he was laughing at his own hopes, the folly of them.

But Billie Paxton was still thinking, and had begun to swing one foot, contemplating the moist weight of water still seeping up, dark, through the close weave of her black dress. Then she stopped jiggling and looked from Murdo to Geordie. She said, "He was tucking in the tail of his shirt. As he came up the ladder from the hold. That Macleod man. He came after the pilot and he was tucking in the tail of his shirt and closing his belt buckle."

This was rather uncomfortable, Geordie thought, any way you looked at it. Any questions proceeding from such information were likely to be more than a little delicate. Geordie didn't care to see how Murdo handled it—he only wanted to spare Billie Paxton any embarrassment. He cleared his throat, but found he hadn't any speech with which to follow his noise.

Billie said to Murdo, "I think I'm the only one who saw."

"And what did you make of it?" Murdo asked.

"Nothing. Do you think it matters?"

"We have so little to go on. Please try to think."

Billie frowned, then looked about her for a chair and sat down. "Look," she said, "if it matters—have you thought—do you remember that the captain pointed out to the pilot Lord Hallowhulme's automobile? It was tied down on the stern deck . . ."

"Yes?"

"The captain told the pilot—by the by—that its seats were in the hold, where they'd be safe from the weather."

Geordie managed to start his voice again by complimenting Billie on her memory.

She was impatient. "I'm always having to remember when people tell me what something says—trains leaving at ten after four, or best mustard seed at tuppence a pound. My memory makes up a little for my muddle about words." She looked back at Murdo. "I'm sure you won't mind me being coarse. If Mr. Macleod didn't like Lord Hallowhulme perhaps he did something to the leather seats. Something that required him to pull his pants down."

Murdo frowned at Billie. Geordie said that he thought it was very unlikely. The pilot wouldn't want to risk his job. *Surely not.*

"No," said Murdo.

Billie Paxton kicked the leg of her chair with the heel of her boot. To cover her impatience she got up. Her face was pink. She said that *that* wasn't the only thing she could think of. She could imagine another thing—but none of it was relevant. Her sentences became a series of stuttered hisses. She said, "It wasn't sin or sh . . . shank that sip . . . sank that ship," then, recovering, "whether it was malice and dirtiness, or . . . or they went down there and liked the leather so much they . . ." She trailed off, stared from Geordie to Murdo, her throat working, swallowing over and over as though she were about to be sick. "There's no answer in what I saw Macleod do or what I thought he might have done."

Geordie started toward her, full of concern, but Billie put her hand in her pocket, found something and held it out, straight-armed, between them. Geordie saw a button made of plaited pigskin, which she gripped by its looped brass post. She held it out between her and them as a priest brandishes a crucifix at armed heathens. "This is a button from Henry's jacket. It was found in Edith's hand," she said. And then, pocketing the button once more, she bolted from the room. She slammed the door on her skirt, and the men heard her fall. They watched as the door opened again, just enough to free the skirt, and listened to her blunder away down the hall.

Geordie turned back to Murdo. He was about to say he thought Miss Paxton hadn't told *herself* that before telling them. But Geordie saw that Murdo had his eyes closed. "Mr. Hesketh?" Geordie said.

Murdo, quietly, from some very peaceful place, possibly a grave, said, "Mr. Betler."

"I'm sure you didn't intend to precipitate that crisis."

"How kind of you."

"But it could have been better managed."

Murdo opened his eyes and Geordie found himself looking at Ian's white bear. The snowbank suddenly had eyes, its breath became visible; still, it was impossible to tell what it intended until it moved. "Betler managed, you mean, Geordie," Murdo Hesketh said. For half a minute he was silent, and only stared, then he used Geordie's name again. "Geordie, one minute you say 'two heads are better,' then you say '*you*'—'*you* didn't intend.' It isn't consistent. Are we not allies? Are we not looking for exactly the same thing—a reason for Ian's death—and redress for it? Geordie, haven't you done sorting Ian's affairs? Haven't you seen him decently buried? Why are you still here? You're not my man, Geordie. You're Andrew Tannoy's man."

"Well." Geordie was irritable. "I hadn't realized I was expected to make a declaration of loyalty or to refrain entirely from criticizing your manner of proceeding. Are those the terms of our alliance, Mr. Hesketh? You're being ridiculous. The fact is that you don't want an ally. You hate help so much that Ian had to go about like a mute for these last few years. Deaf and dumb and inoffensive to your dignity." Geordie heard himself say all this with some surprise. He had only thought to defend himself, show some mettle. He watched Murdo Hesketh's eyes pale, turn almost silver in the indoor light, and his lips turn white. Geordie said, quickly, "I beg your pardon."

Murdo went and sat by the fire. He put a hand up to the side of his face, shielding it not from the flames but from Geordie, who watched the orange light shining through fingers, a rosy ear, the thick, glassy hair. "I know what Ian did for me," Murdo said.

"He admired you—too much, I always thought. I've spent the last three years on and off trying to persuade him to leave you."

"Ian didn't drown because he admired me too much."

Geordie wondered if he'd heard that right—Murdo's emphasis on his brother's name. That emphasis said that there was someone else who *had* drowned because they admired him.

Murdo went on, directing his words to the fire. He said, "I want to make this clear. I don't need your help, and I don't want it. Ian was my friend. But I don't want your friendship, and I don't need it. Because we have the same goal we will inevitably find ourselves working together. But just remember: I don't want you."

It was at that moment that Geordie, in a surge of pity mixed with stubborn indignation, decided that he was going to save Murdo's miserable life. He said, "Very well. You can stop now. I understand you."

"Listen." Murdo was about to propose something. Geordie stopped him by saying he'd listen only if Mr. Hesketh looked at him, and Murdo turned from the fire, conscious and ashamed of the signs of tears on his face but determined neither to hide nor show them. And Geordie saw why Ian had loved Murdo Hesketh—he saw nerve, pride independent of dignity, the man who lied to his doomed brother-in-law about his dead sister, the man Karl Borg imagined could somehow save him. Murdo was saying something Geordie had to hear. Geordie held up a hand and made Murdo go back.

"Listen," Murdo said again, and paused to see that he had Geordie's attention. "Miss Paxton couldn't be expected to think of this. Macleod was buckling his belt and tucking his shirt back in. She said he stopped on the ladder to do it. He didn't mean to be seen. She was the only passenger on the windward side of the ship, in the cold, where no one could reasonably be expected to be lurking."

Geordie nearly laughed at the image of Billie Paxton lurking.

"Macleod had something under his shirt. He'd removed it in the hold."

Geordie lifted his brows.

"It was wound around his waist. It was measured, down to

the last minute, and maybe no one was meant to die—but the ship was too slow. It was a fuse."

SUNDAY MORNING WAS CALM AND CLEAR. BILLIE LEFT Henry under the eye of Jane Tegner, who had undertaken to read him the main stories in yesterday's newspaper. Jane hadn't gone to church. She said that with her back she couldn't endure even an hour in Reverend Mulberry's hard pews. No one had pressed Billie to attend. Perhaps they guessed she'd not find God in a church she'd only entered to identify her sister's body.

Billie ran down to the gatehouse. She found Alan and tried for size the half a vest she'd knitted—held it against his back. She said that Minnie should have thought of it, and he said Minnie was too busy *thinking* to have thought. Then he apologized— he'd forgotten about the beach. They pelted back to the castle together, and while Alan harnessed Kirsty, Billie put her knitting away, and fetched the matches and paper that Alan said they'd need.

They hurried Kirsty through town before church was out. As they passed it they heard singing—*Eternal Father, strong to save, Whose arm hath bound the restless wave, Who bid'st the mighty ocean deep, Its own appointed limits keep . . .*

THE SUN WAS HOT, THE AIR STILL. KIRSTY PUT HER NOSE down and blew at the dry sand, each nostril making its own dimple. Billie could see that Alan was disappointed. On the way over they had noticed that the sea wasn't as smooth as it had been on their last visit. But until they got down through the dunes and onto the beach they weren't able to gauge the scale of the surf. Though the air was still, and had been for twelve hours, the sea hadn't yet come down. Steep five-foot waves were breaking at the high-water mark. The beach was steep, too, and the waves broke close into shore once their troughs began to drag and slow and their crests to topple.

Well—Alan said—they were here now, and it was a nice day with no wind so at least the smoke of their fire would go straight up and not whip around and get in their eyes. He went a short way toward the water and chose a spot where the southerly had heaped fine sand up against a tuft of dune grass. He bent the grass to incorporate it into his pyre, and over the grass and balled newspaper he made a cage of the split kindling he'd brought with him. Kindling, and a bag of dried peats. Billie told Alan that the sea she knew best was often like this—its shelved stony beaches, beaches built up with river stones and broken roof tiles. There was usually a strip of pebbles where the waves broke, on which it was possible to stand upright. But of course the larger stones were often spherical, or near to it, and, as the beach was shelved, it was impossible to walk into the water. "People limp, as if lame," Billie said. "Or they sit down where the surf is creaming—I've seen boys whose backsides are dappled with bruises from being lifted a little on each wave then dropped back down on the stones." She laughed at Alan's look. "I was little— we were all ragged and savage—though my backside was always covered."

Alan grinned at her, he poked the fire.

Billie realized that she'd laughed. Several times now. She went on to say that those who could swim—when the sea was high like this—would time their entry so as not to be knocked back into the broken water by the breakers. The trick was timing, to jump out over a lower wave and swim beyond where they were breaking. Then to tread water, sometimes for hours, going up and down and only slapped in passing by the peaks of the waves. *This* kind of sea was, in fact, safer, because there was no undertow. "See," said Billie, "the water is only white at the shore, and all along the beach rollers are coming in even furrows. And there's no smooth patch, no false quiet of a rip."

Alan's fire was going well, and noisily. The driftwood wasn't wholly dry. It sang and smoked, but its smoke went straight up.

Then Billie asked how Ingrid Hallow had drowned.

"It was 'death by misadventure.' That was what the coroner said. Lord Hallowhulme got a coroner up from Edinburgh. It was August—hot weather. She was wading and took a fall. Her skirts hampered her movements. That was what the Edinburgh man found."

"Do you think he was right?"

Alan wasn't surprised by her question. He said that Kissack men saw sin everywhere. "Believing as they do that any sin you commit you carry around your whole life. Some of them even think that God has all our sins set out for us from the hour of our birth, so that some men are born damned." Alan spat in the fire. He wiped his lips. Then, because of course he, too, had heard Minnie say that she thought Murdo Hesketh had something to do with her sister's death, he went on. "These Kissack men want to think badly of Mr. Hesketh because they don't like what he does for Lord Hallowhulme. Lord Hallowhulme is here at Christmas and rides around town with a dray full of hampers, and he's putting heating in the old customhouse and has turned it into a meeting hall. Mr. Hesketh hires and fires and lures men away from reliable work so that the barley goes in late and the peat is cut late and is still damp in October. So of course he has to be a seducer, too." Alan added, "Minnie knows you hate him. She's just throwing fuel on the fire. But—but you should understand that Minnie doesn't hate him. She likes him really."

Billie wanted to know why, if Ingrid Hallow drowned on Scouse Beach, Alan wanted to go swimming there?

"You said 'I can teach you,' Miss Paxton."

"Billie."

"I take up all offers to be taught."

"All I know is needlework, knitting, the piano, swimming, and how to cheat at cards." Billie said. "I'm sure you won't want me to teach you all of that." Alan didn't answer; he fed the fire and stood on his dignity. Billie watched him for a moment, then alarmed him by saying she was going to go in.

She wrestled with the buttons on the back of her dress, then asked for Alan's help, waited patiently as he fumbled, clumsy despite his small fingers. Then Billie pulled the dress off over her head, and sat down to remove her shoes and stockings. She left her hair in its long plait. It wouldn't do any good to pin it up—it wasn't the kind of sea you could go in and keep your hair dry. She told Alan she'd be quick, because the water would be cold. He said he'd get more wood to build up the fire. Then he ran up the beach to get a blanket from the box under the seat of the dogcart. While he was gone Billie went down to the water. She'd remembered modesty—that the moment her drawers and camisole were wet they'd be transparent. She didn't want to embarrass Alan.

The water was warmer than it had been the other day. A rough sea in the sun is always warmer—as if the waves chafe a little heat into each other, or the warm sun kneads warmth into the water. The sand was coarse and heavy, but packed firm so that Billie was able to wade in, braced for the waves that broke and rushed to embrace her thighs, groin, belly. Then she was where they were breaking and she jumped in over the white, striated, pouring arch of one, arms out, straight into the gleaming green wall of the following wave. It stopped her dead, bent her back and rolled her right over in itself as it collapsed. Billie slid back up the beach feetfirst. The water parted her hair and pushed a ridge of sand up against her forehead. She raised her face. The foam was deafening, a harsh hissing. Cold water streamed out of her nose and she shouted, delight and fear mixed. She lifted herself out of the softer liquid of foam and went back into the hard water.

Again she jumped, turned herself this time in the trough between one wave and the next and rose up, cut the crest with her shoulder and swam out. She was soon out of her depth, still near the loud water but now in a procession of whole leaning waves. The sea was terribly cold—as forceful as she knew it was, a force she had the measure of, and adored. But the cold was draining. She knew she should go in.

She jumped up with each crest to crane out to sea, looking for a worthy wave, one to carry her in, one she'd let turn her around again and spit her out on the beach. She saw it, gleaming and growing, streaked with foam. One wave had joined another, the foam formed by their collision. Billie saw that the wave would break before it reached her, it was already tilting sloppily. The trough it pushed before it was too deep, the water at its base dragged back while the crest kept its old open ocean speed. Billie took a deep breath. The wave collapsed, trapped air bursting through it. Billie was flipped. Her plait unraveled, she felt her hair clinging to her bare feet as she went over, her eyes open, in a world without geometry or fixtures or gravity, just green light and churning power. Her knees scraped the sand. Then she was seized; someone caught her and lifted her out of the water.

MURDO HESKETH WAS ON HIS WAY TO THE ALGINATE FAC-tory. He was quite sure that he wasn't the only one at this end of the island who had failed to keep the Sabbath. It was always on Sundays that tools or lumber disappeared from the site. He'd look in. Besides, his horse needed the exercise.

Murdo emerged from the biggest gap in the sand hills and found Kirsty, and Minnie's dogcart. He saw that Alan Skilling had already attached to it a horn salvaged from James's sunken auto-mobile. Murdo stooped and gave the horn a squeeze to rouse Alan, wherever he was, and to see if the horn's voice had sur-vived. It still had water in its rubber bulb. It made a spluttering fart—not enough sound to summon anyone.

There was a fire on the beach, topped by a plume of thick smoke. By the fire was a pile of clothes. Murdo's eye caught movement of an unwatery sort at the waterline. He saw Billie Paxton, in her underclothes, drenched already, her head hanging, weighed down by wet hair. He saw her marching into the sea. He kicked his horse, galloped her down to the water, into the water—where the animal balked, not liking her footing, the mo-bile surface of a broken wave clawing back the reaching foam of the wave before it. The horse turned despite Murdo's urging and was soon out where only her hooves were wet. Murdo stood up in the stirrups and scanned the sea. He saw Billie, saw white cot-ton, pale flesh, and red hair, but mixed into the green water, churned under, drowned already.

Murdo jumped out of his saddle and into the waves. He forged forward wading and swimming to grab hold of Billie. He lifted her up and turned toward the shore. A big wave slapped his back, hips to neck, and pushed him under. He felt Billie Paxton's hair stream up around his wrists. She was under him, his knees were on either side of her body. The wave passed and her face emerged from its racing water. Her eyes were open, smooth and glazed in a face blistered with bursting bubbles of foam. She spat out seawater at Murdo and climbed, crawled, wriggled out from under him.

Murdo struggled up again, snatched her around her waist, and carried her up the beach and away from the water. "*No*," he said to her. He put her down by the fire and kept hold of her. "I'm not going to let you," he panted.

She was difficult to subdue, small but flexible and—in her state of mind—unmindful of the possibility of injury. She writhed, and he adjusted his hold as carefully as he was able. She coated herself in sand and, as her skin and clothes became gritty, Murdo's grip became firmer. Finally, she bit him on the arm. But he was dressed for June on Kissack and she only managed to close her teeth on cloth. Murdo was reminded of Karl. He heard the tendons in her jaw click as she bore down hard. She glared up at him, her brow creased. Then she let go and lay still. "Alan," she said.

Alan Skilling was beside them, his arms full of driftwood. He dropped the wood to circle them, he was trying to explain something, or to intervene.

Murdo rounded on him. "What do you think you were doing?" He'd seen the boy—a moment before he jumped from the saddle and into the sea—one arm around his firewood, and one hand covering his mouth.

Alan said he'd dropped the box lid on his fingers when he'd fetched the blanket from the cart. He was sucking them.

"She even had time to get out of her clothes while you were woolgathering," Murdo shouted.

"Wood-gathering, actually." Alan was airy. "And I was there when she took off her clothes."

Murdo let go of Billie Paxton and lunged at Alan, hand raised. He was knocked sideways. Billie Paxton held Murdo's arm and pummeled him with her knees and elbows. She threw her resilient, clammy body against him and tried to do him damage. Murdo caught her wrists and pushed them back behind her head. They were yelling at each other—or she was making a sound somewhere between growl and whine, while he yelled that he wasn't about to let her destroy herself just because she'd lost a sister. "You're alive!" he shouted. "You don't owe her your life!" Murdo could hear himself, his voice rough with its unaccustomed volume and vehemence.

Billie Paxton dropped her head, hung limp from Murdo's hands. He heard her say, "I was only swimming." He let go. Alan, who had been dancing around them like a little dog around a dogfight, darted in to take her from Murdo, but then lurched back, afraid to touch, for Billie Paxton had fallen on all fours in the sand, her skin red with cold and shining through the wet cotton of her clothes. She pushed her forehead into the beach, then raised her face, sand coating her thick wet loose locks of hair, and screamed with grief or rage. She knelt, wrapped her hands, gloved and softened by dry sand, around her own back and began to rock and howl, her chin wet with seawater and with spit.

Alan stared at her, his eyes wide, and seemed to lean in against the barrier of her noise like someone inclining on strong wind.

Billie Paxton's despair shoved Murdo from her, lifted him on to his feet, sent him down the beach after his horse, and then into the saddle and back past Kirsty and away through the notch in the dunes. His clothes were sodden, his flesh cold, coming back to life only to feel that something was beating him. That he had—again—been pulled hard against the bars between him and those he owed. Those he loved. Only Clara was on his side of the bars now—whole and hollowed-out and impossible to talk to, but at least silent, not a miserable, howling, damp, self-destructive wretch like that girl.

Murdo put his head down and kicked his horse into a canter.

AND BILLIE? BILLIE WAS ASKING HERSELF, IN HER OWN way, what she was doing in the sea that had smothered her sister? Must she lose swimming, too? Edith had the world, once, Edith could read, Edith had Henry. Now Edith had swallowed the sea—was swollen with Billie's sea.

AFTER A LONG WHILE BILLIE SAID TO ALAN, WHO WAS holding her, that he was far too thin. Alan answered that he was only sometimes able to eat well. He had to forage, but was good at it. He said he'd show her, and then he helped her dress, and together they kicked sand on the fire.

He led her along the beach past the factory and out over sand and mud mixed, to a little island of rocks. Alan climbed a rock face, kept close to it even when the gulls came and made loud passes at his back. There were eggs in the gulls' nests which the boy, suspended by one hand and dodging birds, removed one at a time and threw down to Billie.

The eggs traveled back to the gatehouse in Billie's skirt. She and Alan made an omelette. At dusk Billie pushed back her plate and said to Alan that *that was good*, now she could afford to miss dinner. She'd be off now—would let herself into the castle where she'd be least likely to meet anyone she couldn't face.

In the ballroom the chairs were still in their circle, but the actors had gone. Billie opened the piano. She tried a note—it went back and forth in the room like a lark drawing predatory attention from its nest in a meadow. She tried another, and the second was like a lost voice saying the word "dear" in the interrogative. "Are you there, dear?" "Dear, is that you?"

Henry didn't remember the kiss. Billie wondered whether she hadn't told him because she wanted to spare him, or because she wanted him to find his way to her again, with nothing between them—not Edith, nor guilt at their disloyalty to Edith.

Billie played a few more notes, which became chords, the beginning of a tune, not one she'd learned, nor one she'd ever heard. It was hers, this phrase, she had only just dreamed it up, and it was her own. The music—perhaps the opening of a song—was like something winding out from her, a path or a trail. Billie remembered the Chemin du Rosaire in one of the little Mediterranean towns of her childhood. A path of smooth curves, whose paving stones were almost covered by tides of silt; a path of dark culverts, surfaced with sinewy tree roots; a path of steps and landings, of shrines, the Stations of the Cross; a trail that crisscrossed the new carter's road which ran between villas and vines, all the way up to a monastery on the flat, tonsured top of a hill. The Chemin, sometimes beside the road, sometimes diverging from it, was a way through the world that wasn't the world's way.

Billie played her few phrases over and remembered the monastery. Edith had liked its view and would take her little sister there in the evenings, when no one was about, but before the gates closed. Billie remembered the cracked plaster on the monastery walls, the young eucalyptus trees among older olives, and vines on terraces right up to the monastery's high defensive wall. As the light faded the sea would pale and its currents appear as smooth haloes around the nearest cape. The mountains would grow, becoming solid and featureless in the hazy air, and the lights of a certain mountain village would show faintly reflected on a cliff face. Then, perhaps, a nightingale would start up singing . . .

Billie played her tune over—her beginning. A tune like a lifeline, a way through the world, but not the world's way.

The actors had left a branch of candles lit. Maybe they'd intended to come back. Billie closed the lid over the keys and looked at the candle flames, watched them stretch, perhaps like children eager to see, but more like animals up after rest, limbering up, indolent, gaining volume and ferocity—but with no object, no prey in sight. The flames grew slowly in the still air.

9 ⚜ Clo Mor (The Big Cloth)

In mid-July Geordie wrote a letter to his dead brother. In it he explained how he'd managed to continue to postpone his departure from Kiss Castle. Geordie had found that what he missed most about Ian was all he'd really had of him—his letters. Whenever Geordie sat down to write to Andrew and Meela Tannoy he felt his loss. Here he was, with Ian's cast of characters, plus a few new additions, and he wasn't able to do them justice. He wanted to reread Ian's letters, but had only his own *to* Ian. So he reread these instead, looking for clues in the questions he'd put to his brother, questions inspired by Ian's accounts of Lord Hallowhulme's industrious tampering; the islanders' views of Hallowhulme; Murdo Hesketh's long, mute, enduring mourning for his sister; and Ingrid Hallow's character and fate. Geordie saw that he'd asked all the wrong questions, and that *this* Geordie Betler, Ian's correspondent, was incurious, prim, and settled to the point of smugness.

Yet, by the time Geordie had read his way back through ten years of his side of the correspondence, he found he was missing *himself* as much as Ian. It was a curious experience. It was like finding, at the back of the cupboard, the last surviving piece of a fine set of dishes. Impossible to use it. Impossible to put it out, alone, on the table again. The well-mannered, patient man who talked with warmth about Mrs. Tannoy's artists, Mr. Tannoy's health, or with passion about the rust on his lilies or the greenfly on his roses—who would hear from him again?

Geordie decided to *continue* writing to Ian. He'd sort out his thoughts, tell Ian everything, then send an edited version to Andrew and Meela Tannoy.

"I managed to stay on at Kiss," Geordie wrote. "More in a minute on *how*. It was well I did. Our Murdo has decided to apply himself to a deliberate and organized investigation into the sinking. His investigation is now quite independent of those being conducted by the owner's insurance company, and the more hobbyist effort of Lord Hallowhulme and his secretary Gutthorm. Despite his—and you will understand me—*charismatic ingratitude*, Murdo seems to have decided to deign to depend on me."

Geordie's pen paused, and he smiled. Murdo Hesketh was on the far side of the library, in the long patch of sectioned sunlight that came through one of the room's tall windows. Murdo was writing a letter—in Swedish—to the Swedish factory responsible for the manufacture of instantaneous fuses. With Henry Maslen's help he had located an engineering gazette with an advertisement by the manufacturer, containing a table of reliable rates of burn in its detonators, fuses, and special junctions. Murdo was still in pursuit of his fuse. Geordie could see it sometimes, a burning calligraphic line, like a signature, in Murdo's eyes. Geordie noticed that Murdo was wearing gloves. Murdo was on his way out, but had sat down to write, quick and to the point. He'd hand the letter unsealed to Geordie—as he now did with every letter concerning their investigation. He'd forget that Geordie didn't read Swedish. It was characteristic behavior. Murdo was energetic, his focus fierce, but his attention was somehow delicate and depressed. It seemed to Geordie that when Murdo ignited, as often as not the concussion of ignition would extinguish him—he'd put himself out.

Murdo had begun to drift. He'd raised his head to stare through Henry Maslen, who was at the long teak table in the center of the room, busy with cataloging cards, and a felt-lined vise into which books were clamped while he marked their spines with numbers in gold leaf. Billie Paxton was on the other side of the table. She held the sheet of gold leaf steady while Henry plied his stylus. They were wearing white cotton gloves and were absorbed in their task.

Geordie went back to his letter. He told Ian that, so far, he and Murdo had been disappointed in their efforts to interview Macleod. Macleod was out fishing every day. The weather had been calm and mild since the end of June. Geordie and Murdo had spoken to the pilot, who claimed he'd taken Macleod along because Macleod, a friend of his, had wanted to intercept the mailbag and take early receipt of a letter addressed to him, but somehow sensitive. No, he hadn't asked Macleod about the letter's contents, the pilot said—by this time backing into a little cave of reserve and disapproval. He said that the captain of the *Gustav Edda* hadn't been sympathetic to Macleod's request. The captain had refused to open the bag, saying that he was required to deliver it to the postmaster at Stolnsay with all its seals intact. "For any more information you have to apply to Macleod himself. And . . ." the pilot was red and congested with anger ". . . as for the lass's *buckles* and *breeches* story, you should look at it as some mischief of her own. I mean—what kind of woman is she?"

That, Geordie wrote to Ian, was a question he'd returned to often over the last few weeks. Billie Paxton was industrious. She was helping Henry Maslen in the few hours each day he had the strength to devote to his paid employment. And she made sure Henry limited his work to only a few hours. She would accompany her brother-in-law on his walks, every day a little farther in distance and longer in duration. Geordie walked to the town himself each day. It had become his habit to deliver his letters, and any Murdo had, to the post office. Deliver them personally—not leave them with every other letter on the tray in the lower hall. (Johan Gutthorm franked the household's mail himself, business and personal, and passed it over to the postmaster's boy, who came to Kiss morning and afternoon five days a week.) On his daily stroll to town Geordie would sometimes come upon Billie and Henry going slowly arm in arm by the seawall, or sitting—Henry on Billie's folded shawl—on the long, shallowly sloping green lawn below the ha-ha. Geordie also saw Billie every day at the rehearsals of Minnie's play, for which she was providing piano music, and *in* which he was to play the patriarch.

This was how Geordie had contrived to stay at Kiss.

On the afternoon of the same Sunday that Billie Paxton went swimming in the cold waves at Scouse Beach, Geordie had stalked Minnie.

After lunch, Minnie carried her easel out into the walled garden to make another attempt at painting her flowers. Geordie took a turn around the garden, then spread his handkerchief on the wall behind Minnie and sat down. After a time she said to him that she didn't suppose he was there for the spectacle—the application of pigment to parchment.

Geordie told Minnie that he wanted to speak to her about her play. It seemed to him that Mr. Shaw had drawn his patriarch with a little less—*gusto*—than he might.

Minnie remarked how so much depended on the performance, and she, as director, had to admit there were difficulties there, since Elov lacked natural authority. But, Minnie said, was Geordie suggesting she should alter the text of Mr. Shaw's play? "Would you like to read it?" Minnie asked. "Or read *for* it?"

Geordie made a noncommittal noise.

Minnie dipped her brush and made inky dots at the top of the petals of each blossom. She didn't look at the flowers in front of her, and Geordie saw she'd done this a number of times. She had a firm notion of how the flowers should look. Hers were a botanical painting; those in front of her, in their pot, were flames on a hob, a thicket of green lines and linear shadows topped by hazy blue.

Minnie said, "I'll give you a script, Mr. Betler. And if you like what you read you might like to—*help* us in a rehearsal or two. Stand in for Elov perhaps. And if you want to argue by proxy with the absent playwright, well, I'm sure *I'm* open to suggestions for improvements."

So Geordie got his part in Minnie's play. And, though the whole cast was in on the secret, its real authorship stayed in their circle, stayed secret. Geordie sometimes believed that it was possible that Billie Paxton didn't know. She'd never seen a play in rehearsal and thought nothing of alterations to the text without the author present. Billie seemed to have a relation to text like that of believers to God. She had *faith* in the presence, in writing, of the spoken word, invisible to her. And, as the players learned and refined their lines and their performances, what Billie seemed to register was the moment she was first utterly convinced by what she heard and saw. So that, after a time, Geordie noticed that Minnie would turn to Billie, behind the piano, sometimes poised over its keys, other times knitting something for Alan—Minnie would turn and say, "How was that, Billie?" And Billie would say, "Well—that will do. But what is Elov doing with his feet?"

("There is nothing essential," said Elov, now playing the patriarch's disciple. "We all slowly appear, in outline, distinguished in the light of our pasts." He jiggled his foot, then complained: "I cannot say 'pasts,' Minnie, like a lisping Finnish sentry!")

MURDO PUT HIS LETTER DOWN ON THE DESK BY GEORdie's elbow; on top of the letter was a penny for the post. Geordie said, quietly, "I do hope you're not one of those people who never *take* because they hope to be permanently acquitted of *giving*."

"When I took James's offer of employment I was able to repay your brother. Debts are damnation."

Maslen, overhearing this last remark, said his wife would have liked to hear it.

The previous evening, at the dinner table, Henry had disagreed, in a mild way, with Lord Hallowhulme's musing on "shiftlessness." Was shiftlessness an inherited trait? One that contributed to pauperism?

"I can't see how it could be, Lord Hallowhulme," Henry said. "At least not *strictly* inherited. My wife was very dutiful and frugal, and Billie is hardworking, but their father was a wandering invalid, and not entirely honest."

And Minnie said, "The only reason people inherit a tendency to poverty is that they don't inherit any money."

"Minnie!" said Clara, warning.

Minnie apologized to her father and Mr. Maslen for interrupting.

But James had, as usual, taken their dissent only as an indication that they hadn't understood him. They didn't agree with him; perhaps he hadn't expressed himself clearly. He repeated himself.

In the library, Murdo moved closer to the big table to watch Henry restore the membrane of gold leaf to its case. Henry was finished for the day. He said—to Murdo—that Billie's young friend, Alan Skilling, had offered to drive them along Alesund Head, where Henry could look at the rocks. He continued to talk in his light voice about the consolation of knowledge. "It's silly, I realize. But I find what I know about the age of certain rocks very reassuring. I *appreciate* their age—not timeless, but ancient in date. I can lay my hand on a piece of gneiss and be touching both today and a remote time—eons, inanimate eons."

Murdo said that Henry was a considering soul. Murdo's voice was warm—for him—but he was watching Henry, blank of face and bright of eye. "Me," Murdo said, "I take comfort from the fit of this glove." He flexed his hand, and the leather made its accommodating creak. "It's an article of faith, the fit of this glove."

Geordie was fascinated. Murdo and Henry were being kind to each other.

Henry went on to say that, of course, Murdo's was only a different kind of consideration. Less philosophical, perhaps, but no less considering.

Geordie saw they were fencing with flattery—making some kind of competitive display of mutual respect. Murdo, talking about clothes, characterized himself as shallow and effete, and Henry said, in effect, *no, no*—*really I know you're a fine person.*

Billie interrupted them. "Mr. Hesketh, have you considered

that if you wear your gloves indoors you won't get the benefit of their warmth outdoors?"

"I'd better hurry outdoors then," he said, and left the library.

"Billie," Henry chided her, gentle, "he was only passing the time."

"Oh yes, the eons, the inanimate eons," she said.

"I don't want you barking at people on my behalf. I'm much better, dear. I don't need protection."

Billie shrugged. She was at the door before Henry and waited, meekly, for him to open it.

"What kind of woman is Billie Paxton?" Geordie wrote to Ian. "Now that she has found her feet, and has at least half her family, she is, I think, a woman who knows her duty and her place, but expresses herself incorrectly. She is helping Mr. Maslen to work, to sink himself in his work. But she's like a dog in a dinghy above a diver. She is above her brother-in-law, defending his boat, the place he'll again occupy once he's completed his dive, once he's come up for air. Billie Paxton is a dog in her master's dinghy, barking at all comers. But, Ian—" Geordie wrote, "—why do I disapprove of behavior I'd find acceptable in Minnie Hallow, who can be just as assertive and uncomfortable? Is it only because Minnie's portion, her share in the world, and her place in it, is so much larger?"

Geordie tapped his pen on the page of his letter, which slid to show the sheet below it. A list of names. Geordie remembered there was something he meant to talk to Murdo about, when he had him alone. He pushed Murdo's letter and coin into his pocket and followed Murdo out of the castle.

◆　　◆　　◆

MURDO HEARD GEORDIE HURRYING AFTER HIM IN THE
high street. He had just parted ways with the investigator of the
Gustav Edda's insurers. He saw that Geordie was out of breath.
Geordie came to a stop, his hand on Murdo's arm, blowing hard.
He said, "What did that man have to say?"

Murdo asked for his letter.

"I have undertaken to post your letter, Mr. Hesketh."

Murdo told the elder Betler not to be so testy. He said
he was losing conviction about his own ideas faster than Geordie
was losing body heat. There was another northerly, and Geordie had hurried out in shirt and waistcoat. Murdo took off his
own jacket and wrapped it around Geordie's shoulders. Ian's
brother wasn't mollified, but he did give Murdo his letter and—
ostentatiously—his penny. Murdo went into the post office,
bought a stamp, sealed his letter, and passed it across the counter.
He went back out to Geordie. "We have to hurry." He took
Geordie's arm and walked him briskly up the road toward Mr.
Mulberry's church. He explained that the insurance investigator
had said he was now focusing his investigation on a passenger, one
of the missing. "One of the three sportsmen from Stockholm who
occupied the other cabins. They were supposed to be in their
cabins when the ship berthed—but their bodies weren't found."

"They are all on my list," Geordie said. "The list I've pressed
on you, time and again, wanting you to sit down and go over
it with me. But *you* insist on thinking that someone planted a
murderous device in the ship's hold with the intention only of
sending a cargo of small gauge rails, wire-reinforced windows,
telephone equipment, batteries, cable, and a car to the bottom of
the sea. For myself, when I see corpses I see either an act of
God, human mismanagement, or the intent to kill."

Murdo said, "And what do you see when corpses aren't

found where they should be?" He said that, apparently, the insurance investigator was suspicious of only one of the Stockholm sportsmen, because, before they arrived at Luag, the man asked—as he had before—for warm water to wash and shave, but hadn't, as before, merely tidied the edges of his beard. When the steward removed the cold water from the empty cabin he found the basin full of a soup of soap and long red whiskers.

"He shaved off his beard?"

"Yes. He shaved off his beard, then went ashore at Luag, and came back in the dark of night. He said he'd forgotten his keys, and the steward let him into his cabin. That was an hour before the *Gustav Edda* sailed."

Murdo stopped in the church porch and removed his jacket from Geordie's shoulders. He put it back on, straightened Geordie's tie, and his own, and cupped his hands to scrape back his hair—slick, almost transparent with macassar but still too thick to lie flat. He said to Geordie that, naturally, when the investigator ran into him outside the post office they talked. "His English is good—but the islanders have a knack for making any mainlander feel like an interloper. He was a little lonely. He wanted to speak Swedish. Wanted to ask me who would have the effects of this drowned sportsman, the effects themselves, or the responsibility for shipping them back to his family. I sent him up to the castle to speak to Gutthorm." Murdo shouldered the church door open and walked through the chapel to Mr. Mulberry's study. He said, "Of course, if they *haven't* been sent to his family, the fellow's belongings will still be here."

THEY FOUND THREE FLAT-BOTTOMED LEATHER BAGS WITH three boxed fishing rods above them, propped upright against the paneled wall of the vestry, like swords over graves, swords in lieu of crosses.

Mr. Mulberry said, "They all kept rooms at a club in Stockholm. We directed our letters there—but there's no answer yet." He said he'd leave them to it; he had a christening at two o'clock.

When Mulberry had gone Geordie stepped up by Murdo and put his list into Murdo's hands. A list of the names of the dead. Eighteen lives. The black gang, the six stokers and two greasers who were in the boiler and engine rooms; the seamen at the gangplank when the explosion occurred, who went into the sea unconscious; the three-year-old girl who had spent the trip from Luag to Stolnsay sick in the salon; the girl's mother, who came out of the sea alive but died several hours later; Ian—the ship had rolled over on him. The remaining five had—like the black gang—been below when the *Gustav Edda* sank. There was another steward, who had been at the hatch with Henry Maslen's luggage, he'd kept his hand on it when he went into the sea, and had been found pinned between the pier and Henry's trunk. That left Edith Maslen, and the three sportsmen.

They had come for the fishing, had rented a bothy on Loch Nurry, and hired ghillies. None of them had been to Kissack before. They made all arrangements by mail. They were never seen in the salon. They liked each other enough to play cards for the full five days of the voyage, to take their meals together in one cabin or another, but not to share cabins.

"We scarcely saw them," Murdo told Geordie. "When Rixon and Elov came aboard at Thurso—they'd come up by rail from Invershin, where they had spent a week with another school friend—we were rather cramped. That is why I took rooms at Luag, one for Rixon and his friend, one for me. Ian kept our cabin. That evening, before the ship departed, we gave our cabin up to Mrs. Maslen."

Mrs. Mulberry came into the room. She said that her husband really hadn't any idea where anything was. "I had to take everything out of the bags in order to preserve what I could. It wouldn't do to send the poor souls' linen back to their people in the state it would be in if it was left soaked and packed." She opened one of the bags. It was empty. "Of course the fishing gear could take the weather. It was soon dry."

She opened a series of long shallow drawers where she kept altar cloths and the choir's smocks. She removed several piles of shirts and undergarments. Then she opened a closet and slid her husband's soutanes aside to show suits, jackets, and trousers. "All these clothes belong to *two* of the gentlemen. They are all washed and ironed."

Murdo and Geordie fingered collars, read the embroidered names. Then Geordie's hand crossed Murdo's to look through the shirts Murdo had. "Ha!" Geordie said. He snatched up two shirts and held them together, the collars kissing, the names cheek to cheek, each an initial and a surname. Different surnames.

Murdo was unimpressed. "Well? They had the same tailor, and the names are the work of some girl in his shop whose embroidery is as distinctive as handwriting." He was tired, and exasperated with Geordie.

"I took trouble for the sake of their people," Mrs. Mulberry said. "But also because of the *quality* of the clothes. All new, or nearly so."

"Yes. That's it." Geordie shook the two garments, just once and hard, under Murdo's nose. "What was in the third bag?" he asked Mrs. Mulberry.

"A blanket. It was marked with the name of the ship. I washed it, too, and gave it, with a few other things, to the poor captain when he went back to Stockholm to give an account of the accident."

"*A blanket?*"

"Yes, Mr. Hesketh, bundled up and stuffed into the bag, which was otherwise empty."

"Perhaps the same man who shaved," Geordie said. "And why *are* these clothes all new?"

Murdo closed his eyes. "You can't possibly suspect all three men."

Geordie told him that while suspecting all three sportsmen *and* Macleod wasn't at all commonsensical, common sense hadn't gotten them very far. Miss Paxton jumped from the deck of the *Gustav Edda* before the explosion, so common sense said that she was responsible for it—though she had no more motive than the three sportsmen.

Murdo said that they should concentrate on two men. The man who shaved, who took his clothes but left his luggage and fishing tackle—who went ashore at Luag and didn't return. "He set the charge," Murdo said. "Then Macleod attached the fuse and lit it."

"God save us," said Mrs. Mulberry. "Why?"

Murdo was amused, and malicious. "Why should God save us? Now there's a question."

"IF HE WAS AT ALL PREPARED TO ANSWER HIS OWN QUESTION, he'd answer Mrs. Mulberry's, too," Geordie wrote to his brother. "He has to accept the element of chance, the insults of bad fortune, and of good. In your last letter to me you said you were going with him to Stockholm, where he intended to place a stone on the Borgs' grave. To *seal* it, like a half-cooled jar of preserves. You said you weren't sure whether he was doing 'the ordinary decent thing,' or trying to keep a grief alive—to preserve it, to remind himself. I think Murdo Hesketh is suspended with his dead, with his sister Ingrid and her husband Karl Borg, and with Ingrid Hallow—if she *was* his—and you. He won't ask 'Why am I alive? Why has God preserved me?' because he regards his life as a temporary difficulty. He's alive because he wants to know who took you from him. But he won't ask 'Who meant to kill me?' in case the question makes him *jealous* of his life and desirous of living."

BILLIE AND ALAN LEFT HENRY, IN A STATE OF RAPT INquiry, in the circle of standing stones on Alesund Head. Alan led Billie down a precipitous track to a cove where, he said, people would come in search of timbers for gables, or tables, or boats. "From wrecks," he said. "They still come, that's why the path is clear."

It was a stony cove, and hidden from view in every direction but seaward. Billie and Alan stripped down to their underclothes, balancing on stones greened by algae, and among burst crates and hunks of grayed, unraveling rope. "At least we're out of the wind," Alan said, shivering.

They walked into the sea, Alan to his armpits and Billie only to her waist. Alan lifted his feet off the stones and dropped down into the clear water.

Billie told him that if he pushed his hands down he'd bob up, but he must remember that it was far more effective to move his arms like this. She demonstrated above the water. Alan copied her, and the water closed over his crown. He stood up again.

"Let your head go under between breaths. Rise up on the stroke," Billie said. "Try it."

Alan tried it, bobbed up and down and propelled himself forward. He looked back, grinning to incite her praise, and tried to stand again. He found he was out of his depth. He thrashed about a bit, made a jerky rotation, and struggled in again.

"Good," said Billie. "Watch my legs." She put her shoulders under, gasped, and swam out past him, around him, and back under his nose. Then she stood and held his hands while he stretched out in the water and tried it for himself. Billie had him push her backward for some distance, then she let him go and he followed her.

Billie, with her greater body mass, buoyant and relaxed, wove around Alan's agitated course. She saw him gradually becoming more synchronized. After a time she bumped him, and said, "Go back. I'm cold, and I haven't had my head under."

They swam back in, side by side, and she helped him out. They pulled their boots back on and, hunched with cold, carried their clothes up the track to a place where the sun lay. They inclined against a bank of sea thrift and thawed themselves. Billie was wearing a knitted shift, which drained well, and warmed while still damp. She basked, her eyes closed and her whole body, it seemed, bundled in the rosy cradle of the space under her eyelids. After a time she said, sleepily, that one day she'd own something to swim in.

"A loch?" said Alan.

"A bathing costume."

Alan said he'd like to swim again that evening, by Kiss Castle if he had to. Billie didn't need to get wet herself, but he'd be happier if she was there. He began to put his clothes back on. Billie listened with suspense to stitches popping in his jacket. She dressed herself and unpinned her plait. It dropped to largely conceal the wet tendrils at her nape. She warned Alan not to walk as if his drawers were damp. "Remember—we were only stretching our legs."

It was a strenuous twenty-minute climb back up the track to Henry. But they found him still content, sitting beneath a stone. It was thicker at its top than its base, and seemed to curl over him in a motherly way.

"This isn't the *famous* stone circle," Alan said. "That one is in the west. The Stolnsay fishermen use these to fix their position."

"But that's not what they were for," Henry said.

"Without trees they seem very tall," said Billie.

Alan asked, "Are they religious?"

"Probably."

"They stand out so," Billie said. "They remind me of a light-house on a long sandspit."

"Lighthouses are for navigation," said Henry.

"So are these," said Alan.

"Or they're religious," Billie said. Then, "Churches are tall."

Henry said, "Billie," fondly. He raised a hand to Alan, who helped him up.

MURDO AND GEORDIE WENT THROUGH EVERYTHING: GEOR-die's list, the bags, tackle boxes, every pocket of the jackets, top-coats, and trousers. Then they hurried back to Kiss, along the promontory road. It was the dinner hour, eight, but the sun was still forty degrees above the horizon, a hand above the mountains and high bogland behind Stolnsay. There would be light till ten-thirty or eleven, a long twilight, then a twilit night, the sun rolling along below the horizon, cool and white, radiant, but with no great heat.

Geordie walked briskly and the sleeves of Murdo's jacket sailed behind him. Murdo went along in Geordie's steps, not looking where he was going but at the paper they had found, an envelope, empty, but addressed to one of the sportsmen at that gentlemen's club. On the other side there was a tally, in three columns, a running record of wins and losses in a card game. The amounts were in pounds, not kronor. Large amounts.

Geordie argued that of course the Swedes had pounds. They were coming to fish on Kissack, where the currency was as *sterling* as the rest of Britain.

"But this much?" Murdo insisted. "They couldn't possibly require this much money for a month's fishing." Everything about these people made him suspicious. Especially since he'd seen none of them alive—*or dead.* There were no corpses, nor claimants come to complain to the authorities about defaulting corpses.

Rory Skilling intercepted Murdo at the gatehouse. He flushed red, with embarrassment or with drink. Fiona was behind him on the threshold, her hand draped over his shoulder and pinching his lapel.

"A new coat, Rory?" Murdo said. "It looks well on you."

Rory's flush faded, but only in patches, a lattice of pale skin appearing, so that the drink showed only in bloody cobbles. Rory said he'd found Macleod. Macleod's boat had come in the night before but the man had gone to his people at Ernol on the

Atlantic coast. "Macleod told a friend he has here that he ex-pected to be at Ernol for a week or two. His cousin is poorly, the one he means to marry."

Murdo thanked Rory and told him to go on in. But before Rory went Murdo asked if Alan was with them. He thought he saw the makings of a family in the gatehouse doorway—a father, a stepmother, but no son. Rory said he'd seen Alan in the cove below the castle—nasty place—with that young lady. She was teaching Alan to swim.

AT THE DINNER TABLE IT WAS OBVIOUS TO ANYONE THAT Billie Paxton's hair was still damp at her nape. It was piled, pinned and drooping over one ear, and with one lock escaping at the back like a serpent making a quick exit from a beehive. Murdo, who was opposite her, could even see the dull patches on her skin where salt water had dried in the air, leaving its residue.

James was talking. He was very pleased with Henry Maslen—an inquiring mind, an intellectual, a man who could talk in ways that were apparently congruent with James's own thinking. At least that's how it seemed to Murdo. *What a pair,* Murdo thought, sullen. Henry Maslen reminded him of a man whose job it was to go about a rubber plantation refreshing the wounds on trees. Henry tapped James, and James oozed talk all evening.

THE BALLROOM: AROUND TEN IN THE EVENING. GEORDIE apologized—he'd had to talk to Alan Skilling. He and Mr. Hesketh hadn't been able to beg off the planned picnic, and the visit to

Lord Hallowhulme's salmon hatcheries. Instead they would set out very early for Ernol on the west coast, and would rendezvous with the picnic party later, inland. That was the plan. Geordie said to Minnie that he was sorry they hadn't asked first whether they could borrow her odd boy. "We need him for his Gaelic. I'm as late as I am because I walked the lad back to the gatehouse."

"He's not in any danger, you know," Minnie said. "He's a wee lad, but he goes about like the spirit of the place."

"Of course," Geordie said. "Again I apologize. I'm all yours for the next hour. But I must go at eleven—with our early start."

"We hadn't begun yet, Mr. Betler," said Anne Tegner. "We've been puzzling over Elov's letter." She nodded at Elov, who got up off the floor and gave his letter to Geordie. Elov explained that it had been sent on first from his school, and then again from the house of his friend at Invershin where he and Rixon had stayed before meeting Mr. Hesketh at Thurso. "My friend sent it on. I got it Tuesday, but I sat on it. I didn't want to cause any trouble."

The letter was written to discourage Elov's visit. It spoke of new responsibilities Rixon had, of projects in which he had a share, and that would occupy him all summer. It said that Rixon really shouldn't have offered hospitality he wasn't equal to "at this minute." Rixon was only being a thoughtless lad—but *that* was the issue, and Rixon's father hoped to bring a little more structure and instill a little more direction and discipline into Rixon's life.

"With the letter he enclosed Samuel Smiles's book. By way of—oh, I don't know—*consolation*." Elov turned the book face-up. It was Samuel Smiles's *Self-Help*.

Geordie could see that Elov was unhappy. "It is rather awkward, isn't it?" he said.

"Elov feels unwelcome," Anne said. "And Ailsa just remembered that Clara said there was a letter following us, too. But she *did* say she was only asking our mother if she thought it might be better to stay away after the accident, and the deaths of all those poor people."

Minnie removed the page from Geordie's hand. She seemed anxious about the document itself, as if it were evidence. She said that the point wasn't who was welcome, but what plans their father had for Rixon that he'd now shelved, due either to Elov's appearance, or to events having chased his plans right out of his mind. Geordie, who was nearest her, heard her add, *sotto voce,* "Except that only his brains leaving his head would put his plans out of his mind."

"What do I *do*?" Elov was desperate. "I've had the hiccups all day."

"Father hasn't even noticed you!" Minnie said, to reassure Elov.

"I sit at his table."

"He doesn't see your mouth eating his food, only your ears apparently uncovered and listening to him no matter what expression the face between them wears. You're not a burden to him. You're a tiny pilot fish with its head buried in the blubber of a giant whale. He doesn't even *feel* you."

"You're Rixon's guest, not Lord Hallowhulme's," Billie said, which Geordie thought was practical and kind. He, Elov, Rixon, and the Tegners all smiled at her. But Minnie was less interested in the relief of Elov's anxiety. She said, "I want to know what his plans were."

"Son-and-heir plans." Rixon was gloomy. "He's scarcely

spoken to me all summer—and I prefer it that way. I don't want to join him. I don't want jobs to do."

"Don't you want to *know*?" Minnie wheedled.

"Well, perhaps, if there was something between not knowing and being *ravished* by information. I'm not going to ask him, Min."

"No! Don't!" Elov said.

10 ♣ MILT AND ROE

MURDO TOOK A FEW GOOD BREATHS OF COLD AIR AND opened his eyes to the long view, where the road went on down to the sea, touched, and came away again, a slope sectioned by blackhouses, some whose thatch was dark with mildew, or fallen where the weighted ropes that held all in place had broken and unraveled. Murdo counted ten empty houses. The series of stone dikes defending fields from the sea had been chewed by several winters of wind and ice. Ernol stood in the wind of an open ocean and, without its human numbers, hands whose habit it was to put stones back, it was slowly losing its human shape. Today the sea showed white only at its edge, and Murdo was able to make a quick count of the smoke streaming up from nearly forty houses. Farther off, and more solidly white, he spotted the smoky exhalations of three whales.

"The house!" Murdo hailed in Gaelic, stooped, touched the lintel, and led Geordie and Alan in.

There was only one cow in the byre that formed half the house. A girl was milking it, her forehead against its flank, and her feet clamped to the base of a solid wooden pail. She looked around, scarcely daring to move. Her face was white in the light reflected from the milk. Murdo heard Alan say, "That isn't your cow, is it?"

"No. It's Mary's. She's sick in her bed," the girl answered.

Murdo was pleased to have followed the exchange but knew he couldn't have formulated Alan's question.

The curtain was opened from within. There were several people in the long room beyond. The only illumination came from rushlights—green rushes, their pithy middles impregnated with grease, hung in simple pottery cradles on the walls. Some further light came down through the smoke hole and up from the peats stacked on the stone floor beneath a suspended kettle. The peats glowed but scarcely smoked. The smell in the room was that of the whole island, sharp and savory, and not unlike the pickled walnuts Murdo's mother liked to spread on rye bread, a black grease, like the peat, a smell so robust it seemed to disinfect the island's air.

Murdo squinted and saw two men and an elderly woman, and he thought he saw a pale face peer through the curtains closed over one of the box beds.

Murdo asked after Macleod. He got his words right. He indicated that they had asked at the outermost house and been directed here. "You are Macleod's people?" Murdo could see they didn't want to speak to him. They were closed and angry, but he wasn't reading hostility as such. He had not faced open hostility from the islanders—they stole from factory sites; or signed on, then shirked; they showed no enthusiasm at offers of work or at the prospect of lives led in rooms without these low ceilings, these caves of two stacked stone walls with turf packed between them. They turned their backs, or shrugged, whispered, or laughed outright at Lord Hallowhulme's offers of a prosperous, progressive future *here*—not on the mainland, or Canada, or Australia—but *here*, on the island. Murdo looked into the eyes of the man opposite him and saw anger, impatience, and a righteousness almost religious—this islander's sense of privacy.

"I work for Lord Hallowhulme. I am Murdo Hesketh."

The islander said he knew who Murdo was.

"Tell them you're sorry to intrude when there's illness in the house," said Geordie.

Murdo looked at Alan, who translated, beginning, "Mr Hesketh says . . ."

The islander spoke to Alan. The old woman interrupted, said something additional, and Alan translated. "They say Macleod's gone to the mainland and they wouldn't have any answers to questions you want to put to him. They say that, if we find him, we should ask him did he think of Mary? Did he ever think of Mary? *She* said that," Alan added, and tilted his chin at the old woman, who at this sign of insolence made a move toward him, her hand raised. It was a feint, but Alan pressed himself in under Murdo's arm.

Murdo asked for himself whether they knew *where* on the mainland Macleod had gone. Their answers were brief, but all three answered, furious, and all three turned away as they spoke, not to dismiss their visitors, but to hide something in their faces.

"Wait," said Alan when Murdo looked at him, one brow raised. Alan was trying to work it out—not what they'd said—for they said it in his mother tongue, but the *sense* of it. Alan wanted to know before Murdo and Geordie. Murdo put a hand on the boy's head—not affectionate, nor bullying, but the same way he'd gentle a nervous horse. He said, "I heard them say 'Gutthorm.'"

"Yes." Alan pointed, a little discreet jab in the direction of the woman—he wasn't about to risk anything more than a feinted slap. "She said, 'You can ask his wicked friends.' And *he* said, 'You can ask the other Norse, that Gutthorm.' And *he*—indicating the other man—said that your servant might have told you, were he still able to speak." Alan looked defiantly at all the householders and crossed himself, kissed his knuckle as though he held a rosary.

ALAN KISSED HIS KNUCKLE. IT WAS A REBUKE. ALAN GEStured, "God forgive you." He told the family off. For Geordie this was a distraction. Even in his shock—what had that man meant, mentioning Ian?—Geordie was struck by Alan's behavior. The boy had a very strong sense of how people should act. It wasn't manners or propriety. Alan Skilling wasn't gentle, in either sense, kind *or* well-bred, but he was morally literate, and he wasn't afraid of anyone.

Murdo said something further in his halting Gaelic. It sounded formal, and like thanks. Then he pulled Alan against his side, put one hand over the boy's mouth, and led him out of the blackhouse.

Geordie turned back to the family, and for a long while they all stood, staring at each other. Being in the black house was like being inside a hill, in hot, hazy darkness. Geordie thought of the stories he knew, about Flora MacDonald and Bonnie Prince Charlie, a man with a French accent and manners. Charles came ashore in Britain very near here, arrived by the back door, and spent his first night in the kingdom he hoped to gain as a guest in a blackhouse, cold, stooped, and coughing at the smoke. James Hallow might have the appearance of a boyish hobbyist as he held the floor and discoursed about houses of white brick, timber flooring, and south-facing windows—but he was seeking to improve where there was plenty of room for improvement.

The family looked at Geordie, silent and stubborn, till he be came aware of himself making no lasting impression, like a raindrop on a sheep's back, a neat, domed drop on lanolin-rich wool, shaken free by the first strong movement the animal made.

Geordie found Murdo inclined against a mound of stacked peats, careless of his coat—the coat that by judicious repeated sponging the maids at Kiss had restored to its original black purity. Murdo dropped his hat and ran his hands through his hair. He hadn't oiled it that morning, it was as flyaway as the silver northstars in bloom on the bog they'd passed through. Geordie looked away. The northstars were visible still, above the village, and the bracken covering abandoned fields. The low sun—always there, always low—shone through their white tufts.

Murdo said, "She was right. Miss Paxton was right." He laughed.

Geordie was angry, all at once, angrier than he could ever remember having been. It made him dizzy. A cloud covered the sun, the halo on the bog's horizon—the northstars—went out, everything came clear, suspended in a cold spiritous bronze light.

"Her naive observation—or her vulgar deduction," Murdo said.

"I won't hear you speak ill of her." Geordie glared at Murdo, who just watched him, his face pale against the dark nimbus of his sable collar. Geordie saw a man armored in his perfection, like a landscape of perhaps indifferent or uncertain qualities beautified by snow, a cosmetic frost. Murdo said, "I don't mean to speak ill of her. And perhaps knowledge is as natural as innocence." He shrugged. "Anyway, she was right about Macleod and the pilot. And, apparently, Macleod is an acquaintance of Johan Gutthorm, too."

"Who are you accusing now?" Geordie was in a kind of fury of despair. He took in huge gulps of air yet still felt stifled. The next thing he knew he was caught, he felt a static of softness against his cheek and throat—the collar of Murdo's coat. He was helped along a few paces and set down in the shelter of a stone wall, on a tumbled section of mortared stones. Geordie felt fingers at his nape, his collar stud pop, and the collar pulled away. Murdo undid a button, too, then put his gloved hand on Geordie's. "I'm not accusing anyone. Is that why you're angry?" He sounded concerned, but Geordie heard something beneath that—something like nervous delight. "I think that if we follow these clues, these suggestions, then Macleod is exonerated. He and the pilot were in the hold, trying out the readily warmed leather upholstery of the seats from James's automobile. Look, Geordie. Yes—that man in there did mention Ian. But Ian had a—what I'd have to describe as a proprietorial dislike of Johan Gutthorm."

"*Will* you explain?" Geordie said.

"I don't know that I can," Murdo said, but tried neverthe-less. "Ian seemed to feel he knew Gutthorm better than we did. That he was better able to know and judge Gutthorm."

Geordie heard Alan ask was Mr. Betler unwell? He looked at Alan's cracked, dinted, dusty shoes, saw the rags with which Alan had stuffed the toes poking from their split stitches.

"Can you ask at the house for some water," Murdo said. The shoes thumped away.

"Listen," Murdo said, "Ian understood Gutthorm—and Macleod, and the pilot, too—but he wasn't an *associate* of theirs. Ian kept to himself." Murdo clearly thought this was what Geordie wanted to hear, that Geordie was distressed by Macleod's kinsman's implication, whether slur or truth. But Geordie hadn't known that Ian was—

Was *what*? What did they call it now, now that law and medicine were having their say after all the Church's long-standing sayings. Geordie hadn't known—but what made him wild, what made him feel as violent as he'd ever felt before, was that he had understood for a very long time that Ian had been in love with Murdo Hesketh. He had to face it fully now—that what he had always chosen to think of as friendship, loyalty, fascination, hero worship even, was—of course—also carnal desire. Geordie had read his own letters to Ian—aware of his unease, his unexpressed hope that Ian would see his Mr. Hesketh settled, back on his feet, and would move on himself to another employer. He'd written to Ian: "You are not following a story as it appears in its parts. You need to think of your future, not wonder what will next happen to your employer." Geordie had been able *not to know* before he came to Kissack to bury his brother and found himself in daily contact with Murdo Hesketh—the disappointed, angry, baffled, splendid Murdo Hesketh.

Alan returned with the old woman. She was concerned. She knelt to examine Geordie's face and felt his forehead. Then she spoke sharply to Murdo, who removed his astrakhan and wrapped it around Geordie. As Murdo drew the collar closed he put his face near Geordie's, his eyes laughing, and said, "She's ashamed of her own unkindness, so tells me off about things I've failed to think to do." He took an enameled cup from Alan and wrapped Geordie's hands around it. Tea, not water. The woman hovered—then bustled off for more tea once Geordie had emptied his cup.

Murdo waited to catch Geordie's eye. Then he said, "I knew, Geordie, but I never thought about it. Do you understand?" Then he sat back on his heels and dusted his hands. He was putting the subject aside. He said something about the task in hand. "The pilot was evasive about Macleod because they'd been together, unbuckled, in the hold. Macleod didn't intercept the sensitive letter—which was in the salvaged mailbag. It was delivered and he fell out with his family, and Mary, indoors, whom he meant to wed. And since Macleod was otherwise occupied, we're left with our three Stockholm sportsmen." Murdo stopped speaking. He seemed abruptly tired, and Geordie imagined he saw a light go out in the younger man's eyes—the light of that coiled safety fuse.

"But why would a man—the Swede—set a fuse, then drown?" Geordie said. Then, "But of course he left the ship before it sailed."

"At ten the night before," Murdo said. Then, frowning, "But there are no eleven-hour fuses."

By noon the picnic party was closing on the Broch, which stood on a hill above the loch where Lord Hallowhulme had his salmon hatcheries. The Broch was a great tower, its roof long gone and half its side scooped away. As the picnic party turned off the road and onto the steep track up to the Broch, Billie watched the tower grow. It was an old thing, and she could see its stones were knit without mortar. Billie had an ear idly turned to Lord Hallowhulme, who was giving the Broch's history. How it was built to keep watch on that stretch of Atlantic coast, a fortress against Roman slave traders. How it had a double wall, the two inclined together for strength. "It was impenetrable to the armaments of its time," Hallowhulme said. "But of course time took it down, stone by stone—with a little assistance from crofters looking for nicely chiseled doorsteps."

The track was too steep for the horses, so Hallowhulme and his wife, Minnie, Elov, Billie, Jane Tegner, and her girls all got down from their respective traps, leaving only Henry, cocooned in his travel rug. Most of the young people bounded ahead. Lord Hallowhulme offered his arm to Billie, who said she'd see to Henry, caught up with him, walked by his side, her hand on his wrapped leg. She looked back at Hallowhulme, alone, Clara and Jane arm in arm behind him, their heads turned down and faces hidden by their hat brims. Minnie came last of all, weaving up the track in their wake. She had a book before her face, had been stupefied by it throughout the ride, and now, staggering, seemed drunk of it.

Henry was watching Lord Hallowhulme, peering with the same expression—puzzled, patient—he'd worn when he first came to understand that Edith was neither mistaken nor exaggerating when she said that Billie wasn't able to learn to read.

"What is it?" Billie said.

Henry thought she was asking after his health. He reassured her. The sun was out, and he was enjoying every minute, the views revealed at every bend in the road. He smiled at her, and covered her hand with his own. Billie tried to remember what Henry and Lord Hallowhulme had talked about during the ride. Billie had been relegated to what she found herself thinking of as "the elder persons' carriage" with Henry, James, Clara, and Jane Tegner. She'd spent much of the ride looking back at the others: Rixon bringing his horse at a gambol toward the carriage and trying to snatch the twins' hats, Elov, in the carriage, tussling with Rixon, the Tegners giggling, and Minnie leaning out over the padded sill of the door and turning the pages of her book. As she listened, Billie watched the island open up around them as they crossed beneath its two-and-a-half-thousand-foot divide. Hallowhulme thought that crofting was a fine old way of life—but that it would only thrive if supplemented by new industries. It wasn't that he believed in progress *per se*, but that he thought, since humans were capable of making rational forecasts about the future, they had *choices*. They could retain what worked in tradition but modify their lives by adopting new methods and inventions. He wanted to see stable seasonal employment, better housing, and children under twelve in schools. He talked about how herrings were salted and how alginate was extracted from seaweed. He and Henry discussed a book he'd given Henry to read, *Science and Penology*. Hallowhulme was animated, he said, "After all, we all agree that you can't breed a gun dog from a shambles cur." He insisted on "proofs beyond cavil" of the power of inheritance. Billie had kept half an ear on their talk, recognizing Lord Hallowhulme's argument as an opposite to those of Minnie's Mr. Goodwin in the play. She finally understood what made Elov Jansen so uneasy in rehearsals. As she listened, Billie watched the island open up around them as they ascended toward its two-and-a-half-thousand-foot divide. She could hear that Henry and Lord Hallowhulme were talking without rancor, Hallowhulme enthusiastic, Henry fully engaged and in good voice. Billie didn't feel she needed to keep an eye on Henry.

But, on the last slope up to the Broch, having dispelled Billie's fears for his health, Henry finally tried to explain his frown. He said he'd never thought of himself as someone with social graces, who knew what to do and say in most social situations. "I'm shy, and that's a shortcoming. I'm neither wary nor obsequious to my social superiors—and that is possibly a virtue. But, unless I know someone well, I am too serious. Another shortcoming. I'm serious, but not sober—though sobriety is more acceptable than seriousness." Henry paused and Billie watched his face, watched him formulate a thought. Henry was cheerful and conscientious—he thought well of the world, he was scarcely ever critical. Time and again Billie had listened as Edith was tart about this or that person they knew, and Henry, offering his opinions, encouraged Edith to be more moderate.

Henry said, "Lord Hallowhulme said a number of things that I think he should have thought better of saying. But who am I to criticize?"

"What did he say?"

"We were discussing the book I borrowed." Henry was polite, he had *borrowed* the book, it had not been imposed on him. "A book about artificial selection. Eugenics. Lord Hallowhulme was talking about the need for accurate and standard classifications of persons."

"I don't understand," Billie said.

"I'm sorry, dear. But you don't need to, I'm just giving a context for his remarks. I mean that his remarks followed on from hypothetical talk, they were in no way heated or personal. But he went on to say, 'Man is no more capable of selecting a mate fit to be the mother of his children than are the beasts of the field.' His words. Now—his remark wasn't directed at anyone, he was only explaining the reasoning of the theory of artificial selection. But he was speaking to a man who had just lost his chosen mate. And—worse—he went on to talk about extreme youth and unfitness, imbecility and unfitness, criminality and unfitness—then *inbreeding*, making a remark about the frequent unfortunate marriages between first cousins. Of course I glanced at Lady Hallowhulme. I couldn't help myself. But she didn't even blink."

Billie was laughing. "Oh, the poor man!" she said. "His foot in his mouth." She squeezed Henry's hand, told him he mustn't mind that his employer was imperfect. "Who has all the virtues?"

Both then thought of Edith, and went along in a stunned silence thinking on an angelic flawless Edith who suddenly seemed to have hidden her true human self behind their grief and need. Grief and need were transparent—and Edith had become a dazzling and magnified woman, close only by some optical trick, in fact distant, with lenses, lying lenses, glass between her and those who loved her.

The balance of the picnic party had reached the Broch, where the servants, who'd set out earlier in the day, had laid rugs, and a substantial luncheon, on a patch of springy grass at the base of the tower.

But Henry had one more thing to say before they joined the others. "Since you laugh, Billie—listen to this. This is odd. Odder than your explanations of what you see on a printed page, or fail to see. Lord Hallowhulme and I were talking about meeting people and finding things in common. And he said this: that when he meets a new person, in business or even in a social situation, someone with whom he might expect to have a conversation, he draws a sort of diagram in his head, mapping who *they* are, where they come from, what they know, and what they might be interested in; and what *he* knows, and what interests him; and then he tries to find a place where they can meet. His diagram is like a stepladder. A stepladder with steps on either side. As he climbs his side, the new acquaintance climbs theirs, till they are revealed, standing eye to eye, and can begin to have a proper conversation—one less 'illogical and superficial' than most social conversation. Don't you think that peculiar?"

The driver applied the brake and got down to hand Henry

out of the carriage. Billie and he joined the party, who were taking a turn around the Broch before eating. As they came around its great cylinder they startled some black-faced sheep, who jumped and scrabbled out over the lowest point of the broken wall and bounded down the far slope kicking up turf. A few hundred feet below the Broch was a loch, under the white half of a blue and white sky, and nacreous gray. "Ah!" said Henry, moved, and Billie leaned into him. Then he said, "You didn't laugh."

Billie said she had so many tricks for managing her own weaknesses, that Lord Hallowhulme's didn't seem so funny. She was wondering whether *she* made diagrams. Ever. She said, "I only recently met these people—and I've never had to think how to speak to them."

"Nothing was expected of us when we met them," Henry said. "Except tears."

"Now it's expected that you will get on with your cataloguing *for your own good*. And all I have to do is remember the music for Minnie's play." Billie laughed—because it seemed so easy, and she felt as if, for the first time in years, she'd been left in peace to wander in a big open space. "And that's all!" she said, sharing her delight.

"Yet here's someone who loves you," Henry said, and Billie was startled, because her brother-in-law was pointing at the two horsemen turning off the main road and starting up the slope. She saw the hair, like a thick concentration of the silvery northstars. Then she saw who Henry meant, for Alan slid down from behind Murdo Hesketh and ran, his big shoes like clubs on the ends of his thin ankles. Alan ran up the road, and straight to her.

◆　◆　◆

AFTER LUNCH LORD HALLOWHULME TOOK SOME OF HIS party down the hill's far side to look at his salmon hatcheries. They walked around the edge of the loch, where there were patches of still water, water standing where bog blended with loch, like a dirty lace trim, mud pocked by the sharp hooves of sheep. Here water lilies were growing, flowers of a modest size, but whose petals were robust, unmoved though the water beneath them shivered. The lilies were white, with a yellow center. Billie looked at them and imagined heat; she recalled the garden at Mulrush, a proper July heat, green water, sulky carp.

Lord Hallowhulme's hatcheries were built at the end of a steep valley, where the stream had been piped so that it ran in several strands, gently, through an underwater garden.

The party came first upon a long waist-high tank. They stood and watched young fish appear, in motion, against its graveled bottom, then slow and disappear into shadow and stillness, tail fins synchronized with the movement of weeds in the current.

Hallowhulme let one of the men who ran the hatcheries answer any questions the visitors had, while he took off his jacket, rolled up his sleeves and set to work pounding cooked beef in water to make a paste of it.

Billie leaned over the side of the tank. She was enchanted by the light on the gravel, and the blue-green-pink tessellated shapes of fish. They glowed with life, but played dead—it seemed to her—going nowhere, only hanging in the current like buoyant stones. She wanted to climb in and drift down the tank with them, but only slid along its edge, the smooth lip wetting the fabric under her arms and across her chest, her face so close to the water that her view was intermittently obscured by the ripples her breath made on its surface. She came to the end of the tank, where the water was deeper and there was a stretch of pale sand where the current feinted and made a fist against a weir. The bigger fish were here, more than she'd ever seen, so that her mind began to make strange comparisons—a flight of ducks against a white evening sky. But the salmon had no voyaging formation; they reached the end of the tank, pushed sidelong in the current, then came to life, accelerated, and shot back up the pool.

Billie put her hand in the water, at the invisible line where the salmon chose to turn. James Hallow appeared beside her with a bowl of mashed meat. The twins were feeding cooked meat to the smelt, he said. What he had here was a meal made of raw beef and other, cheaper, fish. This they fed the adult salmon.

Billie put her wet hand into the bowl, scooped out some warm, mealy matter, felt bristles of fine bones scratch her fingers and lodge in her nails. She put her hand back in the water and shook it. She watched fibrous gobs of mince drop away from her, to be snatched out of space by a shadow, a flash, a thick, moving curve.

Lord Hallowhulme stood quietly beside her as she took more, repeating the process till the bowl was empty. He dipped and rinsed it, and she, cooperative, wiped its sides till all the meal was gone. He set it on its edge against the tank and escorted her upstream to show her where the spring came up through the graveled floor of a pool perhaps eight feet deep. The spring was invisible, pure water in purity, but the stones at that place flew up and fluttered down like moths disturbed by someone crossing a meadow.

James Hallow took Billie back downstream to the smaller tanks to watch Geordie—less fastidious than the twins, who only looked on—pinch little portions of boiled beef and drop them through a timber grille, which pressed a grid of glass rods down in water only a little dimpled by a gentle current. Among the glass rods, and batches of eggs still opaque, or spotted with life starting, were tiny translucent fish, salmon smelt, some still attached by umbilical cords to their egg remnants, their transparent bags of provisions. Billie could see the food in their digestive tracts, their spines, their brains behind their eyes—the only wholly solid features emerging out of glassiness, a whole glassy world where everything seemed liquid, water in more forms than she'd ever imagined water could take.

Billie's sleeves were soaked, so she unbuttoned them. They dangled and dripped as she followed the others along the path to the smallest tanks, and a table on which the man who'd hitherto been their guide was setting a flat vessel, a low zinc pan, half full of water.

Geordie said, "What's this?" sounding, for some reason, uneasy.

Billie was nearly asleep in the heat and the silence. She wasn't in need of any kind of information. What this was, for instance. She got it though.

"The primal moment of pisciculture," Hallowhulme said, tense and husky. He made a joke as he plied the net over the tank. He was the spirit moving on the face of the water. But he didn't have any luck, though the fish were confined, so he passed the net to his assistant and called Billie to him. This was something he could teach her, James Hallow said, something she could be taught. Besides, it needed hands, and hers were wet already. He had her lift her arms and rolled her sleeves for her. His assistant had netted a fish. James extracted it from the net, very delicate, and held it carefully, head up and tail down over the pan. He gripped the fish with his left hand and began to pass his right down its length. It was important to apply an even pressure, he said. A grainy transparency appeared under his hand and dribbled into the pan where it gelled and slopped, tiny beads of water in water. James cleaned the salmon's belly of the strings of eggs and put the fish back in its tank. His assistant had another fish ready. James took this one, too, by its head, and held it over the blistered water. He called Billie to his side and set her hand on the creature. She felt its scales, silkiness one way and rough opposition the other. She felt James Hallow's warm, cushiony palms pressing the back of her hands. James said she mustn't be afraid of hurting it. She should be firm, her pressure consistent. His hand guided hers, down the fish's belly, squeezing. This was a male fish. Billie saw the milt, white and creamy, pour from the pouting slit near its tail.

The fish was returned to its tank, and James had Billie stir the pan with her fingers. "Gently," he said, "for a few minutes, until it's fecund."

Billie found she enjoyed the sensation of the slight glutinous globes of eggs brushing against her fingers. She had a sudden memory of eating milk-drowned tapioca with her fingers. This led her to a recollection, very rare for her, of her mother. Billie's mother pulled her hands out of the pudding and wiped them with a cold flannel. Her mother put a spoon in her fist, Billie's baby spoon with its mother-of-pearl handle. Billie could see the spoon quite clearly, but couldn't see her mother, who stood behind her chair. *Turn around and look up*, Billie said to herself. At the same time she took her hand out of the water, roe, milt, and put the tip of one finger in her mouth. The taste of salt burst on her tongue as the egg's membranes ruptured, and she was recalled to the moment, so that when she *did* turn around and look up she saw not her mother but James Hallow, his flushed, fair, expressive skin—like his cousin's—his startled hazel eyes, his gaze wavering away from hers.

Then Geordie Betler thrust his face between them. He was standing behind them, tilted forward from the hips to crane, absurdly, into the small space between Billie and James Hallow. "How *interesting!*" He said. "Do you now place the fertilized eggs in the tank with the glass rods?"

"Yes," Lord Hallowhulme said—and didn't elaborate.

Billie went to the stream to rinse her hands.

There was no breeze at all in the shelter of the Broch, but the sun was too high and hot for midges, and Murdo dozed, roused now and again by the thump of the hoof of one of the grazing horses, telegraphed through the turf, or by a squeaking as Minnie rubbed the corner of a page, preparatory to turning it. He heard the whisper of cloth, a woman's skirt brushing through the seeding grasses. Minnie made no acknowledgment, so it was only her mother, back from a turn around the Broch. Murdo felt his face shaded. Clara didn't stand over him, but she did put her parasol down beside him, so his face was in its shadow. He heard her canvas camp stool creak as she sat back down. He opened his eyes. Clara was behind him, the parasol between him and her. He looked up at its spokes, and the thick streaks of slub in the silk. It was bronze silk, as bright in its way as the unscreened sun.

Murdo asked Clara if she ever thought of their boat.

"I haven't thought about it for a long time," she said.

He heard a flurry of movement, thick female clothes adjusting between body and ground—that was Minnie writhing around to look at them, at last diverted from her book, *The Adventures of*

Sherlock Holmes. But Minnie wouldn't be able to follow them; they'd spoken in their mother tongue.

CLARA AND MURDO HAD BEEN BEYOND REACH IN THEIR boat on the pond at Ulna. As a small boy Murdo hadn't liked being on the water. On his family's regular North Sea crossings his father would settle him below—they always had a cabin nearest the center of the ship. "The vessel's gimbal, its pivot point," his father would explain, "where there is the least movement." Murdo had learned to associate his sickness with being afloat, rather than in motion. He had no such trouble in his grandmother's phaeton. One summer his cousin Clara undertook to cure him of his aversion to water. She was at a confident and crusading age—twelve. Murdo was six and in awe of her. Clara made him a bed in the flat-bottomed boat on the pond at Ulna, their grandfather's country house. Clara had him lie down, his head pillowed on the padded stern board, and rowed them out into the pond's center, the only place where the water was its true green, not striped by the reflections of the birches that all but surrounded it. Murdo wasn't sick. The young Clara was very pleased with herself, flattered by her cousin's obedience, his attention, and his gratitude at her patronage. Her own brother was a nuisance, but Murdo was a pet.

Summer after summer, Clara—a secretive, irritable girl— would abdicate from her affectionate family, from a mother to whom she was always "darling," and a father who called her his little star. She'd go into exile, sometimes all day, afloat in the center of the pond—often with her retinue of one. Clara would read to Murdo—books he'd find too difficult to tackle himself. He would lie draped across the stern and Clara's arrangement of borrowed cushions, and the brocaded curtains she'd stolen from a trunk in the attic, the finery of a former era. Murdo would lie facedown, peering at the green water, his breath making two separate dimples on its surface. Sometimes they would drift from the pond's center, and he'd find himself facing the perfect reflection of birch trunks and would imagine he and his cousin were in their grandfather's library, faceup on its floor, with the tiered shelves towering above them, thick with books, gilded, calf-bound, sectioned spines—continuous columns of spines, like stands of bamboo. Then he'd doze, with the world going around and around the boat: a forest, a library, another forest.

When Murdo was twelve himself, and Clara eighteen, he arrived at Ulna for his usual summer visit to find the furniture moved out of rooms, rugs airing on ropes between the elms, and every sideboard covered with silverware in a condition of high polish. There was to be a ball. Murdo's aunt said Clara was confining her own preparations entirely to her toilette. She was out in the wood, picking wildflowers to supplement the hothouse blooms she'd selected for her posy holder. "They are all the rage at her school. The girls gave each other books on the subject. The language of flowers." Clara's mother chortled. Other adults joined in. There was quite a crowd of them—all family, all people Murdo recognized. They were speaking English, out of politeness to the clumsy young man, Murdo's other cousin James Hallow, whose father owned a grocery, but who had himself made a fortune in soap. The family were laughing now at cousin James's wit—at the notion of Clara performing "a sort of floral semaphore." James seemed surprised that he'd made them laugh.

Murdo found Clara on the jetty, stuffing wetted moss into the silver horn of her posy holder. She was over the water, so had the posy-holder's ring on her finger and its chain looped twice around her wrist.

Murdo sat down beside her and used his leg to hook the boat closer to them. Clara noticed that he was in long pants, and admired his cadet's uniform. He held the boat steady as she got in, and she said, "Lord, Murdo! The size of your knees!" She squeezed his knee under the navy serge. He passed her flowers down to her and got in the boat.

The cushions and curtains had—Murdo saw—been soaked and dried, soaked and dried. He pushed off, pulled in the oars, and let the boat carry on slowly into the deeper water. When he lay back against the stern his head raised the smell of mildew from the cushions. Clara talked about the ball—mathematically, the number of young couples who could stand up together. She discovered a grease of old pencil marks on the fan of bone dance cards attached to the top of her posy holder. She wet her handkerchief with spit and began to polish them. She consulted with Murdo. Should she carry cedar leaves and carnations to say, "I live for thee. Alas, my poor heart"? or little arum, for "ardor," and, to mitigate, scarlet fuchsia for "taste"?

Murdo told her he liked the white rosebuds.

"Yes, aren't they lovely." Clara stroked them. "They mean 'a heart innocent of love.' Unfortunately they can also convey 'girlhood' or 'you're too young for me.'" Clara said she had plans, *real* plans for the evening. This year the girls in her school had practiced kissing as a kind of extension to their dance lessons—in the dormitory, after the lights went out, with the sophisticated and knowledgeable Anna Bergen testing them and judging their form. They practiced prim kisses, and promissory kisses, and even passionate kisses. Anna Bergen would instruct: "Your lips must be firmer," or "Don't put your hand on his ear," or "Melt, girl! Melt!"

Murdo, who had been impressing the water with his breath, rolled over and regarded his cousin out of one eye. He said, experimentally, that he couldn't imagine what she meant.

"No, I suppose you can't," Clara said. She was quiet for a while, only inspected her harvest of flowers. At last she said, defensive, that she preferred to be *prepared*.

"Yes," Murdo said. "I see that. What I mean is that I can't work out how your friend distinguishes one kiss from another. It's all very well in a book where one reads that some hero's kiss is 'forceful' or heroine's kiss is 'melting,' and one thinks ho-hum—is this only the same thing as saying, in a story, that 'the sun beat down'? The sun does no such thing, the sun stays in its own round, thousands of miles removed from us. Surely, Clara, a *prim* kiss is a kiss on the cheek, like the kisses I give your mother. And what on earth is a promissory kiss?"

"Skeptic," Clara said, more amused than irritated. She brushed the flowers from her lap, put down the posy holder, and crawled toward him.

He squinted, so she opened her parasol and set it up beside his head. She bent over him. "This is a prim kiss," she said, and pressed her firm, closed lips briefly against his. "And this"—she held up one finger—"is a promissory kiss—a delicate concoction, like a sorbet between courses." Murdo knew she was quoting Anna Bergen. His cousin touched her lips to his, softer, off center, her lips moving to catch his lower lip momentarily, and pinch it gently.

Murdo took a breath and, for the first time in his life, felt air as a solid, a thick filling obstruction in his head and body, an indigestible richness.

Clara sat back. "And I am *not* going to demonstrate a passionate kiss—because for those, *you* have to be standing, and *taller* than me. Which you are not. Besides, I'll only do so much even to furnish proof to a skeptic."

"I have to stand up over you?" Murdo rallied, he poured on the scorn. "Is that your sophisticated Anna Bergen's whole prescription? What say I'd just fought a duel for you, and was lying on the dew-covered grass at dawn, bleeding from a fatal injury? I beg your pardon, miss, but I can't possibly get up. Is it not your job—no—your *calling*, to cover my face with burning kisses?"

"Well—I've covered it with a parasol," Clara said. "That will have to do. I have to get these flowers out of the sun, and into clean water. Could you row us in, dear?"

He put out the oars and rowed. He handed her ashore. He repressed his hair and restored his cap and helped her carry her flowers.

The next morning he asked her whom she'd kissed. Or—if not whom—how many?

She'd kissed Anders Eglund. It was Anders she'd been planning and practicing for all along. But, feeling her power, she also kissed two others—men, she supposed—anyway, older than her. She'd bitten off more than she could chew with Mr. Trond. This morning after her bath she'd found a spotting of bruises in the small of her back, his fingerprints, and a corresponding thumb print on her side. "His grip was *convulsive*. He was very . . ." Clara's eyes grew opaque as she searched for a word, "very stirred." Then she smiled. "And I kissed cousin James, who is *so* temptingly, so impregnably pompous!"

"All promissory kisses?" Murdo inquired.

"Mr. Trond was passionate. *He* was. I felt tenderized. The others were promissory. Anders is so backward."

"Were you afraid of Trond?"

Clara laughed. "Not at all. I got him behind the big fern by the stairs. I could hear my papa and yours in the billiard room." Clara lay back on the damp cushions and smiled at Murdo. He was at the oars, rowing for exercise, as he had never done before, his shirtsleeves rolled up and sweat printed on the back of his shirt where his elasticized suspenders pressed under his shoulder blades and down his spine.

"I have all summer to study," Clara said, and closed her eyes. She yawned, complained of tiredness.

"Who was best?" Murdo asked.

"You were, dear. And Anna Bergen." Clara brushed a hand along her jaw, added, "No nasty whiskers."

Clara said she didn't often think of their boat. Minnie rolled over to peer at her mother and Murdo. Murdo rolled, too, so that his face was clear of Clara's thoughtfully placed parasol, and he was looking up into Clara's eyes, her face, thin and greenish in the shade of her hat. It was, for just an instant, like looking at his own face in a mirror. He would look at himself and he'd know what he was thinking. He would know because he *was* himself, not because his thoughts showed in his face. Looking at Clara was like that—but only for a moment. Then she was again the Clara *after all these years*, and after Ingrid. She wasn't living foliage anymore, the makings of a posy, leaking green onto a white cotton summer dress. She was one of those concoctions of wax fruit and dried flowers and stuffed hummingbirds, under glass, a deceitful, fading, false thing.

Murdo turned away, over onto his back, stared at the clouds and the broken rim of the Broch.

The hatcheries tour returned. James got the idlers up to stretch their legs before the journey back. He walked his wife, used his hat to herd his daughter. He sent Murdo into the Broch to flush out Alan Skilling, who was climbing between its two walls—not really a safe thing to do.

11 ⚜ *Fortune and the Four Winds*

MURDO HAD HOPED HE COULD GET AWAY FOR A SHORT time without any fuss. The few things he had to do for James he delegated to Rory Skilling. But Rory seemed offended at being left behind. He felt neglected, apparently, or supplanted by Geordie Betler.

It was true that, lately, when Murdo had gone out in the execution of James's business, he'd taken Geordie, even when Rory had presented himself early and eager. Sometimes Rory went, as well, rode behind them, silent and sulky. It seemed that the trip to Ernol was a final insult. Rory wanted to know why Murdo had asked for his son Alan, not him? Did Mr. Hesketh no longer have any confidence in him? "And you went out to Scouse Beach alone on that Sunday. Yet you knew I wouldn't be at Stolnsay Kirk." Rory said all this while scuffing his feet on the gatehouse doorsill and swinging his head, as if checking the front of his new jacket for lint.

Murdo couldn't tell Rory that he had asked for Alan because he hoped Alan would translate while understanding little. Murdo didn't trust *anyone* anymore—except, perhaps, these new acquaintances: Geordie; the innocuous Mr. Maslen; dim, "innocent" Miss Paxton; and the children, of course. But Geordie was the only one Murdo would allow to help him investigate. Besides, the rest of the Kiss household clearly thought the investigation was better left to experts. Clara seemed to consider Murdo's investigation coarse and forward. And to James the sinking was only a puzzle, like a problem in chess, less interesting to him than the schemes he had in hand, or his new projects of patronage, of helping the survivors he had taken under his wing.

Murdo said to Rory Skilling: "Please don't take offense. I asked for Alan because Alan—despite Minnie's silver—is really on his own time. You are in Lord Hallowhulme's employ, and I mustn't have you moonlighting on my investigation."

Rory Skilling nodded. He conceded this. "I have been meaning to tell you, sir, that Lord Hallowhulme has made me a very kind offer—I'm to be a manager at the Southport cannery when it's finished. I'm to have a manager's house. It's on the strength of this that Fiona has said yes to me."

"I am very happy for you, Rory." Murdo was pleased, and rather surprised, that James had recognized Rory's qualities: loyalty and discretion. Murdo offered his hand, and Rory took it, shy. He then said, in a rush, "But for now, I'm still your man, Mr. Hesketh. And you must remember me whenever you are off about anything I can share." His gaze, formerly lacking traction, caught on Murdo's as he said this, and Murdo could see strong feeling, some kind of passion, sullen and reluctant.

Murdo had encountered this look before, at other times, in other people. It made him impatient. He'd done as much as he meant to mollify Rory. He said he'd be back in under a week. They would speak further then.

Murdo had set out from Kiss for the pier and his ship, a wind-dependent sloop, which would catch the tide at eight. He'd left before breakfast, and had slipped a note under Geordie's door. *"I'm off for perhaps a week to Oban. The window glass, rails, car, the materials for Lord Hallowhulme's telephone exchange all came up to Oban by rail, and then went on to Luag, where they sat for a week awaiting the* Gustav Edda. *I want to track that cargo. I'll stop for a day at Luag on my way back to ask about its final period of confinement. I realize you can't be spared from Kiss, and I hope you have confidence in my ability to pursue this matter without you. Yours, MH."*

However, Murdo wasn't able to get quietly away. He was in the vessel, out of the way of the seamen, when Minnie arrived on the pier, alone in her trap and, without waiting for permission, came up the gangplank. She had a brown paper parcel under her arm. "Cousin Murdo, Father says he's surprised you didn't let him in on your intentions. Mr. Betler told us at breakfast that you'd gone. I *missed* my breakfast to come down here and catch you."

"What have you there?" Murdo pointed at the package.

"Oh—this is just something Mr. Gutthorm would like you to take to his aunt, the one who lives near the port in Luag. It's addressed; he was intending to post it." She passed the package to Murdo, who gave it a squeeze—it was heavy, springy, and yielding.

"It's tweed, I believe, a length of big cloth," Minnie said. "It's not why I came. I'm not running messages for Gutthorm." Her gaze, usually forthright, was flitting and lighting from his face to their surrounds. "Damn!" she said, then put her hands on his arms and moved him, bodily, so that his back was to the pier.

"Minnie, you are not *blocking* a scene. I'm not one of your theatrical amateurs."

"Yes, yes, I know. I hate to take liberties, only I have something to say to you."

"Presumptuous, I hope," Murdo teased. Then he looked

over his shoulder, to see what he was being prevented from seeing, what the distraction was.

Billie Paxton was hurrying along the pier, on foot. She was wearing a summer dress, black silk with a thin violet stripe, mourning still, but elegant mourning.

"She didn't buy that," he said.

"It's one of the dresses Father had made for her," Minnie said. Then she stamped her foot. "Our performance is tomorrow evening. You knew that. You'd have enjoyed it. When I chose it I was thinking of you, of you, *too*, that is."

"Minnie," Murdo said. "I didn't think —I'm not—"

"I know—you're not to be entertained. You're not to be included."

Billie Paxton arrived, in a surge, a lovely susurration of silk and breath. Her hair was loose, and everyone was looking at her. Apparently her arrival was the whole of her attack, because once she was on the deck beside them she stopped dead and stood dumb.

Murdo tried to think of something to say to Minnie, something kindly. His own feelings failed him, so he turned his attention to Billie. "And what do you want, Miss Paxton?"

"A quick word."

"Miss," said the sloop's captain to Minnie, "here is the tug. We must move out into the channel before we set our sails."

"I'm listening," said Murdo to Billie.

Again Minnie stamped her foot.

"Really, miss, I must insist," said the captain.

"It's very generous of you, Minnie, to ask me to take an interest in you." Murdo was out of patience with her, and with the captain. He wanted to hear what Billie had to say.

"In private," Billie added.

Minnie glared at her, but Billie wouldn't meet her eyes.

Minnie spun around and stamped off. The captain followed her for a few steps, apologizing. Then he realized he hadn't managed to evict both young women.

Billie hunched her shoulders to hide something. She was fumbling with the purse on her belt.

"One moment," Murdo told the captain, who looked at him with gratitude as Murdo took Billie's arm and led her onto the pier, then, from the deck, with dismay as Murdo crossed the pier with Billie, so that they stood at the harbor's outer wall. Murdo waited for Billie to notice where they were. He had a sudden recollection of himself watching a cat he'd had as a boy and waiting for the moment it discovered that its kittens—five cats too many—had been spirited away. Murdo registered this memory as a moment of conscience, and understood that his curiosity was cruel.

Billie had finally got her fingers into the overstuffed bag. She pulled out a crumpled wad, comprised of newspaper and a pound note. She said, "At a rehearsal the other day Minnie said to Alan, 'Don't you have any respectable shoes?' He doesn't." She put the pound in Murdo's hand then spread out the newspaper—two pieces of it, the scissored-out shapes of a pair of small feet. "I traced his feet. I took my tracings to the shops in Stolnsay, but I was told to make a mail order or to go to Luag." Billie put the scraps into Murdo's hands. "They aren't marked, but you'll know which is right and which is left. Please, Mr. Hesketh. I didn't want to mention it in front of Minnie. I don't want to embarrass her."

Murdo hesitated; didn't immediately put the pound and papers in his pocket. He said, "A package for Gutthorm's aunt. A pound for Alan's shoes." He inclined very deliberately against one leg of the steel derrick that stood over the drowned ship. He saw Billie notice the derrick, then look down into the water. Murdo watched her realize, remember, suffer—but she did it all quietly, with resignation. She said, "Before—I would have left it to Edith to notice what needed doing, and to do it. I owe it to Edith to do what she would've done."

"I see. You mean to fill your sister's shoes, so to speak." Murdo meant to insinuate, but heard his own voice, tense and harsh.

Billie stared at him, then said, with implacable patience, "To do the *kindness* Edith would have done."

Murdo nodded, pocketed the pound and traced feet and walked away from her, bounded down onto the deck just as the tow rope tightened between the sloop and the tug.

GEORDIE WENT TO THE STOLNSAY POST OFFICE AND found a package from Andrew Tannoy, the letters he'd asked for, Ian's to him. Following Geordie's instructions Tannoy had sent only the recent correspondence. Three years' worth.

Geordie opened the package and filled all his pockets, then, as he walked, he began reading from the beginning—Ian's arrival on the island—looking for any mention of Ingrid Hallow.

"She favors her mother," Geordie read. "Minnie is less fortunate, she has her father's brains, but is a noisy, unladylike girl." Ian wrote that Rixon had taken to Murdo right away, and had Murdo teach him to shoot; they were often out after grouse. Murdo was in better spirits, but uncharacteristically docile. Clara was a great comfort to Murdo, Ian thought.

While reading, Geordie had veered to the right, his whole

body following the tendency of the words on the page. He was on the promontory road, its ragged right margin. He had got into the weeds, and a nettle caressed his ankle. Geordie jumped in shock, limped to the seawall, and sat down. He pulled up his trouser leg and looked where the nettle had touched, the welts white on his ankle above his drooping sock. He was annoyed with himself—his slipping standards—he'd neglected to put on his garters not just today, but yesterday, the day of the picnic, when he'd lain rucked and rumpled and unseemly against a wall at Ernol.

Geordie picked a big dock leaf, crushed it, and rubbed its white sap on the welts. Then he opened a few further letters.

Murdo was warm to Ingrid Hallow. She was the only one of James and Clara's children he'd met before. When Minnie was a baby her mother had left her with a nurse and come to visit her own mother in Stockholm. She brought Ingrid with her. This was years before Ian was with Murdo, who was then between military school and the King's Cavalry. His sister Ingrid Hesketh was ten, Ingrid Hallow was four. Murdo told Ian later that his sister had called Ingrid her little fairy—a dark-eyed, wispy, white-haired child in Paris dresses covered in ruffled lace, so that she seemed to carry her own cushion around with her always. Murdo and his sister took Ingrid sledding and skating and to matinees of plays about woodcutters' daughters who fell in love with wolves. Ingrid doted on Ingrid (while Murdo, showing off to his suddenly solemn cousin Clara, fell from his horse and broke his collarbone, which put an end to the skating and sledding for that visit). Clara couldn't dance attention on her daughter. She was tired. Rixon was possibly already on the way. "Clara only came to talk to her mother," Murdo told Ian. Really, he didn't understand why she hadn't left Ingrid at home also, except possibly his aunt had insisted Clara bring her eldest granddaughter. "Something was up. I can see that now, in hindsight," Murdo told Ian. "Or—well—Clara and I were once so alike, despite the differences in our ages, so much in sympathy, I can imagine what she'd have felt after several years of marriage."

Murdo said this, Ian wrote, then saw Ian's surprise. "Don't mistake me," Murdo said, "James was always—is still—a good match. A well-bred, honorable, conscientious man. But Clara had many admirers. Male admirers, and female imitators—valiantly loyal friends. Clara was restless and venturesome and changeable. How could James fully appreciate her? A man who minds so much that doors are either firmly shut or fully open! I see now that James couldn't. That he only differentiates the people around him by ideas he has about people. They're all beads sorted by size in a tray. Valuable to him in all their types and classes. Clara loved to astonish—and she married someone to whom she couldn't ever be sure she'd appear as *herself*, or be heard as *herself*." Murdo said to Ian that he now understood that, when Ingrid was four, and Clara visited her mother, she'd really come to complain about James. "My aunt failed to follow Clara's meaning. James wasn't hard-hearted, he was only impervious—and it was churlish and *girlish* of Clara to object to a fault that was certainly also a virtue in a millionaire."

Geordie put the letters back in his pockets, pulled up his sock, and went on toward Kiss.

AT TWO GEORDIE REPORTED FOR THE FITTING OF HIS false beard. The ballroom was partway through its transformation. Its stage, the foot-high orchestra dais, as yet had no curtains. These were being made, and Geordie took his seat beside long swaths of stiff blue cotton bunting, on which Billie knelt plying a paste brush and tinsel stars.

While the Tegner twins adjusted the gauze and glue and hair on Geordie's face he read the program—typed by Minnie on Gutthorm's machine. *Fortune and the Four Winds: A cautionary comedy, by G. B. Shaw.* There was a cast list in which the patriarch was described as "a social experimenter" and, like a dictionary's secondary meaning of a word, a "serious positive character."

The Tegner twins were giggling. Geordie said his beard must not be ridiculous. Anne held a mirror before his face. There he was, an illusion dependent on poor illumination. With a beard he seemed more a gentleman than a gentleman's gentleman.

Minnie and Rixon were inspecting an arrangement of black screens at the back of the stage. It was from these the fake walls would fall—lengths of real wallpaper, some with washes of watercolor to form fake shadows and angles. The exits were in the obvious places, two hinged pasteboard doors, but there was also a trick exit. "If only we had a trapdoor!" Minnie lamented.

Rixon said she was getting above herself. This wasn't a theater. "And if you hope to suggest the patriarch has a spooky way of coming and going without being immediately noticed, you *can't* do it by the deployment of a device traditionally reserved for devils, ghosts, and witches. Minnie, it's only the other characters who should fail to notice that he's appeared and is listening to them. The audience has to *see* him listening."

Geordie remarked that, since he had his cues by heart, he wished they would settle their ideas. Then he saw that everyone had stopped what they were about. Billie got up. "Excuse me," she said, "I lost track of the time."

Clara was waiting for her at the ballroom door.

◆　◆　◆

CLARA TOOK BILLIE TO THE COTTAGE LORD HALLOW-
hulme had supplied for his cataloguer and family. Under the circumstances, Clara thought Billie should look over the house and
its furnishings before Henry. After all, the house was more Billie's
business. She should examine it, see what alterations were required. They had the rest of the summer to get it up to scratch,
Clara said.

The cottage was whitewashed brick, and stood alone one
street up from the harbor. Its front rooms faced south. The parlor
was papered in a simple blocked floral pattern. The kitchen had a
timber floor and a pump indoors over a copper-lined scullery
sink. The bedrooms were upstairs, and both had gabled windows
that looked out into the trees on the Nose, a belt of green in
which an odd whitened snag showed, and then hid.

Clara reached past Billie to open a window. She did this as
she did everything—stately, deliberate. But Billie could scarcely
feel the woman behind her. Clara stood close only to manage the
window's catch, but did so without imposition. Her presence
lacked palpable intent, or warmth, or impetus, so that Billie felt
that Clara was more shade than person, more ghostly than the
woman whose house the cottage really was.

Clara said that, as Lord Hallowhulme hoped, Henry's first
task looked set to last him through the winter. The family always
left Kiss in late August—though James was back in October for
the shooting, and often came at Christmas, too. Kiss wasn't
closed up, but ran on a reduced staff and, Clara said, she and
Lord Hallowhulme were sure Mr. Maslen and Miss Paxton would
be more comfortable here. The cottage was cozier than the castle, more *suitable*, and nearer the estimable Mrs. Mulberry . . .

Winter in Stolnsay. Billie would put seed in the garden beds she'd glimpsed out back and lay straw over the soil, to keep it warm. She'd done it before, in Crickhowell. She'd watched frost scab a seedbed before. But the snow here would fall thicker than she'd ever seen. She imagined it, the white cottage fastened by snow, mortared in its place. For the last few weeks Billie had sat at her piano, watching Minnie's play, and had felt entitled to *play* herself. But she wasn't Minnie, or Ailsa and Anne—she was neither host nor houseguest. And Billie remembered how, that morning, when dressing Alan in his footman's finery, his stuck-on, tufty muttonchops, Minnie had said, "Alan will just have to *do*." Alan would do. Billie would do—and then she'd be done with. Autumn would find her in the cottage, Edith's sister in Edith's place.

She wondered, did Lady Hallowhulme assume that she and Henry would marry? It wasn't an unreasonable assumption—it happened all the time, that a woman took charge of a sister's widower, usually "for the sake of the children." But surely, without children, wasn't it a little improper for Billie to set up house with Henry—Edith's sister in Edith's place?

Billie had never wanted that, and she wasn't sure now that she had ever really wanted Henry. She wondered: What were her feelings for Henry? She hadn't loved him like a brother, or like her sister's husband. She'd loved Henry as Edith had, persuaded by Edith's love. Billie's love began in her empathy with Edith, and continued in her envy. These were, after all, the most intimate ways people had of living other lives, of walking in other shoes—empathy and envy.

Billie brought Henry to mind—Henry on the mend and on the move, active, radiating heat. She had the oddest feeling, as if

both she and Edith had Henry before them, he making a reasonable appeal for the affection that was his due, that he'd done
nothing to lose. But Billie and her sister were suddenly out of
Henry's scale—Edith was too big, swollen with something, her
own death like an undelivered child. And Billie had lost ten years
of her own life, she was the Wilhelmina Paxton who'd stood beside her father's coffin, wiping her nose on her sleeve. This Billie
wasn't a proper companion for Henry. This Billie's only proper
companion, it seemed, was the person she was happiest with, a
person *her own age*, ten-year-old Alan Skilling.

MINNIE HAD LEFT A HANDFUL OF PROGRAMS ON THE HALL
sideboard, and, an hour before dinner, Lord Hallowhulme, his
interest piqued, paid a visit to the theater. As far as he was able to
see, the ballroom was empty. Minnie and the twins were out
gathering heather with which to make a skirt to hide the base of
the stage. The boys were playing cricket. And Alan was foraging
at the gatehouse table—if he didn't coincide with dinner they
kept nothing back for him.

James Hallow arrived with Henry, who was looking for Billie. And Billie saw them, through the overlapping walls of black
gauze that formed Minnie's optically elusive exit. Billie had
come in to try it out, and had, for the umpteenth time, just
stepped out of sight of her reflection in a full-length mirror
which Minnie and Rixon had carried down from Minnie's
dressing room in order to test their effects. The light was right
and Billie was invisible to the men, although she could see them.

James Hallow was reading Minnie's conniving program
notes. He said he wasn't usually a man for plays. To him a play

sometimes seemed just so much polite conversation. "A demonstration of what society is prepared to accept in terms of intimacy and interaction. And yet no play I've seen has managed to provide a practical blueprint or procedure for that kind of unexceptional talk." He mused, then said, "I've tried to protect my children's integrity of character, Mr. Maslen, by periodically removing them from fashionable society. But my daughter, following instincts that are deeply ingrained in her sex, recreates fashionable society—or at least its diversions—here, on the island."

Henry said that although the starry theater curtains certainly looked the part of parlor theatricals, the play itself sounded rather *less* conventional. He paused to examine the angled lid of the piano. He touched its highly polished surface, frowned, tapped his fingertips together, testing tackiness, not dust. Billie had forgotten to wipe her hands when she went from paste pot to keyboard. She had rested her hand, hot, insulated by spilled glue, on the piano's black ice. In her hiding place, Billie put her hand back to touch the taut edge of the gauze behind her and her fingertips, feathered with flaking glue, caught on the cloth. She wondered would she be seen if she moved, if she wove her way into a thicker weight of fake shadow.

"Yes. Unconventional," James Hallow said. "I've already recognized Mr. Shaw as a dramatist with a coordinated philosophy and *some* constructive ideas."

Henry read out the scenes, in order. "A train, second-class coach. A drawing room. A heath. A hearth," then, quietly, "Heaven."

Billie, who knew the play by heart, all its cues, all its lines, knew there was no scene in Heaven. She wanted to step out and take Henry's hand. She saw herself do it, and what she would see if she did, Henry's warm brown eyes across a short space of quiet air. Instead she made herself less visible by slowly raising a hand to gather her hair at her nape and draw the mass of it behind her body. There was a perceptible dimming in the reflected light about her face and she could see more clearly.

James Hallow, inspecting Minnie's footlights, candles in halved tin cans, came closer to the stage. He glanced up and saw Billie. She didn't move, but kept her hand behind her head, elbow cocked, like a marble caryatid. He, too, was still, staring at her. Then he put his hand up to his mouth—and for a moment Billie thought he'd do something gallant, perhaps kiss his hand at her, but instead she saw him biting a knuckle, his nose wrinkled, his eyes squeezed into slits.

On the far side of the room Henry chuckled. He held up a sheet of newspaper and peered through foot-shaped stencil holes. Then his attention was caught by a headline, or the caption of an illustration. He picked up the remainder of the sheets—just scrap paper to the illiterate Billie—folded them and tucked them under his arm. He said they'd know soon enough what kind of play it was. He only hoped the vapor in the glue would be gone from the room by tomorrow night.

IN A WAREHOUSE IN OBAN, MURDO FOUND JAMES'S AUTO-mobile, or rather its replacement. A two-cylinder, chain-driven Panhard et Levassor. It had high wheels for the island's poor roads, spoked yellow wheels, a single Ducellier headlamp, and cream leather button upholstery with removable flat leather seat cushions *sans* buttons.

The man who let Murdo into the warehouse was an agent of the shipping company that had transported the first vehicle, James's factory fittings, and telephone equipment.

The man opened an office and showed Murdo his manifest book. The relevant page—Lord Hallowhulme's component of the *Gustav Edda*'s cargo—gave Murdo no new information. He left it open on the desk, and he and the agent gravitated back to the car. It was a wonderful object, with its multijointed radiator and green-painted steel—a glistening insectile thing.

"Have you ever taken one out?" the agent asked.

Murdo shook his head.

The agent had, and offered pointers. He'd sprained his wrist on a crank handle. You had to be very careful about that. Murdo had seen a car cranked, but hadn't been at leisure to ask about it. The agent was happy to tell him. The crank turned the engine over. "Then it sparks. The fuel and air ignite in the cylinders, and the pistons jump." The man thrust his hands into his pants pockets, rose on his toes. "When I first saw an automobile I thought, erroneously, that it was like cranking a phone. But when you crank a phone you send a small electrical charge down the wire."

The agent jiggled his hands and jingled his coins. Light shivered on his silver watch chain, a visual equivalent of a thin, tittering laugh. Murdo felt encircled, softly touched and coaxed by all the instruments and artifacts in the warehouse. He focused on the crank, an object named for its shape, its angle—crank, crooked, a crevice, a caprice.

Might not a small electrical charge have the same effect upon explosives as fire delivered by a fuse?

◆   ◆   ◆

GEORDIE, IN BED AND PROPPED UP BY PILLOWS, SUR-
rounded by the crackling mass of Ian's letters, had discovered
why he'd not remembered what Ian had first said about Ingrid
Hallow—Ian scarcely ever mentioned her. Ingrid was merely
"well-bred" and "something of a beauty." She was tall but had a
way of ducking her head and looking up under her brows calcu-
lated to make everyone feel they towered over her. In Minnie's
Twelfth Night Ingrid played a passable Olivia. (Minnie, on the
other hand, was a spirited Viola—"But," Ian wrote, "from the
start she tended to render Viola's speeches in a way that empha-
sized their full philosophical reverberations. She asked, 'What
country, friend, is this?' and I found myself looking at Lord
Hallowhulme.")

It wasn't until Geordie reached the letter written the day after the drowning that he felt—regarding Ingrid Hallow—he was
back in the company of the brother he knew, the sympathetic,
fully alert Ian. He read, he followed his brother's painstaking reasoning, as Ian tried to work out what had happened. Why was
Ingrid at Scouse Beach alone? How did she get into the water?

There was scarcely a mark on her body. She was found only
a few hours after she drowned, rolled up onto the smooth beach
and left by a retreating tide. The people who found her saw no
bruises or abrasions. She hadn't slipped from a rock and knocked
herself silly. She hadn't struggled; all her buttons were still fastened. They found her shoes above the high-tide mark. She'd
been paddling, perhaps.

Lord Hallowhulme called in a coroner from Edinburgh.
Clara's maid Jenny said to Ian, "He wants to know whether Miss
Ingrid suffered." But other servants were already talking about
suicide. Ingrid had been on the beach earlier in the day—had
accompanied her brother and her father, his cousin, and an

engineer, to the spit at the end of Scouse Beach. She'd asked to come for the exercise. They let her help hammer in some boundary pegs—Lord Hallowhulme planned to build a factory at Scouse. He had some scheme, some process to extract a perfect food from seaweed. The men were there about men's business, and Rixon had taken to following Mr. Hesketh. Ingrid's presence was odd, unlikely. The party returned to the castle for lunch. For some reason Ingrid went back. The cook told Ian that Miss Ingrid hadn't dined with the family—she'd not felt well, and Lady Hallow had a syllabub sent up to her. "My syllabub," the cook said. "Lemon, cream, sugar, and Madeira whipped to a froth."

"The recipe is now enshrined in the cook's mind," Ian wrote, "and is what she always tenders in talk about *poor Miss Ingrid*, like a newspaper account of a condemned man's last meal." The syllabub was returned uneaten—the cook's previously infallible temptation to invalids. Ian wrote, "The cook implies that, after rejecting her syllabub, Ingrid's obvious next step was to renounce living." Lady Hallowhulme was concerned about her daughter—Ian wrote—and had looked in on Ingrid after lunch. Nothing further was known, not when Ingrid left the castle, nor how she reached the beach. "Mr. Hesketh says she walked," Ian wrote. "But I will not ask him what he and his cousin James and the boy Rixon have probably all been asked: 'Did anything occur that morning to upset her?' We all assume someone hurt her, and Lord Hallowhulme then compounded the gossip by sending to Edinburgh for a coroner."

The more audible talk was all of the perils of bathing on a full belly, or fatigue and an empty one. "Mr. Hesketh doesn't say anything. I wasn't with him that day. I was plying my iron over his shirts, about which he's so particular, and for the sake of which I've incurred the hostility of the laundress.

"Mr. Hesketh doesn't say a thing," Ian wrote. "He doesn't speculate. Everyone else does. I went into town the other day and talked to a man I know—Duncan Macleod—he told me that Ingrid Hallow's shoes were found just above the heap of charcoal where Mr. Hesketh had made a fire for tea that morning. When I asked Mr. Hesketh if this was true—that she'd left her shoes right where she'd had tea that same morning—he told me that Ingrid fetched driftwood for him when he built the fire.

"I can almost see them, Geordie, Mr. Hesketh putting up a fine fretwork of dried black seaweed over balled newspaper, taking wax matches out of the flat silver box in which he carries them. Ingrid is busy, her hands are full. Is she unhappy? If she's so very unhappy, why is she helping Mr. Hesketh build a fire, why isn't she at home with her head rested on her mother's knee?"

Ian didn't see Ingrid's parents until the funeral. Clara was destroyed. "She'd been in full bloom, now she's a papery flower whose color has bled into the pages between which it is pressed. But no—that's too poetic. It was the way she walked—abruptly old, unoiled, seized up. Whatever it is that has stiffened her, it's not temporary, not condensation, but like the deposit of lime on the sides of a drinking glass. Lord Hallowhulme's appearance was less shocking. He was drawn, black about the eyes, but for once his eyes didn't shy about, as evasive as one of those shining afterimages of a poorly shaded lamp that always darts away when you look—away, away—always to one side of your gaze. All through the graveside service Lord Hallowhulme looked into faces, as attentive as a deaf mute."

For five letters Kiss was called "the sad house." There was no more *matter* about Ingrid Hallow—until this: "She was like *him*—only quieter, unworldly, content to listen to a family who planned and bossed, or rollicked (Rixon), or tended ordinary motherly advice: 'Perhaps a hat with a closer weave, dear, the sun has real heat today.' But still, Geordie, she was more *like him* than the rest of them, like the Murdo Hesketh I knew before his ruin. There was her openness, easily mistaken for simplicity; and her animal confidence, easily mistaken for vanity; and an enjoyment of luxury easily mistaken for inertia or superficiality. I thought Ingrid was a nice, beautiful, slightly banal young woman. Perhaps I thought that because she couldn't act—neither can her sister, but Minnie is pungent with life force. I thought that—and now I think that she *did* walk into the water at Scouse Beach, meaning to die, and resolute in her death."

Then, a further three letters on, this: "Before Ingrid Hallow died there had been signs of a thaw, a shine of ice grown slick in the sun, but he's now taken himself farther north, and wrapped himself up in coldness."

ON THE STEAMER ON HIS RETURN, MURDO ENCOUNTERED the *Gustav Edda*'s surviving steward. The man delivered tea to Murdo's cabin. He recognized Murdo and asked, "How do you do now, Mr. Hesketh?"

"Very well," Murdo said. "And you?"

The steward said he was quite over his bout of pleurisy. The company kept him when he was ill. "The insurers paid *our* compensation in any case."

However, he said, he had parted ways with his former employers. He planned, by changing ships, to work his way farther south before the winter. He reckoned it was see some sun, or be done for.

As Murdo listened, and the steward made passes with the hem of his apron around the edges of the tray, Murdo remembered the fellow doing this, going around the edge of a table in the little salon where the seamen had been fed, scrubbing away, squinting at his handiwork, folding the cloth to find a cleaner patch and rubbing some more. Murdo wanted to work the talk around to a lost set of cabin keys and a basin full of beard hair, so said, "Tell me, did you service the cabins on the *Gustav Edda*? I seem to recall seeing you serving in the seamen's mess."

"We both did everything, mess and cabins. Me and Alfred, God rest him. I was on at eight bells. Came on at five. I was still washing up in the galley when the ship reached port. That's why I'm alive and Alfred isn't. I was slow that day because the purser complained about the tables. It was because of the black gang. They always came to the table without doing much more than making a pass of a dirty cloth over their dirty hands—God rest them, too. By the time they finished their meal the table would be as edged with black as a widow's letter."

Murdo had idly watched the steward, his furious, finicky scrubbing. Murdo should have been on the windward side, where Miss Paxton was, to see Macleod and the pilot emerge from the hold. He was sure he'd have been a better judge of what there was to be seen. He asked, "Was it you the Swede came to tell he'd lost his cabin keys?"

"Yes. And I told the insurance fellow that I thought the Swede only did that in order to convince me he was on board when it sailed. In fact, he left the ship at Luag. He shaved off his beard, you see."

"Would you know him if you saw him again?"

The man nodded, said that *that* was why the company wanted him to keep them posted as to his whereabouts. "They're not bothering with the police, Mr. Hesketh, they've just kept the disability going although I'm on my feet again. They know I'll keep collecting as long as they don't stop the payments. I warned them that the money might—what's the word—*scotch* their case."

"Compromise," said Murdo.

"Aye. That's the word. I'm a bit of a sea lawyer, and that's what I told them."

ON THE LAST DAY OF JULY, WHEN MINNIE'S PLAY WAS DUE to be performed, Murdo arrived at Luag. He spoke to the foreman of the warehouse that briefly stored James's factory and exchange equipment. He spoke to the stevedores who had loaded that cargo. He learned nothing new.

Several hours before his sailing Murdo delivered the package of tweed to Gutthorm's aunt. He found the old lady weeding her window boxes. She asked him to please carry the packet indoors for her. "I wouldn't want to sully it," she said, looking with cupidity at the brown paper as much as its contents. She asked, "You will take tea, Mr. Hesketh?" then went away to wash her hands and rouse her girl.

Murdo was tired, and happy to be fed. He polished off three scones and three boiled eggs and let the old lady work her way around to the subject of the relative worth of Murdo Hesketh and Johan Gutthorm. She was proud of her nephew—Lord Hallowhulme's man of business, at work, or play. Obviously Gutthorm had managed to communicate to his aunt his opinion—that Kissack and Skilling was *play*, whereas London, Edinburgh, and Port Clarity were *business*. She clearly thought of Murdo as the manager of Hallowhulme's island estate, but not a manager who had to do with practical matters like land in pasture and tonnages of wool. Her nephew Gutthorm, on the other hand, closely involved in the affairs of a great man, was himself great by proxy. He must be, since only greatness could compensate his aunt for his increasing neglect of her, his only relative.

Murdo, tranquilized by tiredness, by tea, flour, and butter, was still able to detect this complaint in the old woman's boasting. Now and again, to console herself, she patted the rolled bolt of tweed. Her nephew had *remembered* her. She told Murdo that she'd had a supper to celebrate her seventieth birthday. She hadn't meant to put Johan out—after all he had been in Luag on business. The plan was that he'd come to supper—stay the night—and set out in the morning overland to Dorve, to meet Lord Hallowhulme's English cataloguer and that cataloguer's wife, and see them safely from Dorve to Southport, then overland to Stolnsay. "You see, Johan expected them to wait out the rough weather. The man's wife was in an interesting condition," the aunt added. "Her comfort was an important consideration." Johan had been, from boyhood, quite unusually precise in his habits, punctual and reliable. But on her birthday he had arrived late. A whole forty minutes late. The old lady gestured at the clock on her mantelpiece, a clock from a previous century, with a crazed porcelain face, once yellow perhaps, now browned like mustard left out too long in the air. The face was hand painted, with hunters and harvesters, with girls a-maying and a snowy village street—the four seasons, in fact. Murdo contemplated this clock and remembered Minnie's play, which she said she'd chosen with him in mind—with him, *too*. What could the girl be meaning to try to tell him? Or did Minnie only want to cheer

him up—in her father's way—with something uplifting and in-
spirational. Then Murdo thought of Billie Paxton—how deliberate she'd been, how dignified, determined only to get him to
do what she wanted, to run her message.

Alan's shoes! Murdo started from his chair. "Is that the time?
Are all the shops closed?"

Gutthorm's aunt gasped and reeled back, her corset crackling
in counterpoint to her breath. She got up. "Yes, as I said, that
clock always keeps *correct time.*"

"There's something I must do," Murdo said. He hurried
to the door. Gutthorm's aunt followed him. She snapped her
fingers at the maid who dived for his hat.

"I was sure you must have *finished* your business before coming to me," said Gutthorm's aunt, as if she stood accused of wast-
ing Murdo's time.

"I had another favor not connected to my business. It slipped
my mind. Please excuse me." Murdo took his hat, coat, and
gloves from the maid, a mousy girl whose bobbing curtsy was
more like a flinch. Murdo thanked Gutthorm's aunt and hurried out.

The shops were all shut.

IN PREPARATION FOR THE PERFORMANCE BILLIE HAD
only to put on her best clothes and dress her hair. An hour before curtain she came downstairs carrying the six boards, stiff
with glue, on which she had mapped out, in her personal code,
her cues—thumbnail sketches of scenes, or sometimes of only a
gesture, all underlined in colored inks.

In the ballroom Billie found Minnie, Rixon, the Tegners,
and Elov. Minnie and Rixon were in costume, the Tegners were

greasy with unblended paint. Elov was dressed, and drunk. He was sitting on the floor, his boots unlaced. The others were trying to get him up and out into the garden, where they hoped the cold air would revive him. Billie thought "revive" was the wrong word—Elov wasn't inert, but resistant. And he was loud. He shouted that he would not, *could* not, say that line. "How can you expect me to just stand up and throw it in his teeth?" He flung out an arm, striking Ailsa Tegner in the chest. "Minnie thinks she can do any mortal thing she chooses," he said. He turned to Minnie, overbalanced, and came down on his elbow. He complained, "You're just like him." Then, in a false, declamatory tone, not at all like his delivery in the rehearsals, but perhaps as he thought Minnie really intended it, he said the line, scornful, self-righteous, and amplified: *"Goodwin's hospitality is only a pretext for propaganda."*

Geordie came in behind Billie, said, "Oh dear," and sent her out for some bread and milk from the kitchen. Something to soak up the brandy. As Billie went she saw that, despite his age and slightness, Geordie was stronger than the young people. He got Elov up and led him out into the garden.

WHEN NOT ONSTAGE GEORDIE HAD WAITED BEHIND THE black gauze of Minnie's secret entrance. He'd been able to watch the audience.

Lord Hallowhulme began the evening with an intrusive appearance of attention. He didn't like to sit still and listen. He liked to make himself felt. His attention was so positive it was almost participation. "Hear! Hear!" he cried once, at a speech about the need for a society led by energetic enthusiasts. He chortled and squirmed. He suppressed his urge to interrupt insofar as he remained in the auditorium and in his seat. But in several of the play's quieter moments Geordie could clearly hear James Hallow's loud, dry sniffing.

It was a mannerism Geordie had noticed on a number of earlier occasions. Compelled to listen, James Hallow would sit and sniff. At first Geordie had supposed that his nose was bothering him and he'd forgotten he was in company. Finally, he realized it was only Lord Hallowhulme's way of saying, "I could add something here"—"I know more than you do."

Hallowhulme squirmed and sniffed and laughed as if meaning to *lead* the laughter. He never did—he was always a beat behind the more moderate amusement of others—but laughed louder, and longer.

Two-thirds of the way through the play, after a sad passage of Billie's music, Hallowhulme fell quiet. He stopped attending to the play and watched only Billie, who sat with her hands folded and head raised to follow the action onstage, ready for her next cue. Billie's face and hair were lit by the branch of candles that stood behind her, low enough for their flames to cast a clear light on her music, but make no shining haze in the air through which she might have trouble seeing the stage. In the candlelight Billie wasn't a Rossetti or a Burne-Jones—specific, ornate, wholly apparent, features and costume and background all equal in weight— she was an old devotional painting, softly luminescent.

After the applause Hallowhulme set up his camera and photographed the cast, onstage, Billie sitting on the edge of the stage between footlights and the skirts of ferns and heather. Then the actors posed in *tableaux vivants* of several key scenes, and the second-class rail coach was reassembled from cardboard walls and curtained windows, its leather seats salvaged from

Hallowhulme's automobile. Hallowhulme emerged from the black skirts of his camera in time to see Billie led out of the room by Henry. He called after them, "Remember that there's a supper, Mr. Maslen."

The Mulberrys were making their excuses to Clara—they couldn't stay. They thanked the players and, as they left, they remarked to Hallowhulme how *proud* a parent he must be—such a good performance of such a *creditable* play. The Mulberrys left and Hallowhulme said to Geordie, who was nearby, "One would imagine a minister more sensitive to the social uses of the word 'good.' " The remark was self-confidently dismissive, but Hallowhulme had that look he often wore, the strained expression of someone hard of hearing, or poor in understanding.

Minnie appeared and took Geordie's arm. "Come in to supper, Mr. Betler," she said, a brisk hostess for the benefit of her mother. Then, quieter, "I know what the caption will be for the group photograph: *'Fortune and the Four Winds, by George Bernard Shaw. Kiss Castle, summer, 1903. My house party, who number twelve individuals.'* " She said, "Did he listen, do you think? I don't think he did. When he listens he always shows his top teeth. Look"—pointing at her father's strained expression— "he's listening now."

THE SHEET OF NEWSPAPER FROM WHICH BILLIE HAD CUT the outline of Alan's feet, was from an Edinburgh paper, dated June 4. It was part of an article about the sinking of the *Gustav Edda*. In it Henry had read—around the holes—that a passenger who had embarked at Luag in the company of her sister and her sister's husband had been seen to jump from ship to shore only moments before the explosion that sank the vessel at its moorings. Henry read that this person had declined to speak to journalists.

"Lord Hallowhulme declined on my behalf," Billie told Henry. "I wasn't aware that a newspaper wanted to speak to me."

They stood at the seawall below the long lawn. The evening was overcast. It was after nine, but the sky was the even white it had been since morning. From this angle the town appeared compact, low, no land visible behind it. Built on a spit, spiked with gabled roofs, chimneys, and steeples, Stolnsay looked like a "mariner's elevation," a drawing on white parchment, flat and diagrammatic, and all exaggerated horizontals. Billie stared at this belt of buildings and streets. She didn't want to look at Henry. Her hand stole into her pocket and closed around the plaited pigskin button she carried—*always* carried, transferring it from garment to garment when she changed her clothes. She said, "Do you remember now, Henry?"

"I guessed, dear. I don't remember." He touched her sleeve. He said, "We were always together, Billie. All of us." Henry said that for weeks he'd hoped to remember. He felt that, if he didn't, he wouldn't be much help to her. "It's been more your burden than mine, Billie. What actually *happened*, as well as its aftermath. And, because you remember, you must feel that we are at fault. But, Billie, please listen—"

She shied away from him. He touched one finger to the raised mound of bone on her wrist, and she stopped still.

"It was a *mistake*. A mistake easy to make. It seemed only natural. We were always together. We were together, and we kept to ourselves too much—you, me, and Edith. *Your* remedy was company."

"Yours was Edith," Billie said. Henry was being kind and his kindness was inadequate.

"Please tell me if I'm mistaken!" Henry begged. "What did I do? I need to know. I think I know myself, and what I *would* do. Is it something worse?"

"Worse than a kiss?" Billie said. Edith, drowning, had clung to her husband, and he'd torn himself out of her grasp. Billie had kept the button in order to share it with him. Day after day she'd touched it with her hand and told herself she was sparing him. But she had only been waiting to spare him no more.

Billie took her hand out of her pocket, the button closed in her fingers. She stepped up to the seawall and threw it. It was light even in its flight, more like an acorn than a pebble. It made a splash, then bobbed up in the center of its ring of ripples and floated. Billie told Henry that it was a hazelnut she'd had in her pocket. "Too stale to eat," she said.

The evening was beginning to seem very strange to Billie. It seemed that only what was harmful had any weight, that truth was money, kindness only a token in money's shape—like the tokens Billie's father had bought her and Edith to spend on the rides at a carnival in Marseilles. The tokens were only for the rides. Edith would rather have had a fringed silk scarf, but couldn't buy back her money.

The button was harmless now—impossible to exchange. Billie watched it bob in the slight current of retreating tide. She remembered how Mr. Betler hadn't let her unwrap the bundle in the coffin with Edith. Without looking himself he'd known what it was. He'd put his arms around her to hold her back, because truth was knowing, but kindness was knowing better than to tell.

Billie gave Henry her hand—he'd asked for it. As they walked slowly back up the lawn Henry told her that, although they'd spend the coming winter in Stolnsay, Lord Hallowhulme had asked him if he'd like to replace Johan Gutthorm. Mr. Gutthorm had given his notice. "Family responsibilities, apparently," Henry said. Then, "I'm assured it's all on friendly terms." It was a great opportunity, Henry said. All his life he had schooled himself to accept work of little—or incalculable—influence. He was a teacher or a cataloguer. But, as Lord Hallowhulme's secretary, he'd have work that was varied and challenging, and a more *worldly* life than he had ever dreamed he'd have. "I'll live in London and Edinburgh. I can see you settled somewhere comfortable, like Port Clarity. And, Billie, you can meet people, make a broader acquaintance. You can choose whom to befriend."

"Choose whom to kiss," Billie said.

There was a hitch in Henry's stride. He squeezed her hand. "You should have a choice." Then he went on to say something Billie couldn't quite follow. He said that Edith chose him, but he was her only choice. He knew that Billie could never get far enough away from Edith to sense Edith's *size*. But he had come to understand that Edith was immense—very strong, and beautiful in a way that made her out of place everywhere she was *able* to be.

But Billie *could* see it now, could see Edith stalking over the sliding litter of broken floor tiles that made the beach at Garavan, her shawl shading her head. Billie's beach friends—some Edith's age—falling silent and, if they were tussling, apparently fainting out of their tangles, and lying still, speckled with grit, staring at Edith. It was her sister's scowl, Billie had always thought. But really it was Edith's beauty—scowl, shawl, flapping shade—Edith's density and size, what Billie sensed now when she was puzzled by how to *be* Edith.

"Edith loved me," Henry said. "But she was poor in choices."

Henry meant that Edith was better than they were. And he was saying *be patient. Wait*—but not for him.

They were below the west face of the castle. Above them the glass in its leaded windows shone like a cliff of white scales. In the sky there were two visible streams of cloud, many thousands of feet apart and moving in different directions. One rind of sky wound against the other and reflected in the west windows in sections, in separate panes, a movement of mismatched instants, as if some bits of the whole real world were destined to catch, or falter, or wind down before the rest.

"We should go in," Henry said.

Billie thought: *I should kiss you.* She put her palm against his face, her fingertips forming a grille over his ear, the heel of her hand on his jaw, his springy side whiskers. His skin was soft, and a little tacky to the touch. Its exact temperature reminded Billie of another warmth, and for a minute Billie was adrift, she was in a room that plunged and kicked, her hand on Edith's forehead, wiping Edith's mouth; she was by the ladder with Henry; she was cold and wet, struggling free of a clammy grip not because it was clammy, but because through his wet clothes a specific warmth had surfaced and her own had jumped out to meet it.

Henry put his hand over her own, pressed it briefly, then pulled it down, cheerful, like someone detaching an overexcited kitten from a curtain. He said he'd stay out here for a time.

"I'll stay with you," she said. But it was like trying to pull herself out of water on the air. She couldn't get any purchase. Henry said she should go in.

Billie went in, and upstairs. Three steps below the landing she raised her head and saw a massive shadow, a silhouette, a head with a squared beard, like a trenching tool on a thick haft. Lord Hallowhulme said to her that he thought she was very good.

"Thank you, sir," she said.

He put a hand on her arm. Heavy but unstable, it twitched rather than trembled. He drew her toward him, so that she could smell sherry, cigar, the orange flower water in his hair or beard. He meant to show her something. Below them, on the terrace, Henry still stood where she had left him. James Hallow took Billie's hand and lifted it to his own cheek. He put her hand on his face in a position that corresponded to where she had touched Henry's a moment before. Billie felt a smaller ear, sleeker beard, the bone in James Hallow's blunt jaw.

Billie removed her hand, but he kept her fingertips trapped between his own. No more proper, but less alarming, he kissed her hand. It was ordinary gallantry and had as predictable a trajectory as investigations by the San Remo ragazzi of her nine-year-old knees. There was no boat to overturn, though, and it seemed to Billie that her only available defensive gesture was to return the kiss. Because Henry hadn't wanted to be kissed.

Billie jumped up against her host like a steep wave against stonework. He was tall, so she set her foot on the toe of his blocky boot, got enough elevation, and rose in and up to his face.

He gasped and jerked back as if expecting her to bite him. They both overbalanced and his elbow knocked a pane of glass and shoved it, whole, out of its lead. It fell onto the terrace beside Henry. Billie put both her hands against James Hallow's chest and, launching herself off him, found her feet and clambered away upstairs.

◆ ◆ ◆

MINNIE OBSERVED TO GEORDIE THAT BILLIE HADN'T come back for her slice of cake. "I saved one for her."

Minnie had taken down her playbill. The servants were clearing the tables and carrying away the screens. Alan had finished everything around Billie's saved slice, even clearing the crumbs from plates, pressing them flat and licking them off his fingers.

Minnie asked Alan if he would go and see what had become of Billie.

It was a long while before Alan came back. The servants had gone to their beds. Geordie and Minnie were alone, in an island of candlelight by the ballroom door. Minnie had been talking to Geordie about Ingrid. Or about *after* Ingrid. After Ingrid, Minnie had found it almost impossible to let her brother out of her sight. She was a sore trial to him. But their father insisted that Rixon go away to school. *This* summer was the longest she and her brother had been together for two years.

Alan returned and stood by the cake. The cake was on the seat of a chair drawn up by Geordie and Minnie. Alan was pale, Geordie saw, and his eyelashes were in glistening spikes. "I couldn't find her," he muttered. Then, more audible, but dull, "She must have gone to bed." He hovered, then he asked, "Can I have her cake?"

"Of course," Minnie said. She told him she was sure Mr. Betler wanted his bed. She was about to turn in, and Alan should carry the cake away.

Alan broke the cake in two and put it in either pocket of the made-over jacket that was his costume. He ran out without saying good night.

◆ ◆ ◆

BILLIE TRAVELED ALL NIGHT—AT THE TRACES OF MINNIE'S
trap, Kirsty in harness—and all the next morning, slower. She
managed not to run the trap into a ditch. By afternoon they
were twenty miles from Southport, on the inland road and near a
ruined abbey. Kirsty had stopped, up to her hocks in a burn,
when Billie saw two horsemen on the farthest rise of the rolling
strip of road, coming toward her, going one before the other, as
if the road were too narrow, or they didn't know each other—
were one traveler about to overtake another—or as if they were
companions who'd had a falling-out.

12 ❧ COMING TO GRIEF

MIDAFTERNOON, FROM A HIGH ROAD THAT FOLLOWED the kinked spine of the island, the men saw a black line appear on the horizon, definite, like a lead join in a stained-glass window. The line was the shadow of a thick rain cloud and, before long, a squall swept across that end of the island. Behind the men Southport vanished, its terraced streets and white houses. The corrugated-iron structure of the cannery reappeared for a moment, whitely haloed with rebounding rain.

Murdo turned up the collar of his summer coat and looked back at Rory Skilling, whom he'd met just outside Southport, where its streets turned into road at the top of the town. Murdo had kicked his horse to catch up, and Rory turned with a look of plain friendliness and inquiry. Then his face fell. He said: "Mr. Hesketh, you're expected at Stolnsay!"

Rory had explained why he was at Southport—to look over the cannery. Mr. Hesketh surely remembered that Lord Hallowhulme had offered Rory a manager's job? Rory *hadn't* tried to explain his initial dismay at their unexpected encounter. Murdo was sure that even after his display the other day—of indignation at being left behind—Rory wasn't happy to see him, and didn't really want to ride with him. But they were both bound for Stolnsay, and the road took them along together.

There was another road, the new one James had built, not in its entirety, but connecting several dots and dashes between villages at the heads of the East Coast sea lochs. This road—inclusive, meandering—appeared several times far below them, occasionally linked to their way by a node of houses, a solitary chapel, or a ruined keep. From time to time Murdo glanced at Rory to see if the man would make his excuses and take the other road, but Rory couldn't seem to see his way out of Murdo's company, any more than he looked to his employer for conversation as they went along.

The rain came and made enough noise between them. They passed a herd of red cows and the cattleman, his hat the brimming lip of a fountain.

Later, the sun reappeared, the road steamed, and the turf began to talk, to tick and wheeze. They climbed a long narrow valley beside a burn. The watercourse was at its summer level, and soon absorbed the rain, running with no more sound than the bands of slickness that crossed the road between burn and rock outcrops. The rocks and road gleamed as if greased. It was close in the valley, humid, and whenever the sun wavered midges appeared and pursued the riders. Murdo's hair began to lift as it dried. He felt the heat tampering with it, like admiring fingers. He thought of Clara, of being appreciated, and at a close proximity. He thought of the limits on the intimacy he'd enjoyed with Ian Betler. Ian, who was always at his elbow. Murdo considered Rory, whose eyes he could feel on the back of his head. Was this appreciation? It did seem a kind of covetousness. Rory coveted something about him, as Ian had coveted the air between them, the distance he kept, the space he hadn't dared cross.

Murdo dropped back. Looking at Rory he saw avid attention, and that Rory was touching his teeth together over and over behind sealed lips, not as if chewing, but as a kitten's jaw will tremble as it stalks a fly.

I must speak to him, Murdo thought. *I must clear this up.* Perhaps he could show Alan's shoes to Rory. Murdo touched the bag strapped to his saddle. He felt the bulge of a shoe heel. But the shoes might be a reproach to Rory—even more of a reproach than Billie's unfilled commission had been to Murdo, who had stayed away another day, missed his passage to Stolnsay, and sailed from Dorve to Southport instead.

"Rory—?" Murdo began.

But Rory looked past him, frowning.

Some distance away, where the road swerved toward the ruin of Ormabeg Abbey, there was a horse in harness to a small trap. A *small* horse.

"That's Kirsty and Miss Minnie's trap," Rory said. Then, irritable, "God save us!"

They went on, picked up the pace some. The sun came fully clear of cloud, a sleepy wave of warmth.

Kirsty was cropping at the edge of the road, tender grass, not tussock. Her nose was wet and coated with grit like coffee grounds. Rory dismounted and went a short way toward the ruin, calling his son.

Three fledgling plover shot up out of the heather, went in a wide circle fussing, unbusinesslike, still only practicing fear.

Rory stopped still, stood listening.

Murdo leaned down to see the bag between the seats in the trap. It was old, the surface of its leather crazed with dusty gray cracks. Its owner was a T. P. Paxton.

A tide of shadow started after the men from the south, came making a meal of hilltops and hurrying into hollows.

Murdo stood on his stirrups, looked around at the heath, road, ruin, Rory on the track to it, calling, not anxious, but in the way someone calls when they enter a house they hope is empty.

Murdo took off his coat and draped it over the trap's seat, concealing the bag. Then he dismounted, applied the trap's brake, and looped his reins there to tether his horse.

He caught up with Rory on the tumbled stones heaped by one of the arched eye sockets of the abbey's main nave. Within the shelter of the ruin grew fuchsia bushes, thickly flowered now, in August.

"There is no one," Murdo said. "Who knows how far Kirsty has wandered."

Rory rounded on him. "My son is none of your business! Alan is none of your business!" He was savage.

Murdo stepped back, his foot turned, and a stone clattered down the pile and fell with a hissing thump into the bracken.

Rory went on speaking, but not to Murdo. He spoke to the air, to the roofless nave, to bees wandering among the red and pink pendant blossoms. "I will be wed," he said. "I will be made. A wealthy man." It was as if he was setting out reasons to the still, sunny space of the nave. And Murdo, who hated to be forced back even a step, shrugged, and turned to pick his way back down the piled stones.

He felt the silence consolidate behind him, and looked back—so that the clubbing stone fell on his shoulder blade and not his skull.

◆　◆　◆

AS SHE LISTENED FOR THE HORSES, BILLIE BECAME SLEEPY. The heather was a damp but resilient bed. If they found her, she'd rather they believed she was sleeping, not hiding. The violet-striped silk dress was in her bag. Lord Hallowhulme had wanted her to wear it—had wanted to see her in it. She remembered his lips and the smell of his beard. She turned her head to brush her mouth back and forth on the aromatic heather. Perhaps she *was* asleep, supine on the flank of a big animal whose heart was beating through her own. If Mr. Hesketh opened the bag the dress would foam up. She saw it, glossy, costly, really scarcely even hers—worn only twice—foaming up, as if still partly filled with her flesh, into his gloved hands. She thought she heard it, a hiss of decompression. She thought she understood James Hallow's gift—a man can keep track of a woman who wears silk.

Then she did hear the horses. Rory Skilling called, "Alan!" She heard his boots in the mud, then his calling moved away. Several minutes later she knew they were up at the ruin, on the far side of the road from her. She heard Rory raise his voice to Mr. Hesketh.

There was a pause. Then a thump, stones grating together, the fall of something not stony—of something bony and articulate.

Billie lifted her head. She saw Murdo Hesketh head down and faceup on a slope of piled stones, his hands raised. She saw Rory in the arched window, one arm uplifted, like St. Michael the Archangel above a prostrate Satan.

Billie sprang out of the heather and blundered to the road. She dropped behind the cart and peered through its wheels.

Hesketh deflected the flung stone and rolled heels over head off the broken wall. Rory leapt after him. Before Hesketh found his feet Rory was on top of him, holding him down by his throat and casting about for another stone. Then he had one. But

Hesketh slowed the blow—didn't prevent it, there was something amiss with his braced shaking arm. His shirt cuff was torn and soaked red.

Clawing at the cart, only agitated, without intention, Billie pulled down Hesketh's coat. It slid onto her knees and something dropped out of its pocket, knocked against the spokes of the wheel, and fell with a clang onto a jutting rock in the road. Only an instant in the sun and it was already warm. Then it was in her hand—hot and heavy. She scrambled out from behind the trap, ran across the road, and up the path to the abbey. Her dress had a wider gait than she, and caught in the bracken so that she was wading through cloth more than heath. She wasn't quiet— but they couldn't hear her. They were in a grunting struggle. Then she heard a hollow crack, a groaning gasp, and only one man breathing. Rory had his back to her; he had straddled Mr. Hesketh. She saw his whole body heave as he breathed, saw one fist move slowly to his side, fastidious, a dark separation between each of his fingers, blood seeping from the rock—it seemed— the rock dripping. Rory dropped it and thrust himself off Hesketh. For a moment he held his hands, palms curled, only an inch from his own chest, then he looked down at them, one soaked, the other sprayed red. He remembered evidence of guilt, or perhaps that his jacket was new, and didn't wipe them. He raised the worst hand to his face, dropped his jaw, put out his tongue, perhaps to groom the blood away. Then he noticed Billie.

Billie saw light alive still in the pure fall of Hesketh's hair— and she saw blood pooled in his ear. Then she saw him move. Rory saw it, too, made a sound between whine and howl, and flung himself after his dropped stone.

"No!" Billie yelled. She went forward, her arms straight out before her, a water diviner, but her wand—a gun—waving loose, not yet coming to the point. Billie stumbled, squeezed the trigger, and heard a click as the hammer hit an empty chamber. A spring, a mechanism in the gun, turned the cylinder. Billie watched it roll around as if pushed by invisible fingers.

Hesketh moved. He turned his head. The blood, already viscous, trembled against its own skin at the rim of his ear, then oozed down into his hair. Rory's eyes flicked sideways to take in this movement—then returned to Billie. He made hushing motions. *Don't wake him.* He had the rock in his hand again, wrapped in its blood-varnished scabs of lichen.

"No," Billie said. She squeezed the trigger again and the gun leapt backward and bit her—she thought—at the base of her thumb. She was knocked over, her whole body following her wrist, and a pain like a mooring line that was pulling something vast in toward the firm earth. Billie crouched, crying, and looked at her hand. Her thumb was bent back toward her wrist, white between base and wrist, white with pressure, permanently pinched. She couldn't move her thumb; it felt dead. She shook her hand, as if to dislodge the stark thumb. For a moment the joint was frozen, then she shook it back into place—another sharp pain that settled into a throb. Aubergine bruises began to rise from within the joint and burst onto her skin, like a stain soaking through. Billie couldn't stand to watch it. She sat and wrapped her hand in her skirts.

The men were motionless. Billie heard a whispering, the gossiping commentary of wind in bracken and heather. She thought she heard flies, hundreds of them, among the dark timbers of the pitched roof of Stolnsay Kirk. Her ears had refused the sound when she first heard it, weeks earlier. Now she remembered it perfectly. Then she registered what she really had to hear, the rattle of the trap's wheels. Hesketh's horse, tethered to the brake handle, had reared, raising the whole trap a foot from the road. The trap dropped, the brakes disengaged and Kirsty bolted, the trap and Hesketh's horse going along behind. Billie watched them go, Rory Skilling's horse following at a more sedate pace.

It began to rain again, this time in a thin drizzle, a mist that came across the bogland in yellow curds. The sun was low, on its gradual downward roll along the tops of the mountains. The drizzle settled, and thickened leaves, stems, the folds of Billie's skirt. She watched it silver Hesketh's black waistcoat.

His long, black overcoat was on the road. Billie went to get it, picked it up, and put it on. She was unable to turn up the sleeves to free her good hand. She tried, rubbing her forearms together. Then she stopped what she was doing and looked back.

Rory Skilling was standing behind her. He said, "Where is it? Where is the gun?" Or rather Billie understood him to say that, though the sounds were quite different. Rory had changed. His eyetooth and its neighbor were smashed, his top lip was torn all the way up to his cheekbone, over which the flesh was furrowed, like a fissure in a cake baked too quickly, or at too high a heat. The white of one eye was red, a window to a chamber flooded with blood.

Billie picked up the split tail of the coat and walked backward. Rory followed. As he came on, he cast about for the gun. A number of times he lunged at her, but his balance was impaired, and he lurched to one side, one shoulder drooping as though he dragged a weight. Billie couldn't turn and hurry, she had to keep him under her eye, so she circled, glancing behind her only to check the state of the ground. She crept backward, and Rory shambled after her. They kept an equal distance, like dance partners. Then Billie saw his figure begin to lose color, to fade, become thin and gray, like the shadow cast by a secondary light source. Rory disappeared. The yellow cast left the air, which grew cold. Billie stared. The mist licked her eyeballs, and insinuated the tip of its forked tongue into her nostrils. She stood still and listened, but the limping rustle was everywhere. A scrape, breath bubbling through thickening blood.

They listened to each other.

Billie was fume, she was something unknown, she was air leavening submerged sand. If he didn't step on her, she wouldn't breathe. She would stay put. She would leave later. She would wait for the open air.

Billie heard Rory lunge and blunder on. Had he seen her, or only a momentary change in the consistency of the mist? She ran, facefirst, the tails of Hesketh's coat fidgeting after her, each little catch like imminent capture, like a hand rising out of the heath.

Billie *saw* a hand. It was long, bare, and had a bloodied cuff. She stopped beside Hesketh, not just her only human company, but her only landmark. She sank down beside him, took cover by his body. After a moment she noticed a regular stirring, the rise and fall of his chest. She was afraid to look, so lifted her face to watch her own fingers walk up his shoulder, where the black wool of his waistcoat was still silver-beaded, resisting water. His shirt was soaked, his skin showing pink through it. There was blood on his collar. Her hand crept behind his neck to pull the stud. She pulled his collar away and unfastened a button or two. The shirt was torn where it wasn't reinforced, open already in a rent where threads were mashed into a bloodied contusion in the hollow where his shoulder joined his chest. Billie's breath came in shallow jumps. She focused on her hands, laid them on his bare bloody throat. She felt pulses—carotid and jugular, in fact—but to her more than one life, or one life and the possibility of several more. She looked into his face, took an instant inventory: jaw, lips, nose, cheekbones, eyelids, moth-brown silver-tipped eyelashes, forehead—all intact and unmarked. A streak of blood severed one eyebrow, and there was a thick patch of blood, black in its center, above his ear, his hair crimson there, then pink where it touched the heath.

Billie lay against him and felt his life, the warm breath loitering above his parted lips. She remained quiet. The light began to go, but by notches, as the sun passed along the stony crests, the impositions of each stone having its effect, but diffused through the mist that was flowing north along the road and the channel of the valley. Before long the mist was blue, and cold.

Billie would have stayed put, but it started to rain heavily, and the mist began to go down like the head of foam on a glass of beer as lemonade goes in to make a shandy. The mist was pitted and sank. The air became transparent, and a little way down toward the road Billie saw a big rock stir—Rory lowered the jacket he'd held up over his head and straightened, looking at her.

Billie began to haul at Hesketh. She told him to get up, to please get up at once.

Hesketh rolled over onto his stomach, got his knees and hands under him. Billie pulled him onto his feet and toward the abbey.

Rory Skilling staggered stiffly after them.

Billie clasped Hesketh's arms around her neck, draped him over her stooped back, and supported him as he stumbled. She looked back. A rag, a fast-flying hag of mist moved between them and Rory. Rory stumbled, fell, and said, "Ah Jesus!" in despair and pain.

Billie slowly skirted the abbey wall on a path the sheep had made. She could see the sheep going along the braided paths on a hillside above her. She envied them their calm, their absence of effort.

It began to pour, and Murdo Hesketh seemed to revive some, to support more of his own weight. It was he who led her off a branch in the sheep track and into shelter, first a narrow, wet stone room, roofless, but its walls filtering the rain, then under a lintel, one great slab of stone, beyond which was neither dim stonework nor another green, flower-filled room, but complete blackness relieved only by the gleaming fringe of water falling from the lip of the lintel. He faltered and fell against her. Billie caught their combined weight and inclined against a neat angle of obstructing stones. But Hesketh pushed as well as leaned, and Billie found her hand on a smooth, gritty surface—a step. She stepped up. Her right hand found and identified a stone column from which stone steps fanned. They were in a tower and on a winding stair.

MURDO COULDN'T PLACE HIS OWN FEET. HIS HEAD JARRED hugely, but there was a hand on its crown. He heard a stifled cry when he lifted his head and her knuckles hit the underside of the steps. He said he was sorry. There was absolutely no light. She dropped behind him and helped him set his hands on the steps' cold, abrasive surfaces. The farther in they moved the colder it grew. Then there was light—the deep notch of an arrow-slit window. Beyond the window Murdo saw mist pulsing with shadows, then a slanting squall of rain over the abbey's smaller roofless rooms, and the gravestones that had accumulated over hundreds of years in the ruin, still consecrated ground to the Catholics of Skilling.

There was no mist now, and no ground below, only rods of rain. The tower was the abbey's sole shelter; Rory knew that as well as he did.

"Can you see him?" said Billie Paxton. Then she asked if he could ease his arms into his coat. She shook off the rain and threaded his good arm into its sleeve. Murdo felt her fishing for the hand of his injured arm, and bit his lip as she eased the sleeve on. He sat on the stair and drew Billie up between his legs, pressed her to him, and closed one side of the coat around her, too. After a moment she took its other edge, hooked two fingers through a buttonhole, and drew it closed.

Murdo slumped and dropped his face onto her shoulder, into the throat-catching ozone of her damp hair.

They didn't move. But the narrow window disappeared. When Murdo lifted his head again there was only blackness, the loud rain, water running on the outer edge of the steps, the splash of water above them, a breeze on his face. Then he saw a spark of rain. The window was there, and it was dark outside, the fullest dark of a night utterly overcast.

Billie Paxton put her hand on his cheek, he felt the wind cold between her colder fingers, then their warmth gradually surfaced, a circuit of warmth closed where her flesh lay against his.

"Where is he?" Murdo asked.

"I don't know."

Murdo was dizzy, and his head dipped again and bumped against hers. She held him still. He said he thought he'd be better once he was sick, then he was, neatly, onto the step below. There was very little in him—only tea and bile. He was sleepy, and tried to stretch out on the steps.

"You'll get wet," Billie said, and wrestled him upright. She braced him, and he drifted into unconsciousness.

He came to—he wasn't sure how much later—to find her trembling with cold and effort.

And with fear.

Murdo heard a hoarse, bubbling whisper, magnified in the tower's stone throat. He didn't understand what was said and supposed Rory was speaking Gaelic till Billie answered him. She said, "If you had the gun, you'd be up here already, Mr. Skilling. Besides, I know you don't have the gun because I have it."

Billie was visible. There was a small amount of light coming through the window, a mealy dark gray—morning was on its way. Billie's hair was plastered to her head, so that her ears appeared as interruptions in the smooth mass with its striated shades of soft pinkish red, and gold, and silvery gold. Billie's skin was so white her faint freckles showed. Her lips had no blood in them, were puckered and dry, although she was wet through. She turned her face from the dark stairwell and looked at Murdo. He saw her lips shape, "Please," and knew she didn't have his gun.

He knew without question a second later when a shot hammered up the barrel of the stair, and a bullet chipped the wall beside the window.

Murdo scrambled up, pressed himself against the wall right beside the raw, smoking chisel stroke of bullet just long enough to swing Billie Paxton around him on the narrow inside of the curving stair and out of Rory's line of fire. He shouted to her to go up, then went up after her, away from the window, turn and turn on into smothering blackness.

Red waves pulled taut by the weight of water. Murdo could see her, her hair like a beacon. He caught at her skirt and pulled her back out of the light of the next window. "Stop," he said. They pressed themselves, stooped, under the inverted staircase, the undersides of stairs above them. Murdo put his hand over her mouth and held his own breath.

Rory Skilling's newly resoled boots scraped and banged slowly up the stairs. He was moaning.

Billie nipped Murdo's fingers and, once her mouth was free, whispered, "I shot him. The gun broke my hand, and I dropped it."

He asked for her broken hand and she gave it to him. He felt it gently, rolling her tendons in the oil of flesh over her little bones. Her thumb was tender in its joint, the skin there hot and tight with swelling. He told her that she hadn't broken it. The dislocated joint must have popped in again of its own accord. She could use it even if it did hurt. "You have to use it now, Miss Paxton. Go to the top of the tower, carefully, because the stair terminates without a landing, and the drop is fatal. Find a loose stone. Or loosen one. More than one if you can manage, but hurry, don't linger, bring them straight back down to me."

As soon as his instructions were finished she was gone. He saw her cross the light, then heard her scrabbling directly above him.

Down in the dark a lisping voice said, "So—you're awake now, Mr. Hesketh."

Murdo didn't answer, he didn't intend to give Rory any help in locating him.

"No one saw us together," the voice said.

Murdo was silent. He counted several sounds, the rasp of boot sole on gritty stone, a splash. He subtracted three steps from the distance between him and Rory.

"No one saw us together," Rory said again.

Murdo bit his lip. A boy would answer—the smart boy he'd been, a long time since. *There was the cattleman who saw us. And, Rory, how did you come by those injuries?*

"Are you another one who thinks that if a thing is carefully planned it will go according to plan?" Rory said. "It's all arrogance and error. *None* of you belongs here. You could have chosen somewhere else to play your scenes. But I want to stay, and I've let our croft go. I had to think of my future, Mr. Hesketh. I had to choose."

Murdo shouted then, "What are you saying?"

Another shot struck the stonework above his head, and he fell flat and stayed quiet. He thought he felt the stone quiver—someone running. Above him. He turned his head up and saw her intent white face appear in the faint light. He yelled a warning. Heard himself and Rory Skilling both shout her name, equally concerned, his own voice tinged with horror and Rory's with threat. Billie passed out of the light and dropped in a huddle behind Murdo. She placed one fist-sized stone in his hand.

He whispered, "Help me get my coat off. Quickly."

Billie helped. Murdo felt the break in his collarbone grate and maybe even come apart, one edge perhaps passing behind the other, tearing muscle and pinching flesh between its splintered ends. At least, that was what Murdo imagined was happening. "Oh Christ!" he said. He fainted momentarily, and his head smacked against the wall. The blow roused him some. "Jacket," he said. "Isn't fine enough, I can't make a knot. I need my shirt. Take it off. Yours won't do—your sleeves are too narrow."

Billie didn't bother him with questions. She removed his jacket and his waistcoat. Murdo heard a light, resinous, clicking music as the jet mourning fob and chain he'd inherited from Karl

Borg slid down the steps. He saw Billie Paxton's fingers on his shirt buttons, her head beside them. He saw the patches of blood on his wet, white linen. Somewhere during all this there was a flash—another shot. The bullet passed through Billie's skirts, missing her feet, and hit the stair where she sat. Murdo could smell scorched wool as well as cordite. Billie got his shirt off. But it caught inside out on one hand, and Billie sobbed and fumbled it right way out again to remove his cuff links. Then it was free. Murdo took it, ran it through his hands, made a hard knot in one sleeve at the cuff, and dropped the stone in at the armhole.

He stood up with the weight dangling in his hand and edged down the stairs.

Rory was saving his bullets—or bullet. But he was quiet, and it was no good Murdo going quietly. Murdo chose to trust what he'd always trusted, what he took as his birthright—his strength and agility. He jumped down, around the stairs and swung his shirt. It smashed into the wall. Murdo heard a gasp and hauled back—hauled back and dropped into a crouch as a flash came again and he saw Rory's wide-eyed ruined face, his white-knuckled hand, and the gun barrel pointing up into the darkness *with too much elevation*. The bullet crashed and ricocheted above them. Then it was dark again, and Murdo swung the stone and the stone found something solid and yielding. The shirt and stone rebounded into Murdo's shin. He caught himself against the wall, and heard Rory banging down the stairs. He heard the thump of flesh on stonework and several muffled, wet pops.

Murdo slithered down the wall, the stones scouring his naked back. The rain made a thick hissing, and water trickled down the stairs. There was no other noise. Murdo edged his way downward. Once his own breath materialized before him, cold and grainy in the light from the lower window. The window's notch was wholly covered by a glassy drapery of falling water. As Murdo went on into the dark, he heard a flutter that wasn't flowing water, then touched Rory's foot, a gritty boot that moved against his hand, in a prolonged spasmodic shiver, as if Rory's soul still had him by that foot and was shaking him as a dog shakes what it refuses to drop. Murdo's hand found Rory's warm ankle, hairy, above his sock, and held it.

In time the shaking stuttered away into stillness. Then Murdo tried to ease past Rory. But Rory had come to rest wedged with one leg facing down and one up, bent improbably at the hips, his head jammed into a window niche. Rory's corpse had stopped up the tower stair.

BILLIE SAT IN THE DOWNPOUR AT THE TOP OF THE TOWER, her back against its broken crown. She was on a small platform, the ultimate step. Below her, far below, was a room floored with bright green moss coating tumbled stones. The rain made the same sound as surf on a shallowly sloping sandy beach, or a great organ pipe that the wind has got into. Through the sound Billie could hear the pinched song of fledgling thrushes in all the nests lining the inside walls of the nave below her. The birds were scolding the rain—or the din of gunfire.

As her fright left her, Billie began to plan how she might defend herself. Or rather, her instincts planned, till she felt the drop beside her as a surface, warm and inviting, and lay back against the stone, pliant and defenseless. Her hair lay in a pool beside her, suspended and magnified with rainwater. All the air was water, and Billie was adrift, weightless, and impressed everywhere.

But it was Murdo Hesketh who emerged from the black well of the tower, carrying his jacket and coat, and the shirt, its bloodied sleeve still tightly knotted at one cuff. He knelt on the step below her and dropped the bundled clothes. Rain had cleared the blood from the broken crust of his injuries, above his temple, and on his shoulder. He leaned on his good arm, inclined over Billie. He told her that she was alive—which she seemed to remember him having told her once before. His hair was soaked. Its ends dribbled water on Billie's face. She simply stared at him, because she had been waiting for Rory, her body a boat to be flipped, overturned, the drop beside her a warm sea friendly to swimmers and treacherous to those who couldn't swim.

Billie asked, "Can you swim, Mr. Hesketh?"

He said, "I am swimming." He touched her arm, her side, her throat, her face. "Are you hit?"

"No," she said, she was only waiting for Rory Skilling. "I could do it again if I had to," she explained.

"I need your help," Hesketh said.

"Yes."

He put his good arm under her shoulders and raised her into a sitting position. He coaxed her out of the rain and back down into the dark. Before they'd quite left the light Billie relieved him of the shirt, unknotted the sleeve, and tried to help him with it.

"I can't," he moaned.

"Just the coat then, its sleeves are fuller."

When the coat was on he leaned against her, gasping. She put her head against his, to hold it up, and answered an earlier question. "I wasn't hit." Then, again, "I was waiting for Rory." She explained, "I like your hair"—leaving out several intermediary premises in her argument.

"I like yours, too," he said, and laughed.

"You shouldn't have to kill someone twice," she said, supplying one of her missing premises.

"That's true," Hesketh agreed. "It isn't reasonable."

Billie felt she hadn't made herself understood, but just wiped the rain from his cheeks and tried to follow his instructions.

He told her that he wasn't able to climb past Rory's body. She would have to, she was smaller. He had tried to haul Rory back up the stairs but, what with his arm, he wasn't able to. "We can't leave him, Billie. We have to move him before rigor sets in."

She peered into Hesketh's face, and his eyes avoided hers. Even in the poor light she thought she saw him blush. "While he's still flexible," he added. "Do you understand me?"

Billie nodded. What she did understand was that he'd take her to the place and give her directions.

In the faint light they found Rory, and Billie saw what she would have to do. She would have to wriggle between Rory's scissored legs, under his canted, backward knee, then reach back through to free his other leg. Sure, Mr. Hesketh could sit on the step above and shove with his own feet, but he couldn't guide the jammed limbs into a position where they'd unlock—unlock the space they had obstructed.

Billie got down on her belly and first threaded her feet through the gap. She could smell Rory, then, as her head and hands passed beneath him she came into contact with the crotch of his pants, squelching with a stinking jelly of fecal matter.

Billie delivered herself and, on the far side, put her head down to retch into the warm slime already coating the steps.

Rory seemed to look down at her, quizzical, his head on an angle, one shoulder up in an exaggerated shrug.

Billie didn't want to stretch an arm back through. Hesketh was coaxing again, she could see him, wet, and as clean as water. Billie shook her head at him. For several minutes she only listened to him apparently talking to himself. He had his shirt, he said, he should have covered her hair. He knew that. *Billie,* he said, *I was careless.* He said that she couldn't go for help. That wouldn't do. She couldn't leave him. Someone was trying to kill him. Why would Rory? But he did appreciate that he and she were only on parallel courses, not in the same boat. Geordie Betler had said the same: We're not in the same boat, Geordie had said. "And he said that he had more confidence in *his* vessel, in its instrument of navigation, in the *necessity* of its voyage."

"What did he mean?" Billie finally responded.

"He thought it was wrongheaded of me to investigate the sinking as sabotage, not as murder."

Billie peered up at Murdo through Rory's straddled legs. His shoulders were invisible, black against blackness, but she could see his skin gleam, his chest, face, hair, and his breath, paler than the rest. He told her that he thought that if she stood hard on Rory's cocked knee, his inverted cocked knee, she might free the joint enough so that Rory would finish falling forward.

Billie got up to do it. It was like trying to break a green branch against the angle of a step. She put her hands on Rory's shoulders and used all her weight, bounced up and down until the spring began to give.

It gave, and Murdo pushed, and Rory Skilling sagged, then collapsed onto Billie.

She screamed and fought. She felt the pressure of the floppy form increase and stopped screaming, she used her mouth to bite, she clawed and writhed till she was out from under him.

She tore her skirt free and flew, ran, tumbled down the last steps, and ran out of the tower.

MURDO HAD LUNGED FORWARD IN AN EFFORT TO CATCH the back of Rory's jacket and lift him. The reaching arm worked, but his bad hand couldn't anchor him, so he fell across Rory, and doubled Rory's deadweight. He heard a hitch in the motor of sound and motion that was Billie Paxton, then that small dynamo started up again, growling with effort, seething like a cat in a bag. Rory jerked, jostled, then deflated, and Murdo heard Billie thump away down the tower.

Murdo took a deep breath, clambered over Rory, and slid down Rory's body on his own belly, kicking at the walls to guide himself. He put his hand on Rory's crown, pressed the man's face into the step, and slithered free, greasy with filth. He went down slowly, feeling in the dark for his gun. He found it, cold and spent.

He went out into the dull morning, joined Billie, and did as she was doing, pulled up bunches of thyme and heather and scrubbed his face, hair, hands, and clothes with their damp aromatic leaves.

After a time Billie stopped trying to clean herself. She went on pulling plants and tossed them at him, her face screwed up and eyes streaming. She bawled, as noisy and dirty as an exhausted baby.

Murdo put the revolver back in the pocket of his coat. He thought that perhaps he should comfort Billie, but her clothes were more contaminated than his and, besides, he was too angry to put out his hand to anyone. Instead he told her they should avoid the road. They must make their way back to Southport, across the bog to the coast at Craige Sands, then walk along the Sands to Clodel, where there was a church that was always open, but scarcely used. (And another tower he had climbed with Ingrid Hallow.) "We can spend the night there," he said, "then we'll go on to Southport, where I will put you on the pilot's vessel to Dorve."

Billie wiped her eyes on her wet sleeves.

"I see you still have your purse at your waist," he said.

"I have my banknotes, and Reverend Vause's money order," Billie said.

"You're set then," Murdo said.

She gave him a sullen, stubborn look and remained sitting.

"You're a witness, Miss Paxton." He shrugged, and it hurt him. "To *someone's* crime. Rory Skilling hadn't any personal grievance against me. Nothing I know of."

Drizzle blew against Murdo's face. It felt warm, then hot, and he sat down. His knees had simply given way.

It all came, in a rush, like seawater through a holed hull. Things he'd seen and hadn't observed. Things he'd heard said and hadn't grasped. A blanket in a bag, a man too tempted by the props of *theater*, his *costume*, the new shirts and jackets and pants. The back of an envelope marked with a pencil, a tally of losses and wins, a tally in pounds not kronor, because the men were *paid* in pounds, the three men who filled the cabins but vanished before the last leg of the voyage. Elov's letter—Geordie had mentioned it to Murdo—*"Don't come this summer."* A startled exclamation, *"My cataloger!"*—Henry Maslen, who had been expected at Southport a day earlier, whose wife was in the cabin Murdo would certainly have occupied otherwise, a cabin just below the waterline, at the ship's pivot point, where Murdo customarily lay low when traveling by sea. *"Good God, my cataloger!"*

"Don't come this summer." And the dependable fixity of maritime meals, the men's mess at eight bells in anything but battle or hurricane, so that, just before the ship docked at Stolnsay the steward was still wiping black fingerprints from the edges of the tables where the five stokers and two greasers had sat. Three cabins filled with men who disappeared; Elov discouraged; most of the black gang topside at eight bells. Almost everyone topside when the pilot's boat was alongside, forty minutes before the *Gustav Edda* reached the seawall of Stolnsay Harbor—*all this*—and an old woman's lace-mittened, pointing hand, her clock with its retrievers and ducks and bulrushes, its girls a-maying, and its cottages under snow. Her nephew late by forty minutes for her birthday celebration. *Forty minutes, forty minutes.* It was preposterous—as Murdo had said to Geordie about his suspecting all three sportsmen. It was fussy, and elaborate, and minutely controlled, and mistaken in its essentials. It was James, Lord Hallowhulme.

13 ♣ A CADAVERIC GRIP

AT WHAT WAS NORMALLY HER BREAKFAST TIME, BILLIE stopped to rest. She sat on a bank where the peat cutters had been that spring, making their neat chisel cuts in the black peat. She watched Murdo Hesketh continue away from her, his coat billowing behind him.

Since they'd left Ormabeg he'd scarcely spoken. She had to remind him that he'd meant to lead her away from what they'd done. When she did remind him he took his head out of his hands and stood, and started away on his own—then came back to help her up. They went down the course of the burn where Billie had stopped to water Kirsty. The burn was little more than a wet crease, the slopes between which it ran so closely inter-leaved that Billie wasn't able to see where they were headed. For a time she retained Hesketh's hand, till they reached a long, canted table of bogland where he released her, and she fell into step behind him. Later, at Billie's usual breakfast time, she real-ized it was the fourth meal she'd missed, and she sat down. Mr. Hesketh strode on away from her. She watched him go. Perhaps it was better not to bother him. She knew he had the gun in his pocket, could tell by the way his coat lay close at one thigh and swung thumping as he walked.

As they left Ormabeg, Billie had told him about Alan Skilling. How Alan had hitched Kirsty to Minnie's trap. Alan had been sent to find her, and she forced him to help her run away from Kiss. "He didn't want me to go," Billie said to Murdo Hesketh. "To *leave* him." She thought Mr. Hesketh would answer her, would say, "Why did you leave?" or, "Poor Alan." *Considering.* Considering Alan's father head down on the tower stair at Ormabeg, his broken body a burr twisted into the tower's yarn. But Hesketh was silent.

Billie needed to understand why she'd chosen to help Hesketh and had hurt Rory. She wanted Hesketh at least to meet her eyes again. She remembered his eyes holding hers at several critical moments: in poor light in the tower well; in the draining gray on the tower top, nothing in the air behind his head, birds singing below them, pinned down by rain. He had blushed when he asked her to move Rory, and talked about Rory's malleability. She recognized the blush as shame, remembering his turned, burning cheek when she pushed past him in the passage between chapel and sacristy at Stolnsay Kirk, when Lady Hallowhulme had taken her to see Edith's body. Billie wanted either the warmth of the blush, or to be borne along in the buoyant medium of Hesketh's blue gaze. She wanted to believe she'd made the right choice, not just because one man was striking another, and giving away certain rights with each blow struck, and not because she was *there* and saw it and felt she had to act, but because she was *involved*, and her choice concerned her future. She needed him to confirm something, but he wouldn't speak or meet her eyes. And when, worn-out, she sat down on the lip of a trench in the peat, he went on without her.

She let him go—she'd keep him in sight. He'd take her to

Southport and put her on a ship. He had promised that. He'd secure her escape.

Billie lay down where she was and closed her eyes. She woke
up once to see Mr. Hesketh on the horizon of the farthest hill,
but couldn't wholly rouse herself. When she woke again she
saw him nearer, on his way back to her. She got up and went to
meet him.

He was very pale. "You made me go the distance twice," he
accused. He sounded hopeless. For the second time that day he
sat down in his tracks.

Billie knelt beside him. He passed her a handful of crumpled paper. She smoothed the pieces on her knees. Alan's feet.
She could see that handling had smeared the newsprint. She was
puzzled—even more so when Hesketh asked her if she ever
wondered why the ship sank.

She shook her head. "I don't know why, Mr. Hesketh. I
mean, I don't know why I never wonder. Maybe because only
Edith was mine. And Edith often told me not to concern myself
with other people, though she meant not be *hurt* by them."
Besides, Billie told him, she *had* let him in on what she was
wondering. Hesketh had seen Henry's button. The button from
Henry's jacket that was found in Edith's hand.

Billie saw that she now had Hesketh's attention and that he
was nodding. He said, "A cadaveric grip. Your sister's hand retained the last thing she'd taken hold of."

"You thought the sinking was my fault," she said. "But I
jumped because I kissed Henry. Or—at least—there was kissing."

"I know," said Hesketh. "I guessed."

"I ran away because that's all I could think to do. You see—
when I was little my father was always handing me through win-

dows to Edith. Me, and our suitcases." Billie told Mr. Hesketh that she'd run away again. This time because Henry wouldn't kiss her. "It made nonsense of everything. He wouldn't kiss me. He kept saying that Edith was better than we were."

"Better? Better off? Or you were both bad?"

"Edith was too good for us. Edith could do better than him, anyway. That's what he said. But I never think of people as better or worse. Even you."

"I'm very glad you've not made an exception of me." Hesketh was still gray, but seemed amused.

"But you *are* worse, really," Billie told him. "You're the least kindly person I know." She put her hand on his arm and said, "I shot Alan's father. I did it to save you."

"Thank you," he said.

"No!" Billie shook him. She was angry, and threatened by wordlessness, by muddle and stammering. "Edith wouldn't have shot him."

How could she explain? Billie knew that Edith would have cried, "Stop!" She imagined her sister, appalled, courageous, running forward to plead and reason.

"It was uncivilized," Mr. Hesketh said, as if he had read her mind. His "uncivilized" wasn't a criticism, but he'd failed to understand her. Or—as usual—she'd failed to make herself understood.

Billie frowned at him, and tried to follow what he next said. He couldn't behave either, he said. It was futile to try. He was fatally clumsy. "My whole spastic existence," he said, with calm self-loathing. Then he said something Billie thought was really rather grandiose. That everything had happened through his inattention. He was talking to himself now, not her.

When his father died, he resigned his commission and took his mother to the spa at Vrena. He should have stayed in Stockholm and kept an eye on Karl. He gave his money to Karl, who lost it. Later he should have forced Karl to tell Ingrid they were bankrupt. Instead he'd told himself they were thinking of her health, of the baby. But perhaps Karl was planning never to have to tell Ingrid anything. "Sometimes I think Karl took my revolver to shoot himself," said Murdo Hesketh. He looked at Billie then, really regarded her. "My first revolver, not my double-action Colt." He patted the pocket of his coat. He said, "Karl told me that he only meant to say to his friend—the man who lost our money—that if there was anything left over from the other creditors to give it to Ingrid. But then he pointed the gun and pulled the trigger. I came back from Mother's funeral and found Karl in prison. Ian Betler reappeared. You know, I don't remember when I first really noticed he'd come back. He kept trying to make me see how foul our lodgings were and asking couldn't I find a healthier place in the country for Ingrid."

As he spoke Hesketh subsided slowly; first his shoulders slumped, then he tilted sideways and sagged onto the marshy ground. He moved so slowly that Billie was able to interpose her hand between his cheek and scratchy spurs of grass. She told him that she didn't understand his story. *"Ingrid?"* she said.

"My sister, the other Ingrid," Hesketh went on. "Ian knew his place, though. I hope you never will, Billie. I hope you'll never be civilized. Still, I'm glad Geordie Betler was, and wouldn't let you look at the baby. I would have shown you everything. I'm not the man I was. I *was* kinder. My poor sister. I still can't understand how there can be nothing where someone was. My heart has just gone on with its restless looking about for them. Ingrid and Karl. When I came back to the house after the execution there was a bumblebee in the porch, stumbling about in the morning warmth. I was hearing with Karl's ears, and Ingrid's. It was their world, still there, but not for them." Hesketh began to shiver, and Billie bent over him to help him with her warmth. He told her that it hadn't helped that he'd had to pretend Ingrid was still alive to spare Karl in his last weeks. "I was afraid he'd read my eyes. I loved Karl. Sometimes I think that I could live if only the same teeth could reopen this wound."

Other than his shuddering, Hesketh had been lying completely still, only making music with his voice. But he moved his good hand up between their faces, and Billie shifted her focus to study the white slots of scar tissue—a bite mark. Billie remembered biting Mr. Hesketh's arm on Scouse Beach, when he'd carried her out of the sea. She reminded him. "I bit you."

"But not hard enough," he said. He wasn't joking. This wasn't "repartee"—a word Minnie had taught Billie. He was serious—and very sad. But he was looking at her. Billie had retained his gaze now for long minutes, even while he told her his story and wandered in his past. Time hadn't stopped while he talked, but the minutes moved aside to admit a longer period, perhaps a lifetime. Billie could see it. And she witnessed the instant Hesketh saw it, too. She saw his blue eyes grow bluer, till they were the color of the inhospitable ocean glimpsed through a crack in pack ice.

He put his hand into her hair and held her face against his and kissed her. His mouth moved against hers as if delivering a practical lesson in how to shape certain difficult words. Suddenly, Billie was only her mouth—and breathless, then she was his mouth, too, and their shared, swapped breath was the only breathable air.

◆　◆　◆

THEY WENT HAND IN HAND ALONG CRAIGE SANDS, A long silver beach that terminated in a headland, beyond which was Clodel, where Murdo believed that, by nightfall, they would likely find the church open and empty.

The tide was on its way out, the sea calm, and it had cleared, so that, with each wave, the sand beside them flooded blue. The blue drained back leaving constellations of broken cockleshells.

The walking was easy, they didn't have to lift their feet as high as on the bog. Billie had removed her shoes when she went into the sea to wash. Murdo watched her feet, with their long toes, high arches, and round heels. He could see now how she'd managed to split the tops of Ingrid Hallow's dancing shoes within minutes of her march out of the gatehouse. He realized that, for weeks, he'd watched her closely—but piecemeal. He'd looked at a gesture, the way her shoulder thrust up through the pinkish red waves of her hair when she shrugged, her hands, stretching for a teacup, coming down as slowly as gulls were coming now to land on the sand beside them. Billie didn't trust herself with crockery. But the same hands touched piano keys like a spider laying in the weft of its web. Murdo had watched Billie Paxton, plagued by everything she did, everything he saw nettling him—a pain like pins and needles, numb flesh coming back to life. He'd disliked her, he believed, the sight of her had so irritated him. She was his shame: the young illiterate woman he'd mistreated. She was his weakness: he'd jumped to conclusions as quickly as she'd jumped from ship to shore. Geordie had expressed it well: *"You're hasty, Mr. Hesketh. And not perspicacious."*

What would he do with her?

He'd give her money, so she wouldn't have to spend any of what was in her purse. He'd put her on a ship and tell her to go to Glasgow and find Geordie's Mr. Tannoy.

Murdo had a bad moment. He thought he'd lost his pocketbook, that it was in the jacket he was no longer wearing. Then he put his hand on it, in the coat's other outside pocket. "Where did we leave my shirt and jacket?" he asked—still having his bad moment. He'd remembered the body in the tower at Ormabeg, remembered *incriminating evidence.*

"I carried them to where I sat down. We left them where we were lying."

"I don't want you to say that." Murdo was sharp.

"We *were* lying," Billie insisted.

"It was just a kiss, Billie."

She was quiet for a time, and Murdo watched the water wrung out of the wet sand where she stepped, her feet falling in flashing halos. After a time she said, "Are you thinking of Ingrid Hallow?"

"I wasn't." She'd annoyed him again. She was in possession of the rumors and satisfied with the commonplace. What more could he expect? "Listen," he said, "I was fond of Ingrid Hallow. I approved of her. She was the only one of them who wasn't lazy. She liked to walk and ride. She'd always bounce up and say, 'I'll go with you.' We climbed the tower at Ormabeg—and to the summit of Larg. James had his Austrian oak staff—perhaps he hoped to poke about at snow for hidden crevasses—God knows—but he sat down with the rest of the family and made tea and talked while Ingrid and I went on. Of course James and Minnie *play* furiously, but most of what they do is done sitting down. Ingrid had animal energy, and she'd lacked someone to keep her company outdoors. There are paintings of Minnie's in which Ingrid appears as if she's *several* people, at different distances—on a far hill, on the road in the middle distance, beneath a tree in the foreground. I'm sure you haven't seen them— Minnie put them away. *I've* always hated to sit still, except on a horse, on parade, a disciplined immobility that requires some effort."

Murdo glanced at Billie. She was watching him, bemused, patient.

"Yes," she said. "I see. You only *admired* Miss Ingrid. But did she love you? Are you telling me not to put any great stock in a kiss, because look where kisses got Ingrid Hallow?"

"I didn't kiss Ingrid," Murdo said. "I find you extremely exasperating, Billie."

"I'm only trying to follow you."

Ingrid Hallow did that, Murdo said. She followed him. No one much noticed. They were the kind of family who readily believed what was *said*. They were susceptible to *testimony* rather than evidence. James had some bee in his bonnet about Rixon. He'd come in one evening and, visibly irritated, said, "I suppose Rixon's been following cousin Murdo about all day?" After that everybody, even Rixon, decided that *that* was what happened— that it was Rixon who followed Murdo. Minnie took to teasing them about Murdo's training Rix in the manly arts. "It was ludicrous. They seemed to feel outfaced by my shooting, riding, fishing, swimming. They were scornful because it made them— oh, Hell!—*hot* with admiration. On fire and angry. They took their cues from Clara, I expect. She was always acid, from my cadetship on. I got into long pants and Clara kept trying to cut me down to size."

"But—" Again Billie nudged him—really did nudge, pushed her body against his side, so that momentarily he was in the aura of her odor. "But why was Lord Hallowhulme displeased by the idea that Rixon admired you?"

"Men hope their sons will admire *them* first and foremost," Murdo said, in the tone of someone talking to a much younger person. She was, of course, a good fifteen years younger.

"No," said Billie, still patiently trying to get at what she wanted.

But Murdo had seen it already. He stopped walking and a wave poured its cold foam onto the toes of his boots and buried Billie's feet. He heard her small sigh of pleasure before he said, "James thinks Rixon is my son."

Billie asked why.

Murdo tried to imagine—or to follow James's imagining. He didn't want to tell Billie what he'd guessed—that if James had sent word to Elov, and not to Rixon, then James had *wanted* Rixon in that cabin with Murdo at eight bells, when almost everyone else was topside and the pilot's boat was on hand. James had imagined it that way—people where he wanted them, each object in its appointed place, and everything running according to plan. But what had James imagined *first*, and why?

Murdo's cousin didn't understand intimacy, and scarcely ever saw it. James was blind to expressions of any temperature, to warm looks or cold. But Murdo and Clara were very old friends. When Murdo arrived, his cousin Clara was happy to have him on the island, and determined to help him back to happiness. She was so ardent that even James was able to see it.

"Rixon is so like Lord Hallowhulme—in looks," Billie said, fishing.

"Of course he is."

"Would Lord Hallowhulme have any cause to think Rixon is yours?"

Murdo considered then said, "James did see me jealous of him. Or, at least, disappointed with Clara. Dismayed by their engagement. This was a long time ago, when Clara was married out of our grandfather's house. Clara is six years my senior, so I was fifteen at the time. Clara had always told me everything, her plans and her adventures. But once she was engaged she chose to play the great lady. It was before his peerage, but he was already Sir James Hallow, at the age I am now. Clara enjoyed his fame. She sailed about in jewels and loud bustles and trailing trains on even ordinary evenings. And she took to calling me 'Dear boy,' as James did. She meant to be droll. Maybe even to have me laugh with her at his pompous nonsense. It's possible. Or perhaps she meant it as a provocation. I don't know. Whatever the case, I behaved very badly. I was insolent to James, and surly with Clara. Then—it must have been the night before the wedding day, since my memories of the wedding are quite watery with hangover—I got stinking drunk and did and said I don't know what. I remember that James forgot himself enough to cuff me. And I bloodied his nose. I remember calling him an overbearing bore with terrible taste in clothes. I was a little snob. I remember smirking at Clara as though I were terribly clever, and her looking back with thin-lipped calculation, trying to plot how to get me packed off to bed with as little noise and fuss as possible. And I remember throwing a crown of white rosebuds in the fire. The *kitchen* fire. I'd got into the stillroom, it was cold, and all the flowers were lying there."

Murdo wondered then, as he sometimes did, why he never remembered any servants present. Only Clara, in an outrage, and the heaps—the hills—of quiet flowers.

Billie said, "So—Lord Hallowhulme may have thought you were in love with your cousin?"

Murdo made a noise of assent, then said, "I was miserable. It was the end of our summers, and I held her responsible. But after several dreary years I joined the cavalry and had a fine old time for the next ten."

Billie Paxton had put herself before him and was buttoning his coat closed. She began at the bottom, and her hair blew against his bare chest. He interfered with her buttoning—slow at the best of times—and managed to gather her hair into the coat with him. When she raised her face through the trapped mass he touched her forehead and eyelids with his lips.

"I think poor, young Ingrid Hallow must have been in love with you," Billie said, solemn.

"She *said* she was. And I said, 'Ingrid, dear, I'm very fond of you.' Smug and avuncular. And she drowned herself."

"You thought I was trying to drown myself. At Scouse Beach."

He pulled her closer yet. He hadn't quite meant to, but did, clutched her till his tired arm quaked. He heard her, she sounded deliberate and reasonable, she'd finally found her way through the tricky currents of their mismatched tides—her simplicity, his complexity. She said, "That's why I asked you whether you were thinking about Ingrid Hallow. You want me not to take your kiss seriously, though I understand now that you didn't ever kiss Ingrid. But, you see, you're telling me I mustn't love you."

"Don't," he said. "Don't imagine you do."

THERE WAS NO LIGHT IN THE CHURCH. THEY CAME UP the path from the beach below the headland, a path they could scarcely see, sand already darkened by dew. The small uneven panes in the church windows gave back the last lemony light on the western horizon, a light that moved as they did, sinking from window to window, as though someone was climbing down from the tower carrying a shaded lantern.

"Look, there's a light," Billie said with tears in her voice. "Will we have to speak to someone now?"

Murdo reassured her. It was only the evening.

He took her around to the side door and lifted its latch. The door grated across the sand used to scour the pink Tyree stone flags, then not properly swept out afterward. There was a light on the altar, wick floating in oil in a brass jar, a spot of radiance in the big, bare nave. There were no pews, only rows of rush chairs, recently reseated, the rushes still smelling sweet and fresh.

Murdo led Billie to the low door at one side of the altar. He showed her up the full circle of a first staircase. They were in Clodel's big square tower, its lower room full of chests and the kind of desks where—Murdo imagined—monks once sat copying out sacred texts in their best, self-effacing, anonymous hands. There was a ladder to the next level, a steep angled ladder of black oak. Partway up it Billie began to sob. The moon had appeared at an east-facing window behind her, a bright boil on the smooth skin of horizon, a gold curve, swollen and trembling through thick horizontal air and scaly window glass. Billie was looking down at her shadow, hanging on the ladder's shadow. Murdo clambered up behind her, till his feet were only one rung below hers. He inclined against her and pressed his cheek to hers.

After a time Billie was quiet, and Murdo put his good hand under one of her arms and coaxed her on, rung by rung.

The tower's top room was warm—the heat of the day had

risen up into it and was trapped. Murdo and Billie lay down on a well-swept oak floor, and he fell asleep.

Later Billie said she was hungry—so hungry. Then she told Murdo that sometimes she tried to talk to Edith. "It's as if I want to pray to her. To ask her what she thinks, what she'd do. But when I open my mouth, all that comes out is: *Edith, Edith, Edith.*"

Murdo nodded. She couldn't see the gesture, so he moved closer to her. And closer. He felt her ribs creak. He said that, though the *fact* of the grief was predictable, its manifestations were not. Then he added, delirious, "It's like a bat in the dark, blind, but somehow able to see things we can't."

Billie perked up and asked what, for instance?

Murdo blinked, trying to see her, and saw the underside of her jaw, her firm pale throat, and the dark line dividing it, like a cut. He'd been looking at that all day, and now he put his lips against it, ran the tip of his tongue along the thin, smooth plait of her choker. He knew that it was a plaited lock of hair—the lock Mrs. Mulberry had cut from Billie's sister's corpse. His mouth shaped a name: "Edith." He felt he was asking something. *For something.* But his shoulder and collarbone were aching and he dropped his forehead against the floor by Billie's neck. He saw the faces of the dead—Ingrid, Karl, Ingrid, Ian—rush toward him then roll into themselves, opening like smoke rings. Or like the iron rings he'd had to collect on the head of a long lance—a parade ground exercise from his cavalry days. He was falling through a series of ruptured membranes, smoke, ringing iron, the faces of the dead.

Then the world grew steady. Billie Paxton had rolled him off her and onto his back. She had unbuttoned his coat again. He felt her warm hand run from his chest to his stomach, and rest there.

"No. Don't," he said.

Billie was sure he'd not been aware of what he was doing. As she lay against his immobilized arm, as she spoke, he hooked his good arm under her, too, and leaned on his elbow and loomed over her. His pity was like a light passing through her, their atoms intermingled. He had all these griefs, it turned out; he wasn't only strong and striking, but a man of substance, solid with suffering. Billie had believed that Edith's death was a thing she and Henry held in common, but Henry consoled himself with his unworthiness, spoke about Edith as if, in the end, she'd been spared him, and had gone on to better things. Murdo Hesketh was as sad as she was. Since Edith's death Billie had been shown goodwill and sympathy, but this was a sadness that sang along to hers, another soul with perfect pitch.

When he fainted onto her, Billie lay quiet for a time, breath constricted, and gauged his full weight. She found she'd moved, not to free herself, but to accommodate him differently. It wasn't quite enough that he was with her. She wanted him nearer still, inside her, their molecules mixed, like milt and roe.

She said his name, his first name, at last. But he was unconscious, so she rolled him off her, unfastened the buttons on his coat, and touched his chest. He was panting with pain. She moved her hand. The muscles in his stomach were held hard. He shuddered under her touch, then said, "No. Don't."

She pressed her palms to his pectoral muscles and stooped over him, her face to his. It was experiment and calculation—

Billie had remembered how Henry had mixed his breath with hers.

Murdo said they had another five miles to walk in the morning.

"Mr. Hesketh, I can't follow your thinking," Billie said.

"You mustn't expect to, Billie. Only follow my lead for a few more hours."

She smiled at him, but he seemed not to see it. She asked him was he in much pain?

"You are leaning on my ribs, though I find they're bruised, not broken as I feared."

"Should I not lean?" Billie said, sweet and obtuse.

"I'd be obliged if you didn't. But that's not what I mean. Move your hands, *too,* please. We can't forget ourselves. Tomorrow you must take a ship to Luag, then Oban. I'll pay your passage. You must go by train to Glasgow and find Geordie Betler's Andrew Tannoy. I'll send our friend Geordie to you, Billie. I have to go back to Stolnsay to take care of Clara and Rixon. You'll do very well with Geordie—since you seem to feel you really *must* run away from Henry Maslen, just because the poor man won't continue to flatter you with kisses."

He was in pain and impatient. He was trying to put her away from him.

Billie said, "I didn't run away from Henry, but from Lord Hallowhulme."

Murdo Hesketh was silent.

"He kissed me," Billie said.

"Did he?" Murdo said, expressionless.

Billie didn't reply. Instead she moved, lay down beside him again. He turned his head, waiting.

"I'm so very hungry," she said. Then, after a pause, "I always was hungry. I used to steal fruit from trees. I was still doing it even when the Reverend Vause drove me to the station after his sister dismissed me for theft." She stretched up her arm into the dark volume of air that was the penultimate room of the church tower at Clodel—the room directly below the bells. She plucked something from the air—black cherries, three on one stem. "The Reverend Vause is a man who believes women are naturally immoral, never able to see the garden wall if their eyes are on the fruit."

"You enjoyed it," said Murdo Hesketh.

He meant Lord Hallowhulme's kiss. Billie could feel his sluggish fury. He lay next to her, low in the water it seemed—a boat very nearly swamped.

"I enjoy so many things," Billie answered, and enjoyed a moment of self-congratulation.

Murdo shoved her away from him and struggled up. She seized him by his coat and held on, as he yelled at her to get away from him. "Little animal," he shouted. Billie clung till he toppled. She pulled him down, laid him out, and clambered up him. He gathered himself. She felt his anger and his strength, but she'd somehow tied him up, and he couldn't hurt her. She pressed him down and put her face in easy reach. Billie took a deep breath, and turned seaward to wait for the big wave.

SHE HAD RUN AWAY FROM HER ENJOYMENT. MURDO understood now. He would make her admit it. First he tried to close her wrists in his one hand, to stretch her arms up above her head. She easily freed herself. She had control of her hands—but he warned her not to touch him. He shoved and sifted through her skirts with his good hand, while leaning on the bad. The scabbed injury on his collarbone had cracked and was bleeding. Billie had blood smeared on her chin. Despite his warning she raised her hands, held him off, or perhaps only supported his weight, as a timber props the sagging ceiling of a mine. He found her ready, oily, hotter than he was. The moon was below the window, making webs on its lower mullions. Murdo saw Billie's surprise, her eyes turn dark with trouble. He stopped. She shut her eyes and he put his mouth to hers though he'd meant not to. She pressed up with her hips, with all her robust muscularity, till she had him entirely, his first since that cowardly woman he'd hoped to marry—Stockholm quality of a recent provenance, a good girl of good family, with scruples, tears, generous concessions: *I love you, I love you,* she said, but her skirt was pulled down straight afterward, and she wasn't interested in benefiting from his experience, was strangely undismayed, but miserly and then so swift to run when they met outside the courthouse during Karl Borg's trial. His *first since*—and he hadn't wanted to help himself again. Hadn't because, although the doctor and nurses had pushed him aside, he'd nevertheless seen them packing cloth swabs to stem the blood gushing between his sister's legs. He'd seen the color leave Ingrid's face and throat and chest—a sunset on snow, night climbing a mountain.

Billie Paxton nipped Murdo's earlobe. "Please," she said. "I want to. You mustn't say we mustn't." She put her open mouth against his throat and moved under him.

Nothing Murdo had in his head had this immediacy. He raised her against him, her cloth-covered, stayed upper body, her warm hair gathered against his bare skin. He felt then that it might be possible to grow something in the world's only hospitable place, the space between their bodies, the warm inches of air where they came apart and came together.

The moon was in the room. The floorboards gave tongue. Murdo felt himself vanish. Then the smooth intricacies of Billie's hair choker were against his lips again.

AT FIRST LIGHT, BILLIE GOT UP OFF THE WOODEN FLOOR, where they had slept, teased by cold breezes, indeterminate in direction. When she got up something trickled down her legs, warm, exhausted, no longer viscous. She stooped and wiped with her petticoats.

Murdo helped her on the ladder. And, resting frequently, they helped each other along five miles of paths at the edge of the sea. Though Billie was light-headed when they stopped, she'd turn her face to find his mouth, as starved and sour as hers. They were constantly turning toward each other, like doors hung crooked that always swing shut, or pages in a book with a too stiffly bound spine.

They stopped on the banks of a burn to wash their hands and faces. Murdo brushed the worst of the mud from Billie's hem and boots, wiped his own with grass. He transferred his wallet to an outside pocket, where it swung in lighter counterpoint to the revolver. He buttoned his coat. They walked arm in arm into Southport.

At a draper's and haberdashery Murdo bought a hat, told the youth at the counter his size, tried several, smoothing his hair and tipping each on tenderly over the contusion, now scabbed black, and in a fan of purple-and-brown bruises.

Murdo then went on to buy Billie petticoats, a skirt, a shawl of the big cloth—there were no coats in her size—a bag, stockings, and, at a grocery, soap, scent, and a comb. Then he purchased bread and cheese, apples, a knife, and a big stoneware bottle of ginger beer. They walked down to the pier, where they perched on mooring posts and ate, he handing her bread by the hunk, cheese and apple by the slice, so she wouldn't eat too quickly.

A steamer, small and riding high, stitched its way through the reef between Dorve and Southport. Its stack smoke floated, a dirty wraith over the white sea to the east.

Gulls settled on the pier and began to shuffle nearer to the man and woman. Billie had the hiccups. She jerked periodically, and watched Murdo push packages into her new bag. He pinched its catch closed and put it in her arms. He helped her up and walked her to where the pilot usually moored. Anyone seeing them, standing against the quiet morning sea, her bag a bundle clutched close to her chest, might have asked: "Who are the couple with the baby?"

Billie listened to Murdo's instructions. She'd find twenty pounds in the bag, in the small slot pocket directly under its catch. It was more than enough. She should go by carrier overland from Dorve to Luag, then buy passage for Oban. Lastly, a train to Glasgow, and Andrew Tannoy, at this address. "Repeat it to me, Billie," he said.

She did.

"I can't leave Clara," he said.

Billie could feel his heart beating, so hard it made his body shake. His hand was in hers, his pulse tapping her wherever they came in contact.

"I don't understand," Billie said. "Isn't it quicker for you, too, by sea, Dorve to Stolnsay?"

"The pilot rests before his next leg. I *have* counted the hours.

I have made a comparison, and it's quicker overland," he said. "I will rest," he promised, though she hadn't asked.

The small steamer was at the pier. Murdo moved Billie back from the noise and bustle of landing. The wind blew a smut against Billie's forehead—a burning kiss.

"I chose you," Billie said.

Murdo said, "I'm sorry."

14 ✤ PRIMING CHARGE, BASE CHARGE

FOUR DAYS AFTER BILLIE PAXTON RAN AWAY, AND TWO after Kirsty was found sore-footed in a fan of grass cropped to the nub beside the ditch where the trap's wheels were snagged in a snarl of reeds, Kiss Castle's shy, Gaelic-speaking tweeny tapped on Geordie's door. It was Sunday, and most of the household was at Stolnsay Kirk. Geordie was packing, his own bag and Ian's— dried and aired—with the few things he meant to keep. The packing process was Geordie's second sort-through of his brother's possessions for, at the first, he'd kept not only what was precious, and personal, like correspondence, but anything that might later prove material evidence. As Geordie looked at these discards now, his former judgments seemed less a careful husbandry of evidence than a boyish certainty of *cases* to be put and *culprits* to be confronted. The sea-spoiled objects still seemed to hold the residual heat of his wishful anger.

The tweeny put a finger to her lips and pinched Geordie's sleeve. He followed her to the bathroom on the landing. At its door he heard the sound of water gushing into a tub. The girl opened the door and left him.

The room was already softened by steam, its black-and-white-tiled walls perspiring. Geordie pulled the chain that opened the louvers and sat down beside Murdo on the bench against the wall.

He took stock of Murdo while the man watched his bath fill. Murdo said that it wasn't quite a bed with clean white sheets, but it would do for now. "I need help with my clothes." Then, faintly defensive, "I had a fall from my horse."

Geordie helped him remove his coat. "When you fell was this all you had on your upper half?" he inquired.

Murdo grunted.

Geordie inspected the signs of battering.

Murdo said that the girl would fetch some bandages. He wanted Geordie to bind his shoulder; he'd broken his collarbone.

Geordie got down on his creaking knees to remove Murdo's shoes. Murdo stepped out of the stinking pile of his clothes and said, as he stepped into the bath, "Throw them away."

Geordie said nonsense, he'd send the coat and trousers down to the laundress. Then, in response to a muttered remark, "It isn't parsimonious to spare someone else's expense, Mr. Hesketh. Is the word 'frugal' not in your vocabulary?" Geordie stooped to gather clothes and shoes. He said he'd find a shirt that could spare a sleeve.

"Get my best—shirt, shoes, suit," Murdo said. He was craning about trying to see his injured shoulder. "How bad is it?"

Geordie sat on the edge of the tub and washed his hands, then he began to clear away resinous blood, and lymph, like blistered varnish. He was gentle and took his time. Murdo turned his head at a hard angle and Geordie watched his top lip quiver. Geordie had never known anyone more susceptible to kindness, and less inclined to take it kindly.

"My *best* clothes," said Murdo, "for an interview with James."

"Ah!" said Geordie. "Do you know where Miss Paxton is?"

"I sent her to Glasgow and your Mr. Tannoy."

"Did Lord Hallowhulme . . . offer her insult?" Geordie asked, delicate.

"Yes, that's it. That's all." Murdo stared at the brass taps. He seemed relieved, perhaps that Geordie had simply asked and, answered, hadn't pressed for any further explanation. Geordie picked up Murdo's wet hand and put the soap in it. He said he was sorry now that he hadn't reported what he had seen at Hallowhulme's salmon hatchery. "But you always had a low opinion of the girl, Mr. Hesketh. Billie's manner was unaffected, so you decided that she *knew too much*."

"She was born knowing," Murdo said, "in compensation for her incapacity."

Geordie puffed up and Murdo glared at him, merely irritated, but intimidating—naked, injured, touchy, and still quelling. "Don't defend her," Murdo said. "She ran away as much from Henry Maslen's inattention, as from James's unwanted attentions."

"Then why take your cousin to task?"

"I'm finished with James. And this helps."

Geordie repossessed the bundled clothes. He removed Murdo's wallet and revolver from his coat pockets and put them down on the chair by the tub.

"When you return can you wash my hair, Geordie? I can't lift this arm." The arm stirred, the water in the bath made its harmonious lapping. A tap dripped, the sound reflected sharply from the tiled walls. Geordie looked at Murdo's profile, a face that, although exhausted, remained taut, shaped by confidence and command. Geordie began to have his doubts. He remembered his collapse at Ernol, Murdo practically jollying him out of his distress. There was something in Murdo's face, shining like a clear sky in a high wind, wind without any other weather.

Geordie didn't want to be exposed to it. He questioned his strength. Any knowledge that could transmute Murdo Hesketh's brute vitality might kill Mr. Betler, might strip the flesh from his bones.

Murdo fell asleep while Geordie was washing his hair. The suds spilled and glided on the water, mingled with a silt of dissolved blood, and the black tea stain of peat. Under the water Murdo's form shifted shape and size, like the highest point of a wicked reef, submerged at high tide.

Geordie thought, *Poor Ian.* Then, along the same lines, "Poor Lord Hallowhulme," he said aloud. "He was out of his depth with Billie Paxton. I'm convinced his gallantry did have a gradual design. But in his admiration he was helpless."

Murdo was awake again, he leaned forward while Geordie rinsed the suds from his hair. "James thinks that if a thing is carefully planned, it will go according to plan," Murdo said.

"That's a line from Minnie's play, did you know?"

"Really?" Murdo pushed his wet hair back, subsided while Geordie made lather in a shaving mug. He tilted his chin to Geordie's razor. A minute later he stood, and Geordie gave him a towel. He draped his head and scrubbed his hair, one-handed. His voice was muffled. "Or, rather, James is so involved in his planning—its detail—that he can't imagine deviations. He's thorough in all situations he can *provide for*, but there are things that are invisible to him."

"Like spirits," said Geordie. "The Isle loud with noises."

"He's no Prospero." Murdo emerged from the towel, his thick, fine hair a raised pelt. He told Geordie that, on a picnic several summers ago, there was a little bit of play where each family member had to name his or her favorite character from Shakespeare.

Murdo had finished drying, ineffectually. He was unable to fasten the towel around his waist, and dropped it. Geordie had him step into his drawers. He made a bow in the drawstring.

"Sorry to be so helpless," Murdo said.

Geordie found a spot on Murdo's ribs, free of bruises, and patted him there.

"Minnie chose Jacques from *As You Like It*. An artist and philosopher, she said. And James said, 'All talk. One of Mr. Shakespeare's gloomy, hesitant hairsplitters.' James himself chose the Duke from *Measure for Measure*, and Minnie—fighting back—said, 'That awful man! Who schemes everyone out of their passions and organizes them out of their fate.' "

"Please—only shallow breaths while I bind this. And stand up straight."

Murdo pulled himself erect. When he continued though, his tone was dreamy. "Ingrid chose Antonio from *Twelfth Night*. We thought she'd say Olivia—her part. Antonio was like Ruth in the Bible, she said. *Whither thou goest, I will go*. She said, 'No one in Shakespeare loves like Antonio.' "

Geordie knew why he was being told this. But he kept quiet, only split the end of the bandage and made a neat knot. He worked Murdo's shirt on without sacrificing a sleeve. Then trousers, braces, waistcoat. "Where is your watch?" Geordie asked, and saw the light change in Murdo's face, a storm of pallor. After a moment Murdo said, "My watch hasn't worked since it went in the sea."

"Of course." But Geordie had a very clear recollection of Murdo's fob. The mourning fob, jet, a beautiful piece. Again he felt he was gathering evidence and, to disguise a transparently thoughtful silence, he asked, incidentally, what Shakespearean personage Murdo had chosen?

"I've little imagination and a great deal of vanity, so naturally I chose Hamlet."

"I see. So, when you spring out on James this afternoon that's what you'll declare: *It is I, Murdo the Swede!*"

ONE QUESTION IN PARTICULAR, OF ALL THOSE HE DE-flected, caused Murdo pain. He'd left his watch in the tower at Ormabeg. He'd be caught—but why should that matter to him, who had courted an *end*, who had been full of amorous thoughts where the holes in his Colt's swing gate were black beauty spots on sleek gun steel. What hurt was that, when he gave his lie to Geordie, Murdo remembered that, on the day after the *Gustav Edda* sank, when he asked Johan Gutthorm, "What does your watch say?" Gutthorm had replied, "My watch isn't keeping correct time."

OBERON AND TITANIA, WITH PUCK AND PEASBLOSSOM IN attendance. Geordie saw that Lord and Lady Hallowhulme, Jenny, and Henry Maslen were first through the door. Then the three Tegners, and Rixon and Elov. The men left their hats on the hall table. Jenny gathered the ladies' hats by their ribbons, her hands full of flower baskets, it seemed.

Geordie, watching this sight for the last time, committed it to memory: the figures blending with the hall's dark wood as they moved about shedding outdoor clothes, against the hall window's textured light and modest amount of color, a heraldic device of a salamander in the flames, and a motto about what the "Princes of the Earth" might do with the permission of the last laird. (The man who built Kiss, who imported tons of topsoil for his plantation on the Nose, then had to sell the whole island.) Geordie committed all this to memory and the past, and consoled himself with thoughts about his roses, his cozy butler's pantry, and his cat—even eager for its reproaches.

Minnie had dawdled, and came in last, stumbling on the doorsill. She was still reading Sherlock Holmes.

Geordie stepped up to the family, showed himself. He asked Lord and Lady Hallowhulme if he might have a word with them. He was packed, he said, leading them away down the hall toward Lord Hallowhulme's study. Clara inclined her head. "If there is anything you'd rather have sent on to you?" she said. And, "You will be sure to take leave of the children."

"Certainly, Lady Hallowhulme. I don't sail until seven."

"And you'll remember us to Mr. and Mrs. Tannoy—we had them to dinner once at Port Clarity."

Geordie nodded. He stepped ahead of Clara and opened James's study door. Clara moved her skirt, an ostentatious gesture of unwillingness, so that Geordie felt he was herding and cramming her into the room. She gave him a look of cool inquiry, then went on. Hallowhulme seemed to notice nothing amiss— he simply followed his wife, making a little shuffle around Geordie, and muttering, "Capital houseguest, Betler. Sorry to see you go."

Henry Maslen was already in the study, speaking to Murdo. He spun toward the door, blushed, said, "Excuse me!" to his employer. To Murdo he said, "Thank you, Mr. Hesketh." He then departed in a hurry.

Geordie was glad Murdo had given Henry Maslen news of Billie's whereabouts. He had thought Murdo might leave that more pedestrian task to him. It was clear from Henry's look as he left the room—self-conscious, but relieved, and completely free of rancor—that Murdo hadn't spoken to him about Hallow-hulme's attentions to Billie. *Good man,* Geordie thought of Murdo, *not to scotch Maslen's chance of advancement, and make him feel he should fight a duel.*

Lord Hallowhulme favored Murdo with the astounded and affronted look he often assumed when surprised by an unexpected visitor.

Clara put a finger on Geordie's wrist. "Mr. Betler, could you please tell Ward to go ahead and serve lunch."

"Of course, Lady Hallowhulme."

Murdo moved some books and papers from a chair before James's cluttered desk. He took Clara's hand and had her sit. "Geordie," said Murdo, dismissing him.

"Well—I'll leave you to it," said Geordie. He glanced back from the doorway and saw Lady Hallowhulme looking at him as if in appeal, an expression of desperation breaking through her usual dull breeding. And, with the stern self-assurance of a doctor prescribing an uncomfortable but effective course of treatment, Geordie closed the door on her.

"GEORDIE IS NO LONGER IN MY CONFIDENCE," MURDO began. "He imagines that I mean to take you to task, James, for kissing Billie Paxton."

James paled and began to bluster—a completely natural reaction—and Murdo managed to appear odd and inhuman himself as he pushed on. "Clara, you're here as my witness."

"Murdo. Dear—" said Clara. "Please."

Murdo moved from the window where he had blended, his body with a high-backed chair, his hair with the sun in colorless glass. He felt like a wolf, peeling off from the pack, beginning to trot nonchalantly around into a flanking position, brushing its sides on snowy tree trunks as it goes, coy, as if its only intention is to clean its coat. Murdo stopped in front of James and said, "Rory Skilling is a slovenly man of rather limited ability. That surprised me. Really, I was astonished to see someone clever fall back from a scheme of intricate design on something *crude*— for want of a better word. Besides, I'd have thought that, after Johan Gutthorm's mistake, you'd have preferred to see to things *yourself*."

"I think my wife should not be party to this discussion," James said.

"She's involved, James."

"But I'd never harm Clara!" James was aggrieved.

"Why?"

"Because she's my wife!" James was amazed.

"Attached to you, so exempt."

James looked blank, then he squinted, and his top lip lifted as if he was straining—to hear perhaps, or to follow what was being said, as if Murdo was speaking in a language foreign to him.

Clara said that they had quite lost her, and Murdo said that this was not a moment for courtesy. Then he told James that he still had no idea how James had done it—it was all too complex and specialized. "I'm betting, like a gambler. I'm *calling you*. I'm paying to see your hand."

James remained blank. After a moment he said, "Ah—a figure of speech." Then he began to explain. He couldn't resist explaining.

He said that the device itself was simple but innovative. If he said so himself. The task was always to deliver a flame safely to

the priming charge, and degrees of flame to complement different rates of detonation. "But there's no point in me explaining
the theory of the problem to you. You—who can't guess *how*.
Who can come up with clever figures of speech, but can't
guess." James was *boasting*. He said that his problem was how to
work from a great distance, in space *and* time, and to act without
touching. "To light no touch paper," James said. "To touch off
no fuse." Then, "See, I can do it, too—make matter out of
words." He went on to say that he'd hit on a notion—a notion so
inevitable that he was sure it could stay his secret and still be
copied, copied by human ingenuity itself. He called it his
"timing bomb." The batteries for the telephone exchange supplied the charge, they were attached by wires to an alarm clock,
its hammer and its bell. When the alarm went off and the bell
and striker came into contact, the charge jumped through another wire, delivering fire—in the form of electricity—into a
blasting cartridge. "One of Alfred Nobel's gelignite blasting car-
tridges. Manufactured in Glasgow." This priming charge was, in
turn, attached to a bundle of dynamite. "The batteries—three
feet in height and twenty-five pounds apiece, plus the baled cables and the steel rails, *and* the seats from my beautiful Panhard et
Levassor high-wheeler—all formed a buffer that concentrated
the blast against the hull."

Clara jumped up with a cry and covered her face. She said,
"Please, God, no more." She said it in Swedish.

"The timing was intricately planned," James said. "*Eleven
hours and fifty-nine minutes*. Though I was haunted by an odd fear
that the clock would go backward—as that case clock of your
grandmother's once chose to, Clara." James addressed his wife.
"Do you recall—we came down to breakfast one morning and
found the clock making a senile purr and telling time backward."

He nodded at Murdo. "Prefer to do things for myself. Right about that. Not always easy to find someone to follow the thinking." James gave one of the small grimaces that Murdo had long ago realized was his imitation of what he saw—all he *could* see—when people bared their teeth to smile broadly. James said, "There's plenty of 'confession' material here—eh, Cousin—regarding aspirations to 'testimony' and 'truth.' "

Murdo might normally have said—in as dull and discouraging a way as possible—"I can't follow you." But he knew that when James was under pressure his speech became very odd—for instance pronouns began to vanish from his sentences. Murdo had always thought this was James's way of asserting himself by abdicating into the impersonal—making his views sound universal and inevitable. But it was something else. A quirk. A characteristic. James was full of talk, but not full of himself, so that people who saw him only a little called him "good-natured." For Murdo the "natured" part of the public praise was coming into focus. Was this a product of nature—an accident of birth rather than biography—this heartless, hobbyist attention to detail, this *disease* of visionary confidence?

"I wrote to Elov Jansen," said James. "In time, too—but foreign mails are very unreliable. I filled three cabins with men I paid to leave at Luag. At eight bells there was only one stoker on watch below. One attendant at the furnace."

"That still leaves five dead," Murdo said. "By your intention."

"Four, cousin. The fellow pinned by Mr. Maslen's trunk wouldn't have been moving luggage at eight bells." James seemed to get pleasure from correcting Murdo.

"The steward. I believe his name was Alfred," said Murdo.

"Please," Clara said—in Swedish, perhaps to Murdo, or possibly to the God of her childhood.

"Speak English!" her husband shouted. He balled his fists and beat the air. "Don't be *secret together.*"

Once he'd raised his voice, James was unable to wind it down. He went on, loud, toneless, declamatory. He explained and expounded. That steward would certainly not have been crushed by Mr. Maslen's trunk, since Mr. Maslen had *undertaken* to ship with the Stolnsay pilot from Dorve the day before.

"Your instructions—as conveyed to him by Gutthorm—were so particular that Mr. Maslen took his cue from their tone rather than their substance," Murdo said. "Maslen decided that you were *very particular* about punctuality, and that he must, at all costs, arrive on the appointed day. Or as near to it as possible. And, James, what about the child, the three-year-old in the salon? What about her in the cold sea off Alesund Head?"

James went purple.

Murdo asked, "What was your margin for error?"

James thrust his own hand into his mouth and bit himself. He bore down, grunting with effort, and blood ran from his broken skin. His wife went to him and pulled the hand down, held it. She said, "Don't do that, James." She was so matter-of-fact that Murdo knew she'd seen him do it before.

"Clara—" James said to Murdo, through lips lacquered with wet blood, "—was a breath of fresh air. My feelings were always too strong for the other ladies, who seemed to feel nothing for me. Clara was the crown of my life—perfect, *picture* perfect, until her visit home. You know what visit. I came to fetch her and my"—his voice strangled—"my little Ingrid—and I found the *hussar* at home and banging about with a cord through his jacket sleeves and jacket slung around his shoulders like a person from Pushkin—"

Murdo was able to make sense of this only because his own

thoughts had often returned to that time—Clara's first visit to her mother after her marriage. He said, "I'd broken my collarbone."

"Showing off," said Clara. Then, very low and tentative, "James—Murdo and I were never alone."

"Yes! I prefer to do things for myself!" James shouted. "Including fathering my own children!"

Murdo thought about the theater, men wearing dummy horses they seemed to sit astride, a puppet cavalry wheeling onstage to the crash of tin cymbals. He thought of ice cream and ice-skating; of his eleven-year-old sister Ingrid carrying little Ingrid across the hall, her back arched, little Ingrid's red boots banging against big Ingrid's shins.

"The *hussar* put me in a difficult position," James said. "Required me to exercise aggression. Masculine competition. Difficult for me."

Clara said to her husband, "You've made a terrible mistake."

"In your terrible certainty," said Murdo.

But James wasn't attending at all. He was talking. About the cuckoo in his nest. And about *character*. No matter what he was given, Rixon remained Rixon. There was nothing at which Rixon excelled. The only education that stuck was a conventional mimicry of conventional male behavior. "Always catching him practicing gestures with a cigar. A dandy, like his father," James said. He asked when the world would understand that everything, that *character*, in the modern and the old-fashioned senses— personality, and force of will—were formed from one cell, one germ plasm, at the moment of conception. It was a miracle. Too much of a miracle to go unmonitored, or unchecked.

Clara groped about for something with which to wipe her face. She fumbled with the scarf knotted at her waist. Murdo passed her his handkerchief. "You've made a terrible mistake," she sobbed at her husband.

"And—where was your margin for error?" Murdo asked again, cold.

James peered at him, cockeyed. It was that odd look he had, his eyes wide only because his brows were hitched high. It was as if his eyelids couldn't open fully of their own accord, but required his whole upper face to move, too.

"Rixon is *yours*," Clara told her husband. "I've been true to the vows I made when I married you."

"I see."

"Don't hurt our son," Clara begged.

James peered at her, mouth open, breathing noisily. Then his mouth snapped shut, and he said, "These are *reasons* I'm giving. You wanted me to be magnanimous to Murdo. Our cousin, you reminded me. I was magnanimous. Never suspected. But you bloomed and blushed and flourished. And he debauched our daughter. Tried to, or wanted to. I sent for the coroner from Edinburgh not to see whether Ingrid had taken her own life—I knew she had—but to see whether she was still *intact*."

Clara made a low, pained sound. She began to walk— tottered slowly to the door. Murdo intercepted her. He held her. He watched her hands, picking and picking at his jacket as his mother's had plucked repeatedly at the coverlet of her deathbed.

"As it turned out she was," James said. "It wasn't *that* then. Of course, that would have been a far simpler matter. I racked my brains. I realized that, on Ingrid's part, it was a chaste affection. A noble affection. But while he dallied with her, she guessed, you see. She watched you together. You. You, Clara. Always asking him, 'Will you take Rixon?' She was a loyal daughter, and *ashamed* of her mother."

"No," said Clara.

And Murdo, "Ingrid told me she loved me, and I said, 'Don't love me.' I said I was fond of her, glad of her company, counted her as a friend. And she gave me a big shove, and ran away weeping. I thought she'd be all right. That we'd be awkward. She'd treat me coldly, perhaps, and everyone would wonder what had happened. I anticipated embarrassment. And I thought perhaps she'd renew her attack. Something, anyway, just *something more*." Then, in despair, "Not more nothing!"

Clara touched his back.

"Look at you!" James yelled at them.

Clara drew herself up; she seemed to collect herself. "Well, James, you're not a man who made much of"—she sighed, as if the air were thin and insufficient nourishment—"of my hand on your shoulder. Sometimes you would flinch. Even at first. Affection must have its rewards." She said, "I've been a good wife to you. In fact, I've followed my principles. But I must tell you that I now think my principles are only prison bars. I've incarcerated myself and excluded others."

Murdo tried to take Clara's hand, but she shook it free.

"However," Clara said to James, "I will continue to follow my principles. I'll provide an *example* for you. You won't harm Murdo. He'll go away, and you can stop thinking about him. You won't hurt Rixon—your son, however unsatisfactory you find him. There will be no divorce, no court case, no untoward exclusions from any will you make. You will make no more murderous budgets where a manservant and a stoker are merely 'necessary expenditure.' You will obey me in all this, and I will save you—your life, fortune, and reputation."

James grunted.

"Let yourself be guided," Clara said, measured and firm.

"You *don't know*, James. You were wrong about Rixon. And Murdo didn't touch Ingrid. *You don't know.*"

"You had no margin for error. And Johan Gutthorm didn't have the correct time," Murdo said.

Clara was looking at her husband with an expression of compassion. "James. The death of a child *is* terrible. All of life is its anniversary. Each week I say, 'At this time last week, month, year, I was potting parsley, and Ingrid was walking back to Scouse Beach.' I say, 'A week ago, a month, a year, two years ago at this time my daughter stopped breathing.' I'm living in her time, not my own. At intervals I'm living in her last day, as if that's the only thing left for me to do. James, I know you've felt it, too—felt your life taken. It's what we *must* feel. It doesn't mean that someone—anyone—has stolen from you, or behaved treacherously. You imagine someone must have meant to hurt you—hurt *only* you, since you feel only *your* injuries—but death is terrible."

She turned to Murdo, looked up into his face, tearful, appealing. "Please," she said. "You're safe. He's safe. I can persuade you both."

James was pale, perspiring, his eyes darted about.

"Your reckoning was right out," Murdo said to him. "Here I am, alive. Rixon is at your table eating his lunch. Fifteen people are in their graves—by your murderous incompetence."

James exploded. He picked up a pile of books and papers and threw them on the floor; he overturned his easel and its dust-furred oil painting; he blundered about the room breaking inkwells, vases, instruments of measurement. He flung his leaf press at the wall and showered the study with sere green flakes.

Murdo pulled Clara out of the room and closed the door on the din, the grunts of effort, the aggrieved whining.

"If he had made less money, and merited less indulgence, he might have learned to think twice instead of building and building on his first thought," Murdo said. "God save us from his kind."

"I've made mistakes," Clara said. She had his hand now, was holding it hard in both of hers.

"You chose James."

"I can't take that as a mistake, Murdo, and wish away Rix and Minnie, whom I love."

Murdo looked down at her, the pink scalp showing through the thin hair on her crown, the shadows dappling her skin, as if she were spoiling in pieces. He looked at the skin on the back of the hands that held him, foxed, like an old map. He looked without compassion because he knew she was about to ask him to spare James. To think of her, of Rixon, of Minnie.

"Don't start," he said. "I can't keep what I know from Geordie. I owe Ian that."

Clara shook her head. She said her mistake was her silence. She'd lived so long with James she'd become accustomed to going unheard. First it was a deprivation. Then a form of immunity. Nothing she said made any difference. "I forgot entirely the real effect of speech." She crushed Murdo's hands between her own. "Listen," she said, urgent. "You told me how you felt when you visited Karl Borg. Locked into his cell, you said, and the course of his execution. Monstrous and cold-blooded, you called it. You said that Karl's condemnation saved no lives."

"Karl was hapless. He hadn't handled a pistol. He didn't hunt. He had no former experience of the effect of a well-placed shot. He had a fatal failure of imagination."

"So did James," Clara said.

"James thought it through. He planned minutely. But he

didn't distinguish the *people* from his automobile or the phone cables. He made sacrifices, he set himself back months—his alginate factory and the telephone exchange. And, he said, about the stoker, the man left on watch, 'The devil take him.' "

"Have you nothing on your conscience?" Clara said.

Murdo said nothing.

Clara placed her hand, palm flat, against his shoulder. Its warmth, if it had any, couldn't make its way through the fabric of jacket, shirt, bandages. She began to talk, to tell him something. "I had thought I'd spare you this, Murdo. But you persist in making up your accounts, like James. Blame *me*. I told my secret. I went up after lunch to see how Ingrid was—she'd come in out of sorts and complained of a headache. She was upset, so I went to talk to her. They were never easy to show love to, my children. Rixon was—is still—inclined to say: 'Oh, *Mater*!' He's very English. Minnie reads me lectures on 'the feminine education in self-sacrifice,' or 'Science and Sentiment.' Ingrid didn't say anything—she simply shook my love off. She had grown into her strength and out of being mothered. She was very unhappy—but very dignified. When she told me how she felt about you, and what you had answered to her honest approach, I could see she was serious, and that it wasn't something she'd get over easily. I wanted to—nip it in the bud." Clara paused, then said, in quite another tone, sly, insinuating, "By the way, do you remember the rosebuds I was to wear at my wedding?"

Murdo started, then dipped his head to regard her full in the face. "What?" he said. It was all he could manage.

"I told Ingrid my secret. I told her that she was your daughter."

Murdo frowned at her; he tried to think.

"You were—*great trouble*. You were out of your mind with drink. You threw my rosebuds—my 'girlhood' in the language of flowers—into the kitchen fire. You wept. My dear. The very next morning—my wedding day—I looked into your face and realized you had no memory of what had happened. And I felt as light as air." Clara actually smiled, remembering. "You didn't like James any more than I did. I liked his money. I was a greedy, indolent girl. You wanted me to be some kind of free, fine, noble creature—but *I wasn't like that.* I loved you so much—my miserable, enraged, bawling bobby calf. And when Ingrid was born, with her feathers for hair, I knew she was yours."

Again Clara freed her hand, this time to use her sharp fist to beat herself on the breastbone. "I should have told *you*, not her!" she cried. "I should have made it *your* task to keep her at arm's length till she fell into some other arms. I'd loved you, and given you up—it was easy when you were fifteen. Ingrid saw what I had only seen after my marriage—the man you became. I gave you up—but she couldn't." Clara threw back her head, and sobbed. "*She left me.* My daughter!"

At that moment, hearing herself called, Clara's daughter appeared—she'd been in the upper hall on her way to her room and Conan Doyle's *Final Problem.* Minnie pounded down the lower flight, sailed like a swinging boom around the newel post, and landed near Murdo and her mother. "Mama!" Minnie was horrified. She hugged Clara, held her as Clara's hair collapsed and oozed out of its pins and over her face. Then, with canine alertness, Jenny appeared, too—and between them the younger women began to lead Clara away.

"Come upstairs, Lady Hallowhulme," said Jenny.

"Shall we lie down, Mother?"

Clara turned her ruined face to Murdo and whispered something, something insane, nonsensical: "For thousands of years, man has made a god of Chance—"

Murdo's hair prickled.

"Mother!" said Minnie, moved and flattered.

Her mother patted her shoulder. "Then what does he go on to say—the silly man?"

Minnie quoted: "It's time man made a god of Will."

"Yes. Dreadful," said Clara. Again she looked at Murdo, her eyes so suffused they seemed blind. "Then the clever young man says: 'But sometimes Chance will make a god of a person—or an instrument of God.'"

"That's right," said Minnie.

"That clever Mr. Shaw," said her mother, with a smile at Minnie. Then, to Murdo, "You don't owe me anything. But I am owed—I'm owed a life. One life. And Chance has made a god of you."

GEORDIE HAD AN UNSATISFACTORY LEAVE-TAKING. AFTER lunch he went to the kitchen to give away those things of Ian's he'd decided not to keep. He sat with Mrs. Deet, Cook, Ward the butler, and Robert the footman with whom he was friendly, and talked. Jenny was with Lady Hallowhulme, Mrs. Deet explained. Lady Hallowhulme was in "a taking." "Very unlike her," Deet added. "But I expect you know all about it. Since Agnes tells us Mr. Hesketh's back—Agnes has his muddy clothes to clean—and he had some news of that strange girl, Miss Paxton, and why she ran away."

"It'll all blow over," Geordie told them.

And Robert said, admiring, that the master was human after all.

Geordie could see they were pleased by the thought—that they warmed to the idea of Lord Hallowhulme's human failings.

"What will Mr. Maslen do?" Cook wondered. "Poor man. He needs to stop somewhere. And we'd all rather have him than Johan Gutthorm." This remark set up a quiver of consensual nodding. Then the butler said there wasn't any point in further speculation. Mrs. Deet, for one, would only be able to follow the story like a book with its middle torn out. The rest of them would be back in Edinburgh in three weeks. And London shortly after, since the Lords would be sitting soon.

They all told Geordie he must write, visit—and he took his leave.

He found the Tegners, mother and daughters, and they told him the same—*if he was ever in Malmö.* Jane thanked him for his kindness to her girls and teased him about his alternative career on the stage.

Rixon and Elov had gone riding. Minnie—whom Geordie most wanted to see—was with her mother. He stood at the door with his bags and his coat over his arm, looking back at the empty hall, the fresh flowers doubled, a splash of color on the silver of the hall mirror; the dark-paneled walls. Sunlight angled in the big landing window and raised more color on the dim carpeted stairs where dust hovered like watery midges. *Yet,* he thought, *I've been happy here.* What right had he to be happy where he'd come to bury his brother? But Geordie's shame seemed rebellious, while happiness was the authority against which it rebelled. No one should ever quarrel with happiness. Geordie thought of Billie Paxton, how she'd done something quite different with her grief. He had kept up his conversation with Ian, wrote to him still, because, without Ian, Geordie wasn't wholly himself. Over the years Ian had become not just the repository of Geordie's private self, but the *occasion* of that private self. Geordie wrote to Ian to *be* Geordie—not Mr. Betler the butler. But Billie Paxton had lost the person nearest to her. She'd been so close to Edith, and so dependent, that she'd let her sister carry her soul—or they had lived and breathed in a cloud of each other's souls. It was as if these sisters, not existing wholly and exclusively in themselves, couldn't be separated, or separately extinguished. Now Billie didn't only check herself with thoughts about what her sister would do and say, she simply did as Edith would, because Edith was present to her, as a stain, a preserving medium, a benign contamination.

Geordie would see Billie soon. He and the Tannoys would help her. The thought kept him buoyant. He was carrying something away with him—the intimacy of Kiss—which was a kind of intimacy he'd never known before. Geordie had confidence that, in the course of his life, he'd have further civil conversation with Lady Hallowhulme, and young Rixon, and friendly conversation with Minnie, but he had Billie to care for, to set on her feet, to pass over to the kind patronage of the Tannoys. Ian was gone—but he'd still be Geordie. He'd be Billie Paxton's Geordie.

Alan Skilling was sitting on the gatehouse doorstep. He got up and wrestled one of Geordie's bags out of his grip. "I've got nothing to do today. It's the Sabbath. I'm just waiting," he said.

"Waiting to do something?"

"To be asked to do something. And for my father."

"Where is he?"

"At Southport, I expect, looking over the cannery." Alan went with Geordie around the harbor, both hands on the bag's handle, while it banged on his legs. Once Geordie tried to retrieve it, and Alan growled, "I can manage."

When they got to the ship, Geordie put his bags down at the foot of the gangplank and searched his pockets for a shilling, and for paper and pen. He wrote out the Tannoys' Glasgow address and told Alan that, when he was a little older, and if he had his father's permission, he could come and ask for a job. "If I'm not there, tell the people Mr. Betler wants you."

"Thank you, I might, too," Alan said. "But I don't like to leave the island."

Geordie raised his eyebrows at the boy.

"Father let our croft go—it's all over bracken now. But when I'm old enough to recover it, I'll ask Lord Hallowhulme for it back. I remember that I liked it—though I was too little to be much use. When my mother was alive, we'd put in the barley, then take our cow up to the sheiling to cut peats, then father was on his cousin's boat, after herring, then we'd harvest, and put by everything we'd need."

Geordie looked down at Alan's thin, tense, sober face, and said that whatever Alan chose, he was sure he'd do well.

"Before you go, sir, was there any news of Billie?"

"Billie," said Geordie, smiling, "is in Glasgow with my employers."

"Oh—that villain," said Alan, darkly.

"Lord Hallowhulme?"

"No. Not him," Alan said. Then, "Well, Mr. Betler, give her my love. And my thanks. And tell her that she shouldn't fret—no one has to remember to feed Alan Skilling."

Geordie reached in his pocket and gave the boy another coin. Then he went on board.

At dusk, when the ferry sailed, and Geordie had already installed himself on a padded bench in its small salon, Murdo Hesketh appeared. Murdo threw his one bag into the netted rack in the corner farthest from the stove, his astrakhan on top of it, and sat down well away from Geordie. Geordie kept his eyes turned toward the man, waiting, and eventually Hesketh turned and gave Geordie a look shockingly like the look Geordie had been given by a mangy lion in a damp brick cell in Glasgow Zoo, a look of impotent, weary hatred. Geordie looked away.

At midnight, when Alesund Head was well astern, shrinking, losing all its naked distinction, and the two women nearest Murdo got up to take a turn around the deck, Geordie took their place.

Murdo didn't open his eyes. Geordie could see that the bruise on Murdo's forehead had spilled its yellow into the nearest eye socket. But Murdo knew Geordie was there. He said, "I am going with you."

"Did you see Minnie? Alan?"

"No. I left Alan some shoes. I lost them for a time, but when I retrieved my horse I found them. They were a present from Billie."

"Thoughtful girl."

"She is. I'll go with you to see her settled. Like Mr. Maslen with his 'cottage in Port Clarity.' Settle Billie. Soothe the baby and go back to the book."

"What's *your* book, Murdo?"

Murdo opened his eyes and smiled. "Job, apparently. *'I was not in safety, neither had I rest, neither was I quiet; yet trouble came.'* "

WHEN THEY GOT TO ANDREW TANNOY'S GLASGOW HOUSE, Geordie and Murdo found that Billie wasn't there, and hadn't been heard from.

15 ⚜ Maintaining
a Good Character

Billie finally fell asleep on the train from Oban to Glasgow. On the water some involuntary fear had kept her aroused and awake. When the pilot's steamer came out of the reef into the tail of the Wash there was a faint shock against the port side. Billie was able to reason that away—it was only an adjustment—but she couldn't sleep. The train carriage didn't roll, it jostled. And she was done in. She woke in the outskirts of the city, looked out on sooty brick and—on a bridge—through the undulations of iron girders. She discovered that she'd lost Edith. Had she left her sister in the sea? Or was it that she was doing something of which her sister would not approve?

Billie began to talk to herself. She talked herself off the train and through into the echoing concourse of the station. "Don't sit like that, Billie," she said first, then, "What were you thinking?" And, arguing with her sister, and her sister's ideas: "I'll not go where I'm not wanted." She raised her hot, sticky eyes to the August sun coming through the station's lofty glass ceiling. Pigeons crossed above her, dancing a quadrille in the air, some flying from a discharge of steam on a near platform, others from the complicated metal wrenching of carriages coupling.

Billie found a lady with two girls, all in straw hats and white summer gloves. She stopped before them, put down her bag, and dug in her purse for a paper. She asked could madam please read this letter—she'd forgotten its directions. The timetable, too? She would commit it to memory. No, she wasn't able to read—it was a defect, a kind of disease, "congenital word blindness." Madam said that, of course, the Express left from Edinburgh, Billie should buy a ticket to Edinburgh. She and her girls were going there, second-class, since it wasn't a long journey. There was the ticket office. Billie had ten minutes.

On the train madam and the girls shared their sandwiches and, at Edinburgh, madam stood by Billie as she bought her ticket to London—a space in the sleeper car. Madam took Billie to the tearooms and sat her at a table facing the window, and a clock at the end of the platform with the thickest traffic of porters. Madam said that before Billie left the train at London she must ask a steward for further directions. Madam had, of course, glanced at the paragraphs preceding Reverend Vause's instructions and knew that Billie wasn't running away but taking up an offer of sanctuary. She ordered Billie tea and scones, wished her good luck, and, girls in tow, walked away into the crowd.

The tearooms were noisy, and all the noises were sharp. A boy at a table near Billie kicked the leg of his chair, and someone behind her tapped their spoon on their saucer. Billie drank her tea, but left her scones. Her throat hurt and it was difficult to swallow. She felt dry and exposed, like a stretch of sand from which the sea has retreated. After a time she went out into the din and waited under the clock, then, when the flow of people on her platform began to include passengers, she found her coach and her seat.

Inside her a tide was going out. Appetite departed first—before the train—then, as whistles were blown up and down the platform and, ahead, the engine began to twitch the carriages into place, twitch and tighten and apply its different rule of inertia, the tide took Billie's vitality, and her lucidity. She sat with her head nodding and knocking against the window while time tried to untangle itself from her day, gently, as though not to awaken her, pushing its yarn back through loosened knots, unraveling, following its own thread and rolling her out of its skein as it went.

Billie was hot. Sweltering in the trap on the final slope to the Broch. Henry was telling her about Lord Hallowhulme's stepladder. Then she was on the ladder, and opposite Lord Hallowhulme. He was asking her about herself, in search of a common ground for conversation. But his kindness was lost on her, because her side of the ladder was in the green water under Stolnsay wharf, and she was Edith, hair trailing upward and her fingernails drifting above her like fallen plum blossom suspended on the surface of a pond. She was cold, not drowned, but draining water on a stone tower top in the rain, with Rory Skilling lying on her, heavy and stifling.

Billie woke up when the illumination increased. The scenery was shining in her face—a river mouth under a white sky. She went out into the corridor where a man noticed her confusion and said, informative, "Berwick upon Tweed," and "The dining car is open." Then, to show he meant nothing by it, he shook out his paper and hid his face. Billie watched the attendant make her bed, then lay, aching in every joint, and gently jerked about all night.

At London the train she wanted left from another station. A porter put her in a cab. Another—she paid them well—set her on a seat on the right platform with only an hour to wait. She jumped up once when she saw her father, Edith, herself, hurrying back into the clamor of the main concourse. They'd got off at the wrong stop. Beyond those doors was not the port, but Genoa's old town, where the buildings leaned together so that their shadows could climb them, and flower, and bear fruit. Billie heard her father promising his girls that it wasn't far to walk. The doors flashed, and they were gone.

Someone asked, "Is this your train?" Billie peered about. It was her train. A train from which she saw the sea several times, and on which she was asked *was she unwell?* Yes. But she was nearly there—in her zinc bedstead under the slope of the roof.

"Miss? Miss?" She had to change trains. She splashed her face in the washroom and combed her hair, twisted it into a thick knot at her nape. Four hours, the stationmaster said, and that there was a quiet parlor in the pub on the high street. But Billie took a seat in the station and watched the line back the way her train had come, a canted curve. The oak trees were dark now, in August, but lightening, leaves brown at their limbs' ends. Billie had missed the trees, their temperate confidences, volume, their stayed stirring.

A slow train on a branch line. Billie lay down on the timber slat seat. Then, at her journey's end, she had a little bit of luck. She heard herself saying it—"A little bit of luck"—just as her father had used to, making excuses for the heartless chance to which he was devoted, his luck, every time it turned back for a moment to trifle with him again. Billie even coughed like her father, her voice caught on something as she tried to get it out quickly, when she saw that, at the same time that she had alighted, so had the Reverend Vause. Billie croaked his name, and began to cough. He dropped his bag and started toward her. He caught her. She drooped in his arms, coughing. He called for water and the train was delayed while its tufty-eared ticket taker talked to the stationmaster and the Reverend Vause. Indeed, he'd noticed her, but not that she was sick. Reverend Vause held a glass to Billie's lips. "Why didn't you stop somewhere? Were you short of funds?"

"I still have my forty pounds from Aunt Blazey. Henry kept Edith's. Henry's alive—but you know that."

"Mr. Maslen survived?"

Billie remembered that Lord Hallowhulme had looked over the letter—dictated to Clara—before posting it. She said to the reverend that maybe she was meant to disappear into Lord Hallowhulme's deep pockets.

The Reverend Vause said—very worried, and falsely bright—that *here was Owen*, sent to meet him with Mrs. Wood's trap. "You remember Owen."

Owen: "Wilhelmina."

The Reverend Vause: "I'll carry Miss Paxton, Owen."

A LITTLE OVER A WEEK LATER BILLIE WAS ALLOWED OUT, on a wicker lounger placed in a sheltered corner of the garden. Olive Vause arranged a rug on Billie's legs then put on an apron and gardening gloves, took secateurs in hand, and walked into a frozen fireworks of summer greenery. She began deadheading. The foxgloves were only standing still for their seed, she explained, tapping it out of the rigid brown rods.

Billie watched. The coneflowers were wilted, their ears laid back. The nearest unfinished thing was the mallow, a pink almost white, a plant that had grown well in the walled garden at Kiss. Bumblebees and cabbage whites worked what was left of the garden.

It was Olive who had cared for Billie. Or rather, it was Olive who supervised the doctor's and servants' care. Nothing had been said about the past. Olive and Billie were engaged in a silent tussle where each meant to make it evident to the other that they were forgiven. Billie was too tired to feel offended.

Billie was tired—but the garden wasn't.

"I wasn't much use to Miss Minnie," Billie explained to Olive. "But I suppose that, if I'd offered myself as a lady's companion, she'd have taken me on."

"Well," said Olive, "that would be a step up in the world."

Billie laughed because, when the heroine of Minnie's play talked about "steps up in the world," the hero said he had stature himself, of himself, and didn't need a box to stand on.

The Reverend Vause appeared. He came across the lawn, removed his hat, said good morning to Billie, and waited for his sister to leave. He eyed Olive, turning his hat by the brim. Billie hadn't seen him since her arrival. She'd been too sick. She still felt queasy and colorless.

"Olive, I'd like to speak to Wilhelmina."

"Indeed," said Olive.

"Please," he said, "remove yourself by a bed or two. Go and discipline your loosestrife or coddle your artemesia."

Olive put her secateurs in her apron pocket. "I'll make up an arrangement for your room," she told Billie, and left.

The Reverend Vause sat on the lawn by Billie's chair, one leg cocked, his wrist propped on his knee. "We're pleased you came, Wilhelmina, and happy you're with us. But, I must admit, we're puzzled by the precipitous haste of your journey—and the state you were in when you arrived. Not just your health, mind, but your attire—torn petticoats, a skirt worn over a dress, the bodice of which was—well—filthy, its stitching popped as though you'd been *swimming* in it. And, though your nails are now trim, they were terribly torn—as if you'd been digging with your bare hands. You must realize that all this requires some explanation. We have to know what happened to you in order to decide how best to help you."

Billie looked at her hands, the nails she'd torn prizing a stone from the top of the tower at Ormabeg, and the still-spreading bruise around the thumb dislocated by the revolver's recoil. She didn't make any answer.

"Furthermore, Mrs. Wood is concerned that you've become accustomed to luxury," he said, and, surprised by the tension in his voice she met his eyes. She told him that Kiss wasn't particularly luxurious. It was rather horrible. Grim and over-ornamented. She was quoting Minnie. "The last laird had terrible taste. Lord Hallowhulme has some beautiful things, though. Lovely vases, *favrile lustering*, and one which sat by the ballroom door, that glowed in the dark as though it held a smoky green genie. I only noticed it the night I went in and found only one branch of candles lit." Billie remembered then the song she'd begun, its opening passage. She heard it, saw what it expressed, the moon breaking free of a cloud and a road suddenly coming clear, the road that was *always there*, the earthly whiteness of a well-worn pilgrims' path.

Billie wriggled out from under the rug, "Come with me," she told the Reverend Vause.

He followed her into his sister's music room. Billie sat at the piano—a grand, like Kiss Castle's. She had played this one once, but like a nervous scullery maid set to dry the best glassware—too tentatively. Billie lifted the lid, said, "Listen," and set her damaged fingertips on the cool keys and played her tune.

"It's lovely," said the Reverend Vause. "Is that all you know?"

"It's unfinished," said Billie. She sat, throbbing with breath and smiles, tears in her eyes, because Edith had come back, rekindled, as steady as a flame in quiet air.

The Reverend Vause sat beside her on the piano stool. He put his hand on her shawled shoulder. He said that his sister Olive had told him how she had hidden her own silver-backed brush and mirror beneath the lining in Billie's bag. "When Olive read about the accident she was distraught—quite ill, and she had to tell me."

"Oh," said Billie.

"She's had her troubles," he said. Then he went on to say that his living was modest, his house dowdy—he wasn't rich like the widow Wood—and the country hereabouts was very quiet—

Billie put a hand on his head, pushed her fingers into his hair. His scalp was humid and the smell rising from it recalled other intimacies. He stopped speaking and began to tremble. He took her other hand and kissed her palm. After a moment he said, "I must know what happened to you." Then, at her silence, and as a kind of guess, he quoted Scripture: *"Put not your trust in Princes."*

Billie told the Reverend Vause about a day they had rowed out to the Old Keep on the island at the mouth of Stolnsay Harbor. Alan Skilling took the first turn at the oars, complaining all the while how the boat was too low at its stern. The Tegners took a turn, remarkably synchronized. Minnie wouldn't row, but gave the Old Keep's history. In the days of its old occupation it was the custom of the laird to send a man to the top of the Keep each night to call out: *"The O'Neil of Kissack has supped; the Princes of the Earth may dine."* "It was a low place," said Billie. "What *pride* they must have had—Minnie said—ruling crofters and paupers, in a tiny treeless town at the edge of Europe, and practicing this ceremony of precedence."

The Reverend Vause gazed at her, waiting.

"I don't know that I can explain," she said, trying to reassure him, and herself. "I couldn't stay there. But, I'm afraid that, without Minnie's talk, I'll start to shrink." She stared at Reverend Vause, very earnest. "I couldn't stay, and I couldn't take anyone away with me, and I didn't want Henry to keep me, like his conscience, in a cottage in Port Clarity." While she spoke Billie left her fingers in his hair, not seeing how he marveled at this, her detached confidence. Instead she took the measure of Mrs. Wood's garden, its cultivated acres, its deep green fathoms. "This is a good place," she said, "and you're a good person."

The Reverend Vause promised that he wouldn't press her, he'd give her time.

THE FOLLOWING DAY, WHEN BILLIE WAS AGAIN INSTALLED in the cane chair in the purple corner the garden, Mrs. Wood came to her with a sewing basket and "a few bits and pieces." She might as well keep her hands occupied. Billie edged a square of cambric, used a crochet hook to make rudimentary lace.

Mrs. Wood looked in on them in the late morning, indoors now—it was hot—and topped up Billie's tasks. A pair of her evening gloves had lost one button, she said, but that only afforded her the opportunity of making a change she'd meant to anyway. Could Billie replace the round buttons with flat?

Over lunch Mrs. Wood asked Billie how she was getting on. "William is expected this afternoon. He will, no doubt, make claims on your attention."

"I'll finish the gloves while he's here," Billie promised. Though, she said, one shouldn't hurry a needle through kid, which too readily tore.

When the Reverend Vause was with her, Billie was glad of the gloves. She didn't want to say anything more to him. She felt as though her talk had, so far, managed to make a safe way through a reef. She had mentioned Lord and Lady Hallowhulme, Minnie and Rixon Hallow, Alan Skilling, Geordie Betler, and the Tegners—but she'd steered clear of that submerged rock. She answered the reverend only as politeness required. Then Mrs. Wood arrived in the drawing room, where Billie and the reverend had been alone for half an hour. Mrs. Wood pointedly settled with her embroidery basket on her knees. Olive followed her sister. Olive had lost a lot of ground between Billie's sixteenth and twentieth years. Her complexion was so dingy that, until she sat with them, her expression was illegible. But Billie thought she saw Olive smirk at her brother.

For another half hour the room was quiet, but not peaceful. It was the silence of suppression—all vulgar noise excluded, and all sound, too, including speech. Then, outside, at the front of the house, came a swelling, clattering, popping racket, succeeded by an audible flurry—the racing footfalls of a number of servants—and a door banging.

The family sat as though stiffened by insult. No one looked at anyone else. A maid thrust her head around the door, her face radiant. It was *an automobile*, she said. Then the butler appeared behind her, in better order, pushed the door wide, and said that a Mrs. Tannoy had come to make inquiries after Miss Paxton.

"Put her in the music room," said Mrs. Wood. And the reverend demanded of Billie, "Who is this person?"

Billie cast the gloves from her, and got up so quickly she upset the sewing basket. She leapt across the spilled needles—a frost star on the carpet, time stopped with a shock. She ran to the music room. No Mr. Tannoy was mentioned. Mrs. Tannoy

wouldn't travel alone. Billie got to the music room a moment after the butler and the visitors. No one's heels had cooled. The
family had followed her, Mrs. Wood saying, "Wilhelmina! You
forget yourself!" But the woman in the dusty dustcoat, veiled
like a beekeeper, a woman with dark skin and a coiled white
plait, turned around and laughed with pleasure as Billie hurled
herself at Geordie Betler.

"LONDON. LONDON LIKE AN OBSTACLE," GEORDIE complained to Mrs. Tannoy. They had to stop in London to rest.
Mrs. Tannoy said they had to be reasonable—meaning that Billie was still a convalescent. They stayed at a hotel. Billie, in a
dream, and never too used to luxury—though Mrs. Wood had
worried—was exhausted by the long corridors and their carpet's
cardinal glory. At breakfast in the hotel dining room the small
party was discreetly eyed. Meela Tannoy, wrapped in yards of
rosy silk, read her newspaper at the table like a gentleman, not
folded, but fully open and a barrier between herself and the
others at her table. It was a pity, Meela Tannoy said, that they
couldn't stay a day longer. She'd like to see this play, *Man and
Superman*. But Andrew had telephoned to say he was having
trouble keeping his hand on Mr. Hesketh.

"Billie, you're to eat that egg," said Geordie.

In the train, Mrs. Tannoy's big private compartment, Billie
lay in a bed that smelled of eau de cologne. She heard Geordie
at the door asking, "Is that child asleep yet?"

"I believe so," said Meela. "She's still a little febrile." Then
Meela's voice changed; she'd been using the voice in which she
spoke to servants, *"Everything is perfectly satisfactory, thank you."* A
beautifully modulated, clear, calm voice. Now it was warmer.

"Don't go yet, Geordie. We want to speak to you," as if someone else was present, and awake. But of course Mrs. Tannoy meant her husband—they had been talking on the telephone and were of one mind. She asked what Geordie intended to *do* with Billie? Then she said that it seemed to her that he regarded Miss Paxton and Mr. Hesketh as singular creatures of a similar sort—rare, beautiful beasts. He wanted to keep them. "You want to settle them somewhere peaceful to see if they'll breed." Then, when Geordie made a noise of protest, "Come now, isn't that what you want?"

Geordie said he was sure he hadn't thought that far ahead.

They arrived in Glasgow late, and Billie went straight to bed. It seemed to Billie that Mrs. Wood's house, in all its summer finery, rich with flowers, had been not much more than an interval between trains, one of those waiting rooms in which Billie had wilted. The Tannoys' town house was on a sensible scale. Billie was back in clothes that were clean, and which fitted her—reunited with her first good mourning dress. She had breakfast by herself, then Geordie took her to meet Andrew Tannoy, a well turned-out, wizened, jaundiced man. Murdo was there, too, in the room, by the window, a shape as hard for Billie to keep in focus, as shimmering as an ice sculpture.

Mr. Tannoy spoke kindly to Billie, made her welcome. Then he looked at Meela, and both Tannoys looked at Geordie, and Geordie looked at Murdo—then Geordie and the Tannoys left the room. No one said, *"Well, Billie, here is Mr. Hesketh."*

A clock ticked, a clock with a marble case, with a pediment and pillars, like a public building.

Billie said to Murdo that he might as well have been invisible.

"Yes."

"Are they unwilling to have you here?"

"No."

She crossed the room and took his hand, peered up at his face, still in its livery of bruises.

He said he was tired of lying awake thinking about the dead. Thinking and thinking on various absences as if there was a solution to be found by thinking. It wasn't work to which he was particularly suited. Let someone else do it.

Billie said, "I want to lie down with you."

But they just stood there together as though it had been raining, and they were out on the heath, and everything was wet. They looked about them, at the sofa, the hearth rug and, in the shallow grate, the neatly stacked coals of a frugal summer fire. Then Murdo stooped until their foreheads touched. He said that he wanted to keep her. Then, warning her, "But I'm *no good* for anyone."

Billie took his face in her hands and, because she was moved, she made one of her nonsensical replies, a feint at a logical response. Her hands were meanwhile doing, in their small way, everything they knew how. She had the silky, plump cartilage of an earlobe between thumb and index finger and was stroking it. She said, like someone with poor understanding, and with no great faith in words, "What is good? What good is it?"

16 ♣ PORT CLARITY

Billie and Murdo lived quietly for a year on the Tannoys' Ayrshire estate, the reserve Geordie chose for them, where Murdo would walk about on summer evenings with Tannoy's gamekeeper, their guns carried broken over their arms and brass knuckles in their pockets. He and Billie lived in the gatehouse, and their first child was born there. When Tannoy entertained the men with whom he did business—English, French, German—he'd have "my Mr. Hesketh" in to listen. Murdo could speak German fluently, and French well. Tannoy would fret to Geordie, "If he isn't bored he should be! I'm going to take him up to town to that meeting I have with the men from the union." And Geordie would warn, "Just don't use him as Lord Hallowhulme did."

But Tannoy was good with people, and eventually he made better use of Murdo's qualities than Hallowhulme had. He'd refer to Murdo as "my secretary" but, as one old friend of Tannoy's confided to his butler, "There are people who look at Mr. Hesketh more in the light of a protégé."

"They'd be mistaken, sir," said Betler the butler. "Though perhaps not mistaken in Mr. Tannoy's wishes. But Mr. Hesketh doesn't care a fig for patents on, and production of, heavy machinery. He's Mr. Tannoy's ornamental armament, like a dress sword, polished, but still capable of doing its business."

It amused Murdo to go about after Tannoy, whom he enjoyed and admired. It amused him to be set to the task of quelling the people who still persisted in trying to keep Andrew Tannoy in his place—hobbled like a carriage horse, forelegs strapped to hind to shorten its stride. If Andrew was rough, if Andrew's wife wasn't pukka (though at least they had no children to further vex society wives with scruples about whether or not to include them in invitations to *soirees* designed to form marriages), still there was Tannoy's "secretary," a minor aristocrat, who—the wives were in possession of the rumors—had actually been in the hunting lodge at Mayerling when the infamous "accident" occurred. It was easy to believe, for those who saw Murdo standing behind Tannoy, blond in his favored black, like a well-fed—thus good-humored—Arctic bear. (For several winters he had a coat with a white fur collar and a number of rich men's wives used the "bear" code among themselves, in letters, with excitement: "Bear seen!" or in disappointment: "Bear barely seen." Meela Tannoy followed all this with amusement. Meela was in possession of a lady's maid so charming that she was always in receipt of the gossip.) Murdo was completely indifferent to his effect on women. He liked to make their husbands uncomfortable. He enjoyed it enormously. And most of all on the occasions when he sat behind Andrew at some meeting and, on the opposite side of a table—a surface of magisterial darkness—was his cousin, mute and cowed, and, behind James, the perplexed Henry Maslen. In fact, Murdo's enjoyment of these occasions was so savage, and Murdo so disturbed afterward, that Geordie would wonder as well as worry.

Geordie never worried about Billie. The Heskeths bought a house in Glasgow, and when Geordie was in town with the Tannoys he would visit. He spent his days off with the family, and went sometimes in the evening, too—in time to kiss Billie at the door as she rushed out to her own job, playing the piano at a cinema. He'd catch her in the hall when she was pulling on her blue velvet tam-o'-shanter, and he'd embrace both the woman and the score she carried, one of her own color-coded scores with thumbnail sketches—washes in India ink—of Mary Pickford and her New York hat, or Chaplin having trouble with a revolving table. Sometimes Geordie and Murdo would take the children to watch films, and their mother, hunched over a chase, or testing her reflexes on the turns of a sword fight—gawky, effective, engrossed—the rhythmonome moving its pointer over the score in time with the action on the screen. And on some Sunday evenings, Geordie would arrive at the Heskeths' to find Murdo reading to the children—looking, in the firelight, like an advertisement for Clarity soap—while Billie and the musical director of the Majestic pored over the studio's cue sheet and argued the different merits of "The Dance of the Skeletons" or "The Hesitation Waltz."

THE WAR CAME. RIXON HALLOW WAS KILLED ON THE Marne at the age of twenty-six and two years out of Oxford. Minnie was at the Slade, painting peaches as faceted as cut gems. When Rixon died she left art school and went back to her mother at Port Clarity. Less than a year later Clara followed her son into the grave. It was a big funeral, big enough to absorb Geordie and Billie and Murdo. Sitting in the cathedral, Geordie had the strangest feeling that he shouldn't be seen. Lord Hallowhulme was behaving quite unlike himself, looking at each speaker with attention, and casting his eye around the cathedral for faces—or *a* face. Hallowhulme found them eventually, looked for a long moment at Billie—thirty-three then and as striking as she'd been at twenty. Then he looked at Murdo. Geordie, glancing sidelong at his friend, saw Murdo shake his head, not in mockery or provocation, nor sympathy and sadness. The gesture was, "No, I won't"—not a refusal, but an agreement.

That spring Geordie's master died. Andrew Tannoy had helped the army—in secret—with the design and manufacture of *tread*, steel belts of clawed plates that wrapped around wheels. He designed the tread for earthmoving machines, but it appeared first on the first tanks. Andrew Tannoy had plotted the course of his working life. For decades he had known what he wanted to do, what to make, and what he wanted to be remembered for. He'd imagined his machines clawing out cuttings for the better, straighter roads required by automobiles. He'd imagined roads built and rivers dammed. He saw his life as a man-made lake, a reservoir of blue water behind a wall of cement. But his earthmoving machines paved the way for tanks, and he read newspaper reports of men trapped and crushed in their trenches. "*The enemy.*" It killed him. He had a series of strokes, first losing the power to articulate his complaint: that he'd made the terrain possible for monsters. Those who loved him could see that even his capacity to *feel* had diminished. It wasn't as if he was losing the world but—as Geordie said to Murdo—as if a world was being lost in him. *The* world. It was like watching the world end.

After Tannoy died, his wife went to stay with friends in Ireland. Murdo and Geordie kept everything ticking over, business and households. Geordie knuckled down, busy in his grief again.

Billie, sad herself, dug out her old song. She finished it. She took her song and played it to some musical friends. The friends were impressed. It was recorded—a tenor singing—and it made Billie a tidy sum. For a year it was heard everywhere, the sad song the soldiers were heard singing when walking up the line. They were singing sad songs by then, much of the drollery drained out of them by the summer of 1916. Geordie tried to explain to himself the success of Billie's song. He considered its generalized sentiment. It was a song whose sorrowing heart was pure, a song that put out its suckers, its venous tendrils, into the paradisal peace of soldiers' daydreams. A song like a lifeline.

Late in the summer of 1916 Alan Skilling came to visit Geordie at the only address he had for him, the Tannoys' Glasgow house. Geordie was there, his rooms the only ones still unshrouded. Geordie didn't recognize Alan at first—a sergeant of the Seaforth Highlanders who stood on his back doorstep. Of course Alan was instantly recognizable when he spoke, his voice improbably soft for a sergeant, the lovely gargling accent of an islander.

Over tea Alan said he had seen Miss Minnie on his last furlough. They had always stayed in touch; after all, he was Minnie's odd boy for five more summers after the one Geordie spent on the island. There were no more plays, though. Both Tegner girls were long married, and with their own twins. Apparently they had signed up for some study, along the lines of Lord Hallowhulme's—what was it?—*eugenics.* They had written to Minnie describing how they did different things with each twin, to determine how much was *environment* and how much *inheritance.* "Minnie said they were very blithe about it all—as though they'd completely forgotten her play."

Alan put four sugar lumps in his cup. He said he shouldn't—he was having trouble with his teeth. "And, you know, I did sometimes write to Billie—I sent my letters care of Mrs. Tannoy. At first I hated to think of Mr. Hesketh having to read everything to her."

"They've been happy," Geordie said.

Alan said that he was going back soon, to France, and the front. "I came *about* something," he said. "Things keep—till they won't." He unbuttoned one of the many flaps inside his tunic and took out a handkerchief, unfolded it, and spilled something into Geordie's hand, a slithering black glitter.

It was Murdo Hesketh's jet fob and chain.

In December 1903, an English photographer, who had come to make some studies of Ormabeg, found human remains in the abbey's tower. Rory Skilling hadn't been seen for five months, and so his surviving brother went with Southport's doctor to fetch the corpse and make an identification. Alan saw only his father's closed coffin. The doctor recorded the cause of death as an accidental fall and, the following summer, Lord Hallowhulme had the tower door stopped up with cement and stones. A mason from Stolnsay had the task—and Alan went with him. Alan carried a torch up the tower's shaft. He tried to imagine what had happened. It had been a dry summer and, for once, the interior of the tower hadn't glistened with moisture. Alan was able to see the glitter in the dark—he crouched, and picked up Murdo's fob.

Geordie was conscious of Alan's gaze. Alan wasn't just waiting on a reaction, but weighing and measuring. "But, by then, they had their baby," Alan said. "Edie." Alan waited some more, then added, "So I left it for later. Billie kept in touch. He'd write down what she said. They were happy. So I just kept letting it lie."

IN THE SPRING OF 1917 ALAN WAS BACK WITH A SHRAPNEL wound, nothing very bad, once the pus stopped coming and the wound closed. Geordie, in London with Meela, visited Alan at Brockenhurst. He passed on Meela's invitation—would Alan like to spend his convalescence in Ayrshire? Alan would. But he asked if, on the way, they could stop at Port Clarity. He had regular letters from Minnie, who was still there. "Sequestered. Playing patience on a monument." Meela was happy to oblige him. She said she'd take a room in the hotel, though, because she no longer had the stamina for Lord Hallowhulme. "Andrew used to tell people—I think to elicit their opinions—that we once had dinner at Hallowhulme's Port Clarity residence. But, to tell the truth, I always felt that I was *had*, at his table, that I was milked of my possibility, that while I had my head in the trough something was being done to my other end."

A SPRING NIGHT, THE MOONLIGHT FILTERED BY A LOW cloud cover. There was drizzle, drops that swarmed in the cow-catcher of light from Minnie's car's low-browed headlamps. From the air the headlamps would appear only as a dapple of moonlight through a threadless area of cloud.

Minnie said that she'd have liked to show them the plant by daylight—it was quite something, a great open-air boiler room, Hell's steaming basement.

They swept along a little faster, following the rails of the trams that took Lord Hallowhulme's workers to his factory. It was formerly a soap factory, now its kitchens were wholly given over to the war effort, and the production of glycerine. At dinner Geordie had conveyed to Minnie Meela's invitation. "Come on," Alan said, "how can you resist a couple of weeks of my conversation?" Then, "I'll teach you to drive." Only, there was a paper Minnie wanted signed, a permission to James's banker in Edinburgh. "I want to get Mother's diamonds," she said.

"Do they need airing?" asked Alan.

Minnie's father was in his office, at his plans, some private project of improvement. "A memorial gallery," Minnie said. "Lady Hallowhulme Gallery."

A watchman met them at the factory's iron gates. They drove up onto a terrace paved with cobbles. Below them was the plant, a huddle of saw-toothed buildings, and chimneys, some smoking, others topped by melting, speedy emissions of steam. The sea was the same shade as the sky, only lower, the port's cranes apparently perched at the edge of a chasm full of cloud.

Minnie went up to the manager's office and secured her father's signature. She came back down the outside stair, and got in beside Alan. Alan was driving; Minnie's chauffeur had the evening off.

"He's alone," she said. "He's busy with a list of prices from some Dutch collector." Then she went on, musing, "He had me look at a catalogue. He wanted to know if I thought Mother would have liked the paintings he plans to buy."

Somewhere down below, at the port, a siren sounded. Then another. Searchlights came on and swung up into the air and onto the woolly underbelly of the clouds.

They all got out of the car.

A silent, taut cylinder pushed down through the cloud, dragging cloud with it, vapor streaming up its black-painted sides. Now that Geordie could see it he realized he'd been hearing its engines for the better part of a minute. The engines of a "height-climbing" zeppelin dropping down from its operational altitude—above the reach of planes—right over its target.

People began to spill out of the factory buildings. Most of them were women, Geordie saw, lasses with their hair wrapped up and out of the way.

"I'll get your father," Alan said to Minnie. He set off. Geordie pursued, hollering. Hampered by his stiff leg, Alan was quite easy to catch. Geordie stopped him. "Let me go," he said. "I can't drive. But see—" he pointed, "—that beauty over there with all the white brass is Lord Hallowhulme's car. I'll get him, and he'll drive us both. You go back and take Minnie in her car." Geordie gripped Alan's shoulder and gave him one hard shake. "I doubt Hallowhulme would want you to wait for him with his only surviving child in the car."

Alan the soldier saw the sense of this, and Alan the odd boy obeyed the butler Betler. But there was a hawthorn tree that grew under the angle of the first flight of steps up to the factory offices, its roots making an eruption in the paving. The tree stopped Alan, it snatched his cap from his head—so that Geordie was able to see his face just once more as he turned back to tear the cap out of the blossom hiding the light-fingered thorn.

The zeppelin was near. It wasn't interested in the port, only the factory.

Geordie went up the stairs, and into the offices. He followed a light, a small crack of light beneath the door of a room cantilevered out over the road up which they had come.

The beam of a searchlight ran ahead of Geordie along the corridor, the light of its far-off, hugely magnified circle still strong, strong enough for Geordie to feel its warmth on his cheek as it swept across him. In its light Geordie saw a billboard, an advertisement depicting the two products on which the Hallowhulme fortune was founded; oblong and oval, a yellow opacity and a tan transparency—bars of soap.

Through the copper-framed panes of the long window, Geordie watched Minnie's car go quickly down the hill, bouncing in potholes, its headlamps now wide-open in alarm and casting wildly about. The car slowed at the gate, seemed to gather and herd the turbaned workers. Geordie saw that Alan actually pulled up and idled a moment at the gate—collecting the watchmen, who thrust their arms through the car's open windows, gripped its door handles, and clung, balanced on its running board as its sped away.

Geordie opened the door to Lord Hallowhulme's office.

Hallowhulme stood in the center of the room, a bundle of plans gathered to his chest. James Hallow—millionaire philanthropist and murderer.

Geordie stopped, still in the doorway.

James Hallow dropped his plans and retreated around his desk. "Who are you?" he said. "What do you want?"

Come away quickly, Geordie thought, but didn't say it aloud. There was something else he meant to say first, only he couldn't think how best to put it. He glanced past Lord Hallowhulme out the tall, broad window. He could see the zeppelin's control car now, bristling with machine guns. He could see where they pointed, firing back at the source of a line of phosphorescent bullets, a dotted line that cracked like a whip.

Lord Hallowhulme picked up the receiver of his phone. He threatened to summon help. He wound its handle.

A great bright wave got up beyond the window. Geordie saw it pass through the glass without breaking it. Swift, it engulfed the thick figure of Lord Hallowhulme, who stood at his desk with his phone to his ear. Then the window shattered, and the wave took Geordie, too.

BILLIE WATCHED HER YOUNGEST CLIMB OUT OF THE SEA. The stones rolled from under Soren's feet, and his hips swayed, gimpy, till he'd stepped up on the shelf the tide had built. He came up the beach on his toes. She handed him his towel, and slipped her hand under the back strap of his wet bathing costume. Soren leaned on her, dripping. He said that the people talking to Edie had tossed him off the raft. "They said I was a cheeky kid."

Meela Tannoy passed him some grapes, in consolation or reward.

Soren's father arrived, came down the wooden steps from the promenade, in his white suit, but without his hat. The sun had nearly gone. Murdo asked what Edie was doing out there with those people, and how long she'd been there.

"They're Americans," Soren said—as if that answered his father's question.

"This boy is very refreshing," Billie said, meaning his skin, not his manner.

Murdo told Meela and Billie that he'd been to the English library at St. John's to look at the latest papers. But there was nothing further about the sinking.

The young men of Kissack and Skilling hadn't all signed up

together, unlike those from the sad shires to the south—a platoon in Kitchener's army might contain the very same individuals as the cricket team of some village in Dorset. The islanders were never so keen, they waited for conscription, and went in dribs and drabs. But the survivors of Kissack were repatriated together—at once and in haste in the early months of 1919. They were dispatched from Inverness to Stolnsay, and a few Skilling men, who wanted to be home quickly, went with them—meaning to walk or beg rides back down to "their island." A hundred and four soldiers sailed in an overloaded and unseaworthy ship, the *Iona*, which foundered in heavy seas off Alesund Head. One powerful young islander, Sergeant Alan Skilling, carried a line from the ship to the shore. He went back through the surf himself and got six other men off before the line snapped and the ship was smashed on the rocks around the headland.

"Billie has had a letter from Minnie," Meela said. She waved it at Murdo, drew him closer and, as he took the pages, she picked his pocket, lifted his cigarettes and said "hmmm" to herself, in satisfaction. She removed one from his case and pushed it, creaking, into her cigarette holder. Murdo sat beside her sunbed and lit it for her. She said she had to use the contraption to preserve what little moisture she had left in her lips. She puffed, slitting her eyes against the smoke, and remarked that it was so hot she might as well have stayed in India. (Meela had gone back to Bombay as soon she was able, at the very end of the war. She lasted only a month, dismayed to find herself a foreigner and homesick for Scotland. Now she was on an extended stay on the shore of the Mediterranean, where it seemed that every fifth person was orphaned of country.)

Murdo had the letter in his hand, but Billie was telling him what it said. Minnie had heard from Alan. He'd been walking down the island, from village to village, all empty of men of a certain age. Everywhere he went he was looked at with longing. Minnie transcribed what he'd written. "Mothers and fathers, wives and sweethearts, siblings and children, all stare at me," he wrote. Minnie said she could feel it—that firmament of eyes. "All of them blame the Imperial Power that has been such a hard master and poor mother," Alan wrote. "Even after another century of discouragements—and they will come, I look at the fallen roofs and know—the grievance will still be alive. *Only the grievance is living.*"

Murdo read Minnie's letter himself, looked up only once to watch his daughter make her dive and surface, followed by all the air she'd pulled down with her. She kicked out for the shore, changing gear as she came, fast and straight. She, too, hobbled out of the sea.

Soren had spotted a boy on the promenade selling apple pastries. He shuffled across the stones and slipped a wet hand into one of his father's jacket pockets. Before Murdo was able to clap his hand to his side Soren was out again. He spread his fingers and showed his father the coins. Murdo took some back. He'd like a pastry, too, he said.

"Not for me," Billie said. She was going back in. She waited for Murdo to pin up her plait, then went down to the water. She left her robe and rope sandals on the last shelf of stones and stepped down, her heels skidding across pebbles loose and lubricated by waves. When she was in over her hips Billie took her feet off the bottom and eased out past the Americans, who were lurking in a line, at eye level with Edie's bare knees. Edie was wringing out her plait. Billie saw that her daughter's hair was bleached and brassy in the sun—saw why, whenever they went out, Murdo would drop back a pace to adjust the veil of her own hat down to where her bunched hair lay against her neck.

Billie swam out, far from shore, then lay on her back and floated. From here she had her favorite view of the old town and the slopes behind it. Now, at evening, the terraces were thick, dark bands rimmed with shining green. Below them were the pale walls of stacked houses, their open shutters rigged with square sails of shadow, warm roofs with round tiles, and the tower of Saint Michael's, polished, elegant, not quite upright.

Billie saw that the composition of the population of the promenade had changed in the eight weeks they'd been there. There were now fewer convalescent soldiers and more tanned, bare-armed men and women.

Billie watched Edie straighten, fling back her plait, and face the Americans, her shoulders back and head at a combative, quizzical tilt—she looked like her father issuing one of his now playful challenges. Murdo was watching Edie, too, still reclined, but up on an elbow and aimed her way.

Billie lay back in the water, forgetful of her carefully fastened hair. She let the water into her ears. The town's sharp sounds became blurry, voices unidentifiable and unintelligible. She looked up at the sky. *At last, enough blue,* she thought—as she'd been thinking for weeks. It was like that blessing: "God before me, God behind me . . ." but blue instead, above and below. Then, because she was thinking how easy everything was now, Billie lifted her head again and looked to the shore, for the two of her children on the beach. She found them, farther from her these days, and bigger, which was a paradox of perspective.

This reminded Billie of Minnie—and of Alan. What should she do about them? It was clear to Billie that Minnie was as afraid of Alan's suffering as he was of hers—both of them without family, Minnie rattling about one of several huge houses and Alan on a pilgrimage from Kissack to Skilling in the company of phantoms. Alan wrote to Minnie, and Minnie wrote to her. All this writing for advice—this delayed, translated concern.

Billie swam into shore, retrieved her robe and sandals, and picked her way up the beach. Murdo took her towel and began to pat her hair dry.

The sun had gone. The mountains had leapt forward and lifted their backs.

"I was wondering if we could do something for Alan," Billie said.

"Or about Minnie," said Murdo. He'd finally managed to catch his daughter's eye. Billie saw him touch the sparkling black beads looped on his waistcoat—Karl Borg's mourning fob. (It had been found among Geordie's things, in a package addressed to Murdo.) Edie's father didn't go so far as to signal his daughter by consulting his watch.

Meela said, "Andrew would say, 'We must have him here.' But I don't think that's quite right."

"I want you to write to Minnie," Billie said to Murdo, "and tell her to go to Alan. Just go and find him."

Murdo nodded.

Billie remembered Henry telling her that, in the end, he had been very glad to stop spending his summers on Kissack. He'd begun to sympathize with the ancient people who, living with all those long horizons, were hungry for verticals, so set up tall stones to stand in for groves of trees they'd never seen. Billie imagined Alan Skilling as a standing stone, still there on an island that, for her, was washed clean of people.

On the beach at Menton Billie began turning over the stones, to find those underneath, whose heat she released—warm round stones, like freshly boiled eggs.